Miracle

and Other Christmas Stories

Also by Connie Willis

Miracle

and Other Christmas Stories

CONNIE WILLIS

Bantam Books

NEW YORK   TORONTO   LONDON   SYDNEY   AUCKLAND

MIRACLE AND OTHER CHRISTMAS STORIES

A Bantam Spectra Book / November 1999

SPECTRA and the portrayal of a boxed "s" are trademarks of Bantam Books, a division of Random House, Inc.

BOOK DESIGN BY CASEY HAMPTON.

Library of Congress Cataloging-in-Publication Data
Willis, Connie.
Miracle, and other Christmas stories / Connie Willis.
p.   cm.—(A Bantam spectra book)
Contents: Miracle—Inn—In Coppelius's toyshop—The pony—Adaptation—Cat's paw—Newsletter—Epiphany—A final word—Twelve terrific things to read at Christmas—And twelve to watch.
ISBN 0-553-11111-6
1. Christmas stories, American.   I. Title.
PS3573.I45652M57   1999
813'.54—dc21   99-15686
                                                             CIP

Published simultaneously in the United States and Canada

Bantam Books are published by Bantam Books, a division of Random House, Inc. Its trademark, consisting of the words "Bantam Books" and the portrayal of a rooster, is Registered in U.S. Patent and Trademark Office and in other countries. Marca Registrada. Bantam Books, 1540 Broadway, New York, New York 10036.

PRINTED IN THE UNITED STATES OF AMERICA
BVG   10   9   8   7   6   5   4   3   2   1

CONTENTS

Introduction

I love Christmas. All of it—decorating the tree and singing in the choir and baking cookies and wrapping presents. I even like the parts most people hate—shopping in crowded malls and reading Christmas newsletters and seeing relatives and standing in baggage check-in lines at the airport.

Okay, I lied. Nobody likes standing in baggage check-in lines. I love seeing people get off the plane, though, and holly and candles and eggnog and carols.

But most of all, I love Christmas stories and movies. Okay, I lied again. I don't love *all* Christmas stories and movies. *It's a Wonderful Life,* for instance. And Hans Christian Andersen's "The Fir Tree."

But I love *Miracle on 34th Street* and Christopher Morley's "The Christmas Tree That Didn't Get Trimmed" and Christina Rosetti's poem "Midwinter." My family watches *The Sure Thing* and *A Christmas Story* each year, and we read George V. Higgins's

"The Snowsuit of Christmas Past" out loud every Christmas Eve, and eagerly look for new classics to add to our traditions.

There aren't a lot. This is because Christmas stories are much harder to write than they look, partly because the subject matter is fairly limited, and people have been writing them for nearly two thousand years, so they've just about rung all the changes possible on snowmen, Santas, and shepherds.

Stories have been told from the point of view of the fourth wise man (who got waylaid on the way to Bethlehem), the innkeeper, the innkeeper's wife, the donkey, and the star. There've been stories about department-store Santas, phony Santas, burned-out Santas, substitute Santas, reluctant Santas, and dieting Santas, to say nothing of Santa's wife, his elves, his reindeer, and Rudolph. We've had births at Christmas (natch!), deaths, partings, meetings, mayhem, attempted suicides, and sanity hearings. And Christmas in Hawaii, in China, in the past, the future, and outer space. We've heard from the littlest shepherd, the littlest wise man, the littlest angel, and the mouse who wasn't stirring. There's not a lot out there that hasn't already been done.

In addition, the Christmas-story writer has to walk a narrow tightrope between sentiment and skepticism, and most writers end up falling off into either cynicism or mawkish sappiness.

And, yes, I am talking about Hans Christian Andersen. He invented the whole three-hanky sob story, whose plot Maxim Gorki, in a fit of pique, described as taking a poor girl or boy and letting them "freeze somewhere under a window, behind which there is usually a Christmas tree that throws its radiant splendor upon them." Match girls, steadfast tin soldiers, even snowmen (melted, not frozen) all met with a fate they (and we) didn't deserve, especially at Christmas.

Nobody, before Andersen came along, had thought of writing such depressing Christmas stories. Even Dickens, who had killed a fair number of children in his books, didn't kill Tiny Tim. But

Andersen, apparently hell-bent on ruining everybody's holidays, froze innocent children, melted loyal toys into lumps of lead, and chopped harmless fir trees who were just standing there in the forest, minding their own business, into kindling.

Worse, he inspired dozens of imitators, who killed off saintly children (some of whom, I'll admit, were pretty insufferable and deserved to die) and poor people for the rest of the Victorian era.

In the twentieth century, the Andersen-style tearjerker moved into the movies, which starred Margaret O'Brien (who definitely deserved to die) and other child stars, chosen for their pallor and their ability to cough. They had titles like *All Mine to Give* and *The Christmas Tree*, which tricked hapless moviegoers into thinking they were going to see a cheery Christmas movie, when really they were about little boys who succumbed to radiation poisoning on Christmas Eve.

When television came along, this type of story turned into the "Very Special Christmas Episode" of various TV shows, the worst of which was *Little House on the Prairie*, which killed off huge numbers of children in blizzards and other pioneer-type disasters every Christmas for years. Hadn't any of these authors ever heard that Christmas stories are supposed to have happy endings?

Well, unfortunately, they had, and it resulted in improbably sentimental and saccharine stories too numerous to mention.

So are there any good Christmas stories out there? You bet, starting with the original. The recounting of the first Christmas (you know, the baby in the manger) has all the elements of great storytelling: drama, danger, special effects, dreams and warnings, betrayals, narrow escapes, and—combined with the Easter story—the happiest ending of all.

And it's got great characters—Joseph, who's in over his head but doing the best he can; the wise men, expecting a palace and getting a stable; slimy Herod, telling them, "When you find this king, tell me where he is so I can come and worship him," and then sending out his thugs to try to murder the baby; the ambivalent innkeeper. And Mary, fourteen years old, pondering all of the above in her heart. It's a great story—no wonder it's lasted two thousand years.

Modern Christmas stories I love (for a more complete list, see the end of this book) include O. Henry's "The Gift of the Magi," T. S. Eliot's "Journey of the Magi," and Barbara Robinson's *The Best Christmas Pageant Ever*, about a church Nativity pageant overrun by a gang of hooligans called the Herdmans. The Herdmans bully everybody and smoke and cuss and come only because they'd heard there were refreshments afterward. And they transform what was a sedate and boring Christmas pageant into something extraordinary.

Since I'm a science-fiction writer, I'm of course partial to science-fiction Christmas stories. Science fiction has always had the ability to make us look at the world from a different angle, and Christmas is no exception. Science fiction has looked at the first Christmas from a new perspective (Michael Moorcock's classic "Behold the Man") and in a new guise (Joe L. Hensley and Alexei Panshin's "Dark Conception").

It's shown us Christmas in the future (Cynthia Felice's "Track of a Legend") and Christmas in space (Ray Bradbury's wonderful "The Gift"). And it's looked at Christmas itself (Mildred Clingerman's disturbing "The Wild Wood").

My favorite science-fiction Christmas stories are Arthur C. Clarke's "The Star," which tells the story of the Christmas star that guided the wise men to Bethlehem, and Thomas Disch's hilarious story "The Santa Claus Compromise," in which two intrepid six-year-old investigative reporters expose the shocking scandal behind Santa Claus.

I also love mysteries. You'd think murder and Christmas wouldn't mesh, but the setting and the possibility of mistletoe/plum pudding/Santa Claus–connected murders has inspired any number of mystery writers, starting with Arthur Conan Doyle and his "The Adventure of the Blue Carbuncle," which involves a Christmas goose. Some of my favorite mysteries are Dorothy Sayers's "The Necklace of Pearls," Agatha Christie's *Murder for Christmas*, and Jane Langton's *The Shortest Day: Murder at the Revels*. My absolute favorite is John Mortimer's comic "Rumpole and the Spirit of Christmas," which stars the grumpy old Scrooge of a barrister, Horace Rumpole, and his wonderful wife, She Who Must Be Obeyed.

Comedies are probably my favorite kind of Christmas story. I love Damon Runyon's "Dancing Dan's Christmas." (Actually, I love everything Damon Runyon ever wrote, and if you've never read him, you need to go get *Guys and Dolls* immediately. Ditto P. G. Wodehouse, whose "Jeeves and the Christmas Spirit" and "Another Christmas Carol," are vintage Wodehouse, which means they're indescribable. If you've never read Wodehouse either, what a treat you're in for! He wrote over a hundred books. Start anywhere.) Both Runyon and Wodehouse balance sentiment and cynicism, irony, and the Christmas spirit, human nature and happy endings, without a single misstep.

And then there's Christopher Morley's "The Christmas Tree That Didn't Get Trimmed," which was clearly written in reaction to Hans Christian Andersen's "The Fir Tree." Unlike Andersen, however, Morley understands that the purpose of Christmas is to remind us not only of suffering but of salvation. His story makes you ache, and then despair. And then rejoice.

Almost all great stories (Christmas or otherwise) have that one terrible moment when all seems lost, when you're sure things won't work out, the bad guys will win, the cavalry won't arrive in time, and they (and we) won't be saved. John Ford's Christmas Western, *The Three Godfathers*, has a moment like that. So does *The Miracle of Morgan's Creek*, and *Miracle on 34th Street*, which I consider to be The Best Christmas Movie Ever.

I know, I know, *It's a Wonderful Life* is supposed to be The Best Christmas Movie Ever, with ten million showings and accompanying merchandising. (I saw an *It's a Wonderful Life* mouse pad this last Christmas.) And I'm not denying that there are some great scenes in it (see my story "Miracle" on this subject), but the movie has real problems. For one thing, the villainous Mr. Potter is still loose and unpunished at the end of the movie, something no good fairy tale ever permits. The dreadful little psychologist in *Miracle on 34th Street* is summarily, and very appropriately, fired, and the DA, who after all was only doing his job, repents.

But in *It's a Wonderful Life*, not only is Mr. Potter free, with his villainy undetected, but he has already proved to be a vindictive and malicious villain. Since this didn't work, he'll obviously try something else. And poor George is still faced with embezzlement charges, which the last time I looked don't disappear just because you pay back the money, even if the cop is smiling in the last scene.

But the worst problem seems to me to be that the ending depends on the goodness of the people of Bedford Falls, something that (especially in light of previous events) seems like a dicey proposition.

Miracle on 34th Street, on the other hand, relies on no such thing. The irony of the miracle (and let's face it, maybe what really galls my soul is that *It's a Wonderful Life* is a work *completely* without irony) is that the miracle happens not because of people's behavior, but in spite of it.

Christmas is supposed to be based on selflessness and innocence, but until the very end of *Miracle on 34th Street*, virtually no one except Kris Kringle exhibits these qualities. Quite the opposite. Everyone, even the hero and heroine, acts from a cynical, very modern self-interest. Macy's Santa goes on a binge right before Macy's Thanksgiving Day Parade, Doris hires Kris to get herself out of a jam and save her job, John Payne invites the little girl Susan to watch the parade as a way to meet the mother.

And in spite of Kris Kringle's determined efforts to restore the true spirit of Christmas to the city, it continues. Macy's and then Gimbel's go along with the gag of recommending other stores, not because they believe in it, but because it means more money. The judge in Kris's sanity case makes favorable rulings only because he wants to get re-elected. Even the postal workers who provide the denouement just want to get rid of stuff piling up in the dead-letter office.

But in spite of this (actually, in a delicious irony, *because* of it) and with only very faint glimmerings of humanity from the principals, and in spite of how hopeless it all seems, the miracle of Christmas occurs, right on schedule. Just as it does every year.

It's this layer of symbolism that makes *Miracle on 34th Street* such a satisfying movie. Also its script (by George Seaton) and perfect casting (especially Natalie Wood and Thelma Ritter) and any number of delightful moments (Santa's singing a Dutch carol to the little Dutch orphan and the disastrous bubble-gum episode and Natalie Wood's disgusted expression when she's told she has to have faith even when things don't work out). Plus, of course, the fact that Edmund Gwenn could make anyone believe in Santa Claus. All combine to make it The Best Christmas Movie Ever Made.

Not, however, the best story. That honor belongs to Dickens and his deathless "A Christmas Carol." The rumor that Dickens invented Christmas is not true, and neither, probably, is the story that when he died, a poor costermonger's little girl sobbed, "Dickens dead? Why, then, is Christmas dead, too?" But they should be.

Because Dickens did the impossible—not only did he write a masterpiece that captures the essence of Christmas, but one that was good enough to survive its own fame. There have been a million, mostly awful TV, movie, and musical versions and variations, with Scrooge played by everybody from Basil Rathbone to the Fonz, but even the worst of them haven't managed to damage the wonderful story of Scrooge and Tiny Tim.

One reason it's such a great story is that Dickens loved Christmas. (And no wonder. His childhood was Oliver Twist's and Little Dorrit's combined, and no kindly grandfather or Arthur Clennam in sight. His whole adult life must have seemed like Christmas.) I think you have to love Christmas to write about it.

For another, he knew a lot about human nature. Remembering the past, truly seeing the present, imagining the consequences of our actions are the ways we actually grow and change. Dickens knew this years before Freud.

He also knew a lot about writing. The plot's terrific, the dialogue's great, and the opening line—"Marley was dead: to begin with"—is second only to "Call me Ishmael" as one of the great opening lines of literature. He knew how to end stories, too, and that Christmas stories were supposed to have happy endings.

Finally, the story touches us because we want to believe people can change. They don't. We've all learned from bitter experience (though probably not as bitter as Dickens's) that the world is full of money-grubbers and curtain-ring stealers, that Scrooge stays Scrooge to the bitter end, and nobody will lift a finger to help Tiny Tim.

But Christmas is about someone who believed, in spite of overwhelming evidence, that humanity is capable of change and worth redeeming. And Dickens's Christmas story is in fact *The Christmas Story*. And the hardened heart that cracks open at the end of it is our own.

If I sound passionate (and sometimes curmudgeonly) about Christmas stories, I am. I *love* Christmas, in all its complexity and irony, and I *love* Christmas stories.

So much so that I've been writing them for years. Here they are—an assortment of stories about church choirs and Christmas presents and pod people from outer space, about wishes that come true in ways you don't expect and wishes that don't come true and wishes you didn't know you had, about stars and shepherds, wise men and Santa Claus, mistletoe and *It's a Wonderful Life* and Christmas cards on recycled paper. There's even a murder. And a story about Christmas Yet to Come.

I hope you like them. And I hope you have a very merry Christmas!

—*Connie Willis*

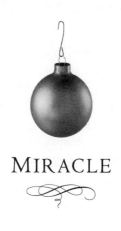

MIRACLE

There was a Christmas tree in the lobby when Lauren got to work, and the receptionist was sitting with her chin in her hand, watching the security monitor. Lauren set her shopping bag down and looked curiously at the screen. On it, Jimmy Stewart was dancing the Charleston with Donna Reed.

"The Personnel Morale Special Committee had cable piped in for Christmas," the receptionist explained, handing Lauren her messages. "I love *It's a Wonderful Life*, don't you?"

Lauren stuck her messages in the top of her shopping bag and went up to her department. Red and green crepe paper hung in streamers from the ceiling, and there was a big red crepe-paper bow tied around Lauren's desk.

"The Personnel Morale Special Committee did it," Evie said, coming over with the catalog she'd been reading. "They're decorating the whole building, and they want us and Document Control to go caroling this afternoon. Don't you think PMS is getting

10

out of hand with this Christmas spirit thing? I mean, who wants to spend Christmas Eve at an office party?"

"I do," Lauren said. She set her shopping bag down on the desk, sat down, and began taking off her boots.

"Can I borrow your stapler?" Evie asked. "I've lost mine again. I'm ordering my mother the Water of the Month, and I need to staple my check to the order form."

"The Water of the Month?" Lauren said, opening her desk drawer and taking out her stapler.

"You know, they send you bottles of a different one every month. Perrier, Evian, Calistoga." She peered into Lauren's shopping bag. "Do you have Christmas presents in there? I hate people who have their shopping done four weeks before Christmas."

"It's four *days* till Christmas," Lauren said, "and I don't have it all done. I still don't have anything for my sister. But I've got all my friends, including you, done." She reached into the shopping bag and pulled out her pumps. "*And* I found a dress for the office party."

"Did you buy it?"

"No." She put on one of her shoes. "I'm going to try it on during my lunch hour."

"If it's still there," Evie said gloomily. "I had this echidna toothpick holder all picked out for my brother, and when I went back to buy it, they were all gone."

"I asked them to hold the dress for me," Lauren said. She put on her other shoe. "It's gorgeous. Black off-the-shoulder. Sequined."

"Still trying to get Scott Buckley to notice you, huh? I don't do things like that anymore. Nineties women don't use sexist tricks to attract men. Besides, I decided he was too cute to ever notice somebody like me." She sat down on the edge of Lauren's desk and started leafing through the catalog. "Here's something your sister might like. The Vegetable of the Month. February's okra."

"She lives in southern California," Lauren said, shoving her boots under the desk.

"Oh. How about the Sunscreen of the Month?"

"No," Lauren said. "She's into New Age stuff. Channeling. Aromatherapy. Last year she sent me a crystal pyramid mate selector for Christmas."

"The Eastern Philosophy of the month," Evie said. "Zen, Sufism, tai chi—"

"I'd like to get her something she'd really like," Lauren mused. "I always have a terrible time figuring out what to get people for Christmas. So this year, I decided things were going to be different. I wasn't going to be tearing around the mall the day before Christmas, buying things no one would want and wondering what on earth I was going to wear to the office party. I started doing my shopping in September, I wrapped my presents as soon as I bought them, I have all my Christmas cards done and ready to mail—"

"You're disgusting," Evie said. "Oh, here, I almost forgot." She pulled a folded slip of paper out of her catalog and handed it to Lauren. "It's your name for the Secret Santa gift exchange. PMS says you're supposed to bring your present for it by Friday so it won't interfere with the presents Santa Claus hands out at the office party."

Lauren unfolded the paper, and Evie leaned over to read it. "Who'd you get? Wait, don't tell me. Scott Buckley."

"No. Fred Hatch. And I know just what to get him."

"Fred? The fat guy in Documentation? What is it, the Diet of the Month?"

"This is supposed to be the season of love and charity, not the season when you make mean remarks about someone just because he's overweight," Lauren said sternly. "I'm going to get him a videotape of *Miracle on 34th Street*."

Evie looked uncomprehending.

"It's Fred's favorite movie. We had a wonderful talk about it at the office party last year."

"I never heard of it."

"It's about Macy's Santa Claus. He starts telling people they can get their kids' toys cheaper at Gimbel's, and then the store psychiatrist decides he's crazy—"

"Why don't you get him *It's a Wonderful Life*? That's *my* favorite Christmas movie."

"Yours and everybody else's. I think Fred and I are the only two people in the world who like *Miracle on 34th Street* better. See, Edmund Gwenn, he's Santa Claus, gets committed to Bellevue because he thinks he's Santa Claus, and since there isn't any Santa Claus, he has to be crazy, but he *is* Santa Claus, and Fred Gailey, that's John Payne, he's a lawyer in the movie, he decides to have a court hearing to prove it, and—"

"I watch *It's a Wonderful Life* every Christmas. I love the part where Jimmy Stewart and Donna Reed fall into the swimming pool," Evie said. "What happened to the stapler?"

They had the dress and it fit, but there was an enormous jam-up at the cash register, and then they couldn't find a hanging bag for it.

"Just put it in a shopping bag," Lauren said, looking anxiously at her watch.

"It'll wrinkle," the clerk said ominously and continued to search for a hanging bag. By the time Lauren convinced her a shopping bag would work, it was already 12:15. She had hoped she'd have a chance to look for a present for her sister, but there wasn't going to be time. She still had to run the dress home and mail the Christmas cards.

I can pick up Fred's video, she thought, fighting her way onto the escalator. That wouldn't take much time, since she knew what she wanted, and maybe they'd have something with Shirley MacLaine in it she could get her sister. Ten minutes to buy the video, she thought, tops.

It took her nearly half an hour. There was only one copy, which the clerk couldn't find.

"Are you sure you wouldn't rather have *It's a Wonderful Life*?" she asked Lauren. "It's my favorite movie."

"I want *Miracle on 34th Street*," Lauren said patiently. "With Edmund Gwenn and Natalie Wood."

The clerk picked up a copy of *It's a Wonderful Life* from a huge display. "See, Jimmy Stewart's in trouble and he wishes he'd never been born, and this angel grants him his wish—"

"I know," Lauren said. "I don't care. I want *Miracle on 34th Street*."

"Okay!" the clerk said, and wandered off to look for it, muttering, "Some people don't have any Christmas spirit."

She finally found it, in the M's, of all places, and then insisted on giftwrapping it.

By the time Lauren made it back to her apartment, it was a quarter to one. She would have to forget lunch and mailing the Christmas cards, but she could at least take them with her, buy the stamps, and put the stamps on at work.

She took the video out of the shopping bag and set it on the coffee table next to her purse, picked up the bag, and started for the bedroom.

Someone knocked on the door.

"I don't have time for this," she muttered, and opened the door, still holding the shopping bag.

It was a young man wearing a "Save the Whales" T-shirt and khaki pants. He had shoulder-length blond hair and a vague expression that made her think of southern California.

"Yes? What is it?" she asked.

"I'm here to give you a Christmas present," he said.

"Thank you, I'm not interested in whatever you're selling," she said, and shut the door.

He knocked again immediately. "I'm not selling anything," he said through the door. "Really."

I don't have *time* for this, she thought, but she opened the door again.

"I'm not a salesguy," he said. "Have you ever heard of the Maharishi Ram Das?"

A religious nut.

"I don't have time to talk to you." She started to say, "I'm late for work," and then remembered you weren't supposed to tell strangers your apartment was going to be empty. "I'm very busy," she said and shut the door, more firmly this time.

The knocking commenced again, but she ignored it. She started into the bedroom with the shopping bag, came back and pushed the deadbolt across and put the chain on, and then went in to hang up her dress. By the time she'd extricated it from the tissue paper and found a hanger, the knocking had stopped. She hung up the dress, which looked just as deadly now that she had it home, and went back into the living room.

The young man was sitting on the couch, messing with her TV remote. "So, what do you want for Christmas? A yacht? A pony?" He punched buttons on the remote, frowning. "A new TV?"

"How did you get in here?" Lauren said squeakily. She looked at the door. The deadbolt and chain were both still on.

"I'm a spirit," he said, putting the remote down. The TV suddenly blared on. "The Spirit of Christmas Present."

"Oh," Lauren said, edging toward the phone. "Like in *A Christmas Carol*."

"No," he said, flipping through the channels. She looked at the remote. It was still on the coffee table. "Not Christmas Present. Christmas *Present*. You *know*, Barbie dolls, ugly ties, cheese logs, the stuff people give you for Christmas."

"Oh, Christmas *Present*. I see," Lauren said, carefully picking up the phone.

"People *always* get me confused with him, which is really insulting. I mean, the guy obviously has a really high cholesterol level. Anyway, I'm the Spirit of Christmas Present, and your sister sent me to—"

Lauren had dialed nine one. She stopped, her finger poised over the second one. "My sister?"

"Yeah," he said, staring at the TV. Jimmy Stewart was sitting in the guard's room, wrapped in a blanket. "Oh, wow! *It's a Wonderful Life*."

My sister sent you, Lauren thought. It explained everything. He was not a Moonie or a serial killer. He was this year's version of the crystal pyramid mate selector. "How do you know my sister?"

"She channeled me," he said, leaning back against the sofa. "The Maharishi Ram Das was instructing her in trance-meditation, and she accidentally channeled my spirit out of the astral plane." He pointed at the screen. "I love this part where the angel is trying to convince Jimmy Stewart he's dead."

"I'm not dead, am I?"

"No. I'm not an angel. I'm a spirit. The Spirit of Christmas Present. You can call me Chris for short. Your sister sent me to give you what you really want for Christmas. You know, your heart's desire. So what is it?"

For my sister not to send me any more presents, she thought. "Look, I'm really in a hurry right now. Why don't you come back tomorrow and we can talk about it then?"

"I hope it's not a fur coat," he said as if he hadn't heard her. "I'm opposed to the killing of endangered species." He picked up Fred's present. "What's this?"

"It's a videotape of *Miracle on 34th Street*. I really have to go."

"Who's it for?"

"Fred Hatch. I'm his Secret Santa."

"Fred Hatch." He turned the package over. "You had it gift-wrapped at the store, didn't you?"

"Yes. If we could just talk about this later—"

"This is a great part, too," he said, leaning forward to watch the TV. The angel was explaining to Jimmy Stewart how he hadn't gotten his wings yet.

"I *have* to go. I'm on my lunch hour, and I need to mail my Christmas cards, and I have to be back at work by"—she glanced at her watch—"oh my God, fifteen minutes ago."

He put down the package and stood up. "Gift-wrapped presents," he said, making a "tsk"-ing noise, "everybody rushing around spending money, rushing to parties, never stopping to have some eggnog or watch a movie. Christmas is an endangered species." He looked longingly back at the screen, where the angel was trying to convince Jimmy Stewart he'd never been alive, and then wandered into the kitchen. "You got any Evian water?"

"No," Lauren said desperately. She hurried after him. "Look, I really have to get to work."

He had stopped at the kitchen table and was holding one of the Christmas cards. "Computer-addressed," he said reprovingly. He tore it open.

"Don't—" Lauren said.

"Printed Christmas cards," he said. "No letter, no quick note, not even a handwritten signature. That's exactly what I'm talking about. An endangered species."

"I didn't have time," Lauren said defensively. "And I don't have time to discuss this or anything else with you. I have to get to work."

"No time to write a few words on a card, no time to think about what you want for Christmas." He slid the card back into the envelope. "Not even on recycled paper," he said sadly. "Do you know how many trees are chopped down every year to send Christmas cards?"

"I am *late* for—" Lauren said, and he wasn't there anymore.

He didn't vanish like in the movies, or fade out slowly. He simply wasn't there.

"—work," Lauren said. She went and looked in the living room. The TV was still on, but he wasn't there, or in the bedroom. She went into the bathroom and pulled the shower curtain back, but he wasn't there either.

"It was a hallucination," she said out loud, "brought on by stress." She looked at her watch, hoping it had been part of the hallucination, but it still read 1:15. "I will figure this out later," she said. "I *have* to get back to work."

She went back in the living room. The TV was off. She went into the kitchen. He wasn't there. Neither were her Christmas cards, exactly.

"You! Spirit!" she shouted. "You come back here this minute!"

"You're late," Evie said, filling out a catalog form. "You will not believe who was just here. Scott Buckley. God, he is so cute." She looked up. "What happened?" she said. "Didn't they hold the dress?"

"Do you know anything about magic?" Lauren said.

"What *happened*?"

"My sister sent me her Christmas present," Lauren said grimly. "I need to talk to someone who knows something about magic."

"Fat . . . I mean Fred Hatch is a magician. What did your sister send you?"

Lauren started down the hall to Documentation at a half-run.

"I told Scott you'd be back any minute," Evie said. "He said he wanted to talk to you."

Lauren opened the door to Documentation and started looking over partitions into the maze of cubicles. They were all empty.

"Anybody here?" Lauren called. "Hello?"

A middle-aged woman emerged from the maze, carrying five rolls of wrapping paper and a large pair of scissors. "You don't have any Scotch tape, do you?" she asked Lauren.

"Do you know where Fred Hatch is?" Lauren asked.

The woman pointed toward the interior of the maze with a roll of reindeer-covered paper. "Over there. Doesn't *anyone* have any tape? I'm going to have to staple my Christmas presents."

Lauren worked her way toward where the woman had pointed, looking over partitions as she went. Fred was in the center one, leaning back in a chair, his hands folded over his ample stomach, staring at a screen covered with yellow numbers.

"Excuse me," Lauren said, and Fred immediately sat forward and stood up.

"I need to talk to you," she said. "Is there somewhere we can talk privately?"

"Right here," Fred said. "My assistant's on the 800 line in my office, placing a catalog order, and everyone else is next door in Graphic Design at a Tupperware party." He pushed a key, and the computer screen went blank. "What did you want to talk to me about?"

"Evie said you're a magician," she said.

He looked embarrassed. "Not really. The PMS Committee put me in charge of the magic show for the office party last year, and I came up with an act. This year, luckily, they assigned me to play Santa Claus." He smiled and patted his stomach. "I'm the right shape for the part, and I don't have to worry about the tricks not working."

"Oh, dear," Lauren said. "I hoped . . . do you know any magicians?"

"The guy at the novelty shop," he said, looking worried. "What's the matter? Did PMS assign you the magic show this year?"

"No." She sat down on the edge of his desk. "My sister is into New Age stuff, and she sent me this spirit—"

"Spirit," he said. "A ghost, you mean?"

"No. A person. I mean he looks like a person. He says he's the Spirit of Christmas Present, as in Gift, not Here and Now."

"And you're sure he's not a person? I mean, tricks can sometimes really look like magic."

"There's a Christmas tree in my kitchen," she said.

"Christmas tree?" he said warily.

"Yes. The spirit was upset because my Christmas cards weren't on recycled paper. He asked me if I knew how many trees were chopped down to send Christmas cards, then he disappeared, and when I went back in the kitchen there was this Christmas tree in my kitchen."

"And there's no way he could have gotten into your apartment earlier and put it there?"

"It's *growing* out of the floor. Besides, it wasn't there when we were in the kitchen five minutes before. See, he was watching *It's a Wonderful Life* on TV, which, by the way, he turned on without using the remote, and he asked me if I had any Evian water, and he went into the kitchen and . . . this is ridiculous. You have to think I'm crazy. *I* think I'm crazy just listening to myself tell this ridiculous story. Evian water!" She folded her arms. "People have a lot of nervous breakdowns around Christmastime. Do you think I could be having one?"

The woman with the wrapping-paper rolls peered over the cubicle. "Have you got a tape dispenser?"

Fred shook his head.

"How about a stapler?"

Fred handed her his stapler, and she left.

"Well," Lauren said when she was sure the woman was gone, "do you think I'm having a nervous breakdown?"

"That depends," he said.

"On what?"

"On whether there's really a tree growing out of your kitchen floor. You said he got angry because your Christmas cards weren't on recycled paper. Do you think he's dangerous?"

"I don't know. He says he's here to give me whatever I want for Christmas. Except a fur coat. He's opposed to the killing of endangered species."

"A spirit who's an animal-rights activist!" Fred said delightedly. "Where did your sister get him from?"

"The astral plane," Lauren said. "She was trance-channeling or something. I don't care where he came from. I just want to get rid of him before he decides my Christmas presents aren't recyclable, too."

"Okay," he said, hitting a key on the computer. The screen lit up. "The first thing we need to do is find out what he is and how he got here. I want you to call your sister. Maybe she knows some New Age spell for getting rid of the spirit." He began to type rapidly. "I'll get on the Net and see if I can find someone who knows something about magic."

He swiveled around to face her. "You're sure you want to get rid of him?"

"I have a *tree* growing out of my kitchen floor!"

"But what if he's telling the truth? What if he really can get you what you want for Christmas?"

"What I *wanted* was to mail my Christmas cards, which are now shedding needles on the kitchen tile. Who knows what he'll do next?"

"Yeah," he said. "Listen, whether he's dangerous or not, I

think I should go home with you after work, in case he shows up again, but I've got a PMS meeting for the office party—"

"That's okay. He's an animal-rights activist. He's not dangerous."

"That doesn't necessarily follow," Fred said. "I'll come over as soon as my meeting's over, and meanwhile I'll check the Net. Okay?"

"Okay," she said. She started out of the cubicle and then stopped. "I really appreciate your believing me, or at least not saying you don't believe me."

He smiled at her. "I don't have any choice. You're the only other person in the world who likes *Miracle on 34th Street* better than *It's a Wonderful Life*. And Fred Gailey believed Macy's Santa Claus was really Santa Claus, didn't he?"

"Yeah," she said. "I don't think this guy is Santa Claus. He was wearing Birkenstocks."

"I'll meet you at your front door," he said. He sat down at the computer and began typing.

Lauren went out through the maze of cubicles and into the hall.

"*There* you are!" Scott said. "I've been looking for you all over." He smiled meltingly. "I'm in charge of buying gifts for the office party, and I need your help."

"My help?"

"Yeah. Picking them out. I hoped maybe I could talk you into going shopping with me after work tonight."

"Tonight?" she said. "I can't. I've got—" A Christmas tree growing in my kitchen. "Could we do it tomorrow after work?"

He shook his head. "I've got a date. What about later on tonight? The stores are open till nine. It shouldn't take more than a couple of hours to do the shopping, and then we could go have a late supper somewhere. What say I pick you up at your apartment at six-thirty?"

And have the spirit lying on the couch, drinking Evian water and watching TV? "I can't," she said regretfully.

Even his frown was cute. "Oh, well," he said, and shrugged. "Too bad. I guess I'll have to get somebody else." He gave her another adorable smile and went off down the hall to ask somebody else.

I hate you, Spirit of Christmas Present, Lauren thought, standing there watching Scott's handsome back recede. You'd better not be there when I get home.

A woman came down the hall, carrying a basket of candy canes. "Compliments of the Personnel Morale Special Committee," she said, offering one to Lauren. "You look like you could use a little Christmas spirit."

"No, thanks, I've already got one," Lauren said.

The door to her apartment was locked, which didn't mean much, since the chain and the deadbolt had both been on when he got in before. But he wasn't in the living room, and the TV was off.

He had been there, though. There was an empty Evian water bottle on the coffee table. She picked it up and took it into the kitchen. The tree was still there, too. She pushed one of the branches aside so she could get to the wastebasket and threw the bottle away.

"Don't you know plastic bottles are nonbiodegradable?" the spirit said. He was standing on the other side of the tree, hanging things on it. He was dressed in khaki shorts and a "Save the Rain Forest" T-shirt, and had a red bandanna tied around his head. "You should recycle your bottles."

"It's your bottle," Lauren said. "What are you doing here, Spirit?"

"Chris," he corrected her. "These are organic ornaments," he said. He held one of the brown things out to her. "Handmade by the Yanomamo Indians. Each one is made of natural by-products found in the Brazilian rain forest." He hung the brown thing on the tree. "Have you decided what you want for Christmas?"

"Yes," she said. "I want you to go away."

He looked surprised. "I can't do that. Not until I give you your heart's desire."

"That is my heart's desire. I want you to go away and take this tree and your Yanomamo ornaments with you."

"You know the biggest problem I have as the Spirit of Christmas Present?" he said. He reached into the back pocket of his shorts and pulled out a brown garland of what looked like coffee beans. "My biggest problem is that people don't know what they want."

"I know what I want," Lauren said. "I don't want to have to write my Christmas cards all over again—"

"You didn't write them," he said, draping the garland over the branches. "They were printed. Do you know that the inks used on those cards contain harmful chemicals?"

"I don't want to be lectured on environmental issues, I don't want to have to fight my way through a forest to get to the refrigerator, and I don't want to have to turn down dates because I have a spirit in my apartment. I want a nice, quiet Christmas with no hassles. I want to exchange a few presents with my friends and go to the office Christmas party and . . ." And dazzle Scott Buckley in my off-the-shoulder black dress, she thought, but she decided she'd better not say that. The spirit might decide Scott's clothes weren't made of natural fibers or something and turn him into a Yanomamo Indian.

". . . and have a nice, quiet Christmas," she finished lamely.

"Take *It's a Wonderful Life*," the spirit said, squinting at the tree. "I watched it this afternoon while you were at work. Jimmy Stewart didn't know what he wanted."

He reached into his pocket again and pulled out a crooked star made of Brazil nuts and twine. "He thought he wanted to go to college and travel and get rich, but what he *really* wanted was right there in front of him the whole time."

He did something, and the top of the tree lopped over in front of him. He tied the star on with the twine, and did something else. The tree straightened up. "You only think you want me to leave," he said.

Someone knocked on the door.

"You're right," Lauren said. "I don't want you to leave. I want you to stay right there." She ran into the living room.

The spirit followed her into the living room. "Luckily, being a spirit, I know what you really want," he said, and disappeared.

She opened the door to Fred. "He was just here," she said. "He disappeared when I opened the door, which is what all the crazies say, isn't it?"

"Yeah," Fred said. "Or else, 'He's right there. Can't you see him?' " He looked curiously around the room. "Where was he?"

"In the kitchen," she said, shutting the door. "Decorating a tree which probably isn't there either." She led him into the kitchen.

The tree was still there, and there were large brownish cards stuck all over it.

"You really do have a tree growing in your kitchen," Fred said, squatting down to look at the roots. "I wonder if the people downstairs have roots sticking out of their ceiling." He stood up. "What are these?" he said, pointing at the brownish cards.

"Christmas cards." She pulled one off. "I told him I wanted mine back." She read the card aloud. " 'In the time it takes you to read this Christmas card, eighty-two harp seals will have been clubbed to death for their fur.' " She opened it up. " 'Happy Holidays.' "

"Cheery," Fred said. He took the card from her and turned it over. " 'This card is printed on recycled paper with vegetable inks and can be safely used as compost.' "

"Did anyone on the Net know how to club a spirit to death?" she asked.

"No. Didn't your sister have any ideas?"

"She didn't know how she got him in the first place. She and her Maharishi were channeling an Egyptian nobleman and he suddenly appeared, wearing a 'Save the Dolphins' T-shirt. I got the idea the Maharishi was as surprised as she was." She sat down at the kitchen table. "I tried to get him to go away this afternoon, but he said he has to give me my heart's desire first." She looked up at Fred, who was cautiously sniffing one of the organic ornaments. "Didn't you find out anything on the Net?"

"I found out there are a lot of loonies with computers. What *are* these?"

"By-products of the Brazilian rain forest." She stood up. "I told him my heart's desire was for him to leave, and he said I didn't know what I really wanted."

"Which is what?"

"I don't know," she said. "I went into the living room to answer the door, and he said that luckily he knew what I wanted because he was a spirit, and I told him to stay right where he was, and he disappeared."

"Show me," he said.

She took him into the living room and pointed at where he'd been standing, and Fred squatted down again and peered at the carpet.

"How does he disappear?"

"I don't know. He just . . . isn't there."

Fred stood up. "Has he changed anything else? Besides the tree?"

"Not that I know of. He turned the TV on without the remote," she said, looking around the room. The shopping bags were still on the coffee table. She looked through them and pulled out the video. "Here. I'm your Secret Santa. I'm not supposed to give it to you till Christmas Eve, but maybe you'd better take it before he turns it into a snowy owl or something."

She handed it to him. "Go ahead. Open it."

He unwrapped it. "Oh," he said without enthusiasm. "Thanks."

"I remember last year at the party we talked about it, and I was afraid you might already have a copy. You don't, do you?"

"No," he said, still in that flat voice.

"Oh, good. I had a hard time finding it. You were right when you said we were the only two people in the world who liked *Miracle on 34th Street*. Everybody else I know thinks *It's a Wonderful Life* is—"

"You bought me *Miracle on 34th Street*?" he said, frowning.

"It's the original black-and-white version. I hate those colorized things, don't you? Everyone has gray teeth."

"Lauren." He held the box out to her so she could read the front. "I think your friend's been fixing things again."

She took the box from him. On the cover was a picture of Jimmy Stewart and Donna Reed dancing the Charleston.

"Oh, no! That little rat!" she said. "He must have changed it when he was looking at it. He told me *It's a Wonderful Life* was his favorite movie."

"Et tu, Brute?" Fred said, shaking his head.

"Do you suppose he changed all my other Christmas presents?"

"We'd better check."

"If he has . . ." she said, darting into the kitchen. She dropped to her knees and started rummaging through them.

"Do you think they look the same?" Fred asked, squatting down beside her.

"*Your* present looked the same." She grabbed a package wrapped in red-and-gold paper and began feeling it. "Evie's present is okay, I think."

"What is it?"

"A stapler. She's always losing hers. I put her name on it in Magic Marker." She handed it to him to feel.

"It feels like a stapler, all right," he said.

"I think we'd better open it and make sure."

Fred tore off the paper. "It's still a stapler," he said. looking at it. "What a great idea for a Christmas present! Everybody in Documentation's always losing their staplers. I think PMS steals them to use on their Christmas memos." He handed it back to her. "Now you'll have to wrap it again."

"That's okay," Lauren said. "At least it wasn't a Yanomamo ornament."

"But it might be any minute," Fred said, straightening up. "There's no telling what he might take a notion to transform next. I think you'd better call your sister again, and ask her to ask the Maharishi if *he* knows how to send spirits back to the astral plane, and I'll go see what I can find out about exorcism."

"Okay," Lauren said, following him to the door. "Don't take the videotape with you. Maybe I can get him to change it back."

"Maybe," Fred said, frowning. "You're sure he said he was here to give you your heart's desire?"

"I'm sure."

"Then why would he change my videotape?" he said thoughtfully. "It's too bad your sister couldn't have conjured up a nice, straightforward spirit."

"Like Santa Claus," Lauren said.

Her sister wasn't home. Lauren tried her off and on all evening, and when she finally got her, she couldn't talk. "The Maharishi and I are going to Barbados. They're having a harmonic divergence there on Christmas Eve, so you need to send my Christmas present to Barbados," she said, and hung up.

"I don't even have her Christmas present bought yet," Lauren said to the couch, "and it's all your fault."

She went into the kitchen and glared at the tree. "I don't even dare go shopping because you might turn the couch into a humpbacked whale while I'm gone," she said, and then clapped her hand over her mouth.

She peered cautiously into the living room and then made a careful circuit of the whole apartment, looking for endangered species. There were no signs of any, and no sign of the spirit. She went back into the living room and turned on the TV. Jimmy Stewart was dancing the Charleston with Donna Reed. She picked up the remote and hit the channel button. Now Jimmy Stewart was singing, "Buffalo Gals, Won't You Come Out Tonight?"

She hit the automatic channel changer. Jimmy Stewart was on every channel except one. The Ghost of Christmas Present was on that one, telling Scrooge to change his ways. She watched the rest of A Christmas Carol. When it reached the part where the Cratchits were sitting down to their Christmas dinner, she remembered she hadn't had any supper and went into the kitchen.

The tree was completely blocking the cupboards, but by mightily pushing several branches aside she was able to get to the refrigerator. The eggnog was gone. So were the Stouffer's frozen entrées. The only thing in the refrigerator was a half-empty bottle of Evian water.

She shoved her way out of the kitchen and sat back down on the couch. Fred had told her to call if anything happened, but it was after eleven o'clock, and she had a feeling the eggnog had been gone for some time.

A Christmas Carol was over, and the opening credits of the

Miracle 29

next movie were starting. "Frank Capra's *It's a Wonderful Life*. Starring Jimmy Stewart and Donna Reed."

She must have fallen asleep. When she woke up, *Miracle on 34th Street* was on, and the store manager was giving Edmund Gwenn as Macy's Santa Claus a list of toys he was supposed to push if Macy's didn't have what the children asked Santa for.

"Finally," Lauren said, watching Edmund Gwenn tear the list into pieces, "something good to watch," and promptly fell asleep. When she woke up again, John Payne as Fred Gailey was kissing Doris, a.k.a. Maureen O'Hara, and someone was knocking on the door.

I don't remember anyone knocking on the door, she thought groggily. Fred told Doris how he'd convinced the State of New York that Edmund Gwenn was Santa Claus, and then they both stared disbelievingly at a cane standing in the corner. "The End" came on the screen.

The knocking continued.

"Oh," Lauren said, and answered the door.

It was Fred, carrying a McDonald's sack.

"What time is it?" Lauren said, blinking at him.

"Seven o'clock. I brought you an Egg McMuffin and some orange juice."

"Oh, you wonderful person!" she said. She grabbed the sack and took it over to the coffee table. "You don't know what he did." She reached into the sack and pulled out the sandwich. "He transformed the food in my refrigerator into Evian water."

He was looking curiously at her. "Didn't you go to bed last night? He didn't come back, did he?"

"No. I waited for him, and I guess I fell asleep." She took a huge bite of the sandwich.

Fred sat down beside her. "What's that?" He pointed to a pile of dollar bills on the coffee table.

"I don't know," Lauren said.

Fred picked up the bills. Under them was a handful of change and a piece of pink paper. " 'Returned three boxes Christmas cards for refund,' " Lauren said, reading it. " '$38.18.' "

"That's what's here," Fred said, counting the money. "He didn't turn your Christmas cards into a Douglas fir after all. He took them back and got a refund."

"Then that means the tree isn't in the kitchen!" she said, jumping up and running to look. "No, it doesn't."

She came back and sat down on the couch.

"But at least you got your money back," Fred said. And it fits in with what I learned on the Net last night. They think he's a friendly spirit, probably some sort of manifestation of the seasonal spirit. Apparently these are fairly common, variations of Santa Claus being the most familiar, but there are other ones, too. All benign. They think he's probably telling the truth about wanting to give you your heart's desire."

"Do they know how to get rid of him?" she asked, and took a bite.

"No. Apparently no one's ever wanted to exorcise one." He pulled a piece of paper out of his pocket. "I got a list of exorcism books to try, though, and this one guy, Clarence, said the most important thing in an exorcism is to know exactly what kind of spirit it is."

"How do we do that?" Lauren asked with her mouth full.

"By their actions," Clarence said. "He said appearance doesn't mean anything because seasonal spirits are frequently in disguise. He said we need to write down everything the spirit's said and done, so I want you to tell me exactly what he did." He took a pen and a notebook out of his jacket pocket. "Everything from the first time you saw him."

"Just a minute." She finished the last bite of sandwich and took a drink of the orange juice. "Okay. He knocked on the door, and when I answered it, he told me he was here to give me a Christmas present, and I told him I wasn't interested, and I shut the door and started into the bedroom to hang up my dress and—my dress!" she gasped and went tearing into the bedroom.

"What's the matter?" Fred said, following her.

She flung the closet door open and began pushing clothes madly along the bar. "If he's transformed this—" She stopped pushing hangers. "I'll kill him," she said and lifted out a brownish collection of feathers and dried leaves. "Benign??" she said. "Do you call that benign??"

Fred gingerly touched a brown feather. "What was it?"

"A dress," she said. "My beautiful black, off-the-shoulder, drop-dead dress."

"Really?" he said doubtfully. He lifted up some of the brownish leaves. "I think it still is a dress," he said. "Sort of."

She crumpled the leaves and feathers against her and sank down on the bed. "All I wanted was to go to the office party!"

"Don't you have anything else you can wear to the office party? What about that pretty red thing you wore last year?"

She shook her head emphatically. "Scott didn't even notice it!"

"And that's your heart's desire?" Fred said after a moment. "To have Scott Buckley notice you at the office party?"

"Yes, and he would have, too! It had sequins on it, and it fit perfectly!" She held out what might have been a sleeve. Greenish-brown lumps dangled from brownish strips of bamboo. "And now he's ruined it!"

She flung the dress on the floor and stood up. "I don't care what this Clarence person says. He is not benign! And he is not trying to get me what I want for Christmas. He is trying to ruin my life!"

She saw the expression on Fred's face and stopped. "I'm sorry," she said. "None of this is your fault. You've been trying to help me."

"And I've been doing about as well as your spirit," he said. "Look, there has to be some way to get rid of him. Or at least get the dress back. Clarence said he knew some transformation spells. I'll go on to work and see what I can find out."

He went out into the living room and over to the door. "Maybe you can go back to the store and see if they have another dress like it." He opened the door.

"Okay." Lauren nodded. "I'm sorry I yelled at you. And you have been a lot of help."

"Right," he said glumly, and went out.

"Where'd you get that dress?" Jimmy Stewart said to Donna Reed.

Lauren whirled around. The TV was on. Donna Reed was showing Jimmy Stewart her new dress.

"Where are you?" Lauren demanded, looking at the couch. "I want you to change that dress back right now!"

"Don't you like it?" the spirit said from the bedroom. "It's completely biodegradable."

She stomped into the bedroom. He was putting the dress on the hanger and making little "tsk"-ing noises. "You have to be careful with natural fibers," he said reprovingly.

"Change it back the way it was. This instant."

"It was handmade by the Yanomamo Indians," he said, smoothing down what might be the skirt. "Do you realize that their natural habitat is being destroyed at the rate of 750 acres a day?"

"I don't care. I want my dress back."

He carried the dress on its hanger over to the chest. "It's so interesting. Donna Reed knew right away she was in love with

Jimmy Stewart, but he was so busy thinking about college and his new suitcase, he didn't even know she existed." He hung up the dress. "He practically had to be hit over the head."

"I'll hit you over the head if you don't change that dress back this instant, Spirit," she said, looking around for something hard.

"Call me Chris," he said. "Did you know sequins are made from nonrenewable resources?" and disappeared as she swung the lamp.

"And good riddance," she shouted to the air.

They had the dress in a size three. Lauren put herself through the indignity of trying to get into it and then went to work. The receptionist was watching Jimmy Stewart standing on the bridge in the snow and weeping into a Kleenex. She handed Lauren her messages.

There were two memos from the PMS Committee—they were having a sleigh ride after work, and she was supposed to bring cheese puffs to the office party. There wasn't a message from Fred.

"Oh!" the receptionist wailed. "This part is so sad!"

"I hate *It's a Wonderful Life*," Lauren said, and went up to her desk. "I hate Christmas," she said to Evie.

"It's normal to hate Christmas," Evie said, looking up from the book she was reading. "This book, it's called *Let's Forget Christmas*, says it's because everyone has these unrealistic expectations. When they get presents, they—"

"Oh, that reminds me," Lauren said. She rummaged in her bag and brought out Evie's present, fingering it quickly to make sure it was still a stapler. It seemed to be. She held it out to Evie. "Merry Christmas."

"I don't have yours wrapped yet," Evie said. "I don't even have my wrapping paper bought yet. The book says I'm suffering from an avoidance complex." She picked up the package. "Do I have to open it now? I know it will be something I love, and you won't like what I got you half as well, and I'll feel incredibly guilty and inadequate."

"You don't have to open it now," Lauren said. "I just thought I'd better give it to you before—" She picked her messages up off her desk and started looking through them. "Before I forgot. There haven't been any messages from Fred, have there?"

"Yeah. He was here about fifteen minutes ago looking for you. He said to tell you the Net hadn't been any help, and he was going to try the library." She looked sadly at the present. "It's even wrapped great," she said gloomily. "I went shopping for a dress for the office party last night, and do you think I could find anything off-the-shoulder or with sequins? I couldn't even find anything I'd be caught dead in. Did you know the rate of stress-related illnesses at Christmas is seven times higher than the rest of the year?"

"I can relate to that," Lauren said.

"No, you can't. You didn't end up buying some awful gray thing with gold chains hanging all over it. At least Scott will notice me. He'll say, 'Hi, Evie, are you dressed as Marley's ghost?' And there you'll be, looking fabulous in black sequins—"

"No, I won't," Lauren said.

"Why? Didn't they hold it for you?"

"It was . . . defective. Did Fred want to talk to me?"

"I don't know. He was on his way out. He had to go pick up his Santa Claus suit. Oh, my God." Her voice dropped to a whisper. "It's Scott Buckley."

"Hi," Scott said to Lauren. "I was wondering if you could go shopping with me tonight."

Lauren stared at him, so taken aback she couldn't speak.

"When you couldn't go last night, I decided to cancel my date."

"Uh . . . I . . ." she said.

"I thought we could buy the presents and then have some dinner."

She nodded.

"Great," Scott said. "I'll come over to your apartment around six-thirty."

"No!" Lauren said. "I mean, why don't we go straight from work?"

"Good idea. I'll come up here and get you." He smiled meltingly and left.

"I think I'll kill myself," Evie said. "Did you know the rate of suicides at Christmas is four times higher than the rest of the year? He is so cute," she said, looking longingly down the hall after him. "There's Fred."

Lauren looked up. Fred was coming toward her desk with a Santa Claus costume and a stack of books. Lauren hurried across to him.

"This is everything the library had on exorcisms and the occult," Fred said, transferring half of the books to her arms. "I thought we could both go through them today, and then get together tonight and compare notes."

"Oh, I can't," Lauren said. "I promised Scott I'd help him pick out the presents for the office party tonight. I'm sorry. I could tell him I can't."

"Your heart's desire? Are you kidding?" He started awkwardly piling the books back on his load. "You go shopping. I'll go through the books and let you know if I come up with anything."

"Are you sure?" she said guiltily. "I mean, you shouldn't have to do all the work."

"It's my pleasure," he said. He started to walk away and then stopped. "You didn't tell the spirit Scott was your heart's desire, did you?"

"Of course not. Why?"

"I was just wondering . . . nothing. Never mind." He walked off down the hall. Lauren went back to her desk.

"Did you know the rate of depression at Christmas is sixteen times higher than the rest of the year?" Evie said. She handed Lauren a package.

"What's this?"

"It's from your Secret Santa."

Lauren opened it. It was a large book entitled *It's a Wonderful Life: The Photo Album*. On the cover, Jimmy Stewart was looking depressed.

"I figure it'll take a half hour or so to pick out the presents," Scott said, leading her past two inflatable palm trees into The Upscale Oasis. "And then we can have some supper and get acquainted." He lay down on a massage couch. "What do you think about this?"

"How many presents do we have to buy?" Lauren asked, looking around the store. There were a lot of inflatable palm trees, and a jukebox, and several life-size cardboard cutouts of Malcolm Forbes and Leona Helmsley. Against the far wall were two high-rise aquariums and a bank of televisions with neon-outlined screens.

"Seventy-two." He got up off the massage couch, handed her the list of employees and went over to a display of brown boxes tied with twine. "What about these? They're handmade Yanomamo Christmas ornaments."

"No," Lauren said. "How much money do we have to spend?"

"The PMS Committee budgeted six thousand, and there was five hundred left in the Sunshine fund. We can spend . . ." He picked up a pocket calculator in the shape of Donald Trump and punched several buttons. "Ninety dollars per person, including tax. How about this?" He held up an automatic cat feeder.

"We got those last year," Lauren said. She picked up a digital umbrella and put it back down.

"How about a car fax?" Scott said. "No, wait. This, this is it!"

Lauren turned around. Scott was holding up what looked like a gold cordless phone. "It's an investment pager," he said, punching keys. "See, it gives you the Dow Jones, treasury bonds, interest rates. Isn't it perfect?"

"Well," Lauren said.

"See, this is the hostile takeover alarm, and every time the Federal Reserve adjusts the interest rate it beeps."

Lauren read the tag. " 'Portable Plutocrat. $74.99.' "

"Great," Scott said. "We'll have money left over."

"To invest," Lauren said.

He went off to see if they had seventy-two of them, and Lauren wandered over to the bank of televisions.

There was a videotape of *Miracle on 34th Street* lying on top of the VCR/shower massage. Lauren looked around to see if anyone was watching and then popped the *Wonderful Life* tape out and stuck in *Miracle.*

A dozen Edmund Gwenns dressed as Macy's Santa Claus appeared on the screens, listening to twelve store managers tell them which overstocked toys to push.

Scott came over, lugging four shopping bags. "They come gift-wrapped," he said happily, showing her a Portable Plutocrat wrapped in green paper with gold dollar signs. "Which gives us a free evening."

"That's what I've been fighting against for years," a dozen Edmund Gwenns said, tearing a dozen lists to bits, "the way they commercialize Christmas."

•   •   •

"What I thought," Scott said when they got in the car, "was that instead of going out for supper, we'd take these over to your apartment and order in."

"Order in?" Lauren said, clutching the bag of Portable Plutocrats on her lap to her.

"I know a great Italian place that delivers. Angel-hair pasta, wine, everything. Or, if you'd rather, we could run by a grocery store and pick up some stuff to cook."

"Actually, my kitchen's kind of a mess," she said. There is a Christmas tree in it, she thought, with organic by-products hanging on it.

He pulled up outside her apartment building. "Then Italian it is." He got out of the car and began unloading shopping bags. "You like prosciutto? They have a great melon and prosciutto."

"Actually, the whole apartment's kind of a disaster," Lauren said, following him up the stairs. "You know, wrapping presents and everything. There are ribbons and tags and paper all over the floor and—"

"Great," he said, stopping in front of her door. "We have to put tags on the presents, anyway."

"They don't need tags, do they?" Lauren said desperately. "I mean, they're all exactly alike."

"It personalizes them," he said, "it shows the gift was chosen especially for them." He looked expectantly at the key in her hand and then at the door.

She couldn't hear the TV, which was a good sign. And every time Fred had come over, the spirit had disappeared. So all I have to do is keep him out of the kitchen, she thought.

She opened the door and Scott pushed past her and dumped the shopping bags onto the coffee table. "Sorry," he said. "Those were really heavy." He straightened up and looked around the living room. There was no sign of the spirit, but there were three Evian water bottles on the coffee table. "This doesn't look too messy. You should see my apartment. I'll bet your kitchen's neater than mine, too."

Lauren walked swiftly over to the kitchen and pulled the door shut. "I wouldn't bet on it. Aren't there still some more presents to bring up?"

"Yeah. I'll go get them. Shall I call the Italian place first?"

"No," Lauren said, standing with her back against the kitchen door. "Why don't you bring the bags up first?"

"Okay," he said, smiling meltingly, and went out.

Lauren leaped to the door, put the deadbolt and the chain on, and then ran back to the kitchen and opened the door. The tree was still there. She pulled the door hastily to and walked rapidly into the bedroom. He wasn't there, or in the bathroom. "Thank you," she breathed, looking heavenward, and went back in the living room.

The TV was on. Edmund Gwenn was shouting at the store psychologist.

"You know, you were right," the spirit said. He was stretched out on the couch, wearing a "Save the Black-Footed Ferret" T-shirt and jeans. "It's not a bad movie. Of course, it's not as good as *It's a Wonderful Life*, but I like the way everything works out at the end."

"What are you doing here?" she demanded, glancing anxiously at the door.

"Watching *Miracle on 34th Street*," he said, pointing at the screen. Edmund Gwenn was brandishing his cane at the store psychiatrist. "I like the part where Edmund Gwenn asks Natalie Wood what she wants for Christmas, and she shows him the picture of the house."

Lauren picked up Fred's video and brandished it at him. "Fine. Then you can change Fred's video back."

"Okay," he said, and did something. She looked at Fred's video. It showed Edmund Gwenn hugging Natalie Wood in front of a yellow moon with Santa Claus's sleigh and reindeer flying across it. Lauren put the video hastily down on the coffee table.

"Thank you," she said. "And my dress."

"Natalie Wood doesn't really want a house, of course. What she really wants is for Maureen O'Hara to marry John Payne. The house is just a symbol for what she really wants."

On the TV Edmund Gwenn rapped the store psychologist smartly on the forehead with his cane.

There was a knock on the door. "It's me," Scott said.

"I also like the part where Edmund Gwenn yells at the store manager for pushing merchandise nobody wants. Christmas presents should be something the person wants. Aren't you going to answer the door?"

"Aren't you going to disappear?" she whispered.

"Disappear?" he said incredulously. "The movie isn't over. And besides, I still haven't gotten you what you want for Christmas." He did something, and a bowl of trail mix appeared on his stomach.

Scott knocked again.

Lauren went over to the door and opened it two inches.

"It's me," Scott said. "Why do you have the chain on?"

"I . . ." She looked hopefully at Chris. He was eating trail mix and watching Maureen O'Hara bending over the store psychologist, trying to wake him up.

"Scott, I'm sorry, but I think I'd better take a rain check on supper."

He looked bewildered. And cute. "But I thought . . ." he said.

So did I, she thought. But I have a spirit on my couch who's perfectly capable of turning you into a Brazilian rain forest by-product.

"The Italian take-out sounds great," she said, "but it's kind of late, and we've both got to go to work tomorrow."

"Tomorrow's Saturday."

"Uh . . . I meant go to work on wrapping presents. Tomorrow's Christmas Eve, and I haven't even started my wrapping. And I have to make cheese puffs for the office party and wash my hair and . . ."

"Okay, okay, I get the message," he said. "I'll just bring in the presents and then leave."

She thought of telling him to leave them in the hall, and then closed the door a little and took the chain off the door.

Go *away*! she thought at the spirit, who was eating trail mix.

She opened the door far enough so she could slide out, and pulled it to behind her. "Thanks for a great evening," she said, taking the shopping bags from Scott. "Good night."

"Good night," he said, still looking bewildered. He started down the hall. At the stairs he turned and smiled.

I'm going to kill him, Lauren thought, waving back, and took the shopping bags inside.

The spirit wasn't there. The trail mix was still on the couch, and the TV was still on.

"Come back here!" she shouted. "You little rat! You have ruined my dress and my date, and you're not going to ruin anything else! You're going to change back my dress and my Christmas cards, and you're going to get that tree out of my kitchen right *now!*"

Her voice hung in the air. She sat down on the couch, still holding the shopping bags. On the TV, Edmund Gwenn was sitting in Bellevue, staring at the wall.

"At least Scott finally noticed me," she said, and set the shopping bags down on the coffee table. They rattled.

"Oh, no!" she said. "Not the Plutocrats!"

"The problem is," Fred said, closing the last of the books on the occult, "that we can't exorcise him if we don't know which seasonal spirit he is, and he doesn't fit the profiles of any of these. He must be in disguise."

"I don't want to exorcise him," Lauren said. "I want to kill him."

"Even if we did manage to exorcise him, there'd be no guarantee that the things he's changed would go back to their original state."

"And I'd be stuck with explaining what happened to six thousand dollars' worth of Christmas presents."

"Those Portable Plutocrats cost six thousand dollars?"

"$5895.36."

Fred gave a low whistle. "Did your spirit say why he didn't like them? Other than the obvious, I mean. That they were non-biodegradable or something?"

"No. He didn't even notice them. He was watching *Miracle on 34th Street*, and he was talking about how he liked the way things worked out at the end and the part about the house."

"Nothing about Christmas presents?"

"I don't remember." She sank down on the couch. "Yes, I do. He said he liked the part where Edmund Gwenn yelled at the store manager for talking people into buying things they didn't want. He said Christmas presents should be something the person wanted."

"Well, that explains why he transformed the Plutocrats then," Fred said. "It probably also means there's no way you can talk him into changing them back. And I've got to have something to pass out at the office party, or you'll be in trouble. So we'll just have to come up with replacement presents."

"Replacement presents?" Lauren said. "How? It's ten o'clock, the office party's tomorrow night, and how do we know he won't transform the replacement presents once we've got them?"

"We'll buy people what they want. Was six thousand all the money you and Scott had?"

"No," Lauren said, rummaging through one of the shopping bags. "PMS budgeted sixty-five hundred."

"How much have you got left?"

She pulled out a sheaf of papers. "He didn't transform the purchase orders or the receipt," she said, looking at them. "The investment pagers cost $5895.36. We have $604.64 left." She handed him the papers. "That's $8.39 apiece."

He looked at the receipt speculatively and then into the shopping bag. "I don't suppose we could take these back and get a refund from The Upscale Oasis?"

"They're not going to give us $5895.36 for seventy-two 'Save the Ozone Layer' buttons," Lauren said. "And there's nothing we can buy for eight dollars that will convince PMS it cost sixty-five hundred. And where am I going to get the money to pay back the difference?"

"I don't think you'll have to. Remember when Chris changed your Christmas cards into the tree? He didn't really. He returned them somehow to the store and got a refund. Maybe he's done the same thing with the Plutocrats and the money will turn up on your coffee table tomorrow morning."

"And if it doesn't?"

"We'll worry about that tomorrow. Right now we've got to come up with presents to pass out at the party."

"Like what?"

"Staplers."

"Staplers?"

"Like the one you got Evie. Everybody in my department's always losing their staplers, too. And their tape dispensers. It's an office party. We'll buy everybody something they want for the office."

"But how will we know what that is? There are seventy-two people on this list."

"We'll call the department heads and ask them, and then we'll go shopping." He stood up. "Where's your phone book?"

"Next to the tree." She followed him into the kitchen. "How are we going to go shopping? It's ten o'clock at night."

"Bizmart's open till eleven," he said, opening the phone book, "and the grocery store's open all night. We'll get as many of the presents as we can tonight and the rest tomorrow morning, and that still gives us all afternoon to get them wrapped. How much wrapping paper do you have?"

"Lots. I bought it half-price last year when I decided this Christmas was going to be different. A stapler doesn't seem like much of a present."

"It does if it's what you wanted." He reached for the phone.

It rang. Fred picked up the receiver and handed it to Lauren.

"Oh, Lauren," Evie's voice said. "I just opened your present, and I *love* it! It's exactly what I wanted!"

"Really?" Lauren said.

"It's perfect! I was so depressed about Christmas and the office party and still not having my shopping done. I wasn't even going to open it, but in *Let's Forget Christmas* it said you should open your presents early so they won't ruin Christmas morning, and I did, and it's wonderful! I don't even care whether Scott notices me or not! Thank you!"

"You're welcome," Lauren said, but Evie had already hung up. She looked at Fred. "That was Evie. You were right about people liking staplers." She handed him the phone. "You call the department heads. I'll get my coat."

He took the phone and began to punch in numbers, and then put it down. "What exactly did the spirit say about the ending of *Miracle on 34th Street*?"

"He said he liked the way everything worked out at the end. Why?"

He looked thoughtful. "Maybe we're going about this all wrong."

"What do you mean?"

"What if the spirit really does want to give you your heart's desire, and all this transforming stuff is some roundabout way of doing it? Like the angel in *It's a Wonderful Life*. He's supposed to save Jimmy Stewart from committing suicide, and instead of doing something logical, like talking him out of it or grabbing him, he jumps in the river so Jimmy Stewart has to save *him*."

"You're saying he turned seventy-two Portable Plutocrats into 'Save the Ozone Layer' buttons to help me?"

"I don't know. All I'm saying is that maybe you should tell him you want to go to the office party in a black sequined dress with Scott Buckley, and see what happens."

"See what happens? After what he did to my dress? If he knew I wanted Scott, he'd probably turn him into a harp seal." She put on her coat. "Well, are we going to call the department heads or not?"

The Graphic Design department wanted staplers, and so did Accounts Payable. Accounts Receivable, which was having an outbreak of stress-related Christmas colds, wanted Puffs Plus and cough drops. Document Control wanted scissors.

Scott looked at the list, checking off Systems and the other departments they'd called. "All we've got left is the PMS Committee," he said.

"I know what to get them," Lauren said. "Copies of *Let's Forget Christmas*."

They got some of the things before Bizmart closed, and Fred was back at nine Saturday morning to do the rest of it. At the bookstore they ran into the woman who had been stapling presents together the day Lauren enlisted Fred's help.

"I completely forgot my husband's first wife," she said, looking desperate, "and I don't have any idea of what to get her."

Fred handed her the videotape of *It's a Wonderful Life* they were giving the receptionist. "How about one of these?" he said.

"Do you think she'll like it?"

"*Everybody* likes it," Fred said.

"Especially the part where the bad guy steals the money, and Jimmy Stewart races around town, trying to replace it," Lauren said.

It took them most of the morning to get the rest of the presents and forever to wrap them. By four they weren't even half done.

"What's next?" Fred asked, tying the bow on the last of the staplers. He stood up and stretched.

"Cough drops," Lauren said, cutting a length of red paper with Santa Clauses on it.

He sat back down. "Ah, yes. Accounts Receivable's heart's desire."

"What's your heart's desire?" Lauren asked, folding the paper over the top of the cough drops and taping it. "What would you ask for if the spirit inflicted himself on you?"

Fred unreeled a length of ribbon. "Well, not to go to an office party, that's for sure. The only year I had an even remotely good time was last year, talking to you."

"I'm serious," Lauren said. She taped the sides and handed the package to Fred. "What do you really want for Christmas?"

"When I was eight," he said thoughtfully, "I asked for a computer for Christmas. Home computers were new then and they were pretty expensive, and I wasn't sure I'd get it. I was a lot like Natalie Wood in *Miracle on 34th Street*. I didn't believe in Santa Claus, and I didn't believe in miracles, but I really wanted it."

He cut off the length of ribbon, wrapped it around the package, and tied it in a knot.

"Did you get the computer?"

"No," he said, cutting off shorter lengths of ribbon. "Christmas morning I came downstairs, and there was a note telling me to look in the garage." He opened the scissors and pulled the ribbon across the blade, making it curl. "It was a puppy." He smiled, remembering. "The thing was, a computer was too expensive, but there was an outside chance I'd get it, or I wouldn't have asked for it. Kids don't ask for stuff they *know* is impossible."

"And you hadn't asked for a puppy because you knew you couldn't have one?"

"No, you don't understand. There are things you don't ask for because you know you can't have them, and then there are things so far outside the realm of possibility, it would never even occur to you to want them." He made the curled ribbon into a bow and fastened it to the package.

"So what you're saying is your heart's desire is something so far outside the realm of possibility, you don't even know what it is?"

"I didn't say that," he said. He stood up again. "Do you want some eggnog?"

"Yes, thanks. If it's still there."

He went into the kitchen. She could hear forest-thrashing noises and the refrigerator opening. "It's still here," he said.

"It's funny Chris hasn't been back," she called to Fred. "I keep worrying he must be up to something."

"Chris?" Fred said. He came back into the living room with two glasses of eggnog.

"The spirit. He told me to call him that," she said. "It's short for Spirit of Christmas Present." Fred was frowning. "What's wrong?" Lauren asked.

"I wonder . . . nothing. Never mind." He went over to the TV. "I don't suppose *Miracle on 34th Street*'s on TV this afternoon?"

"No, but I made him change your video back." She pointed. "It's there, on top of the TV."

He turned on the TV, inserted the video in the VCR, and hit play. He came and sat down beside Lauren. She handed him the wrapped cough drops, but he didn't take them. He was watching the TV. Lauren looked up. On the screen, Jimmy Stewart was walking past Donna Reed's house, racketing a stick along the picket fence.

"That isn't *Miracle*," Lauren said. "He told me he changed it back." She snatched up the box. It still showed Edmund Gwenn hugging Natalie Wood. "That little sneak! He only changed the box!"

She glared at the TV. On the screen Jimmy Stewart was glaring at Donna Reed.

"It's all right," Fred said, taking the package and reaching for the ribbon. "It's not a bad movie. The ending's too sentimental, and it doesn't really make sense. I mean, one minute everything's hopeless, and Jimmy Stewart's ready to kill himself, and then the angel convinces him he had a wonderful life, and suddenly everything's okay." He looked around the table, patting the spread-out wrapping paper. "But it has its moments. Have you seen the scissors?"

Lauren handed him one of the pairs they'd bought. "We'll wrap them last."

On the TV Jimmy Stewart was sitting in Donna Reed's living room, looking awkward. "What I have trouble with is Jimmy Stewart's being so self-sacrificing," she said, cutting a length of red paper with Santa Clauses on it. "I mean, he gives up college so his brother can go, and then when his brother has a chance at a good job, he gives up college *again*. He even gives up committing suicide to save Clarence. There's such a thing as being too self-sacrificing, you know."

"Maybe he gives up things because he thinks he doesn't deserve them."

"Why wouldn't he?"

"He's never gone to college, he's poor, he's deaf in one ear. Sometimes when people are handicapped or overweight they just assume they can't have the things other people have."

The telephone rang. Lauren reached for it and then realized it was on TV.

"Oh, hello, Sam," Donna Reed said, looking at Jimmy Stewart.

"Can you help me with this ribbon?" Fred said.

"Sure," Lauren said. She scooted closer to him and put her finger on the crossed ribbon to hold it taut.

Jimmy Stewart and Donna Reed were standing very close together, listening to the telephone. The voice on the phone was saying something about soybeans.

Fred still hadn't tied the knot. Lauren glanced up at him. He was looking at the TV, too.

Jimmy Stewart was looking at Donna Reed, his face nearly touching her hair. Donna Reed looked at him and then away. The voice from the phone was saying something about the chance of a lifetime, but it was obvious neither of them was hearing a word. Donna Reed looked up at him. His lips almost touched her forehead. They didn't seem to be breathing.

Lauren realized she wasn't either. She looked at Fred. He was holding the two ends of ribbon, one in each hand, and looking down at her.

"The knot," she said. "You haven't tied it."

"Oh," he said. "Sorry."

Jimmy Stewart dropped the phone with a clatter and grabbed Donna Reed by both arms. He began shaking her, yelling at her, and then suddenly she was wrapped in his arms, and he was smothering her with kisses.

"The knot," Fred said. "You have to pull your finger out."

She looked uncomprehendingly at him and then down at the

package. He had tied the knot over her finger, which was still pressing against the wrapping paper.

"Oh. Sorry," she said, and pulled her finger free. "You were right. It does have its moments."

He yanked the knot tight. "Yeah," he said. He reached for the spool of ribbon and began chopping off lengths for the bow. On the screen Donna Reed and Jimmy Stewart were being pelted with rice.

"No. You were right," he said. "He is too self-sacrificing." He waved the scissors at the screen. "In a minute he's going to give up his honeymoon to save the building and loan. It's a wonder he ever asked Donna Reed to marry him. It's a wonder he didn't try to fix her up with that guy on the phone."

The phone rang. Lauren looked at the screen, thinking it must be in the movie, but Jimmy Stewart was kissing Donna Reed in a taxicab.

"It's the phone," Fred said.

Lauren scrambled up and reached for it.

"Hi," Scott said.

"Oh, hello, Scott," Lauren said, looking at Fred.

"I was wondering about the office party tonight," Scott said. "Would you like to go with me? I could come get you and we could take the presents over together."

"Uh . . . I . . ." Lauren said. She put her hand over the receiver. "It's Scott. What am I going to tell him about the presents?"

Fred motioned her to give him the phone. "Scott," he said. "Hi. It's Fred Hatch. Yeah, Santa Claus. Listen, we ran into a problem with the presents."

Lauren closed her eyes.

"We got a call from The Upscale Oasis that investment pagers were being recalled by the Federal Safety Commission."

Lauren opened her eyes. Fred smiled at her. "Yeah. For excessive cupidity."

Lauren grinned.

"But there's nothing to worry about," Fred said. "We replaced them. We're wrapping them right now. No, it was no trouble. I was happy to help. Yeah, I'll tell her." He hung up. "Scott will be here to take you to the office party at seven-thirty," he said. "It looks like you're going to get your heart's desire after all."

"Yeah," Lauren said, looking at the TV. On the screen, the building and loan was going under.

They finished wrapping the last pair of scissors at six-thirty, and Fred went back to his apartment to change clothes and get his Santa Claus costume. Lauren packed the presents in three of the Upscale Oasis shopping bags, said sternly, "Don't you dare touch these," to the empty couch, and went to get ready.

She showered and did her hair, and then went into the bedroom to see if the spirit had biodegraded her red dress, or, by some miracle, brought the black off-the-shoulder one back. He hadn't.

She put on her red dress and went back into the living room. It was only a little after seven. She turned on the TV and put Fred's video into the VCR. She hit play. Edmund Gwenn was giving the doctor the X-ray machine he'd always wanted.

Lauren picked up one of the shopping bags and felt the top pair of scissors to make sure they hadn't been turned into bottles of Evian water. There was an envelope stuck between two of the packages. Inside was a check for $5895.36. It was made out to the Children's Hospital fund.

She shook her head, smiling, and put the check back into the envelope.

On TV, Maureen O'Hara and John Payne were watching Natalie Wood run through an empty house and out the back door to look for her swing. They looked seriously at each other. Lauren held her breath. John Payne moved forward and kissed Maureen O'Hara.

Someone knocked on the door. "That's Scott," Lauren said to John Payne, and waited till Maureen O'Hara had finished telling him she loved him before she went to open the door.

It was Fred, carrying a foil-covered plate. He was wearing the same sweater and pants he'd worn to wrap the presents. "Cheese puffs," he said. "I figured you couldn't get to your stove." He looked seriously at her. "I wouldn't worry about not having your black dress to dazzle Scott with."

He went over and set the cheese puffs on the coffee table. "You need to take the foil off and heat them in a microwave for two minutes on high. Tell PMS to put the presents in Santa's bag, and I'll be there at eleven-thirty."

"Aren't you going to the party?"

"Office parties are your idea of fun, not mine," he said. "Besides, *Miracle on 34th Street*'s on at eight. It may be the only chance I have to watch it."

"But I wanted you—"

There was a knock on the door. "That's Scott," Lauren said.

"Well," Fred said, "if the spirit doesn't do something in the next fifteen seconds, you'll have your heart's desire in spite of him." He opened the door. "Come on in," he said. "Lauren and the presents are all ready." He handed two of the shopping bags to Scott.

"I really appreciate your helping Lauren and me with all this," Scott said.

Fred handed the other shopping bag to Lauren. "It was my pleasure."

"I wish you were coming with us," she said.

"And give up a chance of seeing the real Santa Claus?" He

held the door open. "You two had better get going before something happens."

"What do you mean?" Scott said, alarmed. "Do you think these presents might be recalled, too?"

Lauren looked hopefully at the couch and then the TV. On the screen Jimmy Stewart was standing on a bridge in the snow, getting ready to kill himself.

"Afraid not," Fred said.

It was snowing by the time they pulled into the parking lot at work. "It was really selfless of Fred to help you wrap all those presents," Scott said, holding the lobby door open for Lauren. "He's a nice guy."

"Yes," Lauren said. "He is."

"Hey, look at that!" Scott said. He pointed at the security monitor. "*It's a Wonderful Life.* My favorite movie!" On the monitor Jimmy Stewart was running through the snow, shouting, "Merry Christmas!"

"Scott," Lauren said, "I can't go to the party with you."

"Just a minute, okay?" Scott said, staring at the screen. "This is my favorite part." He set the shopping bags down on the receptionist's desk and leaned his elbows on it. "This is the part where Jimmy Stewart finds out what a wonderful life he's had."

"You have to take me home," Lauren said.

There was a gust of cold air and snow. Lauren turned around.

"You forgot your cheese puffs," Fred said, holding out the foil-covered plate to Lauren.

"There's such a thing as being too self-sacrificing, you know," Lauren said.

He held the plate out to her. "That's what the spirit said."

"He came back?" She shot a glance at the shopping bags.

"Yeah. Right after you left. Don't worry about the presents.

He said he thought the staplers were a great idea. He also said not to worry about getting a Christmas present for your sister."

"My sister!" Lauren said, clapping her hand to her mouth. "I completely forgot about her."

"He said since you didn't like it, he sent her the Yanomamo dress."

"She'll love it," Lauren said.

"He also said it was a wonder Jimmy Stewart ever got Donna Reed, he was so busy giving everybody else what they wanted," he said, looking seriously at her.

"He's right," Lauren said. "Did he also tell you Jimmy Stewart was incredibly stupid for wanting to go off to college when Donna Reed was right there in front of him?"

"He mentioned it."

"What a great movie!" Scott said, turning to Lauren. "Ready to go up?"

"No," Lauren said. "I'm going with Fred to see a movie." She took the cheese puffs from Fred and handed them to Scott.

"What am I supposed to do with these?"

"Take the foil off," Fred said, "and put them in a microwave for two minutes."

"But you're my date," Scott said. "Who am I supposed to go with?"

There was a gust of cold air and snow. Everyone turned around.

"How do I look?" Evie said, taking off her coat.

"Wow!" Scott said. "You look terrific!"

Evie spun around, her shoulders bare, the sequins glittering on her black dress. "Lauren gave it to me for Christmas," she said happily. "I love Christmas, don't you?"

"I *love* that dress," Scott said.

"He also told me," Fred said, "that his favorite thing in *Miracle on 34th Street* was Santa Claus's being in disguise—"

"He wasn't in disguise," Lauren said. "Edmund Gwenn told everybody he was Santa Claus."

Fred held up a correcting finger. "He told everyone his name was Kris Kringle."

"Chris," Lauren said.

"Oh, I love this part," Evie said.

Lauren looked at her. She was standing next to Scott, watching Jimmy Stewart standing next to Donna Reed and singing "Auld Lang Syne."

"He makes all sorts of trouble for everyone," Fred said. "He turns Christmas upside down—"

"Completely disrupts Maureen O'Hara's life," Lauren said.

"But by the end, everything's worked out, the doctor has his X-ray machine, Natalie Wood has her house—"

"Maureen O'Hara has Fred—"

"And no one's quite sure how he did it, or if he did anything."

"Or if he had the whole thing planned from the beginning." She looked seriously at Fred. "He told me I only thought I knew what I wanted for Christmas."

Fred moved toward her. "He told me just because something seems impossible doesn't mean a miracle can't happen."

"What a great ending!" Evie said, sniffling. "*It's a Wonderful Life* is my favorite movie."

"Mine, too," Scott said. "Do you know how to heat up cheese puffs?" He turned to Lauren and Fred. "Cut that out, you two, we'll be late for the party."

"We're not going," Fred said, putting his arm around Lauren. They started for the door. "*Miracle*'s on at eight."

"But you can't leave," Scott said. "What about all these presents? Who's going to pass them out?"

There was a gust of cold air and snow. "Ho ho ho," Santa Claus said.

"Isn't that your costume, Fred?" Lauren said.

"Yes. It has to be back at the rental place by Monday morning," he said to Santa Claus. "And no changing it into rainforest by-products."

"*Merry* Christmas!" Santa Claus said.

"I like the way things worked out at the end," Lauren said.

"All we need is a cane standing in the corner," Fred said.

"I have no idea what you're talking about," Santa Claus said. "Where are all these presents I'm supposed to pass out?"

"Right here," Scott said. He handed one of the shopping bags to Santa Claus.

"Plastic shopping bags," Santa Claus said, making a "tsk"-ing sound. "You should be using recycled paper."

"Sorry," Scott said. He handed the cheese puffs to Evie and picked up the other two shopping bags. "Ready, Evie?"

"We can't go yet," Evie said, gazing at the security monitor. "Look, *It's a Wonderful Life* is just starting." On the screen Jimmy Stewart's brother was falling through the ice. "This is my favorite part," she said.

"Mine, too," Scott said, and went over to stand next to her.

Santa Claus squinted curiously at the monitor for a moment and then shook his head. "*Miracle on 34th Street*'s a much better movie, you know," he said reprovingly. "More realistic."

INN

Christmas Eve. The organ played the last notes of "O Come, O Come Emmanuel," and the choir sat down. Reverend Wall hobbled slowly to the pulpit, clutching his sheaf of yellowed typewritten sheets.

In the choir, Dee leaned over to Sharon and whispered, "Here we go. Twenty-four minutes and counting."

On Sharon's other side, Virginia murmured, " 'And all went to be taxed, every one into his own city.' "

Reverend Wall set the papers on the pulpit, looked rheumily out over the congregation, and said, " 'And all went to be taxed, every one into his own city. And Joseph also went up from Galilee, out of the city of Nazareth, into Judea, unto the city of David, which is called Bethlehem, because he was of the house and lineage of David. To be taxed with Mary, his espoused wife, being great with child.' " He paused.

"We know nothing of that journey up from Nazareth," Virginia whispered.

"We know nothing of that journey up from Nazareth," Reverend Wall said, in a wavering voice, "what adventures befell the young couple, what inns they stopped at along the way. All we know is that on a Christmas Eve like this one they arrived in Bethlehem, and there was no room for them at the inn."

Virginia was scribbling something on the margin of her bulletin. Dee started to cough. "Do you have any cough drops?" she whispered to Sharon.

"What happened to the ones I gave you last night?" Sharon whispered back.

"Though we know nothing of their journey," Reverend Wall said, his voice growing stronger, "we know much of the world they lived in. It was a world of censuses and soldiers, of bureaucrats and politicians, a world busy with property and rules and its own affairs."

Dee started to cough again. She rummaged in the pocket of her music folder and came up with a paper-wrapped cough drop. She unwrapped it and popped it into her mouth.

". . . a world too busy with its own business to even notice an insignificant couple from far away," Reverend Wall intoned.

Virginia passed her bulletin to Sharon. Dee leaned over to read it, too. It read, "What happened here last night after the rehearsal? When I came home from the mall, there were police cars outside."

Dee grabbed the bulletin and rummaged in her folder again. She found a pencil, scribbled "Somebody broke into the church," and passed it across Sharon to Virginia.

"You're kidding," Virginia whispered. "Were they caught?"

"No," Sharon said.

The rehearsal on the twenty-third was supposed to start at seven. By a quarter to eight the choir was still standing at the back of the sanctuary, waiting to sing the processional, the shepherds and angels were bouncing off the walls, and Reverend Wall, in his chair behind the pulpit, had nodded off. The assistant minister, Reverend Lisa Farrison, was moving poinsettias onto the chancel steps to make room for the manger, and the choir director, Rose Henderson, was on her knees, hammering wooden bases onto the cardboard palm trees. They had fallen down twice already.

"What do you think are the chances we'll still be here when it's time for the Christmas Eve service to start tomorrow night?" Sharon said, leaning against the sanctuary door.

"I can't be," Virginia said, looking at her watch. "I've got to be out at the mall before nine. Megan suddenly announced she wants Senior Prom Barbie."

"My throat feels terrible," Dee said, feeling her glands. "Is it hot in here, or am I getting a fever?"

"It's hot in these *robes*," Sharon said. "Why *are* we wearing them? This is a rehearsal."

"Rose wanted everything to be exactly like it's going to be tomorrow night."

"If I'm exactly like this tomorrow night, I'll be dead," Dee said, trying to clear her throat. "I *can't* get sick. I don't have any of the presents wrapped, and I haven't even *thought* about what we're having for Christmas dinner."

"At least you *have* presents," Virginia said. "I have eight people left to buy for. Not counting Senior Prom Barbie."

"I don't have anything done. Christmas cards, shopping, wrapping, baking, nothing, and Bill's parents are coming," Sharon said. "Come *on*, let's get this show on the road."

Rose and one of the junior choir angels hoisted the palm trees to standing. They listed badly to the right, as if Bethlehem were experiencing a hurricane. "Is that straight?" Rose called to the back of the church.

"Yes," Sharon said.

"Lying in church," Dee said. "Tsk, tsk."

"All right," Rose said, picking up a bulletin. "Listen up, every-body. Here's the order of worship. Introit by the brass quar-tet, processional, opening prayer, announcements—Reverend Farrison, is that where you want to talk about the 'Least of These' Project?"

"Yes," Reverend Farrison said. She walked to the front of the sanctuary. "And can I make a quick announcement right now?" She turned and faced the choir. "If anybody has anything else to donate, you need to bring it to the church by tomorrow morning at nine," she said briskly. "That's when we're going to deliver them to the homeless. We still need blankets and canned goods. Bring them to the Fellowship Hall."

She walked back down the aisle, and Rose started in on her list again. "Announcements, 'O Come, O Come, Emmanuel,' Reverend Wall's sermon—"

Reverend Wall nodded awake at his name. "Ah," he said, and hobbled toward the pulpit, clutching a sheaf of yellowed type-written papers.

"Oh, no," Sharon said. "Not a Christmas pageant *and* a ser-mon. We'll be here forever."

"Not *a* sermon," Virginia said. "*The* sermon. All twenty-four minutes of it. I've got it memorized. He's given it every year since he came."

"Longer than that," Dee said. "I swear last year I heard him say something in it about World War I."

" 'And all went to be taxed, every one into his own city,' Rever-end Wall said. " 'And Joseph also went up from Galilee, out of the city of Nazareth.' "

"Oh, *no*," Sharon said. "He's going to give the whole sermon right now."

"We know nothing of that journey up from Bethlehem," he said.

"Thank you, Reverend Wall," Rose said. "After the sermon, the choir sings 'O Little Town of Bethlehem' and Mary and Joseph—"

"What message does the story of their journey hold for us?" Reverend Wall said, picking up steam.

Rose was hurrying up the aisle and up the chancel steps. "Reverend Wall, you don't need to run through your sermon right now."

"What does it say to us," he asked, "struggling to recover from a world war?"

Dee nudged Sharon.

"Reverend *Wall*," Rose said, reaching the pulpit. "I'm afraid we don't have time to go through your whole sermon right now. We need to run through the pageant now."

"Ah," he said, and gathered up his papers.

"All right," Rose said. "The choir sings 'O Little Town of Bethlehem' and Mary and Joseph, you come down the aisle."

Mary and Joseph, wearing bathrobes and Birkenstocks, assembled themselves at the back of the sanctuary, and started down the center aisle.

"No, no, Mary and Joseph, not that way," Rose said. "The wise men from the East have to come down the center aisle, and you're coming up from Nazareth. You two come down the side aisle."

Mary and Joseph obliged, taking the aisle at a trot.

"No, no, slow *down*," Rose said. "You're tired. You've walked all the way from Nazareth. Try it again."

They raced each other to the back of the church and started again, slower at first and then picking up speed.

"The congregation won't be able to see them," Rose said, shaking her head. "What about lighting the side aisle? Can we do that, Reverend Farrison?"

"She's not here," Dee said. "She went to get something."

"I'll go get her," Sharon said, and went down the hall.

Miriam Hoskins was just going into the adult Sunday school room with a paper plate of frosted cookies. "Do you know where Reverend Farrison is?" Sharon asked her.

"She was in the office a minute ago," Miriam said, pointing with the plate.

Sharon went down to the office. Reverend Farrison was standing at the desk, talking on the phone. "How soon can the van be here?" She motioned to Sharon she'd be a minute. "Well, can you find out?"

Sharon waited, looking at the desk. There was a glass dish of paper-wrapped cough drops next to the phone, and beside it a can of smoked oysters and three cans of water chestnuts. Probably for the 'Least of These' Project, she thought ruefully.

"Fifteen minutes? All right. Thank you," Reverend Farrison said, and hung up. "Just a minute," she told Sharon, and went to the outside door. She opened it and leaned out. Sharon could feel the icy air as she stood there. She wondered if it had started snowing.

"The van will be here in a few minutes," Reverend Farrison said to someone outside.

Sharon looked out the stained-glass panels on either side of the door, trying to see who was out there.

"It'll take you to the shelter," Reverend Farrison said. "No, you'll have to wait outside." She shut the door. "Now," she said, turning to Sharon, "what did *you* want, Mrs. Englert?"

Sharon said, still looking out the window, "They need you in the sanctuary." It *was* starting to snow. The flakes looked blue through the glass.

"I'll be right there," Reverend Farrison said. "I was just taking care of some homeless. That's the second couple we've had tonight. We always get them at Christmas. What's the problem? The palm trees?"

"What?" Sharon said, still looking at the snow.

Reverend Farrison followed her gaze. "The shelter van's coming for them in a few minutes," she said. "We can't let them stay in here unsupervised. First Methodist's had their collection stolen twice in the last month, and we've got all the donations for the 'Least of These' Project in there." She gestured toward the Fellowship Hall.

I thought they were for the homeless, Sharon thought. "Couldn't they just wait in the sanctuary or something?" she said.

Reverend Farrison sighed. "Letting them in isn't doing them a kindness. They come here instead of the shelter because the shelter confiscates their liquor." She started down the hall. "What did they need me for?"

"Oh," Sharon said, "the lights. They wanted to know if they could get lights over the side aisle for Mary and Joseph."

"I don't know," she said. "The lights in this church are such a mess." She stopped at the bank of switches next to the stairs that led down to the choir room and the Sunday school rooms. "Tell me what this turns on."

She flicked a switch. The hall light went off. She switched it back on and tried another one.

"That's the light in the office," Sharon said, "and the downstairs hall, and that one's the adult Sunday school room."

"What's this one?" Reverend Farrison said.

There was a yelp from the choir members. Kids screamed.

"The sanctuary," Sharon said. "Okay, that's the side aisle lights." She called down to the sanctuary. "How's that?"

"Fine," Rose called. "No, wait, the organ's off."

Reverend Farrison flicked another switch, and the organ came on with a groan.

"Now the side lights are off," Sharon said, "and so's the pulpit light."

"I told you they were a mess," Reverend Farrison said. She flicked another switch. "What did that do?"

"It turned the porch light off."

"Good. We'll leave it off. Maybe it will discourage any more homeless from coming," she said. "Reverend Wall let a homeless man wait inside last week, and he relieved himself on the carpet in the adult Sunday school room. We had to have it cleaned." She looked reprovingly at Sharon. "With these people, you can't let your compassion get the better of you."

No, Sharon thought. Jesus did, and look what happened to him.

"The innkeeper could have turned them away," Reverend Wall intoned. "He was a busy man, and his inn was full of travelers. He could have shut the door on Mary and Joseph."

Virginia leaned across Sharon to Dee. "Did whoever broke in take anything?"

"No," Sharon said.

"Whoever it was urinated on the floor in the nursery," Dee whispered, and Reverend Wall trailed off confusedly and looked over at the choir.

Dee began coughing loudly, trying to smother it with her hand. He smiled vaguely at her and started again. "The innkeeper could have turned them away."

Dee waited a minute, and then opened her hymnal to her bulletin and began writing on it. She passed it to Virginia, who read it and then passed it back to Sharon.

"Reverend Farrison thinks some of the homeless got in," it read. "They tore up the palm trees, too. Ripped the bases right off. Can you imagine anybody doing something like that?"

"As the innkeeper found room for Mary and Joseph that Christmas

Eve long ago," Reverend Wall said, building to a finish, "let us find room in our hearts for Christ. Amen."

The organ began the intro to "O Little Town of Bethlehem," and Mary and Joseph appeared at the back with Miriam Hoskins. She adjusted Mary's white veil and whispered something to them. Joseph pulled at his glued-on beard.

"What route did they finally decide on?" Virginia whispered. "In from the side or straight down the middle?"

"Side aisle," Sharon whispered.

The choir stood up. " 'O little town of Bethlehem, how still we see thee lie,' " they sang. " 'Above thy deep and dreamless sleep, the silent stars go by.' "

Mary and Joseph started up the side aisle, taking the slow, measured steps Rose had coached them in, side by side. No, Sharon thought. That's not right. They didn't look like that. Joseph should be a little ahead of Mary, protecting her, and her hand should be on her stomach, protecting the baby.

They eventually decided to wait on the decision of how Mary and Joseph would come, and started through the pageant. Mary and Joseph knocked on the door of the inn, and the innkeeper, grinning broadly, told them there wasn't any room.

"Patrick, don't look so happy," Rose said. "You're supposed to be in a bad mood. You're busy and tired, and you don't have any rooms left."

Patrick attempted a scowl. "I have no rooms left," he said, "but you can stay in the stable." He led them over to the manger, and Mary knelt down behind it.

"Where's the baby Jesus?" Rose said.

"He's not due till tomorrow night," Virginia whispered.

"Does anybody have a baby doll they can bring?" Rose asked.

One of the angels raised her hand, and Rose said, "Fine. Mary, use the blanket for now, and, choir, you sing the first verse of 'Away in a Manger.' Shepherds," she called to the back of the sanctuary, "as *soon* as 'Away in a Manger' is over, come up and stand on *this* side." She pointed.

The shepherds picked up an assortment of hockey sticks, broom handles, and canes taped to one-by-twos and adjusted their headcloths.

"All right, let's run through it," Rose said. "Organ?"

The organ played the opening chord, and the choir stood up.

"A-way," Dee sang and started to cough, choking into her hand. "Do—cough—drop?" she managed to gasp out between spasms.

"I saw some in the office," Sharon said, and ran down the chancel steps, down the aisle, and out into the hall.

It was dark, but she didn't want to take the time to try to find the right switch. She could more or less see her way by the lights from the sanctuary, and she thought she knew right where the cough drops were.

The office lights were off, too, and the porch light Reverend Farrison had turned off to discourage the homeless. She opened the office door, felt her way over to the desk and patted around till she found the glass dish. She grabbed a handful of cough drops and felt her way back out into the hall.

The choir was singing "It Came Upon a Midnight Clear," but after two measures they stopped, and in the sudden silence Sharon heard knocking.

She started for the door and then hesitated, wondering if this was the same couple Reverend Farrison had turned away earlier, coming back to make trouble, but the knocking was soft, almost diffident, and through the stained-glass panels she could see it was snowing hard.

She switched the cough drops to her left hand, opened the door a little, and looked out. There were two people standing on the porch, one in front of the other. It was too dark to do more than make out their outlines, and at first glance it looked like two women, but then the one in front said in a young man's voice, *"Erkas."*

"I'm sorry," Sharon said. "I don't speak Spanish. Are you looking for a place to stay?" The snow was turning to sleet, and the wind was picking up.

"Kumrah," the young man said, making a sound like he was clearing his throat, and then a whole string of words she didn't recognize.

"Just a minute," she said, and shut the door. She went back into the office, felt for the phone, and, squinting at the buttons in the near-darkness, punched in the shelter number.

It was busy. She held down the receiver, waited a minute, and tried again. Still busy. She went back to the door, hoping they'd given up and gone away.

"Erkas," the man said as soon as she opened it.

"I'm sorry," she said. "I'm trying to call the homeless shelter," and he began talking rapidly, excitedly.

He stepped forward and put his hand on the door. He had a blanket draped over him, which was why she'd mistaken him for a woman. *"Erkas,"* he said, and he sounded upset, desperate, and yet somehow still diffident, timid.

"Bott lom," he said, gesturing toward the woman who was standing back almost to the edge of the porch, but Sharon wasn't looking at her. She was looking at their feet.

They were wearing sandals. At first she thought they were barefoot and she squinted through the darkness, horrified. Barefoot in the snow! Then she glimpsed the dark line of a strap, but they still might as well be. And it was snowing hard.

She couldn't leave them outside, but she didn't dare bring them into the hall to wait for the van either, not with Reverend Farrison around.

The office was out—the phone might ring—and she couldn't put them in the Fellowship Hall with all the stuff for the homeless in there.

"Just a minute," she said, shutting the door, and went to see if Miriam was still in the adult Sunday school room. It was dark, so she obviously wasn't, but there was a lamp on the table by the door. She switched it on. No, this wouldn't work either, not with the communion silver in a display case against the wall, and anyway, there was a stack of paper cups on the table, and the plates of Christmas cookies Miriam had been carrying, which meant there'd be refreshments in here after the pageant. She switched off the light, and went out into the hall.

Not Reverend Wall's office—it was locked anyway—and certainly not Reverend Farrison's, and if she took them downstairs to one of the Sunday school rooms, she'd just have to sneak them back up again.

The furnace room? It was between the adult Sunday school room and the Fellowship Hall. She tried the doorknob. It opened, and she looked in. The furnace filled practically the whole room, and what it didn't was taken up by a stack of folding chairs. There wasn't a light switch she could find, but the pilot light gave off enough light to maneuver by. And it was warmer than the porch.

She went back to the door, looked down the hall to make sure nobody was coming, and let them in. "You can wait in here," she said, even though it was obvious they couldn't understand her.

They followed her through the dark hall to the furnace room, and she opened out two of the folding chairs so they could sit down, and motioned them in.

"It Came Upon a Midnight Clear" ground to a halt, and Rose's voice came drifting out of the sanctuary. "Shepherd's crooks are not weapons. All right. Angel?"

"I'll call the shelter," Sharon said hastily, and shut the door on them.

She crossed to the office and tried the shelter again. "Please, please answer," she said, and when they did, she was so surprised, she forgot to tell them the couple would be inside.

"It'll be at least half an hour," the man said. "Or forty-five minutes."

"Forty-five minutes?"

"It's like this whenever it gets below zero," the man said. "We'll try to make it sooner."

At least she'd done the right thing—they couldn't possibly stand out in that snow for forty-five minutes. The right thing, she thought ruefully, sticking them in the furnace room. But at least it was warm in there and out of the snow. And they were safe, as long as nobody came out to see what had happened to her.

"Dee," she said suddenly. Sharon was supposed to have come out to get her some cough drops.

They were lying on the desk where she'd laid them while she phoned. She snatched them up and took off down the hall and into the sanctuary.

The angel was on the chancel steps, exhorting the shepherds not to be afraid. Sharon threaded her way through them up to the chancel and sat down between Dee and Virginia.

She handed the cough drops to Dee, who said, "What took you so long?"

"I had to make a phone call. What did I miss?"

"Not a thing. We're still on the shepherds. One of the palm trees fell over and had to be fixed, and then Reverend Farrison stopped the rehearsal to tell everybody not to let homeless people into the church, that Holy Trinity had had its sanctuary vandalized."

"Oh," she said. She gazed out over the sanctuary, looking for Reverend Farrison.

"All right, now, after the angel makes her speech," Rose said, "she's joined by a multitude of angels. That's *you*, junior choir. No. Line up on the steps. Organ?"

The organ struck up "Hark, the Herald Angels Sing," and the junior choir began singing in piping, nearly inaudible voices.

Sharon couldn't see Reverend Farrison anywhere. "Do you know where Reverend Farrison went?" she whispered to Dee.

"She went out just as you came in. She had to get something from the office."

The office. What if she heard them in the furnace room and opened the door and found them in there? She half stood.

"Choir," Rose said, glaring directly at Sharon. "Will you help the junior choir by humming along with them?"

Sharon sat back down, and after a minute Reverend Farrison came in from the back, carrying a pair of scissors.

" 'Late in time, behold Him come,' " the junior choir sang, and Miriam stood up and went out.

"Where's Miriam going?" Sharon whispered.

"How would I know?" Dee said, looking curiously at her. "To get the refreshments ready, probably. Is something the matter?"

"No," she said.

Rose was glaring at Sharon again. Sharon hummed, " 'Light and life to all He brings,' " willing the song to be over so she could go out, but as soon as it was over, Rose said, "All right, wise men," and a sixth-grader carrying a jewelry box started down the center aisle. "Choir, 'We Three Kings.' Organ?"

There were four long verses to "We Three Kings of Orient Are." Sharon couldn't wait.

"I have to go to the bathroom," she said. She set her folder on her chair and ducked down the stairs behind the chancel and through the narrow room that led to the side aisle. The choir called it the flower room because that was where they stored the out-of-season altar arrangements. They used it for sneaking out when they needed to leave church early, but right now there was barely room to squeeze through. The floor was covered with music stands and pots of silk Easter lilies, and a huge spray of red roses stood in front of the door to the sanctuary.

Sharon shoved it into the corner, stepping gingerly among the lilies, and opened the door.

"Balthazar, lay the gold in front of the manger, don't drop it. Mary, you're the Mother of God. Try not to look so scared," Rose said.

Sharon hurried down the side aisle and out into the hall, where the other two kings were waiting, holding perfume bottles.

" 'Westward leading, still proceeding, guide us to thy perfect light,' " the choir sang.

The hall and office lights were still off, but light was spilling out of the adult Sunday school room all the way to the end of the hall. She could see that the furnace-room door was still shut.

I'll call the shelter again, she thought, and see if I can hurry them up, and if I can't, I'll take them downstairs till everybody's gone, and then take them to the shelter myself.

She tiptoed past the open door of the adult Sunday school room so Miriam wouldn't see her, and then half-sprinted down to the office and opened the door.

"Hi," Miriam said, looking up from the desk. She had an aluminum pitcher in one hand and was rummaging in the top drawer with the other. "Do you know where the secretary keeps the key to the kitchen? It's locked, and I can't get in."

"No," Sharon said, her heart still pounding.

"I need a spoon to stir the Kool-Aid," Miriam said, opening and shutting the side drawers of the desk. "She must have taken them home with her. I don't blame her. First Baptist had theirs stolen last month. They had to change all the locks."

Sharon glanced uneasily at the furnace-room door.

"Oh, well," Miriam said, opening the top drawer again. "I'll have to make do with this." She pulled out a plastic ruler. "The kids won't care."

She started out and then stopped. "They're not done in there yet, are they?"

"No," Sharon said. "They're still on the wise men. I needed to call my husband to tell him to take the turkey out of the freezer."

"I've got to do that when I get home," Miriam said. She went across the hall and into the library, leaving the door open. Sharon waited a minute and then called the shelter. It was busy. She held her watch to the light from the hall. They'd said half an hour to forty-five minutes. By that time the rehearsal would be over and the hall would be full of people.

Less than half an hour. They were already singing "Myrrh is mine, its bitter perfume." All that was left was "Silent Night" and then "Joy to the World," and the angels would come streaming out for cookies and Kool-Aid.

She went over to the front door and peered out. Below zero, the woman at the shelter had said, and now there was sleet, slanting sharply across the parking lot.

She couldn't send them out in that without any shoes. And she couldn't keep them up here, not with the kids right next door. She was going to have to move them downstairs.

But where? Not the choir room. The choir would be taking their folders and robes back down there, and the pageant kids would be getting their coats out of the Sunday school rooms. And the kitchen was locked.

The nursery? That might work. It was at the other end of the hall from the choir room, but she would have to take them past the adult Sunday school room to the stairs, and the door was open.

" 'Si-i-lent night, ho-oh-ly night,' " came drifting out of the sanctuary, and then was cut off, and she could hear Reverend Farrison's voice lecturing, probably about the dangers of letting the homeless into the church.

She glanced again at the furnace-room door and then went into the adult Sunday school room. Miriam was setting out the paper cups on the table. She looked up. "Did you get through to your husband?"

"Yes," Sharon said. Miriam looked expectant.

"Can I have a cookie?" Sharon said at random.

"Take one of the stars. The kids like the Santas and the Christmas trees the best."

She grabbed up a bright yellow–frosted star. "Thanks," she said, and went out, pulling the door shut behind her.

"Leave it open," Miriam said. "I want to be able to hear when they're done."

Sharon opened the door back up half as far as she'd shut it, afraid any less would bring Miriam to the door to open it herself, and walked quietly to the furnace room.

The choir was on the last verse of "Silent Night." After that there was only "Joy to the World" and then the benediction. Open door or no open door, she was going to have to move them now. She opened the furnace-room door.

They were standing where she had left them between the folding chairs, and she knew, without any proof, that they had stood there like that the whole time she had been gone.

The young man was standing slightly in front of the woman, the way he had at the door, only he wasn't a man, he was a boy, his beard as thin and wispy as an adolescent's, and the woman was even younger, a child of ten maybe, only she had to be older, because now that there was light from the half-open door of the adult Sunday school room Sharon could see that she was pregnant.

She regarded all this—the girl's awkward bulkiness and the

boy's beard, the fact that they had not sat down, the fact that it was the light from the adult Sunday school room that was making her see now what she hadn't before—with some part of her mind that was still functioning, that was still thinking how long the van from the shelter would take, how to get them past Reverend Farrison, some part of her mind that was taking in the details that proved what she had already known the moment she opened the door.

"What are you *doing* here?" she whispered, and the boy opened his hands in a gesture of helplessness. *"Erkas,"* he said.

And that still-functioning part of her mind put her fingers to her lips in a gesture he obviously understood because they both looked instantly frightened. "You have to come with me," she whispered.

But then it stopped functioning altogether, and she was half-running them past the open door and onto the stairs, not even hearing the organ blaring out "Joy to the world, the Lord is come,'" whispering, "Hurry! Hurry!" and they didn't know how to get down the steps, the girl turned around and came down backwards, her hands flat on the steps above, and the boy helped her down, step by step, as if they were clambering down rocks, and she tried to pull the girl along faster and nearly made her stumble, and even that didn't bring her to her senses.

She hissed, "Like this," and showed them how to walk down the steps, facing forward, one hand on the rail, and they paid no attention, they came down backwards like toddlers, and it took forever, the hymn she wasn't hearing was already at the end of the third verse and they were only halfway down, all of them panting hard, and Sharon scurrying back up above them as if that would hurry them, past wondering how she would ever get them up the stairs again, past thinking she would have to call the van and tell them not to come, thinking only, Hurry, hurry, and How did they *get* here?

She did not come to herself until she had herded them some-how down the hall and into the nursery, thinking, It can't be locked, please don't let it be locked, and it wasn't, and gotten them inside and pulled the door shut and tried to lock it, and it didn't have a lock, and she thought, That must be why it wasn't locked, an actual coherent thought, her first one since that moment when she opened the furnace-room door, and seemed to come to herself.

She stared at them, breathing hard, and it *was* them, their never having seen stairs before was proof of that, if she needed any proof, but she didn't, she had known it the instant she saw them, there was no question.

She wondered if this was some sort of vision, the kind people were always getting where they saw Jesus' face on a refrigerator, or the Virgin Mary dressed in blue and white, surrounded by roses. But their rough brown cloaks were dripping melted snow on the nursery carpet, their feet in the useless sandals were bright red with cold, and they looked too frightened.

And they didn't look at all like they did in religious pictures. They were too short, his hair was greasy and his face was tough-looking, like a young punk's, and her veil looked like a grubby dishtowel and it didn't hang loose, it was tied around her neck and knotted in the back, and they were too young, almost as young as the children upstairs dressed like them.

They were looking around the room frightenedly, at the white crib and the rocking chair and the light fixture overhead. The boy fumbled in his sash and brought out a leather sack. He held it out to Sharon.

"How did you *get* here?" she said wonderingly. "You're sup-posed to be on your way to Bethlehem."

He thrust the bag at her, and when she didn't take it, untied the leather string and took out a crude-looking coin and held it out.

"You don't have to pay me," she said, which was ridiculous. He couldn't understand her. She held a flat hand up, pushing the coin away and shaking her head. That was a universal sign, wasn't it? And what was the sign for welcome? She spread her arms out, smiling at the youngsters. "You are welcome to stay here," she said, trying to put the meaning of the words into her voice. "Sit down. Rest."

They remained standing. Sharon pulled the rocking chair. "Sit, please."

Mary looked frightened, and Sharon put her hands on the arms of the chair and sat down to show her how. Joseph immediately knelt, and Mary tried awkwardly to.

"No, no!" Sharon said, and stood up so fast she set the rocking chair swinging. "Don't kneel. I'm nobody." She looked hopelessly at them. "How did you *get* here? You're not supposed to be here."

Joseph stood up. *"Erkas,"* he said, and went over to the bulletin board.

It was covered with colored pictures from Jesus' life: Jesus healing the lame boy, Jesus in the temple, Jesus in the Garden of Gethsemane.

He pointed to the picture of the Nativity scene. *"Kumrah,"* he said.

Does he recognize himself? she wondered, but he was pointing at the donkey standing by the manger. *"Erkas,"* he said. *"Erkas."*

Did that mean "donkey," or something else? Was he demanding to know what she had done with theirs, or trying to ask her if she had one? In all the pictures, all the versions of the story, Mary was riding a donkey, but she had thought they'd gotten that part of the story wrong, as they had gotten everything else wrong, their faces, their clothes, and above all their youth, their helplessness.

"Kumrah erkas," he said. *"Kumrah erkas. Bott lom?"*

"I don't know," she said. "I don't know where Bethlehem is."

Or what to do with you, she thought. Her first instinct was to hide them here until the rehearsal was over and everybody had gone home. She couldn't let Reverend Farrison find them.

But surely as soon as she saw who they were, she would—what? Fall to her knees? Or call for the shelter's van? "That's the second couple tonight," she'd said when she shut the door. Sharon wondered suddenly if it was them she'd turned away, if they'd wandered around the parking lot, lost and frightened, and then knocked on the door again.

She couldn't let Reverend Farrison find them, but there was no reason for her to come into the nursery. All the children were upstairs, and the refreshments were in the adult Sunday school room. But what if she checked the rooms before she locked up?

I'll take them home with me, Sharon thought. They'll be safe there. If she could get them up the stairs and out of the parking lot before the rehearsal ended.

I got them down here without anybody seeing them, she thought. But even if she could manage it, which she doubted, if they didn't die of fright when she started the car and the seat belts closed down over them, home was no better than the shelter.

They had gotten lost through some accident of time and space, and ended up at the church. The way back—if there was a way back, there had to be a way back, they had to be at Bethlehem by tomorrow night—was here.

It occurred to her suddenly that maybe she shouldn't have let them in, that the way back was outside the north door. But I couldn't *not* let them in, she protested, it was snowing, and they didn't have any shoes.

But maybe if she'd turned them away, they would have walked off the porch and back into their own time. Maybe they still could.

She said, "Stay here," putting her hand up to show them what she meant, and went out of the nursery into the hall, shutting the door tightly behind her.

The choir was still singing "Joy to the World." They must have had to stop again. Sharon ran silently up the stairs and past the adult Sunday school room. Its door was still half-open, and she could see the plates of cookies on the table. She opened the north door, hesitating a moment as if she expected to see sand and camels, and leaned out. It was still sleeting, and the cars had an inch of snow on them.

She looked around for something to wedge the door open with, pushed one of the potted palms over, and went out on the porch. It was slick, and she had to take hold of the wall to keep her footing. She stepped carefully to the edge of the porch and peered into the sleet, already shivering, looking for what? A lessening of the sleet, a spot where the darkness was darker, or not so dark? A light?

Nothing. After a minute she stepped off the porch, moving as cautiously as Mary and Joseph had going down the stairs, and made a circuit of the parking lot.

Nothing. If the way back had been out here, it wasn't now, and she was going to freeze if she stayed out here. She went back inside, and then stood there, staring at the door, trying to think what to do. I've got to get help, she thought, hugging her arms to herself for warmth. I've got to tell somebody. She started down the hall to the sanctuary.

The organ had stopped. "Mary and Joseph, I need to talk to you for a minute," Rose's voice said. "Shepherds, leave your crooks on the front pew. The rest of you, there are refreshments in the adult Sunday school room. Choir, don't leave. I need to go over some things with you."

There was a clatter of sticks and then a stampede, and Sharon was overwhelmed by shepherds elbowing their way to the refreshments. One of the wise men caught his Air Jordan in his robe and nearly fell down, and two of the angels lost their tinsel halos in their eagerness to reach the cookies.

Sharon fought through them and into the back of the sanctuary. Rose was in the side aisle, showing Mary and Joseph how to walk, and the choir was gathering up their music. Sharon couldn't see Dee.

Virginia came down the center aisle, stripping off her robe as she walked. Sharon went to meet her. "Do you know where Dee is?" she asked her.

"She went home," Virginia said, handing Sharon a folder. "You left this on your chair. Dee's voice was giving out completely, and I said, 'This is silly. Go home and go to bed.' "

"Virginia . . ." Sharon said.

"Can you put my robe away for me?" Virginia said, pulling her stole off her head. "I've got exactly ten minutes to get to the mall."

Sharon nodded absently, and Virginia draped it over her arm and hurried out. Sharon scanned the choir, wondering who else she could confide in.

Rose dismissed Mary and Joseph, who went off at a run, and crossed to the center aisle. "Rehearsal tomorrow night at 6:15," she said. "I need you in your robes and up here right on time, because I've got to practice with the brass quartet at 6:40. Any questions?"

Yes, Sharon thought, looking around the sanctuary. Who can I get to help me?

"What are we singing for the processional?" one of the tenors asked.

" '*Adeste Fideles*,' " Rose said. "Before you leave, let's line up so you can see who your partner is."

Reverend Wall was sitting in one of the back pews, looking at the notes to his sermon. Sharon sidled along the pew and sat down next to him.

"Reverend Wall," she said, and then had no idea how to start. "Do you know what *erkas* means? I think it's Hebrew."

He raised his head from his notes and peered at her. "It's Aramaic. It means 'lost.'"

"Lost." He'd been trying to tell her at the door, in the furnace room, downstairs. "We're lost."

"Forgotten," Reverend Wall said. "Misplaced."

Misplaced, all right. By two thousand years, an ocean, and how many miles?

"When Mary and Joseph journeyed up to Bethlehem from Nazareth, how did they go?" she asked, hoping he would say, "Why are you asking all these questions?" so she could tell him, but he said, "Ah. You weren't listening to my sermon. We know nothing of that journey, only that they arrived in Bethlehem."

Not at this rate, she thought.

"Pass in the anthem," Rose said from the chancel. "I've only got thirty copies, and I don't want to come up short tomorrow night."

Sharon looked up. The choir was leaving. "On this journey, was there anyplace where they might have gotten lost?" she said hurriedly.

"'*Erkas*' can also mean 'hidden, passed out of sight,'" he said. "Aramaic is very similar to Hebrew. In Hebrew, the word—"

"Reverend Wall," Reverend Farrison said from the center aisle. "I need to talk to you about the benediction."

"Ah. Do you want me to give it now?" he said, and stood up, clutching his papers.

Sharon took the opportunity to grab her folder and duck out. She ran downstairs after the choir.

There was no reason for any of the choir to go into the nursery, but she stationed herself in the hall, sorting through the music in her folder as if she were putting it in order, and trying to think what to do.

Maybe, if everyone went into the choir room, she could duck into the nursery or one of the Sunday school rooms and hide until everybody was gone. But she didn't know whether Reverend Farrison checked each of the rooms before leaving. Or worse, locked them.

She could tell her she needed to stay late, to practice the anthem, but she didn't think Reverend Farrison would trust her to lock up, and she didn't want to call attention to herself, to make Reverend Farrison think, "Where's Sharon Englert? I didn't see her leave." Maybe she could hide in the chancel, or the flower room, but that meant leaving the nursery unguarded.

She had to decide. The crowd was thinning out, the choir handing Rose their music and putting on their coats and boots. She had to do something. Reverend Farrison could come down the stairs any minute to search the nursery. But she continued to stand there, sorting blindly through her music, and Reverend Farrison came down the steps, carrying a ring of keys.

Sharon stepped back protectively, the way Joseph had, but Reverend Farrison didn't even see her. She went up to Rose and said, "Can you lock up for me? I've got to be at Emmanuel Lutheran at 9:30 to collect their Least of These contributions."

"I was supposed to go meet with the brass quartet—" Rose said reluctantly.

Don't let Rose talk you out of it, Sharon thought.

"Be sure to lock *all* the doors, including the Fellowship Hall," Reverend Farrison said, handing her the keys.

"No, I've got mine," Rose said. "But—"

"And check the parking lot. There were some homeless hanging around earlier. Thanks."

She ran upstairs, and Sharon immediately went over to Rose. "Rose," she said.

Rose held out her hand for Sharon's anthem.

Sharon shuffled through her music and handed it to her. "I

82 *Connie Willis*

was wondering," she said, trying to keep her voice casual, "I need to stay and practice the music for tomorrow. I'd be glad to lock up for you. I could drop the keys by your house tomorrow morning."

"Oh, you're a godsend," Rose said. She handed Sharon the stack of music and got her keys out of her purse. "These are the keys to the outside doors, north door, east door, Fellowship Hall," she said, ticking them off so fast, Sharon couldn't see which was which, but it didn't matter. She could figure them out after everybody left.

"This is the choir-room door," Rose said. She handed them to Sharon. "I *really* appreciate this. The brass quartet couldn't come to the rehearsal, they had a concert tonight, and I really need to go over the introit with them. They're having a terrible time with the middle part."

So am I, Sharon thought.

Rose yanked on her coat. "And after I meet with them, I've got to go over to Miriam Berg's and pick up the baby Jesus." She stopped, her arm half in her coat sleeve. "Did you need me to stay and go over the music with you?"

"No!" Sharon said, alarmed. "No, I'll be fine. I just need to run through it a couple of times."

"Okay. Great. Thanks again," she said, patting her pockets for her keys. She took the keyring away from Sharon and unhooked her car keys. "You're a godsend, I mean it," she said, and took off up the stairs at a trot.

Two of the altos came out, pulling on their gloves. "Do you know what I've got to face when I get home?" Julia said. "Putting up the tree."

They handed their music to Sharon.

"I hate Christmas," Karen said. "By the time it's over, I'm worn to a frazzle."

They hurried up the stairs, still talking, and Sharon leaned into the choir room to make sure it was empty, dumped the music and Rose's robe on a chair, took off her robe, and went upstairs.

Miriam was coming out of the adult Sunday school room, carrying a pitcher of Kool-Aid. "Come on, Elizabeth," she called into the room. "We've got to get to Buymore before it closes. She managed to completely destroy her halo," she said to Sharon, "so now I've got to go buy some more tinsel. Elizabeth, we're the last ones *here*."

Elizabeth strolled out, holding a Christmas-tree cookie in her mittened hand. She stopped halfway to the door to lick the cookie's frosting.

"Elizabeth," Miriam said. "Come *on*."

Sharon held the door for them, and Miriam went out, ducking her head against the driving sleet. Elizabeth dawdled after her, looking up at the sky.

Miriam waved. "See you tomorrow night."

"I'll be here," Sharon said, and shut the door. I'll *still* be here, she thought. And what if they are? What happens then? Does the Christmas pageant disappear, and all the rest of it? The cookies and the shopping and the Senior Prom Barbies? And the church?

She watched Miriam and Elizabeth through the stained-glass panel till she saw the car's taillights, purple through the blue glass, pull out of the parking lot, and then tried the keys one after the other, till she found the right one, and locked the door.

She checked quickly in the sanctuary and the bathrooms, in case somebody was still there, and then ran down the stairs to the nursery to make sure *they* were still there, that they hadn't disappeared.

They were there, sitting on the floor next to the rocking chair and sharing what looked like dried dates from an unfolded cloth. Joseph started to stand up as soon as he saw her poke her head in the door, but she motioned him back down. "Stay here," she said softly, and realized she didn't need to whisper. "I'll be back in a few minutes. I'm just going to lock the doors."

She pulled the door shut, and went back upstairs. It hadn't occurred to her they'd be hungry, and she had no idea what they were used to eating—unleavened bread? Lamb? Whatever it was, there probably wasn't any in the kitchen, but the deacons had had an Advent supper last week. With luck, there might be some chili in the refrigerator. Or, better yet, some crackers.

The kitchen was locked. She'd forgotten Miriam had said that, and anyway, one of the keys must open it. None of them did, and after she'd tried all of them twice she remembered they were Rose's keys, not Reverend Farrison's, and turned the lights on in the Fellowship Hall. There was tons of food in there, stacked on tables alongside the blankets and used clothes and toys. And all of it was in cans, just the way Reverend Farrison had specified in the bulletin.

Miriam had taken the Kool-Aid home, but Sharon hadn't seen her carrying any cookies. The kids probably ate them all, she thought, but she went into the adult Sunday school room and looked. There was half a paper-plateful left, and Miriam had been right—the kids liked the Christmas trees and Santas the best—the only ones left were yellow stars. There was a stack of paper cups, too. She picked them both up and took them downstairs.

"I brought you some food," she said, and set the plate on the floor between them.

They were staring in alarm at her, and Joseph was scrambling to his feet.

"It's food," she said, bringing her hand to her mouth and pretending to chew. "Cakes."

Joseph was pulling on Mary's arm, trying to yank her up, and they were both staring, horrified, at her jeans and sweatshirt. She realized suddenly they must not have recognized her without her choir robe. Worse, the robe looked at least a little like their clothes, but this getup must have looked totally alien.

"I'll bring you something to drink," she said hastily, showing them the paper cups, and went out. She ran down to the choir room. Her robe was still draped over the chair where she'd dumped it, along with Rose's and the music. She put the robe on and then filled the paper cups at the water fountain and carried them back to the nursery.

They were standing, but when they saw her in the robe, they sat back down. She handed Mary one of the paper cups, but she only looked at her fearfully. Sharon held it out to Joseph. He took it, too firmly, and it crumpled, water spurting onto the carpet.

"That's okay, it doesn't matter," Sharon said, cursing herself for being an idiot. "I'll get you a real cup."

She ran upstairs, trying to think where there would be one. The coffee cups were in the kitchen, and so were the glasses, and she hadn't seen anything in the Fellowship Hall or the adult Sunday school room.

She smiled suddenly. "I'll get you a real cup," she repeated, and went into the adult Sunday school room and took the silver Communion chalice out of the display case. There were silver plates, too. She wished she'd thought of it sooner.

She went into the Fellowship Hall and got a blanket and took the things downstairs. She filled the chalice with water and took it in to them, and handed Mary the chalice, and this time Mary took it without hesitation and drank deeply from it.

Sharon gave Joseph the blanket. "I'll leave you alone so you can eat and rest," she said, and went out into the hall, pulling the door nearly shut again.

She went down to the choir room and hung up Rose's robe and stacked the music neatly on the table. Then she went up to the furnace room and folded up the folding chairs and stacked them against the wall. She checked the east door and the one in the Fellowship Hall. They were both locked.

She turned off the lights in the Fellowship Hall and the office, and then thought, "I should call the shelter," and turned them back on. It had been an hour since she'd called. They had probably already come and not found anyone, but in case they were running really late, she'd better call.

The line was busy. She tried it twice and then called home. Bill's parents were there. "I'm going to be late," she told him. "The rehearsal's running long," and hung up, wondering how many lies she'd told so far tonight.

Well, it went with the territory, didn't it? Joseph lying about the baby being his, and the wise men sneaking out the back way, the Holy Family hightailing it to Egypt and the innkeeper lying to Herod's soldiers about where they'd gone.

And in the meantime, more hiding. She went back downstairs and opened the door gently, trying not to startle them, and then just stood there, watching.

They had eaten the cookies. The empty paper plate stood on the floor next to the chalice, not a crumb on it. Mary lay curled up like the child she was under the blanket, and Joseph sat with his back to the rocking chair, guarding her.

Poor things, she thought, leaning her cheek against the door. Poor things. So young, and so far away from home. She wondered what they made of it all. Did they think they had wandered into a palace in some strange kingdom? There's stranger yet to come, she thought, shepherds and angels and old men from the east, bearing jewelry boxes and perfume bottles. And then Cana. And Jerusalem. And Golgotha.

But for the moment, a place to sleep, out of the weather, and something to eat, and a few minutes of peace. How still we see thee lie. She stood there a long time, her cheek resting against the door, watching Mary sleep and Joseph trying to stay awake.

His head nodded forward, and he jerked it back, waking himself up, and saw Sharon. He stood up immediately, careful not to wake Mary, and came over to her, looking worried. *"Erkas kumrah,"* he said. *"Bott lom?"*

"I'll go find it," she said.

She went upstairs and turned the lights on again and went into the Fellowship Hall. The way back wasn't out the north door, but maybe they had knocked at one of the other doors first and then come around to it when no one answered. The Fellowship Hall door was on the northwest corner. She unlocked it, trying key after key, and opened it. The sleet was slashing down harder than ever. It had already covered up the tire tracks in the parking lot.

She shut the door and tried east door, which nobody used except for the Sunday service, and then the north door again. Nothing. Sleet and wind and icy air.

Now what? They had been on their way to Bethlehem from Nazareth, and somewhere along the way they had taken a wrong turn. But how? And where? She didn't even know what direction they'd been heading in. Up. Joseph had gone *up* from Nazareth, which meant north, and in "The First Nowell" it said the star was in the northwest.

She needed a map. The ministers' offices were locked, but there were books on the bottom shelf of the display case in the adult Sunday school room. Maybe one was an atlas.

It wasn't. They were all self-help books, about coping with grief and codependency and teenage pregnancy, except for an ancient-looking concordance and a Bible dictionary.

The Bible dictionary had a set of maps at the back. Early Israelite Settlements in Canaan, The Assyrian Empire, The Wanderings of the Israelites in the Wilderness. She flipped forward.

The Journeys of Paul. She turned back a page. Palestine in New Testament Times.

She found Jerusalem easily, and Bethlehem should be northwest of it. There was Nazareth, where Mary and Joseph had started from, so Bethlehem had to be farther north.

It wasn't there. She traced her finger over the towns, reading the tiny print. Cana, Kedesh, Jericho, but no Bethlehem. Which was ridiculous. It had to be there. She started down from the north, marking each of the towns with her finger.

When she finally found it, it wasn't at all where it was supposed to be. Like them, she thought. It was south and a little west of Jerusalem, so close it couldn't be more than a few miles from the city.

She looked down at the bottom of the page for the map scale, and there was an inset labeled "Mary and Joseph's Journey to Bethlehem," with their route marked in broken red.

Nazareth was almost due north of Bethlehem, but they had gone east to the Jordan River, and then south along its banks. At Jericho they'd turned back west toward Jerusalem through an empty brown space marked Judean Desert.

She wondered if that was where they had gotten lost, the donkey wandering off to find water and them going after it and losing the path. If it was, then the way back lay southwest, but the church didn't have any doors that opened in that direction, and even if it did, they would open on a twentieth-century parking lot and snow, not on first-century Palestine.

How had they gotten here? There was nothing in the map to tell her what might have happened on their journey to cause this.

She put the dictionary back and pulled out the concordance.

There was a sound. A key, and somebody opening the door. She slapped the book shut, shoved it back into the bookcase, and went out into the hall. Reverend Farrison was standing at the door, looking scared. "Oh, Sharon," she said, putting her hand to her chest. "What are you still doing here? You scared me half to death."

That makes two of us, Sharon thought, her heart thumping. "I had to stay and practice," she said. "I told Rose I'd lock up. What are you doing here?"

"I got a call from the shelter," she said, opening the office door. "They got a call from us to pick up a homeless couple, but when they got here there was nobody outside."

She went in the office and looked behind the desk, in the corner next to the filing cabinets. "I was worried they got into the church," she said, coming out. "The last thing we need is someone vandalizing the church two days before Christmas." She shut the office door behind her. "Did you check all the doors?"

Yes, she thought, and none of them led anywhere. "Yes," she said. "They were all locked. And anyway, I would have heard anybody trying to get in. I heard you."

Reverend Farrison opened the door to the furnace room. "They could have sneaked in and hidden when everyone was leaving." She looked in at the stacked folding chairs and then shut the door. She started down the hall toward the stairs.

"I checked the whole church," Sharon said, following her.

She stopped at the stairs, looking speculatively down the steps.

"I was nervous about being alone," Sharon said desperately, "so I turned on all the lights and checked all the Sunday school rooms and the choir room and the bathrooms. There isn't anybody here."

She looked up from the stairs and toward the end of the hall. "What about the sanctuary?"

"The sanctuary?" Sharon said blankly.

She had already started down the hall toward it, and Sharon followed her, relieved, and then, suddenly, hopeful. Maybe there was a door she'd missed. A sanctuary door that faced southwest. "Is there a door in the sanctuary?"

Reverend Farrison looked irritated. "If someone went out the east door, they could have gotten in and hidden in the sanctuary. Did you check the pews?" She went into the sanctuary. "We've had a lot of trouble lately with homeless people sleeping in the pews. You take that side, and I'll take this one," she said, going over to the side aisle. She started along the rows of padded pews, bending down to look under each one. "Our Lady of Sorrows had their Communion silver stolen right off the altar."

The Communion silver, Sharon thought, working her way along the rows. She'd forgotten about the chalice.

Reverend Farrison had reached the front. She opened the flower-room door, glanced in, closed it, and went up into the chancel. "Did you check the adult Sunday school room?" she said, bending down to look under the chairs.

"Nobody could have hidden in there. The junior choir was in there, having refreshments," Sharon said, and knew it wouldn't do any good. Reverend Farrison was going to insist on checking it anyway, and once she'd found the display case open, the chalice missing, she would go through all the other rooms, one after the other. Till she came to the nursery.

"Do you think it's a good idea us doing this?" Sharon said. "I mean, if there is somebody in the church, they might be dangerous. I think we should wait. I'll call my husband, and when he gets here, the three of us can check—"

"I called the police," Reverend Farrison said, coming down the steps from the chancel and down the center aisle. "They'll be here any minute."

The police. And there they were, hiding in the nursery, a bearded punk and a pregnant teenager, caught redhanded with the Communion silver.

Reverend Farrison started out into the hall.

"I didn't check the Fellowship Hall," Sharon said rapidly. "I mean, I checked the door, but I didn't turn on the lights, and with all those presents for the homeless in there . . ."

She led Reverend Farrison down the hall, past the stairs. "They could have gotten in the north door during the rehearsal and hidden under one of the tables."

Reverend Farrison stopped at the bank of lights and began flicking them. The sanctuary lights went off, and the light over the stairs came on.

Third from the top, Sharon thought, watching Reverend Farrison hit the switch. Please. Don't let the adult Sunday school room come on.

The office lights came on, and the hall light went out. "This church's top priority after Christmas is labeling these lights," Reverend Farrison said, and the Fellowship Hall light came on.

Sharon followed her right to the door and then, as Reverend Farrison went in, Sharon said, "You check in here. I'll check the adult Sunday school room," and shut the door on her.

She went to the adult Sunday school room door, opened it, waited a full minute, and then shut it silently. She crept down the hall to the light bank, switched the stairs light off and shot down the darkened stairs, along the hall, and into the nursery.

They were already scrambling to their feet. Mary had put her hand on the seat of the rocking chair to pull herself up and had set it rocking, but she didn't let go of it.

"Come with me," Sharon whispered, grabbing up the chalice. It was half-full of water, and Sharon looked around hurriedly, and then poured it out on the carpet and tucked it under her arm.

"Hurry!" Sharon whispered, opening the door, and there was no need to motion them forward, to put her fingers to her lips. They followed her swiftly, silently, down the hall, Mary's head ducked, and Joseph's arms held at his sides, ready to come up defensively, ready to protect her.

Sharon walked to the stairs, dreading the thought of trying to get them up them. She thought for a moment of putting them in the choir room and locking them in. She had the key, and she could tell Reverend Farrison she'd checked it and then locked it to make sure no one got in. But if it didn't work, they'd be trapped, with no way out. She had to get them upstairs.

She halted at the foot of the stairs, looking up around the landing and listening. "We have to hurry," she said, taking hold of the railing to show them how to climb, and started up the stairs.

This time they did much better, still putting their hands on the steps in front of them instead of the rail, but climbing up quickly. Three-fourths of the way up, Joseph even took hold of the rail.

Sharon did better, too, her mind steadily now on how to escape Reverend Farrison, what to say to the police, where to take them.

Not the furnace room, even though Reverend Farrison had already looked in there. It was too close to the door, and the police would start with the hall. And not the sanctuary. It was too open.

She stopped just below the top of the stairs, motioning them to keep down, and they instantly pressed themselves back into the shadows. Why was it those signals were universal—danger, silence, run? Because it's a dangerous world, she thought, then and now, and there's worse to come. Herod, and the flight into Egypt. And Judas. And the police.

She crept to the top of the stairs and looked toward the sanctuary and then the door. Reverend Farrison must still be in the Fellowship Hall. She wasn't in the hall, and if she'd gone in the adult Sunday school room, she'd have seen the missing chalice and sent up a hue and cry.

Sharon bit her lip, wondering if there was time to put it back, if she dared leave them here on the stairs while she sneaked in and put it in the display case, but it was too late. The police were here. She could see their red and blue lights flashing purply through the stained-glass door panels. In another minute they'd be at the door, knocking, and Reverend Farrison would come out of the Fellowship Hall, and there'd be no time for anything.

She'd have to hide them in the sanctuary until Reverend Farrison took the police downstairs, and then move them—where? The furnace room? It was still too close to the door. The Fellowship Hall?

She waved them upward, like John Wayne in one of his war movies, along the hall and into the sanctuary. Reverend Farrison had turned off the lights, but there was still enough light from the chancel cross to see by. She laid the chalice in the back pew and led them along the back row to the shadowed side aisle, and then pushed them ahead of her to the front, listening intently for the sound of knocking.

Joseph went ahead with his eyes on the ground, as if he expected more sudden stairs, but Mary had her head up, looking toward the chancel, toward the cross.

Don't look at it, Sharon thought. Don't look at it. She hurried ahead to the flower room.

There was a muffled sound like thunder, and the bang of a door shutting.

"In here," she whispered, and opened the flower-room door.

She'd been on the other side of the sanctuary when Reverend Farrison checked the flower room. Sharon understood now why she had given it only the most cursory of glances. It had been full before. Now it was crammed with the palm trees and the manger. They'd heaped the rest of the props in it—the innkeeper's lantern and the baby blanket. She pushed the manger back, and one of its crossed legs caught on a music stand and tipped it over. She lunged for it, steadied it, and then stopped, listening.

Knocking out in the hall. And the sound of a door shutting. Voices. She let go of the music stand and pushed them into the flower room, shoving Mary into the corner against the spray of roses and nearly knocking over another music stand.

She motioned to Joseph to stand on the other side and flattened herself against a palm tree, shut the door, and realized the moment she did that it was a mistake.

They couldn't stand here in the dark like this—the slightest movement by any of them would bring everything clattering down, and Mary couldn't stay squashed uncomfortably into the corner like that for long.

She should have left the door slightly open, so there was enough light from the cross to see by, so she could hear where the police were. She couldn't hear anything with the door shut except the sound of their own light breathing and the clank of the lantern when she tried to shift her weight, and she couldn't risk opening the door again, not when they might already be in the sanctuary, looking for her. She should have shut Mary and Joseph in here and gone back into the hall to head the police off. Reverend Farrison would be looking for her, and if she didn't find her, she'd take it as one more proof that there was a dangerous homeless person in the church and insist on the police searching every nook and cranny.

Maybe she could go out through the choir loft, Sharon thought, if she could move the music stands out of the way, or at least shift things around so they could hide behind them, but she couldn't do either in the dark.

She knelt carefully, slowly, keeping her back perfectly straight, and put her hand out behind her, feeling for the top of the manger. She patted spiky straw till she found the baby blanket and pulled it out. They must have put the wise men's perfume bottles in the manger, too. They clinked wildly as she pulled the blanket out.

She knelt farther, feeling for the narrow space under the door, and jammed the blanket into it. It didn't quite reach the whole length of the door, but it was the best she could do. She straightened, still slowly, and patted the wall for the light switch.

Her hand brushed it. Please, she prayed, don't let this turn on some other light, and flicked it on.

Neither of them had moved, not even to shift their hands. Mary, pressed against the roses, took a caught breath, and then released it slowly, as if she had been holding it the whole time.

They watched Sharon as she knelt again to tuck in a corner of the blanket and then turned slowly around so she was facing into the room. She reached across the manger for one of the music stands and stacked it against the one behind it, working as gingerly, as slowly, as if she were defusing a bomb. She reached across the manger again, lifted one of the music stands, and set it on the straw so she could push the manger back far enough to give her space to move. The stand tipped, and Joseph steadied it.

Sharon picked up one of the cardboard palm trees. She worked the plywood base free, set it in the manger, and slid the palm tree flat along the wall next to Mary, and then did the other one.

That gave them some space. There was nothing Sharon could do about the rest of the music stands. Their metal frames were tangled together, and against the outside wall was a tall metal cabinet, with pots of Easter lilies in front of it. She could move the lilies to the top of the cabinet at least.

She listened carefully with her ear to the door for a minute, and then stepped carefully over the manger between two lilies. She bent and picked up one of them and set it on top of the cabinet and then stopped, frowning at the wall. She bent down again, moving her hand along the floor in a slow semicircle.

Cold air, and it was coming from behind the cabinet. She stood on tiptoe and looked behind it. "There's a door," she whispered. "To the outside."

"Sharon!" a muffled voice called from the sanctuary.

Mary froze, and Joseph moved so he was between her and the door. Sharon put her hand on the light switch and waited, listening.

"Mrs. Englert?" a man's voice called. Another one, farther off, "Her car's still here," and then Reverend Farrison's voice again, "Maybe she went downstairs."

Silence. Sharon put her ear against the door and listened, and then edged past Joseph to the side of the cabinet and peered behind it. The door opened outward. They wouldn't have to move the cabinet out very far, just enough for her to squeeze through and open the door, and then there'd be enough space for all of them to get through, even Mary. There were bushes on this side of the church. They could hide underneath them until after the police left.

She motioned Joseph to help her, and together they pushed the cabinet a few inches out from the wall. It knocked one of the Easter lilies over, and Mary stooped awkwardly and picked it up, cradling it in her arms.

They pushed again. This time it made a jangling noise, as if there were coat hangers inside, and Sharon thought she heard voices again, but there was no help for it. She squeezed into the narrow space, thinking, What if it's locked? and opened the door.

Onto warmth. Onto a clear sky, black and pebbled with stars.

"How—" she said stupidly, looking down at the ground in front of the door. It was rocky, with bare dirt in between. There was a faint breeze, and she could smell dust and something sweet. Oranges?

She turned to say, "I found it. I found the door," but Joseph was already leading Mary through it, pushing at the cabinet to make the space wider. Mary was still carrying the Easter lily, and

Sharon took it from her and set it against the base of the door to prop it open and went out into the darkness.

The light from the open door lit the ground in front of them and at its edge was a stretch of pale dirt. The path, she thought, but when she got closer, she saw it was the dried bed of a narrow stream. Beyond it the rocky ground rose up steeply. They must be at the bottom of a draw, and she wondered if this was where they had gotten lost.

"Bott lom?" Joseph said behind her.

She turned around. *"Bott lom?"* he said again, gesturing in front and to the sides, the way he'd done in the nursery. Which way?

She had no idea. The door faced west, and if the direction held true, and if this was the Judean Desert, it should lie to the southwest. "That direction," she said, and pointed up the steepest part of the slope. "You go that way, I think."

They didn't move. They stood watching her, Joseph standing slightly in front of Mary, waiting for her to lead them.

"I'm not—" she said, and stopped. Leaving them here was no better than leaving them in the furnace room. Or out in the snow. She looked back at the door, almost wishing for Reverend Farrison and the police, and then set off toward what she hoped was the southwest, clambering awkwardly up the slope, her shoes slipping on the rocks.

How did they do this, she thought, grabbing at a dry clump of weed for a handhold, even with a donkey? There was no way Mary could make it up this slope. She looked back, worried.

They were following easily, sturdily, as certain of themselves as she had been on the stairs.

But what if at the top of this draw there was another one, or a dropoff? And no path. She dug in her toes and scrambled up.

There was a sudden sound, and Sharon whirled around and looked back at the door, but it still stood half-open, with the lily at its foot and the manger behind.

The sound scraped again, closer, and she caught the crunch of footsteps and then a sharp wheeze.

"It's the donkey," she said, and it plodded up to her as if it were glad to see her.

She reached under it for its reins, which were nothing but a ragged rope, and it took a step toward her and blared in her ear, "Haw!" and then a wheeze that was practically a laugh.

She laughed, too, and patted his neck. "Don't wander off again," she said, leading him over to Joseph, who was waiting where she'd left them. "Stay on the path." She scrambled on up to the top of the slope, suddenly certain the path would be there, too.

It wasn't, but it didn't matter. Because there to the southwest was Jerusalem, distant and white in the starlight, lit by a hundred hearthfires, a thousand oil lamps, and beyond it, slightly to the west, three stars low in the sky, so close they were almost touching.

They came up beside her, leading the donkey. *"Bott lom,"* she said, pointing. "There, where the star is."

Joseph was fumbling in his sash again, holding out the little leather bag.

"No," she said, pushing it back to him. "You'll need it for the inn in Bethlehem."

He put the bag back reluctantly, and she wished suddenly she had something to give them. Frankincense. Or myrrh.

"Hunh-*haw*," the donkey brayed, and started down the hill. Joseph lunged after him, grabbing for the rope, and Mary followed them, her head ducked.

"Be careful," Sharon said. "Watch out for King Herod." She raised her hand in a wave, the sleeve of her choir robe billowing out in the warm breeze like a wing, but they didn't see her. They went on down the hill, Mary with her hand on the donkey for steadiness, Joseph a little ahead. When they were nearly at the bottom, Joseph stopped and pointed at the ground and led the donkey off at an angle out of her sight, and Sharon knew they'd found the path.

She stood there for a minute, enjoying the scented breeze, looking at the almost-star, and then went back down the slope, skidding on the rocks and loose dirt, and took the Easter lily out of the door and shut it. She pushed the cabinet back into position, took the blanket out from under the door, switched off the light, and went out into the darkened sanctuary.

There was no one there. She went and got the chalice, stuck it into the wide sleeve of her robe, and looked out into the hall. There was no one there either. She went into the adult Sunday school room and put the chalice back into the display case and then went downstairs.

"*Where* have you been?" Reverend Farrison said. Two uniformed policemen came out of the nursery, carrying flashlights.

Sharon unzipped her choir robe and took it off. "I checked the Communion silver," she said. "None of it's missing." She went into the choir room and hung up her robe.

"We looked in there," Reverend Farrison said, following her in. "You weren't there."

"I thought I heard somebody at the door," she said.

By the end of the second verse of "O Little Town of Bethlehem," Mary and Joseph were only three-fourths of the way to the front of the sanctuary.

"At this rate, they won't make it to Bethlehem by Easter," Dee whispered. "Can't they get a move on?"

"They'll get there," Sharon whispered, watching them. They paced slowly, unperturbedly, up the aisle, their eyes on the chancel. " 'How silently, how silently,' " Sharon sang, " 'the wondrous gift is given.' "

They went past the second pew from the front and out of the choir's sight. The innkeeper came to the top of the chancel steps with his lantern, determinedly solemn.

> " 'So God imparts to human hearts,
>   The blessings of his heaven.' "

"Where did they go?" Virginia whispered, craning her neck to try and see them. "Did they sneak out the back way or something?"

Mary and Joseph reappeared, walking slowly, sedately, toward the palm trees and the manger. The innkeeper came down the steps, trying hard to look like he wasn't waiting for them, like he wasn't overjoyed to see them.

> " 'No ear may hear his coming,
>   But in this world of sin . . .' "

At the back of the sanctuary, the shepherds assembled, clanking their staffs, and Miriam handed the wise men their jewelry box and perfume bottles. Elizabeth adjusted her tinsel halo.

> " 'Where meek souls will receive him still,
>   The dear Christ enters in.' "

Joseph and Mary came to the center and stopped. Joseph stepped in front of Mary and knocked on an imaginary door, and the innkeeper came forward, grinning from ear to ear, to open it.

IN COPPELIUS'S TOYSHOP

$\mathcal{S}$o here I am, stuck in Coppelius's Toyshop, the last place I wanted to be. Especially at Christmas.

The place is jammed with bawling babies and women with shopping bags and people dressed up like teddy bears and Tinkerbell. The line for Santa Claus is so long, it goes clear out the door and all the way over to Madison Avenue, and the lines at the cash registers are even longer.

There are kids everywhere, running up and down the aisles and up and down the escalators, screaming their heads off, and crowding around Rapunzel's tower, gawking up at the row of little windows. One of the windows opens, and inside it there's a ballerina. She twirls around, and the little window closes, and another one opens. This one has a mouse in it. A black cat rears up behind it with its mouth open and the mouse leans out the window and squeaks, "Help, help!" The kids point and laugh.

And over the whole thing the Coppelius's Toyshop theme song plays, for the thousandth time:

"Come to Dr. Coppelius's
Where all is bright and warm,
And there's no fear
For I am here
To keep you safe from harm."

I am not supposed to be here. I am supposed to be at a Knicks game. I had a date to take Janine to see them play the Celtics this afternoon, and instead, here I am, stuck in a stupid toy store, because of a kid I didn't even know she had when I asked her out.

Women always make this big deal about men being liars and not telling them you're married, but what about them? They talk about honesty being the most important thing in a "relationship," which is their favorite word, and they let you take them out and spend a lot of money on them and when they finally let you talk them into going up to their apartment, they trot out these three little brats in pajamas and expect you to take them to the zoo.

This has happened to me about ten times, so before I asked Janine out, I asked Beverly, who works in Accounting with her, whether she lived alone. Beverly, who didn't tell me about *her* kid till we'd been going out over a month and who was really bent out of shape when I dumped her, said, yeah, Janine lived alone and she'd only been divorced about a year and was very "vulnerable" and the last thing she needed in her life was a jerk like me.

She must've given Janine the same line because I had to really turn on the old charm to get her to even talk to me and had to ask her out about fifteen times before she finally said yes.

So, anyway, the Knicks game is our third date. Bernard King is playing and I figure after the game I'm gonna get lucky, so I'm feeling pretty good, and I knock on her door, and this little kid answers it and says, "My mom's not ready."

I should've turned around right then and walked out. I could've scalped Janine's ticket for fifteen bucks, but she's already coming to the door, and she's wiping her eyes with a Kleenex and telling me to come in, this is Billy, she's so sorry she can't go to the game, this isn't her weekend to have the kid, but her ex-husband made her switch, and she's been trying to call me, but I'd already left.

I'm still standing in the hall. "You can't get tickets to Knicks games at the last minute," I say. "Do you know what scalpers charge?" She says, no, no, she doesn't expect me to get an extra ticket, and I breathe a sigh of relief, which I shouldn't have, because then she says she just got a call, her mom's in the hospital, she's had a heart attack, and she's got to go to Queens right away and see her, and she tried to get her ex on the phone but he's not there.

"You better not expect me to take the *kid* to the Knicks game," I say, and she says, no, she doesn't, she's already called Beverly to watch him, and all she wants me to do is take the kid to meet her on the corner of Fifth Avenue and Fifty-eighth.

"I wouldn't ask you to do this if I had anybody else I could ask, but they said I needed to come"—she starts to cry again—"right . . . away."

The whole time she's telling me this, she's been putting on her coat and putting the kid's coat on him and locking the door. "I'll say hi to Grandma for you," she says to the kid. She looks at me, her eyes all teary. "Beverly said she'll be there at noon. Be a good boy," she says to the kid, and is down the stairs and out the door before I can tell her no way.

So I'm stuck with taking this kid up to Fifth Avenue and Fifty-eighth, which is the corner Coppelius's Toyshop is on. Coppelius's is the biggest toy store in New York. It's got fancy red-and-gold doors, and two guys dressed up like toy soldiers standing on both sides of them, saluting people when they walk in, and a chick dressed like Little Red Riding Hood with a red cape and a basket, passing out candy canes to everybody who walks by.

There's a whole mob of people and kids looking at the windows, which they decorate every Christmas with scenes from fairy tales. You know the kind, with Goldilocks eating a bowl of porridge, lifting a spoon to her mouth over and over, and stuffed bears that turn their heads and blink their eyes. It looks like half of New York is there, looking in the windows. Except for Beverly.

I look at my watch. It's noon, and Beverly better get here soon or the kid can wait by himself. The kid sees the windows and runs over to them. "Come back here!" I yell, and grab him by the arm and yank him away from the windows. "Get over here!" I drag him over to the curb. "Now stand there."

The kid is crying and wiping his nose, just like Janine. "Aunt Beverly said she was going to take me to look at the windows," he says.

"Well, then, *Aunt Beverly* can," I say, "when she finally gets here. Which better be pretty damn soon. I don't have all day to wait around."

"I'm cold," he says.

"Then zip up your coat," I say, and I zip up mine and stick my hands in my pockets. There's one of these real cold New York winds whipping around the corner, and it's starting to snow. I look at my watch. It's a quarter past twelve.

"I hafta go to the bathroom," he says.

I tell him to shut up, that he's not going anywhere, and he starts in crying again.

"And quit crying or I'll give you something to cry about," I say.

Right then Red Riding Hood comes over and hands the kid a candy cane. "What's the matter, honey?" she says.

The kid wipes his nose on his sleeve. "I'm cold and I hafta go to the bathroom," he says, and she says, "You just come with me to Coppelius's," and takes hold of his hand and takes him into the store before I can stop her.

"Hey!" I say, and go after them, but the toy-soldier guys are already shutting the doors behind them, and they go through their whole stiff-armed saluting routine before they open them again and I can get in.

When I finally do, I wish I hadn't. The place is a nightmare. There are about a million kids hollering and running around this huge room full of toys and people in costumes demonstrating things. A magician is juggling glow-in-the-dark balls and Raggedy Ann is passing out licorice sticks and a green-faced witch is buzzing the customers with a plane on a string. Around the edges of the room, trains are running on tracks built into the walls, hooting and whistling and blowing steam.

In the middle of this mess is a round purple tower, at least two stories high. There's a window at the very top and a mechanical Rapunzel is leaning out of it, combing her blonde hair, which hangs all the way down to the bottom of the tower. Underneath Rapunzel's window there's a row of little windows that open and close, one after the other, and different things poke out, a baby doll and a white rabbit and a spaceship. All of them do something when their window opens. The doll says "Ma-ma," the rabbit pulls out a pocket watch and looks at it, shaking his head, the spaceship blasts off.

A whole bunch of kids are standing around the tower, but Janine's kid isn't one of them, and I don't see him or Red Riding Hood anywhere. Along the back wall there's a bunch of escalators leading up and down to the other floors, but I don't see the kid on any of them and I don't see any signs that say "Bathrooms," and the lines for the cash registers are too long to ask one of the clerks.

A chick dressed up like Cinderella is standing in the middle of the aisle, winding up green toy frogs and setting them down on the floor to hop all over and get in everybody's way.

"Where are your toilets?" I say, but she doesn't hear me, and no wonder. Screaming kids and hooting trains and toy guns that go rat-a-tat-tat, and over the whole thing a singsongy tune is playing full blast:

> *"I am Dr. Coppelius.*
> *Welcome to my shop.*
> *Where we have toys*
> *For girls and boys,*
> *And the fun times never stop."*

It's sung in a croaky old man's voice and after the second verse finishes, the first one starts in again, over and over and over.

"How do you stand that godawful noise?" I shout to Cinderella, but she's talking to a little kid in a snowsuit and ignores me.

I look around for somebody else I can ask and just then I catch sight of a red cape at the top of one of the escalators and take off after it.

I'm about to step on, when an old guy dressed in a long red coat and a gray ponytail wig moves in front of me and blocks my way. "Welcome to Coppelius's Toyshop," he says in a phony accent. "I am Dr. Coppelius, the children's friend." He does this stupid bow. "Here in Coppelius's, children are our first concern. How may I assist you?"

"You can get the hell out of my way," I say, and shove past him and get on the escalator.

The red cape has disappeared by now, and the escalator's jammed with kids. Half of them are hanging over the moving handrail, looking at the stuffed animals along the sides, teddy bears and giraffes and a life-size black velvet panther. It's got a pink silk tongue and real-looking teeth with a price tag hanging from one of its fangs. "One of a kind," the price tag says. Four thousand bucks.

When I get to the top of the escalator, I can't see Janine's kid or Red Riding Hood anywhere, but there's a red-and-gold sign-post with arrows pointing off in all directions that say "To Hot Wheels Country" and "To Babyland" and "To the Teddy Bears' Picnic." One of them says "To the Restrooms" and points off to the left.

I go in the direction the sign says, but the place is a maze, with aisles leading off in all directions and kids jamming every aisle. I go through fire engines and chemistry sets and end up in a big room full of *Star Wars* stuff, blasters and swords that light up and space fighters. But no signposts.

I ask a gold-colored robot for directions, feeling like an idiot, and he says, "Go down this aisle and turn left. That will bring you to Building Blocks. Turn left at the Tinker Toys and left again. The restrooms are right next to the Lego display."

I go down the aisle and turn left, but it doesn't bring me to Building Blocks. It brings me to the doll department and then the stuffed animals, more giraffes and bunnies and elephants, and every size teddy bear you've ever seen.

Holding on to one of them is a toddler bawling its head off. The kid's been eating candy, and the tears are running down into the chocolate for a nice sticky mess.

It's wailing, "I'm lost," and as soon as it sees me, it lets go of the teddy bear and heads straight for me with its sticky hands. "I can't find my mommy," it says.

The last thing I need is chocolate all over my pants. "You shoulda stayed with your mommy, then," I say, "instead of running off," and head back into the doll department, and old Coppelius must've been lying about the panther, because there, right in the middle of the Barbie dolls, is another one, staring at me with its yellow glass eyes.

I head back through the dollhouses and end up in Tricycles, and this is getting me nowhere. I could wander around this place forever and never find Janine's kid. And it's already one o'clock. If I don't leave by one-thirty, I'll miss the start of the game. I'd leave right now, but Janine would be steamed and I'd lose any chance I had of getting her in the sack on one of those weekends when her ex has the kid.

But I'm not going to find him by wandering around like this. I need to go back down to the main room and wait for Red Riding Hood to bring him back.

I find a down escalator in the sled department and get on it, but when I get off, it's not the main floor. I'm in Babyland with the baby buggies and yellow rubber ducks and more teddy bears.

I must not have gone down far enough. "Where's the escalator?" I say to a chick dressed like Little Bo Peep. She's kootchy-cooing a baby, and I have to ask her again. "Where's the down escalator?"

Bo-peep looks up and frowns. "Down?"

"Yeah," I say, getting mad. "Down. An escalator."

Still nothing.

"I want to get the hell out of this place!"

She makes a move toward the baby, like she's going to cover its ears or something and says, "Go down past the playpens and turn left. It's at the end of Riding Toys."

I do what she says, but when I get there, it goes up, not down. I decide to take it anyway and go back up to the tricycles and find the right escalator myself, but Babyland must be in the basement because at the top is the main room.

The place is even crazier and more crowded than it was before. A clown's demonstrating bright orange yo-yos, Humpty Dumpty's winding up toy dinosaurs, and there are so many kids and baby buggies and shopping bags, it takes me fifteen minutes to make it over to Rapunzel's tower.

There's no sign of Red Riding Hood and the kid or Beverly, but

I can see the door from here and all the escalators. Dr. Coppelius is standing over at the foot of them, bowing to people and passing out big red suckers.

The kids around the tower shout and point, and I look up. A puppet with a hooked nose and a pointy hat is leaning out of one of the windows. He's holding a stick between his puppet hands, and he waves it around. The kids laugh.

The window shuts and another one opens. The ballerina twirls. The black cat, with teeth as sharp as a panther's, rears up behind the mouse, and the mouse squeaks, "Help, help!" Rapunzel combs her hair. And over it all, in time to the squeaking and the twirling and the combing, the song plays over and over:

> ". . . For girls and boys,
> And the fun times never stop."

And after I've been standing there five minutes, the whole thing is stuck in my head.

I look at my watch. It's one-fifteen. How the hell long does it take to take a kid to the bathroom?

The first verse finishes and the second one starts in:

> "Come to Dr. Coppelius's
> Where all is bright and warm . . ."

I'm going to go crazy if I have to stand here and listen to this gas much longer, and where the hell is Beverly?

I look at my watch again. It's one-thirty. I'm going to give it five more minutes and then take one more look around, and then I'm going to the game, kid or no kid.

Somebody yanks on my coat. "Well, it's about time," I say. "Where the hell have you been?" I look down.

It's a kid with dishwater-blonde hair and glasses. "When will he come and get her?" she says.

"Get who?" I say.

She pushes the glasses up on her nose. "Rapunzel in her tower. When will the prince come and get her down?"

I stoop down and get real close. "Never," I say.

The kid blinks at me through her glasses. "Never?" she says.

"He got sick of waiting around for her," I say. "He waited and waited, and finally he got fed up and went off and left her there."

"All alone?" she squeaks, just like the mouse.

"All alone. Forever and ever."

"Doesn't she ever get out of the tower?"

"She's not going anywhere, and it serves her right. It's her own fault."

The kid backs away and looks like she's going to bawl, but she doesn't. She just stares at me through her glasses and then looks back up at the tower.

The rabbit checks his watch. A dragon breathes orange tin-foil flames. The baby doll goes, "Ma-ma." The singsongy tune bellows, *"To keep you safe from harm,"* and starts over, *"I am Dr. Coppelius,"* and I shove my way over to where he's standing at the foot of the escalators.

"How do I find a lost kid?" I say to Dr. Coppelius.

"Up this escalator to Painter's Corner," he says in his phony accent. "Turn right at the modeling-clay display and go all the way to the end." He puts his hand on my arm. "And don't worry. He's perfectly safe. No child ever comes to harm in Coppelius's Toyshop."

"Yeah, well, I know one who's going to when I finally find him," I say, and get on the escalator.

I thought it was the same one I went up before, but it's not. There's no panther, and no signpost at the top, but I can see paints and crayons down one of the halls, and I head that way. Halfway there, the aisle's blocked with kids and mothers pushing strollers.

"What the hell's this?" I say to a guy dressed up like an elf.

"It's the line for Santa Claus," he says. "You'll have to go around. Halfway down that aisle to the basketballs and turn left."

So I go down, but there aren't any basketballs, there's a big Atari sign and a bunch of kids playing Pac-Man, and when I turn left, I run into a room full of toy tanks and bazookas. I go back and turn left and run smack into the Santa Claus line again.

I look at my watch. It's a quarter past two. The hell with this. I've already missed the start of the game, and I'm not going to miss the rest of it. Beverly can try and find the kid, if and when she ever gets here. I'm leaving.

I squeeze through the line to the nearest escalator and take it down, but I must have gotten up on the third floor somehow, because here's the *Star Wars* stuff. I find an escalator and go down it, but when I get to the bottom, I'm back in Babyland and now I have to take the escalator up. But at least I know where it is. I go down past the playpens and over to Riding Toys, and sure enough, there's the escalator. I start to get on it.

The panther is standing at the bottom of the escalator, the price tag dangling from his sharp teeth.

I change my mind and go back through the riding toys and turn left, and now I'm back in Dolls, which can't be right. I backtrack to the playpens, but now I can't find them either. I'm in Puzzles and Games.

I look around for somebody to ask, but there aren't any clerks or Mother Gooses around, and no kids either. They must all be in line to see Santa Claus. I decide to go back to the doll department and get my bearings, and I go up the jigsaw puzzle aisle, but I can't seem to find a way out, and I am getting kind of worried when I see Dr. Coppelius.

He walks past the Candyland display and into a door in the wall between Jeopardy! and Sorry! and I catch a glimpse of gray walls and metal stairs. I figure it must be an employee stairway.

I wait a few minutes so the clown won't see me and then open the door. It's an employee stairway, all right. There are stacks of boxes and wooden crates piled against the wall, and on the stairs there's a big sign headed "Store Policy." I look up the metal stairway, and it has to lead up to the main floor because I can hear the sound of the song jangling far above:

> ". . . For girls and boys,
> And the fun times never stop."

I shut the door behind me, and start up the stairs. It's dark with the door shut, and it gets darker as I climb, and narrower, but the song is getting steadily louder. I keep climbing, wondering what kind of stairway this is. It can't be for bringing up stock because it keeps making all these turns and when I decide I'd better turn around and go back down, somebody's locked the door at the bottom, so I have to keep climbing up, and it keeps getting narrower and narrower and darker and darker, till I can feel the walls on both sides and the last few steps I practically have to squeeze through, but I can see the door up ahead, there's light all around the edges, and the song is getting really loud.

> "Come to Dr. Coppelius's
> Where all is bright and warm . . ."

I squeeze up the last few steps and open the door, only it isn't a door. It's one of the little windows the mouse and the ballerina and the white rabbit come out of, and I have somehow gotten inside of Rapunzel's tower. This must be the stairs they use to come fix the mechanical toys when they break down.

Kids are looking up, and when I open the window, they point and laugh like I was one of the toys. I shut the window and squeeze back down the stairs. I break a piece of wood off one of the crates on the stairs to use to pry the door open, but I must have made a wrong turn somewhere, because I end up back in the same place. I open the door and yell, "Hey! Get me out of here!" but nobody pays any attention.

I look around, trying to spot Red Riding Hood or the robot or Dr. Coppelius to signal them to come help me, and I see Beverly going out the front door. She's got Janine's kid, and he is wiping his nose on his sleeve and clutching a red sucker. Beverly squats down and wipes his eyes with a Kleenex. She zips up his coat, and they start out the door, which a toy soldier is holding open for them.

"Wait!" I shout, waving the piece of wood to get their attention, and the kids point and laugh.

I am going to have to climb out the window and down the side of the tower, hanging on to Rapunzel's hair. I put my foot up over the windowsill. It's a tight squeeze to get my leg up onto the sill, but I manage to do it, and when I get out of here, I know a little boy with a sucker who's going to be really sorry. I hitch my leg over and start to hoist my other foot up over the sill.

I look down. The panther is sitting at the foot of the tower, crouched and waiting. He licks his velvet chops with his pink silk tongue. His sharp teeth glitter.

So here I am, stuck in Coppelius's Toyshop, for what seems like forever, with kids screaming and running around and trains whistling and that stupid song playing over and over and over,

"I am Dr. Coppelius.
Welcome to my shop . . ."

I take out my watch and look at it. It says five to twelve. I've kind of lost track of how long I've been stuck here. It can't be more than two days, because on Monday Janine or Beverly or one of the chicks at work will notice I'm not there, and they'll figure out this is the last place anybody saw me. But it seems longer, and I am getting kind of worried.

Every time the window opens there seem to be different toys, fancy games you play on computers and cars that run by remote control and funny-looking roller skates with only one row of wheels. And the people demonstrating them and handing out candy canes are different, too, mermaids and turtles wearing headbands and a hunchback in a jester's hat and a purple cape.

And the last time I looked out, a woman with dishwater-blonde hair and glasses was standing under the tower, looking up at me. "When I was little," she said to the guy she was with, "I hated this place. I was so worried about Rapunzel."

She pushed her glasses up on her nose. "I didn't know she was a toy. I thought she was real, and I thought the prince had just gone off and abandoned her. I thought he'd gotten fed up and gone off and left her there. All alone."

She said it to the guy, but she was looking straight at me. "Forever and ever. And it served her right. It was her own fault."

But there are lots of people who wear glasses, and even if Janine's mother died and she had to go to the funeral, she'd still be back at work by Wednesday.

I look over at the exit. The toy soldiers are still there, saluting, on either side of the door, and in between them Dr. Coppelius smiles and bows. Overhead the song screeches:

> *"And there's no fear*
> *For I am here*
> *To keep you safe from harm."*

And starts in on the first verse again.

I take out my watch and look at it, and then I shut the window and go look for a way out, but I get confused on the stairs and make a wrong turn and end up in the same place. The little window opens, and I lean out. "Help! Help!" I shout.

The kids point and laugh.

THE PONY

"Well, aren't you going to open it?" Suzy demanded. Barbara obediently pulled off the red-and-green-plaid bow, bracing herself for the twinge of disappointment she always felt when she opened Christmas presents.

"I always just tear the paper, Aunt Barbara," Suzy said. "I picked out this present all by myself. I knew what you wanted from the Macy's parade when your hands got so cold."

Barbara got the package open. Inside was a pair of red-and-purple striped mittens. "It's just what I wanted. Thank you, Suzy," she said. She pointed at the pile of silver boxes under the tree. "One of those is for you, I think."

Suzy dived under the tree and began digging through the presents.

"She really did pick them out all by herself," Ellen whispered, a smile quirking the corners of her mouth. "As you could probably tell by the colors."

Barbara tried on the mittens. I wonder if Joyce got gloves, she thought. At her last session Joyce had told Barbara that her mother always got her gloves, even though she hated gloves and her mother knew it. "I gave one of my patients your phone number," Barbara said to Ellen. "I hope you don't mind."

"Just a little," said her sister. Barbara clenched her mittened fists.

Suzy dumped a silver box with a large blue bow on it in Barbara's lap. "Does this one say 'To Suzy'?" she asked.

Barbara unfolded the silver card. "It says 'To Suzy from Aunt Barbara.' " Suzy began tearing at the paper.

"Why don't you open it on the floor?" Ellen said, and Suzy snatched the package off Barbara's lap and dropped to the floor with it.

"I'm really worried about this patient," Barbara said. "She's spending Christmas at home with an unhappy, domineering mother."

"Then why did she go home?"

"Because she's been indoctrinated to believe that Christmas is a wonderful, magical time when everyone is happy and secret wishes can come true," Barbara said bitterly.

"A baseball shirt," Suzy said happily. "I bet now those boys at my preschool will let me play ball with them." She pulled the pin-striped Yankees shirt on over her red nightgown.

"Thank goodness you were able to find the shirt," Ellen said softly. "I don't know what she would have done if she hadn't gotten one. It's all she's talked about for a month."

I don't know what my patient will do either, Barbara thought. Ellen put another red-and-green package in her lap, and she opened it, wondering if Joyce was opening her presents. At Joyce's last session she had talked about how much she hated Christmas morning, how her mother always found fault with all her presents, saying they didn't fit or were the wrong color or that she already had one.

"Your mother's using her presents to express the dissatisfaction she feels with her own life," Barbara had told her. "Of course, everyone feels some disappointment when they open presents. It's because the present is only a symbol for what the person really wants."

"Do you know what I want for Christmas?" Joyce had said as though she hadn't heard a word. "A ruby necklace."

The phone rang. "I hope this isn't your patient," Ellen said, and went into the hall to answer it.

"What does this present say?" Suzy said. She was standing holding another present, a big one with cheap, garish Santa Clauses all over it.

Ellen came back in, smiling. "Just a neighbor calling to wish us a merry Christmas. I was afraid it was your patient."

"So was I," Barbara said. "She's talked herself into believing that she's getting a ruby necklace for Christmas, and I'm very worried about her emotional state when she's disappointed."

"I can't read, you know," Suzy said loudly, and they both laughed. "Does this present say 'To Suzy'?"

"Yes," Ellen said, looking at the tag, which had a Santa Claus on it. "But it doesn't say who it's from. Is this from you, Barbara?"

"It's ominous," Suzy said. "We had ominous presents at my preschool."

"Anonymous," Ellen corrected, untaping the tag and looking on the back. "They had a gift exchange. I wonder who sent this. Mom's bringing her presents over this afternoon and Jim decided to wait and give her his when she goes down there next weekend. Go ahead and open it, honey, and when we see what it is, maybe we'll know who it's from." Suzy knelt over the box and started tearing at the cheap paper. "Your patient thinks she's getting a ruby necklace?" Ellen said.

"Yes, she saw it in a little shop in the Village, and last week when she went in there again, it was gone. She's convinced someone bought it for her."

"Isn't it possible someone did?"

"Her family lives in Pennsylvania, she has no close friends, and she didn't tell anybody she wanted it."

"Did you buy her the necklace?" Suzy said. She was tearing busily at the Santa Claus paper.

"No," Barbara said to Ellen. "She didn't even tell me about the necklace until after it was gone from the shop, and the last thing I'd want to do would be to encourage her in her mother's neurotic behavior pattern."

"I would buy her the necklace," Suzy said. She had all the paper off and was lifting the lid off a white box. "I would buy it and say, 'Surprise!'"

"Even if she got the necklace, she'd be disappointed in it," Barbara said, feeling obscurely angry at Suzy. "The necklace is only a symbol for a subconscious wish. Everyone has those wishes: to go back to the womb, to kill our mothers and sleep with our fathers, to die. The conscious mind is terrified of those wishes, so it substitutes something safer—a doll or a necklace."

"Do you really think it's that ominous?" Ellen asked, the corners of her mouth quirking again. "Sorry, I'm starting to sound like Suzy. Do you really think it's that serious? Maybe your patient really wants a ruby necklace. Didn't you ever want something really special that you didn't tell anybody about? You did. Don't you remember that year you wanted a pony and you were so disappointed?"

"I remember," Barbara said.

"Oh, it's just what I wanted!" Suzy said so breathlessly that they both looked over at her. Suzy pulled a doll out of a nest of pink tissue and held it out at arm's length. The doll had a pink ruffled dress, yellow curls, and an expression of almost astonishing sweetness. Suzy stared at it as if she were half afraid of it. "It is," she said in a hushed tone. "It's just what I wanted."

"I thought you said she didn't like dolls," Barbara said.

"I thought she didn't. She didn't breathe a word of this." Ellen picked up the box and rustled through the pink tissue paper, looking for a card. "Who on earth do you suppose sent it?"

"I am going to call her Letitia," Suzy said. "She's hungry. I'm going to feed her breakfast." She went off into the kitchen, still holding the doll carefully away from her.

"I had no idea she wanted a doll," Ellen said as soon as she was out of sight. "Did she say anything when you took her to Macy's?"

"No," Barbara said, wadding the wrapping paper in her lap into a ball. "We never even went near the dolls. She wanted to look at baseball bats."

"Then how did you know she wanted a doll?"

Barbara stopped with her hands full of paper and plaid ribbon. "I didn't send her the doll," she said angrily. "I bought her the Yankees shirt, remember?"

"Then who sent it to her?"

"How would I know? Jim, maybe?"

"No. He's getting her a catcher's mitt."

The phone rang. "I'll get it," Barbara said. She crammed the red paper into a box and went into the hall.

"I just had to call you!" Joyce shouted at her. She sounded nearly hysterical.

"I'm right here," she said soothingly. "I want you to tell me what's upsetting you."

"I'm not upset!" Joyce said. "You don't understand! I got it!"

"The ruby necklace?" Barbara said.

"At first I thought I hadn't gotten it and I was trying to be cheerful about it even though my mother hated everything I got her and she gave me gloves again, and then, when almost all the presents had been passed out, there it was, in this little box, all wrapped in Santa Claus paper. There was a little tag with a Santa Claus on it, too, and it said 'To Joyce.' It didn't say who it was from. I opened it, and there it was. It's just what I wanted!"

"Surprise, Aunt Barbara," Suzy said, feeding a cookie shaped like Santa Claus to her doll.

"I'll wear the necklace to my next session so you can see it," Joyce said, and hung up.

"Barbara," Ellen's voice called from the living room. "I think you'd better come in here."

Barbara took hold of Suzy's hand and walked into the living room. Ellen was wrestling with a package wrapped in gaudy Santa Claus paper. It was wedged between the Christmas tree and the door. Ellen was behind it, trying to straighten the tree.

"Where did this come from?" Barbara said.

"It came in the mail," Suzy said. She handed Barbara her doll and clambered up on the couch to get to the small tag taped on top.

"There isn't any mail on Christmas," Barbara said.

Ellen squeezed past the tree and around to where Barbara was standing. "I hope it's not a pony," she said, and the corners of her mouth quirked. "It's certainly big enough for one."

Suzy climbed back down, handed Barbara the tag, and took her doll back. Barbara held the tag a little away from her, as if she were afraid of it. It had a Santa Claus on it. It read "To Barbara." The present was big enough to be a pony. Or something worse. Something only your subconscious knew you wanted. Something too frightening for your conscious mind to even know it wanted.

"It's an ominous present," Suzy said. "Aren't you going to open it?"

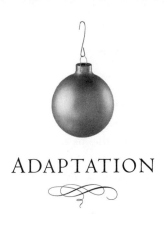

ADAPTATION

"Heap on more wood! The wind is chill;
But let it whistle as it will,
We'll keep our Christmas merry still."

— SIR WALTER SCOTT

*M*arley was dead: to begin with.

Dickens's story, *A Christmas Carol*, however, of which the aforementioned is the first sentence, is alive and well and available in any number of versions. In the books department of Harridge's, where I work, we have nineteen, including *Mickey's Christmas Carol*, *The Muppet Christmas Carol*, the Cuddly-Wuddlys' *Christmas Carol*, and one with photographs of dogs dressed as Scrooge and Mrs. Cratchit.

We also have an assortment of *Christmas Carol* cookbooks, advent calendars, jigsaw puzzles, and an audiotape on which Captain

Picard of the American television series *Star Trek: The Next Generation* takes all the parts.

All of these are, of course, adaptations, shortened and altered and otherwise bowdlerized. No one reads the original, though we carry it, in paperback. In the two years I've worked here, we've only sold a single copy, and that to myself. I bought it last year to read to my daughter, Gemma, when I had her for Christmas, but then I did not have time to do so. My ex-wife, Margaret, came to pick her up early for a pantomime she and Robert were taking her to, and we only got as far as Marley's ghost.

Gemma knows the story, though, in spite of never having read it, and the names of all the characters, as does everyone. They are so well-known, in fact, that at the beginning of the season this year Harridge's management had suggested the staff dress in costume as Scrooge and Tiny Tim, to increase profits and "provide a seasonal atmosphere."

There was a general outcry at this, and the idea had been dropped. But on the morning of the twenty-second when I arrived at work, there was a figure in a floor-dragging black robe and a hood standing by the order desk with Mr. Voskins, who was smiling smugly.

"Good morning, Mr. Grey," Mr. Voskins said to me. "This is your new assistant," and I half-expected him to say, "Mr. Black," but instead he said pleasedly, "the Spirit of Christmas Future."

It is actually Christmas Yet to Come, but Mr. Voskins has not read the original either.

"How do you do?" I said, wondering if Mr. Voskins was going to demand that I wear a costume as well, and why he had hired someone just now. The books department had been shorthanded all of December.

"Mr. Grey will explain things to you," Mr. Voskins said to the spirit. "Harridge's has been able to arrange for an author autographing," he said to me, which explained this hiring three days before Christmas. No doubt the book's being autographed was yet another version of *A Christmas Carol*. "We will be holding it the day after tomorrow."

"On Christmas Eve?" I said. "At what time? I'd arranged to leave early on Christmas Eve."

"It will depend on the author's schedule," Mr. Voskins said. "He's an extremely busy man."

"My daughter's spending the evening with me," I explained. "It's the only time I'll have her." They would be at Robert's parents' in Surrey for the rest of Christmas week.

"I'm discussing the details with the author this morning," he said. "Oh, and your wife telephoned. She wants you to ring her back."

"Ex-wife," I corrected him, but he had already hurried off, leaving me with my new assistant.

"I'm Mr. Grey," I said, extending my hand.

The spirit silently extended a skinny hand for me to shake, and I remembered that the Spirit of Christmas Yet to Come was mute, communicating solely by pointing.

"Have you worked in a books department before?" I asked.

He shook his hooded head. I hoped he didn't plan to stay in character while waiting on the customers, or perhaps that was the idea, and he was here for "seasonal atmosphere" only.

"What am I supposed to call you?" I said.

He extended a bony finger and pointed at the *Wild West Christmas Carol*, on the cover of which a black-hatted spirit stood, pointing at a tombstone with Scrooge's name on it.

"Spirit? Christmas? Yet to Come?" I said, thinking that an "atmospheric" assistant was worse than none at all.

But I was wrong. He proved to be very efficient, learning the cash register and the credit-card procedure with ease, and waiting on customers promptly. They seemed delighted when he extended his bony finger from his black sleeve and pointed at the books they'd asked for. By ten o'clock I felt confident enough to leave him in charge of the department while I went to the employee lounge to telephone Margaret.

The line was engaged. I intended to ring her up again at a quarter past, but we had a surge of shoppers, and although Christmas Yet to Come was extremely helpful, I couldn't get away again till nearly eleven. When I dialed Margaret's flat, there was no answer.

I was almost glad. I wanted to know the time of the autographing before I spoke to her. We had already had two fights over the "visitation schedule," as Margaret calls it. I was originally to have had Gemma on Boxing Day as well as Christmas Eve, but Robert's parents had invited them up to Surrey for the entire week. We had compromised by my having Gemma on Christmas Eve and part of Christmas Day. Then last week Margaret had rung up to say Robert's parents especially wanted them there for church on Christmas morning as it was a family tradition that Robert read the Scripture. "You can have her all Christmas Eve day," Margaret had said.

"I have to work."

"You could insist on having the day off," she'd said, letting her voice die away.

It is a trick she has of leaving a sentence unfinished but her meaning perfectly clear. She used it to excellent account during the divorce, claiming she had not said any of the things I accused her of, as in fact she had not, and though I only see her now when she brings Gemma, I still understand her perfectly.

"You could insist on having the day off," she meant now, "if you really cared about Gemma." And there is no answer to that, no way to make her understand that Christmas Eve is not a day a shopclerk can insist on taking off, to explain to her that it is different from being an accountant. No way to explain why I gave up being an accountant.

And no way to explain to her that I might need to change the schedule because of an autographing. I decided to wait to try again till I had spoken to Mr. Voskins.

He did not come back till after noon. "The autographing will take place from eleven to one," he said, handing us a stack of red-and-green flyers. "Hand these out to the customers," he said.

I read the top flyer, relieved that the autographing wouldn't cause a problem with Gemma. "A Special Signing of Sir Spencer Siddon's latest book," it read. *"Making Money Hand Over Fist."*

"It's on the bestseller list," Mr. Voskins said happily. "We were very lucky to get him. His secretary will be here at half-past one to discuss the arrangements."

"We'll need more staff," I said. "The two of us can't possibly run an autographing and wait on customers at the same time."

"I'll try to hire someone," he said vaguely. "We'll discuss everything when Sir Spencer's secretary arrives."

"Shall I go to lunch now, then?" I said, "and let Mr. . . ." I pointed at the spirit, "go second so I'll be back in time for the meeting?"

"No," he said. "I want you both here. Go now." He waved vaguely in our direction.

"Which?"

"Both of you. I'll get someone from the housewares department to cover your department. Be back by 1:00."

When our replacement came, I told the spirit, "You can go to lunch," stuck *A Christmas Carol*, which I'd been reading on my lunch and tea breaks, in my coat pocket, and went to telephone Margaret. The line was engaged again.

When I came out of the lounge, the spirit was standing there, waiting for me, and I realized he wouldn't know where to go for lunch. Since Harridge's had closed its employee dining room to increase profits, employees had half an hour to get to, partake of, and return from lunch. "I know of a place that's quick," I told him.

He nodded, and I led off through the crowded aisles, hoping he would keep up. I need not have had any fear—he kept pace with me easily, in spite of not saying, as I did, "Sorry," to dozens of shoppers blocking the way. By the time we'd reached the south door, he was even with me, and, before I could turn toward Cavendish Square, he'd moved ahead, his arm extended and his long, bony finger pointing toward Regent Street.

All the luncheon places in Regent Street are expensive and invariably crammed with shoppers resting their feet, and are a good ten minutes' walk away. We would have just enough time to walk there, not get waited on, and return empty-handed.

"I usually go to Wilson's," I said, "it's closer," but he continued to point commandingly and we had no time for arguing either. I followed him down the street, down a lane I hadn't known was there, and into a dismal-looking lunch counter called Mama Montoni's.

It wasn't crowded, at any rate, and the small tables looked comparatively clean, though the made sandwiches on top of the counter looked several days old.

At one of the tables was an enormous man with a full brown beard, and I saw why the spirit had brought me here. The man was dressed as the Spirit of Christmas Present, in a green robe edged with white fur, and a crown of holly.

"Come in! Come in!" he said, even though we were already in, and my companion glided over to him.

The enormous man shook his head and said, "No, he can't make it for lunch today," as if Christmas Yet to Come had spoken.

I wondered who the "he" they referred to was. The Spirit of Christmas Past, perhaps?

"Neither of us got anything, I'm afraid," the enormous man said to Yet to Come, sounding discouraged. "Most of the bank executives are on holiday. But the teller said the Adelphi is holding pantomime auditions this afternoon."

I wondered if the pantomime was *A Christmas Carol*, or if they had previously been in a production and were now trying to find employment that fit the costumes. It was a good costume. The holly crown had the requisite icicles, and the green robe was belted with a rusted scabbard, just as in the original. His chest was not bare, though, and neither were his feet. He had compromised with the weather by wearing sandals with thick socks and had fastened the open robe across his massive chest with a large green button.

I was still standing just inside the door. My companion turned and pointed at me, and the enormous man boomed out, "Come know me better, man," and beckoned me to the table.

I was going to say that I needed to order first, but the old woman behind the counter—Mama Montoni?—had disappeared into the back. I went over to the table. "How do you do?" I said. "I'm Edwin Grey."

"Delighted to meet you," the enormous man said heartily. "Sit down, sit down. My friend tells me you work together."

"Yes." I sat down. "At Harridge's."

"He tells me you are hiring additional staff in your department. Is that right?"

"Possibly," I said, wondering how Sir Spencer Siddon would feel at being confronted with half the characters from *A Christmas Carol*. Would he think he was meant to be Scrooge? "It would be only temporary, though. Just the three days till Christmas."

"Till Christmas," he said, and the old woman emerged from the back with a fistful of silverware and two plates of congealed-looking spaghetti.

"I'll have what they're having," I said, "and a paper cup of tea to take with me."

The old woman, who was clearly related to Yet to Come, didn't answer or even acknowledge that I'd spoken to her, but she disappeared into the back again.

"I didn't know this café was here," I said, so he wouldn't bring up the topic of job openings again.

"Excellent choice of books," he said, pointing at my *Christmas Carol*, which was protruding from my coat pocket.

"I should imagine it's your favorite," I said, laying it on the table, smiling.

He shook his shaggy brown head. "I prefer Mr. Dickens's *Little Dorrit*, so patient and cheerful in her imprisonment, and Trollope's *Barchester Towers*."

"Do you read a good deal?" I asked. It's rare to find anyone who reads the older authors, let alone Trollope.

He nodded. "I find it helps to pass the time," he said. "Especially at this time of year, 'When dark December glooms the day/ And takes our autumn joys away. When short and scant the sunbeam throws/ Upon the weary waste of snows/ A cold and profitless regard . . .' *Marmion*. Sir Walter Scott."

"Fourth canto," I said, and he beamed at me.

"You are a reader, too?" he said eagerly.

"I find books a great comfort," I said, and he nodded.

"Tell me what you think of *A Christmas Carol*," he said.

"I think it has lasted all these years because people want to believe it could happen," I said.

"But you don't believe it?" he said. "You don't believe a man might hear the truth and be changed by it?"

"I think Scrooge seems quite easily reformed," I said, "compared with the Scrooges I have known."

Mama Montoni emerged from the back again, glaring, and slapped down a plate of lukewarm spaghetti and a crockery cup half full of tea.

"So you have read *Marmion*?" the Spirit of Christmas Present said. "Tell me, what did you think of the tale of Sir David Lindesey?" and we launched into an eager discussion that lasted far too long. I would be late getting back for the meeting with Scrooge's secretary.

I stood up, and my assistant did, too. "We must be getting back," I said, pulling on my coat. "It was a pleasure meeting you, Mr. . . . ?"

He extended his huge hand. "I am the Spirit of Christmas Present."

I laughed. "Then you're missing your third. Where's Christmas Past?"

"In America," he said quite seriously, "where he has been much corrupted by nostalgia and commercial interests."

He saw me looking skeptically at his socks and sandals. "You do not see us at our best," he said. "I fear we have fallen on hard times."

Apparently. "I should think these would be good times, with any number of Scrooges you could reform."

"And so there are," he said, "but they are praised and rewarded for their greed, and much admired. And"—he looked sternly at me—"they do not believe in spirits. They lay their visions to Freud and hormonal imbalance, and their therapists tell them they should feel no guilt, and advise them to focus further on themselves."

"Yes, well," I said, "I must be getting back." I pointed at my assistant, not knowing whether Present would expect me to address him as the Spirit of Christmas Yet to Come. "You can stay and talk to your friend if you wish," and made my escape, glad that at least I hadn't suggested he come speak to Mr. Voskins about being taken on, and wondering what Mr. Voskins would do when he found out he had hired a lunatic.

Mr. Voskins wasn't on the floor, and neither was the secretary. I looked at my watch, expecting it to be well past one, but it was only a quarter till. I rang up Margaret. The line was engaged.

My assistant was there when I got back, waiting on a

customer, but there was still no sign of Mr. Voskins. He finally came up at two to tell us the secretary had phoned to change the schedule.

"Of the autographing?" I said anxiously.

"No, of the meeting with us. His secretary won't be here till half-past."

I took advantage of the delay to try Margaret again. And got Gemma.

"Mummy's downstairs talking to the doorman about our being gone," she told me.

"Do you know what she wanted to speak to me about?" I asked her.

"No . . . o," she said, thinking, and added, with a child's irrelevance, "I went to the dentist. She'll be back up in a minute."

"I'll talk to you in the meantime, then," I said. "What shall we have to eat for Christmas Eve?"

"Figs," she said promptly.

"Figs?"

"Yes, and frosted cakes. Like the little princess and Ermengarde and Becky had at the feast. Well, actually, they didn't have it. Horrid Miss Minchin found out and took it all away from them. And red-currant wine. Only I suppose you won't let me have wine. But red-currant drink or red-currant juice. Red-currant *something*."

"And figs," I said distastefully.

"Yes, and a red shawl for a tablecloth. I want it *just* like in the book."

"What book?" I said, teasing.

"A Little Princess."

"Which one is that?"

"You *know*. The one where the little princess is rich and then she loses her father and Miss Minchin makes her live in the garret and be a servant and the Indian gentleman feels sorry for her and sends her things. You *know*. It's my favorite book."

I do know, of course. It has been her favorite for two years now, displacing both *Anne of Green Gables* and *Little Women* in her affections. "It's because we're just alike," she'd told me when I asked her why she liked it so much.

"You both live in a garret," I'd said.

"*No.* But we're both tall for our age, and we both have black hair."

"Of course," I said now. "I forgot. What do you want for Christmas?"

"Not a doll. I'm too old for dolls," she said promptly, and then hesitated. "The little princess's father always gave her books for Christmas."

"Did he?"

Mr. Voskins appeared at my elbow, looking agitated.

"I'll be right there," I said, cupping my hand over the mouthpiece.

"It's nearly half-past," he said.

"I'll be right there." I promised Gemma I'd purchase figs and red-currant *something*, and told her to tell her mother I'd phoned, and went to meet the secretary, wondering if he'd look like Bob Cratchit. That would make the cast complete, except for the Spirit of Christmas Past, of course, who was in America.

The secretary wasn't there yet. At a quarter to three, Mr. Voskins informed us that the secretary had phoned to change the meeting time to four. I used the extra time to purchase Gemma's present, a copy of *A Little Princess*. She owns a paperback, which she has read a dozen times, but this was a reproduction of the original, with a dark blue cloth cover and colored plates. Gemma looked at it longingly every time she came to see me, and had given all sorts of not-very-veiled hints, like her "The little princess's father bought her books," just now.

I had Yet to Come ring the book up for me, and I put it with my coat and went back into the stockroom to get another copy so

Gemma wouldn't see it was gone when she came to the store the day after tomorrow, and guess.

When I came out with the copy, Mr. Voskins was there with Sir Spencer's secretary. I was wrong about the secretary's looking like Bob Cratchit. She was a smartly dressed young woman, with a short, sleek haircut, and a gold Rolex watch.

"Sir Spencer requires a straight-backed chair without arms, with a wood table seventy centimeters high, and two fountain pens with viridian ink. Where did you plan to have him sit?"

I showed her the table in the literature section. "Oh, this won't do at all," she said, looking at the books. "A photographer will be coming. These shelves will all have to be filled with copies of *Making Money Hand Over Fist*. Facing out. And the rest of them *here*," she said, pointing at the history shelves, "so that they're easily accessible from the queue. Who will be in charge of that?"

"He will," I said, pointing at Yet to Come.

"Single file," she said, looking at her notes. "Two books per person. New hardbacks only, no paperbacks and nothing previously owned."

"Do you want them to write the name they wish inscribed on a slip of paper," I said, "so they won't have to spell their names for him?"

She stared at me coldly. "Sir Spencer does not personalize books, he signs them. Sir Spencer prefers Armentières water, *not* Perrier, and some light refreshments—water biscuits and dietetic cheese." She checked off items in her notebook. "We'll need an exit through which he can depart without being seen."

"A trapdoor?" I said, looking at Yet to Come, who seemed positively friendly by comparison.

She turned to Mr. Voskins. "How many staff do you have?"

"I'm hiring additional help," he said, "and we're getting in additional books from the publishers."

She snapped the notebook shut. "Sir Spencer will be here

from eleven to one. You were very lucky to get him. Sir Spencer is very much in demand."

We spent the rest of the day bringing up books and scouring the basement and the furniture department for a table that would meet specifications. I had intended to shop for the ingredients for Gemma's feast after work, but instead I went from shop to shop looking for Armentières water, which I found on the sixth try, and for red-currant juice, which I did not find. I bought a box of black-currant tea and hoped that would do.

It was nearly ten when I got home, but I phoned Margaret twice more. Both times the line was engaged.

Next morning I left Yet to Come in charge of the department and went down to the food hall to arrange for the dietetic cheese and water biscuits. When I got back, Margaret was there, asking Yet to Come where I was.

"I suppose it was *your* idea to have a shopclerk that's mute," Margaret said.

"What are you doing here?" I said. "Is Gemma here, too?"

"Yes," Gemma said, coming up, smiling.

"I needed to speak to you," Margaret said. "Gemma, go over to the children's department and see if you can find a hairbow to match your Christmas dress."

Gemma was looking at Yet to Come, who was pointing at the travel section. "Is that the Spirit of Christmas Yet to Come?" she said. "From *A Christmas Carol*?"

"Yes," I said. "The genuine article."

"*Gemma,*" Margaret said. "Go find a hairbow. Burgundy, to match the dress Robert gave you." She sent her off, watching her till she was a good distance down the aisle, and then turned back to me. "It was obvious you weren't going to return my call."

"I did," I said. "Didn't Gemma tell you I'd phoned?"

"She *told* me you couldn't wait even a few moments till I returned, that you were too *busy*."

Gemma told her no such thing, of course. "What did you want to speak to me about?" I said.

"Your daughter's welfare." She looked pointedly at the boxes of books. "Or are you too busy for that, as well?"

There are times when it is hard for me to imagine that I ever loved Margaret. I know rationally that I did, that when she told me she wanted a divorce it was like a blade going through me, but I cannot call up the feeling, or remember what it was about her that I loved.

I said ploddingly, "What about her welfare?"

"She needs a brace. The dentist says she has an overbite and that it needs to be corrected. It will be expensive," she said, and let her voice die away.

Too expensive for a shopclerk, she means. An accountant could have afforded it.

There is no answer to that, even if she had actually said it. She believes I quit my job as an accountant out of spite, to keep her from collecting a large amount of child support, and there is nothing I could say that would convince her otherwise. Certainly not the truth, which is that having lost her, having lost Gemma, I could not bear to do without books as well.

"Robert has offered to pay for the brace," she said, "which I think is very generous of him, but he was afraid you might object. Do you?"

"No," I said, wishing I could say, "I want to pay for the brace," but, as she had not said, a shopclerk doesn't earn enough to pay for it. "I don't have any objections."

"I told him you wouldn't care," she said. "It's become increasingly clear over the past two years that you don't care about Gemma at all."

"And it's becoming increasingly clear," I said, raising my voice, "that you are systematically attempting to take my daughter away from me. You can't even stand to let me see her on Christmas!" I shouted, and saw Gemma.

She was over in the literature section, standing with her back to the shelves. She was holding the copy of *A Little Princess*, and she had obviously come back to see if it was still there, to see if I'd bought it yet.

And heard her parents trying to tear her in two. She huddled back against the shelves, looking small and hunted, clutching the book.

"Gemma," I said, and Margaret turned and saw her.

"Did you find a burgundy hairbow?" she said.

"No," Gemma said.

"Well, come along. We have shopping to do."

Gemma put the book back carefully, and started toward us.

"I'll see you tomorrow night," I said, trying to smile. "I found some black-currant tea for our feast."

She said solemnly, "Did you get the figs?"

"Come along, Gemma," Margaret said. "Tell your father goodbye."

"Goodbye," she said, and smiled tentatively at me.

"I'll get the figs," I promised.

Which was easier said than done. Harridge's food hall didn't have them, either canned or fresh, and neither did the grocer's down the street. There wasn't time to walk to the market and back on my lunch break. I would have to go after work.

And I didn't want to go to Mama Montoni's. I didn't want Christmas Present making more inquiries about whether we were hiring additional staff. And I didn't feel like talking to anyone, sane or not. I ducked down the alley to Wilson's, intending to get a bacon sandwich to take.

The Spirit of Christmas Present was there, sitting at one of the tiny tables, reading *Making Money Hand Over Fist*. He looked up when I came in and motioned me eagerly over to the table.

"I am supposed to meet Jacob Marley here," he said, waving me over. "Come, we'll discuss *Ivanhoe* and *The Mystery of Edwin Drood*." He pulled a chair out for me. "I have always wondered if Edwin were truly dead, or if he could be brought to life again."

I sat down and picked up *Making Money Hand Over Fist*. "I thought you kept to the older authors."

"Research," he said, taking the book back. "Jacob has high hopes of a job for us. He went to the Old Bailey this morning to speak with a barrister."

"Who specializes in divorce, no doubt," I said. "Or did he go to speak to the barrister about getting his sentence reduced?"

"About repentance," he said.

I laughed humorlessly. "You really believe you're the incarnation of Dickens's spirits."

"Not Dickens's," he said.

"That you're really Christmas Present and my assistant is Christmas Yet to Come? Is that why he never speaks? Because the Spirit of Christmas Yet to Come in Dickens's story is mute?"

"He can speak," he said, quite seriously. "But he does not like to. Many find the sound of his voice distressing."

"And you believe your job is to reform misers and spread Christmas cheer?" I swung my arm wide. "Then why don't you do something?" I said bitterly. "Use your magic powers. Help the needy. House the homeless. Reunite fathers with their children."

"We have no such powers. A little skill with locks, some minor dexterity with time. We cannot change what is, or was. Our power is only to rebuke and to remind, to instruct and to forewarn."

"Like books," I said. "Which no one reads anymore."

"Your daughter."

"My daughter," I said, and brightened. "Do you know where I can find figs?"

"Tinned or fresh?"

"Either," I said.

"Fortnum and Mason's," he said, and as soon as I stood up, went back to reading Sir Spencer's book. There was not time to go to Fortnum's, though when I got back to Harridge's and looked at my watch, I had nearly ten minutes of my lunch break left.

Mr. Voskins was waiting for me.

"Sir Spencer's secretary phoned. Sir Spencer can't be here till half-past one." He handed me a stack of revised flyers. "The autographing will be from half-past one to half-past three."

I looked at the flyers, dismayed.

"It was the only free time in his schedule," he said defensively. "We're lucky he can fit us in at all."

I thought of the cleaning up afterward. "I'll need to leave by four," I said. "My daughter's coming for Christmas Eve."

It was a long afternoon. Yet to Come took the books down from the literature shelves and put up Sir Spencer's books, facing out, bright green volumes with a hundred-pound note design and gold lettering. I taped up flyers and dealt with customers who had gotten a gift they had not expected and who now had, grudgingly, to return the favor, "And nothing over two pounds." I gave them credit-card receipts and flyers, thinking, Only one more day till I have Gemma.

After work I went to Fortnum's, which had both fresh and tinned figs. I bought them both, and frosted cakes, and chocolates, which I intended to tell her the Indian gentleman had sent.

When I got home I rooted out an old red wool scarf to use as a tablecloth, and tidied up the flat. Only one more day.

Which day came at last, and with it a new flyer (half-past one to half-past three) and the Spirit of Christmas Present. "What are you doing here?" I said.

"We have found employment," he said, beaming.

"We?" I said, looking around for Marley. I didn't see anyone who looked the part, and Present was already piling copies of Sir Spencer's book on the display tables.

"What sort of employment?" I said suspiciously. "You're not planning some sort of demonstration against Sir Spencer, are you?"

"I'm your new assistant," he said, stacking books on the floor by the order desk. "I'm supposed to pass out numbers for queueing up."

"I can't imagine that many people will come," I said, but by ten o'clock there were twenty people clutching their numbered chits.

I sold them copies of *Making Money Hand Over Fist* and explained why Sir Spencer wouldn't be there at eleven as advertised. "He's a very busy man," I said. "We're lucky he was able to fit us in at all."

Mr. Voskins came up at eleven to tell us we would have to forgo lunch, which was patently obvious. The department was filled with milling people, Yet to Come had had to go down to the basement for more books, and Present was writing numbers on more chits.

By noon the queue had begun to form according to the numbers and was halfway down the aisle.

"You'd best go get more books," I told Yet to Come, and turned round to find Margaret standing there.

"What are you doing here?" I said blankly. "Where's Gemma?"

"She's up on fifth, looking at dolls," she said.

"I thought she didn't want a doll."

"She said she just wanted to look at them," she said. Yes, I thought, and hide a safe two floors away from her parents' fighting.

"Christmas Eve won't work," Margaret said.

"What?" I said blankly, though I knew already what she meant, felt it like a blade going in.

"We need to take an earlier train. Robert's parents are having a friend of theirs down who's an orthodontist, and he's agreed to look at Gemma's overbite, but he's only going to be there for Christmas Eve."

"I'm to have Gemma Christmas Eve," I said stupidly.

"I *know*. That's why I came, so we can rework the schedule. We're coming back the day after New Year's. You can have her then."

"Why can't she see the orthodontist after New Year's?"

"He's a very busy man. Ordinarily Gemma would have to be put on a waiting list, but he's agreed to see her as a special favor. I think we should be very grateful he was able to fit us in at all."

"I have to work inventory the day after New Year's," I said.

"Of course," she said, and let her voice die away. "The next weekend, then. Whenever you like."

And the next weekend she will have to be fitted for the brace, I thought, and the following one it will have to be tightened or she will have to have bands put on. "I was counting on Gemma's being with me Christmas Eve. Can't you take a later train?" I said, though I already knew it was hopeless, knew I was standing against the bookcase the way Gemma had, looking hunted.

"The only trains are at four and half-past ten. The late one doesn't get in till one o'clock. You can hardly expect Robert to ask his parents and the orthodontist to wait up for us. I really do think you could be a bit more accommodating. . . ."

"Mr. Grey, we're out of chits," Mr. Voskins said. "And I need to speak to you about the queue."

"We'll come back a day early, and you can have Gemma for New Year's," she said.

"It's nearly to the end of the aisle," Mr. Voskins said. "Should we loop it round?"

Margaret started toward the jammed aisle. "Wait," I said, "I have Gemma's present at home. Just a moment."

I hurried over to the literature shelves and then remembered those books had been moved over under Travel. I knelt and looked for the other copy of *A Little Princess*. It wasn't wrapped, but she would at least have it for Christmas.

It wasn't there. I looked through the B's twice, and then ran a finger along the backs, looking for the dark-blue cover. It wasn't there. I checked Children's, thinking Yet to Come might have put it there, but it wasn't, and when I stood up from checking Literature again, Margaret was gone.

"I've made it a double queue," Mr. Voskins said. "This is going to be a great success, isn't it? Mr. Grey?"

"A great success," I said, and went to write more numbers on slips of paper.

Sir Spencer arrived at a quarter till two in a Savile Row suit. He settled himself in the straight-backed chair, looked disdainfully at the table and the queue, and uncapped one of the fountain pens.

He began to sign the books that were placed before him, and to dispense wisdom to the admiring queue.

"Christmas is an excellent time to think about your future," he said, scrawling a squiggle that might have been an S followed by a long, uneven line. "And an excellent time to plan your financial strategy for the new year."

Four persons back in the queue was someone who could only be meant to be Marley, an old-fashioned coat and trousers draped with heavy chains and a good deal of gray-green greasepaint. He had a kerchief tied round his head and jaw and was clutching a copy of *Making Money Hand Over Fist*.

"They're actually going to try to reform him," I thought, and wondered what Sir Spencer would say.

Marley moved to the front of the queue and laid his open book down on the table. "In life . . ." he said, and it was a curious voice, brittle, dry, a voice that sounded as if it had died away once and for all.

"In life I was Jacob Marley," he said, in that faint dead voice, and shook his chain with a gray-green hand, but Sir Spencer was already handing his book back to him and was reaching for the next.

"There are those who say that money isn't everything," Sir Spencer said to the crowd. "It isn't. Money is the *only* thing."

The queue applauded.

At half-past two, Sir Spencer stopped to flex the fingers of his writing hand and drink his Armentières water. He consulted, whispering, with his secretary, looked at his watch, and took another sip.

I went over to the order desk to get another bottle, and when I came back I nearly collided with the Spirit of Christmas Present. He was carrying a huge plum pudding with a sprig of holly on top.

"What are you doing?" I said.

"Christmas is an excellent time to think about your future," he said, winking, and started toward the table, but the sleek secretary interposed herself between him and Sir Spencer.

He tried to give the plum pudding to her, still laughing, but she handed it back. "I specifically requested *light* refreshments," she said sharply, and went back over to Sir Spencer, looking at her watch.

Present followed her. "Come, know me better," he said to her, but she was consulting with Sir Spencer again, and they were both looking at their watches.

She came over to me. "The queue needs to move along more quickly," she said. "Tell them to have their books open to the title page."

I did, working my way back along the queue. There was a

sudden silence, and I looked back at the table. Yet to Come had glided in front of a middle-aged woman at the front of the queue, and she had stepped back, clutching her book to her wide bosom.

He's going to do it, I thought, and almost wished he could. It would be nice to see something good happen.

Sir Spencer reached his hand out for the book, and Yet to Come drew himself up and pointed his finger at him, and it was not a finger, but the bones of a skeleton.

I thought, he's going to speak, and knew what the voice would sound like. It was the voice of Margaret, telling me she wanted a divorce, telling me they had to take an earlier train. The voice of doom.

I drew in my breath, afraid to hear it, and the secretary leaned forward. "Sir Spencer does not sign body parts," she said sternly. "If you do not have a book, please step aside."

And that was that. Sir Spencer signed newly purchased hardbacks until a quarter of three and then stood up in midscrawl and went out the previously arranged back way.

"He didn't finish," the young girl whose book he had been in the midst of signing said plaintively, and I took the book and the pen and started after him, though without much hope.

I caught him at the door. "There are still people in the queue who haven't had their books signed," I said, holding out the book and pen, but the secretary had interposed herself between us.

"Sir Spencer will be signing on the second at Hatchard's," she said. "Tell them they can try again there."

"It's Christmas," I said, and took hold of his sleeve.

He looked pointedly at it.

"You'll miss your plane to Majorca," the secretary said, and he pulled his sleeve free and swept away, looking at his watch.

"Late," I heard the secretary say.

I was still holding the pen and the open book, with its half-finished S. I took it back to the girl. "If you'd like to leave it, I'll try to get it signed for you. Was it a Christmas present?"

"Yes, for my father," she said, "but I won't see him till after Christmas, so that's all right."

I took her name and telephone number, set the books on the order desk, and began taking down the posters.

I had thought perhaps Yet to Come would have disappeared after his failure with Sir Spencer like the others had, but he was still there, putting books into boxes.

He seemed somehow more silent—which was impossible, he had never spoken a word—and downcast, which was ridiculous, as well. The Spirit of Christmas Yet to Come was supposed to be dreadful, terrifying, but he seemed to have shrunk into himself. Like Gemma, shrinking against the shelves.

It's Sir Spencer that's terrifying, I thought, and his secretary. And her gold Rolex watch. "Scrooges are praised and much rewarded for their greed," Present had said, and so they were, with Savile Row suits and knighthoods and Majorca. No wonder the Spirits had fallen on hard times.

"At least you tried," I said. "There are some battles that are lost before they're begun."

Children's came over to buy a gift. "For Housewares. I told her I didn't believe in exchanging with colleagues," she said irritably, "but she's bought me something anyway. And I'd planned on leaving early. I suppose you are, too, so you can spend the evening with your little girl."

I looked at my watch. It was after three. They would be leaving for the station soon, and Robert's parents, and the orthodontist.

I cleared away the refreshments. I put foil over the plum pudding and set it next to the girl's book, which I had no hope of getting signed, and went back to help Yet to Come take *Making Money Hand Over Fist* down from the shelves, trying not to think about Gemma and Christmas Eve.

The spirit stopped suddenly and drew himself up and pointed, the robe falling away from his bony hand. I turned, afraid of more bad news, and there was Gemma in the aisle, working her way toward us.

She was pushing steadily upstream through shoppers who all seemed to be going in the opposite direction, ducking between shopping bags with a determined expression on her narrow face.

"Gemma!" I said, and pulled her safely out of the aisle. "What are you doing here?"

"I wanted to tell you goodbye and that I'm sorry I can't come for Christmas Eve."

I raised my head and tried to see down the aisle. "Where's your mother? You didn't come here alone, did you?"

"Mummy's up on fifth," she said. "With the dolls. I told her I'd changed my mind about wanting one. A bride doll. With green eyes." She looked pleased with herself, as well she might. It was no small accomplishment to have gotten Margaret back here half an hour before they were to meet Robert at the station, and she would never have agreed if she'd known why Gemma wanted to come. I could imagine her arguments—there isn't time, you'll see him the day after New Year's, we can't inconvenience Robert, who after all is paying for your brace—and so could Gemma, apparently, and had sidestepped them neatly.

"Did you tell her you were coming down to third?" I said, trying to look disapproving.

"She told me to go look at games so I wouldn't see her buying the doll," she said. "I wanted to tell you I'd rather be with you Christmas Eve."

I love you, I thought.

"I think when I *do* come," she said seriously, "that we should pretend that it *is* Christmas Eve, like the little princess and Becky."

"They pretended it was Christmas Eve?"

"*No.* When the little princess was cold or hungry or sad she pretended her garret was the Bastille."

"The Bastille," I said thoughtfully. "I don't think they had figs in the Bastille."

"*No.*" She laughed. "The little princess pretended all sorts of things. When she couldn't have what she wanted. So *I* think we should pretend it's Christmas Eve, and wear paper hats and light the tree and say things like, 'It's nearly Christmas,' and 'Oh, listen, the Christmas bells are chiming.' "

"And 'Pass the figs, please,' " I said.

"This is *serious*," she said. "We'll be together next Christmas, but till then we'll have to *pretend*." She paused, and looked solemn. "I'm going to have a good time in Surrey," she said, and her voice died away uncertainly.

"Of *course* you'll have a good time," I said heartily. "You'll get huge heaps of presents, and eat lots of goose. And figs. I hear in Surrey they use figs for stuffing." I hugged her to me.

A thin gray woman with rather the look of Miss Minchin came up. "Pardon me, do you work here?" she said disapprovingly.

"I'll be with you in just a moment," I said.

Yet to Come hurried up, but the woman waved him away. "I'm looking for a book," she said.

I said to Gemma, "You'd best get back before your mother finishes buying the doll and misses you."

"She won't. The bride dolls are all sold. I asked when I was here before." She smiled, her eyes crinkling. "She'll have to send them to check the stockroom," she said airily, looking just like her mother, and I remembered suddenly what I had loved about Margaret—her cleverness and the innocent pleasure she took in it, her resourcefulness. Her smile. And it was like being given a boon, a Christmas gift I hadn't known I wanted.

"I'm looking for a book," Miss Minchin repeated. "I saw it in here several weeks ago."

"I'd better go," Gemma said.

"Yes," I said, "and tell your mother you don't want the doll before she turns the stockroom inside out."

"I do want it, though," she said. "The little princess had a doll," and again that trailing away, as if she had left something unsaid.

"I thought you said all of them had been sold."

"They have," she said, "but there's one in the window display, and you know Mummy. She'll *make* them give it to her."

"*Pardon* me," Miss Minchin said insistently. "It was a green book, green and gold."

"I'd better go," Gemma said again.

"Yes," I said regretfully.

"Goodbye," she said, and plunged into the crush of shoppers, which now was going the other way.

"Hardback," Miss Minchin said. "It was *right* here on this shelf."

Gemma stopped halfway down the aisle, shoppers milling about her, and looked back at me. "You'd better eat the frosted cakes so they won't grow stale. I'm going to have a good time," she said, more firmly, and was swallowed by the crowd.

"It had gold lettering," Miss Minchin said. "It was by an earl, I think."

The book Miss Minchin wanted, after a protracted search, was Sir Spencer's *Making Money Hand Over Fist*. Of course.

"What a sweet little girl you have," she said as I rang up the sale, all friendliness now that she had gotten what she wanted. "You're very lucky."

"Yes," I said, though I did not feel lucky.

I looked at my watch. Five past four. Gemma had already taken the train to Surrey, and I would not see her sweet face again this year, and even if I stayed after closing and put everything back as it had been, there were still all the hours of Christmas Eve to be gotten through. And the day after. And all the days after.

And the rest of the afternoon, and all the shoppers who had left their shopping till too late, who were cross and tired and angry that we had no more copies of *The Outer Space Christmas Carol*, and who had *counted* on our giftwrapping their purchases.

And Mr. Voskins, who came up to say disapprovingly that he had been very disappointed in the sales from the autographing, and that he wanted the shelves back in order.

In between, Yet to Come and I folded chairs and carried boxes of Sir S's books to the basement.

It grew dark outside, and the crush of shoppers subsided to a trickle. When Yet to Come came over to me with his bony hands full of a box of books, I said, "You needn't come back up again," and didn't even have the heart to wish him a happy Christmas.

The trickle of shoppers subsided to two desperate-looking young men. I sold them scented journals and started taking Sir S's books off the literature shelves and putting them in boxes.

On the second shelf from the top, wedged in behind *Making Money Hand Over Fist*, I found the other copy of *A Little Princess*.

And that seemed somehow the final blow. Not that it had been here all along—there was no real difference between its not being there and my not being able to find it, and Gemma would love it as much when I gave it to her next week as she would have Christmas morning—but that Sir Spencer Siddon, Sir Scrawl of the new hardbacks only and the Armentières water, Sir Scrooge and his damnable secretary who had not even recognized the Spirits of Christmas, let alone heeded them, who had no desire to keep Christmas, had cost Gemma hers.

"Hard times," I said, and sank down in the wing chair. "I have fallen on hard times." After a while I opened the book and turned the pages, looking at the colored plates. The little princess and her father in her carriage. The little princess and her father at the school. The little princess and her father.

The birthday party. The little princess huddled against a wall, her doll clutched to her, looking hunted.

"The little princess had a doll," she'd said, and meant, "to help her through hard times."

The way the little princess's doll had helped her when she lost her father. The way the book had helped Gemma.

"I find books a great comfort," I had told the Spirit of Christmas Present. And so had Gemma, who had lost her father.

"I'm going to have a good time in Surrey," she had said, her voice trailing off, and I could finish that sentence, too. "In spite of everything."

Not a hope, but a determination to try to be happy in spite of circumstance, as the little princess had tried to be happy in her chilly garret. "I'm going to have a good time," she'd said again, turning at the last minute, and it was rebuke and reminder and instruction, all at once. And comfort.

I stood a moment, looking at the book, and then closed it and put it carefully back on the shelf, the way Gemma had.

I went over to the order desk and picked up the plum pudding. The book the girl had left for Sir Spencer to finish signing was under it. I opened it and took out the paper with her name and address on it.

Martha. I found the fountain pen, with its viridian ink, uncapped it and drew a scrawl that looked a little like Sir Spencer's. "To Martha's father," I wrote above it. "Money isn't everything!" And I went to find the spirits.

If they could be found. If they had not, after all, found other employment with the barrister or the banker, or taken a plane to Majorca, or gone up to Surrey.

Mama Montoni's had a large Closed sign hanging inside the door, and the light above the counter was switched off, but when I tried the door it wasn't locked. I opened it, carefully, so the buzzer wouldn't sound, and leaned in. Mama Montoni must have switched off the heat as well. It was icy inside.

They were sitting at the table in the corner, hunched forward over it as if they were cold. Yet to Come had his hands up inside his sleeves, and Present kept tugging at his button as if to pull the green robe closer. He was reading to them from *A Christmas Carol*.

" ' "You will be haunted," resumed the Ghost of Marley, "by three spirits," ' " Present read. " ' "Is this the chance and hope you mentioned, Jacob?" he demanded in a faltering voice. "It is." "I—I think I'd rather not," said Scrooge. "Without their visits," said the Ghost, "you cannot hope to shun the path I tread." ' "

I banged the door open and strode in. " 'Come, dine with me, uncle,' " I said.

They all turned to look at me.

"We are past that place," Marley said. "Scrooge's nephew has already gone home, and so has Scrooge."

"We are at the place where Scrooge is being visited by Marley," Present said, pulling out a chair. "Will you join us?"

"No," I said. "You are at the place where you must visit me."

Mama Montoni came rushing out from the back. "I'm closed!" she growled. "It's Christmas Eve."

"It's Christmas Eve," I said, "and Mama Montoni's is closed, so you must dine with me."

They looked at each other. Mama Montoni snatched the Closed sign from the door and brandished it in my face. "I'm *closed!*"

"I can't offer much. Figs. I have figs. And frosted cakes. And Sir Walter Scott. ' 'Twas Christmas broach'd the mightiest ale, 'Twas Christmas told the merriest tale.' "

"'A Christmas gambol oft could cheer the poor man's heart through half the year,'" Present murmured, but none of them moved. Mama Montoni started for the phone, to dial 999, no doubt.

"No one should be alone on Christmas Eve," I said.

They looked at each other again, and then Yet to Come stood up and glided over to me.

"The time grows short," I said, and Yet to Come extended his finger and pointed at them. Marley stood up, and then Present, closing his book gently.

Mama Montoni herded us out the door, looking daggers. I pulled *A Christmas Carol* out of my pocket and handed it to her. "Excellent book," I said. "Instructive."

She banged the door shut behind us and locked it. "Merry Christmas," I said to her through the door, and led the way home, though before we had reached the tube station, Yet to Come was ahead, his finger pointing the way to the train, and my street, and my flat.

"We've black-currant tea," I said, going into the kitchen to put on the kettle. "And figs. Please, make yourselves at home. Present, the Dickens is in that bookcase, top shelf, and the Scott's just under it."

I set out sugar and milk and the frosted cakes I'd bought for Gemma. I took the foil off the plum pudding. "Courtesy of Sir Spencer Siddon, who, unfortunately, remains a miser," I said, setting it on the table. "I'm sorry you failed to find someone to reform."

"We have had some small success," Present said from the bookcase, and Marley smiled slyly.

"Who?" I said. "Not Mama Montoni?"

The kettle whistled. I poured the boiling water over the tea and brought the teapot in. "Come, come, sit down. Present, bring your book with you. You can read to us while the tea steeps." I pulled out a chair for him. "But first you must tell me about this person you reformed."

Marley and Yet to Come looked at each other as if they shared a secret, and both of them looked at Christmas Present.

"You have read Scott's 'Marmion,' have you not?" he said, and I knew that, whoever it was, they weren't going to tell me. One of the people in the queue, perhaps? Or Harridge?

"I always think 'Marmion' an excellent poem for Christmas," Present said, and opened the book.

" 'And well our Christian sires of old,' " he read, " 'loved when the year its course had roll'd, and brought blithe Christmas back again, with all his hospitable train.' "

I poured out the tea.

" 'The wassail round, in good brown bowls,' " he read, " 'garnished with ribbons, blithely trowls.' " He put down the book and raised his teacup in a toast. "To Sir Walter Scott, who knew how to keep Christmas!"

"And to Mr. Dickens," Marley said, "the founder of the feast."

"To books!" I said, thinking of Gemma and *A Little Princess*, "which instruct and sustain us through hard times."

" 'Heap on more wood!' " Present said, taking up his book again, " 'The wind is chill; but let it whistle as it will, we'll keep our Christmas merry still.' "

I poured out more tea, and we ate the frosted cakes and Gemma's figs and half a meat pie I found in the back of the refrigerator, and Present read us "Lochinvar," with sound effects.

As I was bringing in the second pot of tea, the clock began to strike, and outside, church bells began to ring. I looked at the clock. It was, impossibly, midnight.

"Christmas already!" Present said jovially. "Here's to evenings with friends that fly too fast."

"And the friends who make it fly," I said.

"To small successes," Marley said, and raised his cup to me.

I looked at Christmas Present, and then at Yet to Come, whose face I still could not see, and then back at Marley. He smiled slyly.

"Come, come," Present said into the silence. "We have not had a toast from Christmas Yet to Come."

"Yes, yes," Marley said, clanking his chains excitedly. "Speak, Spirit."

Yet to Come took hold of his teacup handle with his bony fingers and raised his cup.

I held my breath.

"To Christmas," he said, and why had I ever feared that voice? It was clear and childlike. Like Gemma's voice, saying, "We'll be together next Christmas."

"To Christmas," the Spirit of Christmas Yet to Come said, his voice growing stronger with each word, "God bless us Every One."

CAT'S PAW

ome, Bridlings," Touffét said impatiently as soon as I arrived. "Go home and pack your bags. We're going to Suffolk for a jolly country Christmas."

"I thought you hated country Christmases," I said.

I had invited him only the week before down to my sister's and gotten a violent rejection of the idea. "Country Christmases! Dreadful occasions!" he had said. "Holly and mistletoe and vile games—blindman's bluff and that ridiculous game where people grab at burning raisins, and even viler food. Plum pudding!" he shuddered. "And wassail!"

I protested that my sister was an excellent cook and that she never made wassail, she made eggnog. "I think you'd have an excellent time," I said. "Everyone's very pleasant."

"I can imagine," he said. "No one drinks, everyone is faithful to his wife, the inheritance is equally and fairly divided, and none of your relatives would ever think of murdering anyone."

"Of course not!" I said, bristling.

"Then I would rather spend Christmas here alone," Touffét said. "At least then I shall not be subjected to roast goose and Dumb Crambo."

"We do not play Dumb Crambo," I replied with dignity. "We play charades."

And now, scarcely a week later, Touffét was eagerly proposing going to the country.

"I have just received a letter from Lady Charlotte Valladay," he said, brandishing a sheet of pale pink notepaper, "asking me to come to Marwaite Manor. She wishes me to solve a mystery for her." He examined the letter through his monocle. "What could be more delightful than murder in a country house at Christmas?"

Actually, I could think of a number of things. I scanned the letter. "You *must* come," she had written. "This is a mystery only you, the world's greatest detective, can solve." Lady Charlotte Valladay. And Marwaite Manor. Where had I heard those names before? Lady Charlotte.

"It doesn't say there's been a murder," I said. "It says a mystery."

Touffét was not listening. "We must hurry if we are to catch the 3:00 train from Euston. There won't be time for you to go home and pack and come back here. You must meet me at the station. Come, don't stand there looking foolish."

"The letter doesn't say anything about my being invited," I said. "It only mentions you. And I've already told my sister I'm spending Christmas with her."

"She does not mention you because it is of course assumed that I will bring my assistant."

"Hardly your assistant, Touffét. You never let me do anything."

"That is because you have not the mind of a detective. Always you see the facade. Never do you see what lies behind it."

"Then you obviously won't need me," I said.

"But I do, Bridlings," he said. "Who will record my exploits if you are not there? And who will point out the obvious and the incorrect, so that I may reject them and find the true solution?"

"I would rather play charades," I said, and picked up my hat. "I hope Lady Charlotte feeds you wassail *and* plum pudding. And makes you play Dumb Crambo."

In the end I went. I had been with Touffét on every one of his cases, and although I still could not place Lady Charlotte Valladay, it seemed to me her name had been connected to something interesting.

And I had never experienced Christmas in a country manor, with the ancient hall decked in holly and Gainsboroughs, a huge Yule log on the fire, an old-fashioned Christmas feast—poached salmon, a roast joint, and a resplendent goose, with a different wine for every course. Perhaps they might even have a boar's head.

The bullet trains to Suffolk were all filled, and we could only get seats on an express. It was filled as well, and every passenger had not only luggage but huge shopping bags crammed with gifts which completely filled all the overhead compartments. I had to hold my bag and Touffét's umbrella on my lap.

I thought longingly of the first-class compartment I had booked on the train to my sister's and hoped Marwaite Manor was at the near end of Suffolk.

Marwaite Manor. Where had I heard that name? And Lady Charlotte's? Not in the tabloids, I decided, though I had a vague idea of something controversial. A protest of some sort. What? Cloning? The revival of fox hunting?

Perhaps she was an actress—they were always getting involved in causes. Or a royal scandal. No, she was too old. I seemed to remember she was in her fifties.

Touffét, across from me, was deep in a book. I leaned forward slightly, trying to read the title. Touffét only reads mystery novels, he says, to study the methods of fictional detectives, but actually to criticize them. And, I suspected, to study their mannerisms. And co-opt them. He had already affected Lord Peter Wimsey's monocle and Hercule Poirot's treatment of his "assistant," and he had met me at the station, wearing a Sherlock Holmesian–Inverness cape. Thank God he had not adopted Holmes's deer-stalker. Or his violin. At least thus far.

The title was in very tiny print. I leaned forward farther, and Touffét looked up irritably. "This Dorothy Sayers, she is ridiculous," he said, "she makes her Lord Peter read timetables of trains, decipher codes, use stopwatches, and it is all, *all* unnecessary. If he would only ask himself, 'Who had a motive to murder Paul Alexis?' he would have no need of all these shirt collar receipts and diagrams."

He flung it down. "It is Sherlock Holmes who has caused this foolish preoccupation with evidence," he said, "with all his tobacco ashes and chemical experiments." He grabbed the carpetbag off my lap and began rummaging through it. "Where have you put my other book, Bridlings?"

I hadn't touched it. I sometimes think he takes me along with him for the same reason that he reads mystery novels—so he can feel superior.

He pulled a book from his bag, Edgar Allan Poe's *The Murders in the Rue Morgue*. No doubt he would find all sorts of things wrong with Inspector Dupin. He would probably think Dupin should have asked himself what motive an orangu—

"Touffét!" I said. "I've remembered who Lady Charlotte Valladay is! She's the ape woman!"

"Ape woman?" Touffét said irritably. "You are saying Lady Charlotte is a carnival attraction? Covered in hair and scratching herself?"

"No, no," I said. "She's a primate-rights activist, claims gorillas and orangutans should be allowed to vote, be given equal standing in the courts, and all that."

"Are you certain this is the same person?" Touffét said.

"Completely. Her father's Lord Alastair Biddle, made his fortune in artificial intelligence. That's how she got interested in primates. They were IA research subjects. She founded the Primate Intelligence Institute. I saw her on television just the other day, soliciting funds for it."

Touffét had taken out Lady Charlotte's pink letter and was peering at it. "She says nothing at all about apes."

"Perhaps one of her orangutans has got loose and committed a murder, just like in *The Murders in the Rue Morgue*," I said. "Looks like she made a monkey out of you, Touffét."

There was no one at the station to meet us. I suggested taking the single taxi parked at the end of the platform, but Touffét said, "Lady Charlotte will of course send someone to meet us."

After a quarter of an hour, during which it began to rain and I thought fondly of how my sister was always on the platform waiting for me, smiling and waving, I telephoned the manor.

A man with a reedy, refined voice said, "Marwaite Manor," and, when I asked for Lady Valladay, said formally, "One moment, please," and Lady Charlotte came on. "Oh, Colonel Bridlings, I am *so* sorry about there not being anyone to meet you. They've refused to issue D'Artagnan a driver's license, which is perfectly ridiculous, he drives better than I do, and there was no one else to send. If you could take a taxi, D'Artagnan will pay the driver when you get here. I'll see you shortly."

By this time, of course, the taxi had long gone, and I had to telephone for one. As I was hanging up, a sunburned middle-aged man with a full red beard and a black shoulder bag accosted me.

"I couldn't help overhearing," he said in a heavy Australian accent. "You're going to Marwaite Manor, are you, mate?"

"Yes," I said warily. Journalists are always trying for interviews with Touffét, and the shoulder bag looked suspiciously like it could contain a vidcam.

"I was wondering if I could bag a ride with you. I'm going to Marwaite Manor, too." He stuck out his hand. "Mick Rutgers."

"Colonel Bridlings," I said, and turned to Touffét, who had walked over to us and was peering at Mr. Rutgers through his monocle. "Allow me to introduce Inspector Touffét."

"Touffét?" Rutgers said sharply. "The detective?"

"You have heard of me in Australia?" Touffét said.

"Everyone has heard of the world's greatest detective," Rutgers said, recovering himself. "This is an honor. What brings you to Marwaite Manor?"

"Lady Charlotte Valladay has asked me to solve a mystery."

"A mystery?" he said. "What mystery?"

"I do not know," Touffét said. "Ah, the taxi arrives."

I picked up our baggage. "I hope it's not far to the manor."

"Only a coupla miles," Rutgers said.

"Ah, you have been here before?" Touffét said.

"No, mate," Rutgers said, the sharpness back in his voice. "Never set foot in England before, as a matter of fact. No, when she invited me she told me the manor was only a coupla miles from the station. Lady Charlotte. I work for the Australian Broadcasting Network."

I *knew* he was a photographer, I thought. "Why are you here?" I asked.

"Lady Charlotte said she had a big story, one we'd be interested in covering."

"And she didn't say what the story was?" Touffét asked.

Rutgers shook his head. "But whatever it is, she was paying all expenses, and I'd never seen England. So here I am."

We piled into the taxi and set out. It was, as Mr. Rutgers had said, "a coupla miles," and in no time we'd arrived at Marwaite Manor.

At least that's what the scrolled wrought-iron sign above the granite gates said. But the buildings in the distance looked more like an industrial compound. There were numerous long metal sheds with parking lots between them and a great many ventilators and pipes. They looked grim in the freezing rain.

The taxi driver drove past the compound and up a long hill and stopped in front of a four-story glass-and-chrome affair that looked like a company headquarters. "Are you certain this is Marwaite Manor?" I asked him as he was taking our bags out of the trunk.

He nodded, handing me Touffét's portmanteau and my bag. "Is the monkey paying me or are you?"

"I *beg* your pardon," I said sternly. I glanced toward Touffét, hoping he hadn't heard the rude remark. He and Rutgers had already gone up to the front door. "Lady Charlotte's butler will pay you," I said stiffly, and followed them over to the door.

It opened. A gorilla was standing there, dressed in a butler's cutaway coat and trousers, and white gloves.

"Good Lord," I said.

"We are here to see Lady Charlotte Valladay," Touffét said, peering at him through his monocle.

The gorilla opened the door farther.

"I am Inspector Touffét and this is Mr. Rutgers."

"I think they understand sign language," I whispered. "Rutgers, do you know any?"

"Come please? Take bags?" the gorilla said, and I was so surprised I just stood there, gaping.

"Take bags, sir?" the gorilla said again.

"The taxi's six pounds," the taxi driver said, reaching past me with his hand outstretched. "And that doesn't include the tip."

"Pay moment," the gorilla said, and turned back to me. "Take bags, sir?"

I had recovered myself sufficiently to hand them to him, trying not to flinch away from those huge paws in their incongruous white gloves, and to murmur, "Thank you."

"This way, sir," the gorilla said, dropping to his gloved knuckles, and led us into an enormous entryway.

"Excuse moment," the gorilla said.

It really was too odd, hearing that refined, upper-class voice coming out of that enormous gray-black gorilla.

"Tell Lady Valladay you here." He started out, still on all fours.

"Good Lord, Touffét—" I had started to say, when a middle-aged woman in khaki and pearls bustled in.

"Oh, Inspector Touffét! I'm *so* glad you're here! Tanny, did you pay the taxi driver?"

"Yes, madam," the gorilla said.

"Good. Stand up straight. Inspector Touffét, I'd like you to meet D'Artagnan."

The gorilla straightened, extended a monstrous gloved hand, and Touffét shook it, albeit a bit gingerly.

"D'Artagnan was orphaned by poachers in Uganda when he was only two weeks old," she said.

"Rescued," D'Artagnan said, pointing at Lady Valladay with a white-gloved finger.

"I found him in Hong Kong in a cage the size of a shoebox," she said, looking fondly at him. "He's been here at the Institute twelve years."

"I thought gorillas couldn't speak," I said.

"He's had a laryngeal implant," she said. "When we tour the compound, you'll see our surgical unit."

"How'd he get the name D'Artagnan?" Rutgers asked.

"He chose it himself. I don't believe in picking names for primates as if they were pets. Our research here at the Institute has shown that primates are extremely intelligent. They are capable of high-level thinking, computation skills, and self-awareness. D'Artagnan is a conscious being, fully capable of making personal decisions. He's scored 95 on IQ tests. He named himself after one of the Three Musketeers. It's his favorite book."

"Good Lord, he can read, too?" I said.

She shook her head. "Only a few words. I read it aloud to him."

D'Artagnan nodded his huge head. "Queen," he said.

"Yes, he loves the part about the Three Musketeers coming to the queen's aid." She turned to Rutgers. "And you must be Colonel Bridlings, who chronicles all his cases."

"Mick Rutgers," he said, extending his sunburnt hand, "of ABN."

She looked confused. "But the press invitations were for the twenty-fifth."

"I'm sure the invitation said the twenty-fourth," he said, fumbling for it in his jacket.

"That's what Ms. Fox said. I really must have Heidi start writing my invitations. Her penmanship is much neater than mine."

"I could come back tomorrow—" Rutgers said.

"No, I'm delighted you're here," she said, and seemed to genuinely mean it. She turned her warm smile on me. "Then *you* must be Colonel Bridlings."

"Yes. How do you do?"

"I'm *so* pleased to meet all of you. Come," she said, taking Touffét's arm, "I want to show you the compound, but first let me introduce you to everyone."

"You spoke of a murder you wished me to solve?" Touffét said.

"A mystery *only* you can solve," she said, smiling that lovely smile. She truly had a gift for making one feel warmly welcome.

I wished I could say the same of Marwaite Manor, but the spacious glass-and-chrome hall she led us into was as welcoming as a dentist's office. And it was cold! The icy rain outside the floor-to-ceiling windows seemed to be falling in the room itself. The only furniture in the room was several uncomfortable-looking chrome-and-canvas chairs and a small glass table with greenery and candles on it.

Two people were huddled in the center of the nearly empty hall, next to the glass table—a stout, balding man, and a pretty young woman in a thin dress. The woman had her arms folded across her bosom, as if trying to keep warm, and the stout man's nose was red. A chimpanzee in a maid's apron, a white collar, and a frilly cap was offering them drinks on a tray.

They all looked up expectantly as we entered. Lady Valladay grabbed Touffét's arm. "I have someone I want you to meet, Inspector," she said, and led him over to the chimpanzee.

"Inspector Touffét, I'd like you to meet Heidi," she said. "She came from a medical research lab, and she's one of your most devoted fans."

Now that we were closer to the chimpanzee, I could see that what I had taken for a collar was actually a white bandage round the chimpanzee's shaved neck.

"She just had her laryngeal implant, so she can't speak yet," Lady Valladay said, "but she has the highest IQ of any primate we've ever had here at the Institute, and she's already reading at a primary school level. She's read *The Cat in the Hat* and all the Curious George books, haven't you, Heidi?" and the chimpanzee grinned widely and bobbed her head up and down. "But *your* books are her favorites, Inspector Touffét. She's constantly after me to read them to her, and sometimes she even tries to read them on her own."

Lady Valladay led Touffét over to the table, her arm linked in his. "Our primates have even outperformed A-level students on higher-level-thinking tests, but in spite of all the studies the Institute has done, in spite of the overwhelming evidence of their intelligence, people persist in thinking of primates as animals instead of sentient creatures. They continue to put them in zoos, experiment on them, kill them for trophies. That's why it's so important that the Institute continue to exist."

"Continue to exist?" Touffét asked.

"I'm afraid we're sadly in need of funds," she said. "If we don't find additional donors soon, we'll be forced to close. We—"

"I beg your pardon," the stout man said. "I didn't mean to interrupt. I only wanted to tell you how much I admire your work."

"This is Sergeant Eustis, our local police detective. Perhaps you two can exchange information about your investigations."

"Oh, no," Sergeant Eustis said, fumbling at his tie, "I haven't had any interesting cases, compared to Mr. Touffét."

"What about—" she began, but the sergeant said, "I'd very much like to hear about the Sappina jewel robbery."

"A very satisfying case," Touffét said, and launched into an account of it.

I wandered over to where the pretty young woman stood by the table and introduced myself.

"Leda Fox," she said, and pointed to a press badge. "I'm a reporter with the *On-Line Times*. And I'm freezing." She leaned forward to warm her hands over one of the candles. "You'd think with all the billions Lord Alastair's got, he could afford to turn up the heat."

"Lord Alastair is a billionaire?"

"Yes. He made his fortune in AI patents."

"I was wondering how the Institute was financed," I said.

"Oh, no, the Institute doesn't get a penny. Lord Alastair never approved of primate research. It's all financed by donations. So, what's this mystery Inspector Touffét's supposed to solve?"

"I'm afraid I have no idea," I said, sipping my drink. "What was the media told?"

"The media?" she said blankly. "Oh. You mean what were we told? Not much. Just that we were all invited to be present at the solving of a mystery by Inspector Touffét. And we were sent a packet of information on primate intelligence." She frowned. "I wonder what the mystery is."

"Something to do with the Institute, perhaps?" I asked. "Lady Charlotte seemed anxious to show us the facilities."

"She dragged me all over them this morning," Leda said.

"You do not like primates?"

She shrugged. "Animals are all right, I suppose, but one tour is enough. She wants me to go again with all of you this afternoon, but there's no way I'm going out in *that*," she said, gesturing at the falling rain. "Tell her I have a headache."

Heidi shambled over with a tray full of silver goblets, one hand under the tray and the other dragging the floor.

"What is it?" I asked Leda, taking one of them.

"Wassail."

Heidi waddled over to Touffét and Sergeant Eustis.

"Poor Touffét," I said.

"Doesn't he like wassail?"

"He doesn't like Christmas."

"Do you think they're really as smart as Lady Charlotte says?" Leda said, watching Heidi offer the tray to the police detective. "She says Heidi can do long division. *I* can't do long division."

"Neither can I," I said, but she wasn't listening. She had turned to look at a tall man in his thirties who had just walked in.

"Who's that?" I asked.

"Lady Charlotte's brother, James," she said. "I met him this morning." She made a face.

"You didn't like him?"

She leaned toward me and whispered, "Drunk."

"Well, well, so this is the Great Detective," James said, walking over to Touffét.

Lady Charlotte looked vexed. "Inspector Touffét, my brother, James."

James ignored her. "Have you solved my sister's mystery yet? I heard you solve them"—he snapped his fingers next to Touffét's nose—"like *that*!"

Touffét stepped back. "Lady Charlotte has not yet informed me of the nature of the mystery."

"Oh, well, then maybe you can solve a mystery for me. Why is it my sister prefers monkeys to her own father and brother?"

"James," Lady Valladay said warningly.

"Heidi!" James said, and snapped his fingers at her. "Bring me a drink."

The chimpanzee hesitated, looking frightened, and then shambled over to him and offered the tray.

James grabbed a drink and turned back to Touffét. "It's a true mystery to me. Why would she rather spend her time with a bunch of dangerous, smelly, stupid—"

"James!" Lady Valladay snapped.

"Oh, that's right. They're not stupid. They can do trigonometry. They can read Shakespeare. Isn't that right, Heidi?" He tweaked her cap. "How much is two plus two, Heidi?"

Heidi looked beseechingly at Lady Charlotte.

"How do you spell 'imbecile,' Heidi?" James persisted.

"That's enough, James," Lady Charlotte said, putting her arm around the chimpanzee. "Heidi, go unpack Inspector Touffét's bags." She took the tray from her. "That's my good girl."

Lady Charlotte set the tray down. "Inspector, you and Colonel Bridlings must both be tired," she said, ignoring James, and he turned on his heel and walked out of the room. "You'll want to get settled in and have a chance to rest before we tour the compound. D'Artagnan will show you to your rooms, and we'll meet in, say, an hour in the entryway."

A door slammed, but she paid no attention. "I do so want you to see our facility." She led us to the door. "D'Artagnan, take them to their rooms."

"Yes, madam," he said. He started to drop to all fours but then straightened.

"An hour, then," she said, smiling, and went down the corridor and into another room, shutting the door behind her.

D'Artagnan pushed the lift button.

"I don't care"—Lady Charlotte's voice drifted down the hall—"I won't have you ruining this. It's too important."

"It's my house," James's voice said.

"It's Father's house."

"It won't be forever," James said, "and when I inherit it, there won't be any monkeys in it. I'm shipping them back to the jungle the day Father dies."

"So this is your idea of a jolly Christmas?" I asked Touffét, waiting for him to put on his Inverness cape. I had spent the promised half hour attempting to find a telephone. I'd left in such a rush, I hadn't had time to telephone my sister to tell her I couldn't come. I attempted to ask Heidi, who was unpacking my things, but couldn't make her understand, so I went downstairs in search of one myself.

There was one in the study, a small frigid room across from the solarium. My sister was disappointed but optimistic. "Perhaps your Inspector Touffét will solve the mystery so quickly you can come tonight, or tomorrow. We could wait dinner."

"Better not," I said. "We haven't even been told what the mystery is yet."

I hung up and started back upstairs. As I came into the entry-way, I caught a glimpse of Leda, in a hooded raincoat, going out the front door. She must have changed her mind about touring the compound, I thought, and wondered if I'd taken so long the others had left without me, but Touffét was in his room, putting on a wool sweater and wrapping a knitted scarf around his neck.

"At least at my sister's house it's warm," I said, "and no one ever threatens to turn anyone else out."

"Exactly," Touffét said. "And there are no mysteries." He put on his cape. "Here already there are several."

"Lady Charlotte's told you why she invited us here?"

He shook his head. "But certain things have struck me. What about you, Bridlings? Have you noticed nothing?"

I thought about it. "I've noticed the brother's a lout. And that Ms. Fox is very pretty."

"Pretty. Alas, Bridlings, once again you see only the facade. You do look at what lies behind. Do you not think it strange that Sergeant Eustis does not wish me to know of his interesting cases? All detectives wish to brag of their exploits."

Well, that's certainly true, I thought.

"And there is this," he said, handing me Lady Charlotte's letter. "Odd, is it not?"

I read it through. "I don't see anything odd about it. She invites us to come and lists the train times."

"Indeed. Look at the second-to-last train time."

"5:48," I said.

"Are you certain?"

"Yes. It says—"

"The five and the four are quite distinct, are they not? And yet both Mr. Rutgers and Ms. Fox say they mistook Lady Charlotte's five for a four and thus came a day early," he said, obviously in his element. "A mystery, yes? Come, we are late."

We went down to the entryway. Lady Charlotte and Mick Rutgers were already there, bundled in coats and scarves. She was telling him about the Institute. "Organizations and ethologists have tried for years to protect primate habitats and regulate the treatment of primates in captivity, but conditions have only gotten worse, and will continue to get worse, so long as people continue to think of them as animals."

She turned to greet us. "Oh, Inspector, Colonel, we're just waiting for D'Artagnan. He's going to drive us down to the compound. I was just telling Mr. Rutgers about the Institute. Some people do not approve of our implanting larynxes and dressing primates in clothing, but the only chance they have of survival is for people to accept them. And to be accepted, unfortunately, they must stand upright, they must have employable skills. They're necessary to make people realize primates are sentient creatures, that they can think and reason and feel as we do. Did you know that humans and pygmy chimpanzees share ninety-nine percent of their genes? Ninety-nine percent. Our genes are their genes. And yet when the University of Oklahoma discontinued their language research project, the apes who had been taught to sign were used in AIDS experiments. Do you remember Lucy?"

"The chimpanzee who was raised as a human and taught to sign?" I asked.

"She was shipped back to Gambia, where she was murdered by poachers." Tears came to Lady Charlotte's eyes. "They cut off her head and hands for trophies. Lucy, who knew three hundred words! Oh, D'Artagnan, there you are," she said.

I turned. D'Artagnan was standing there in the corridor. He was still in his cutaway coat and trousers, but not his white gloves. I wondered how long he'd been there.

"Are you ready to drive us to the compound, Tanny?" Lady Charlotte asked.

"Lord Alastair. Wish meet Inspector," he said in that ridiculously small voice.

"Oh, dear," Lady Charlotte said, as if she'd just heard bad news. She bit her lip, and then, as if she'd realized her response needed some sort of explanation, said, "I'd hoped your arrival hadn't wakened him. My father has so much difficulty sleeping. I'm afraid we'll have to wait until tomorrow morning to tour the compound."

She turned to D'Artagnan. "Tell Nurse Parchtry we'll be up directly," she said, and as he started to leave, "Where are your gloves, Tanny?"

He promptly put his hairy black paws behind his back and hung his head. "Took off. Dishes. Now can't find."

"Well, go and get another pair out of the pantry." She took a bunch of keys out of her pocket and handed them to him.

"D'Artagnan sorry," he said, looking ashamed.

"I'm not angry," she said, putting her arms around his vast back. "You know I love you."

"Love *you*," he said, and flung his huge arms around her.

I looked at Touffét, alarmed after what James had said, but D'Artagnan had already released her and was asking, "Gloves first? Tell first?"

"Tell Nurse Parchtry first, and then go and get a new pair of gloves." She patted his arm.

He nodded and lumbered off, Lady Charlotte smiling affectionately after him. "He's such a dear," she said, and then continued briskly, "Inspector Touffét, if you don't mind, my father's an invalid and gets lonely."

"But of course I should be happy to meet him," he said.

"Can I meet him, too?" Rutgers said. "I've heard so much about his AI work."

"Of course," Lady Valladay said, but she sounded reluctant. "We'll all go up just for a little while. My father tires easily."

She pressed the button for the lift. We stepped inside. "My father's rooms are on the fourth floor," she said, pressing another button. "It used to be the nursery." The lift shot up. "He's been ill for several years."

The lift opened, and Lady Charlotte led the way to a door. "Oh, dear," she said. "I gave my keys to D'Artagnan. Nurse Parchtry will have to let us in."

She knocked. "My father has a wonderful nurse. Marvelously efficient. She's been with us for nearly a year."

The door started to open. I looked curiously at it, wondering if Nurse Parchtry would turn out to be an orangutan in a nurse's cap and stethoscope. But the person who opened the door was a thin, disheveled-looking woman in white trousers and a white smock.

"May we come in, Nurse Parchtry?" Lady Charlotte asked, and the woman nodded and stepped back to let us through into a small room with plastic chairs and a Formica counter along one side.

"You'd best stay here in the anteroom, though," the woman said. "Tapioca for lunch."

If this was Nurse Parchtry, she looked anything but efficient. One pocket of her smock was torn and hanging down, and her fine, gray-brown hair had come out of its bun on one side. There was a huge blob of something yellowish-gray on one trouser leg—the tapioca?

No, the tapioca was splattered across the glass-and-chicken-wire partition that separated the room we were in from the larger one beyond, along with soft brown smears of something. I hoped they weren't what they looked like.

I wondered if I had somehow misunderstood, and Lady Charlotte had taken us to see the primate compound after all instead. The room behind the partition looked almost like a cage, with toys and a large rubber tire in the middle of the floor. No, there was a single bed against the far wall and a rocking chair beside it.

"He heard the taxi," Nurse Parchtry was saying. "I've told that cabbie to drive quietly. I tried to tell him it was just a parcel arriving for Christmas, but he knew it was guests. He always knows, and then there's just no dealing with him till he sees them."

Lady Charlotte nodded sympathetically. "Nurse Parchtry, this is Inspector Touffét."

"I'm *so* pleased to meet you," Nurse Parchtry said, trying to push the straggle of gray-brown hair behind her ear. "I am *such* a fan of your detecting. I adored *The Case of the Clever Cook*. I've always wished I could see you solve one of your murders." She turned to me. "Does he really solve them as quickly as you say, Colonel Bridlings?"

Nurse Parchtry turned to Lady Charlotte. "I was wondering— it *is* Christmas Eve, and I am such a fan of Inspector Touffét's— if I might eat downstairs tonight instead of having a tray."

Lady Charlotte glanced uncertainly at the partition. "I don't know. . . ."

"Lord Alastair always goes to sleep after he's had his cocoa," Nurse Parchtry said, gesturing toward the tray, "and I did so want to hear Inspector Touffét recount some of his celebrated cases. And Lord Alastair's been very good today."

There was a splat, and I looked over at the partition. A large blob of greenish mush was trickling down the center of the glass, and behind it, holding the plastic bowl it had come out of, was Lord Alastair.

If I had been shocked by the sight of a talking gorilla, I was completely overwhelmed by the sight of Lord Alastair, computer genius and billionaire, dressed in wrinkled pajamas, his white hair matted with the greenish stuff he'd just thrown. He was barefoot, and his teeth were bared in a cunning grin.

"Good Lord," I said, and next to me, Rutgers murmured disbelievingly, "Al?"

Lord Alastair stepped back, hunching his shoulders, and I wondered if we had frightened him, but he was still grinning. He reared back and spat at us.

"Oh, *Father*," Lady Charlotte said, and he grinned evilly at her and began smearing the spittle into the tapioca and the brown streaks, as if he were fingerpainting.

"Oh, dear," Nurse Parchtry said, "and you were so good this morning." She pulled a bunch of keys out of her pocket, hastily unlocked a door next to the partition, and disappeared. She reappeared inside a moment later with a wet towel and began wiping Lord Alastair's hands.

I watched, horrified, afraid he was going to spit on her next, but he only struggled to free his hands, slapping weakly at her like a naughty child and shouting a string of garbled obscenities.

Beside me, Rutgers seemed hypnotized. "How long has he been like this?"

"It's gotten gradually worse," Lady Charlotte said. "Ten years."

Nurse Parchtry had Lord Alastair's hands clean and was combing his hair. "You must look nice for your guests," she said, her voice faint but clear through the glass. "Inspector Touffét's here, the famous detective."

She brought him over to the partition, holding his left wrist in a firm grasp. "Lord Alastair, I'd like you to meet Inspector Touffét."

Touffét stepped up to the glass and bowed. "I'm pleased to meet you."

"Inspector Touffét's come to solve a mystery for us, Father," Lady Charlotte said.

"Yes," Touffét said, "I am interested to know more of this mystery."

There was a knock at the door behind us. "Shall I?" I asked Lady Charlotte.

"Please," she said, and I unlocked and opened it. It was Heidi, bearing a tray with a toddler's lidded cup and a plate of graham biscuits on it.

I stepped back so she could enter, and as soon as she did,

Lord Alastair exploded. His left arm came up sharply, clipping Nurse Parchtry on the chin, and she reeled back, cradling her jaw. He began pounding on the glass with both hands and hooting wildly. Heidi watched him, clutching the tray, her eyes wide with fright.

"Oh, dear," Lady Charlotte said. "Heidi, set the tray down on the counter."

Heidi did, her eyes still on Lord Alastair, then bobbed a curtsey and ran awkwardly out on all fours. Lord Alastair continued pounding for a moment and then walked over to the plastic bowl, sat down on the floor, and began licking the inside of the bowl.

Rutgers shook his head sadly. "Ten years," he murmured.

Nurse Parchtry disappeared and then reappeared at the door, her jaw and cheek scarlet.

"He doesn't like Heidi," she said unnecessarily. "Or D'Artagnan." She put her hand wincingly up to her cheek. "He threw the rocking chair the last time D'Artagnan brought in his lunch."

"I think you'd best put some ice on that," Lady Charlotte said. "And with Father so upset, I think perhaps you'd better eat up here tonight."

"Oh, no!" Nurse Parchtry said desperately. "He'll quiet down now. He always does after—"

There was a banging on the door, and Touffét moved to open it. James burst in, clutching his thumb. "You will not believe what that monster just did!"

I wheeled and looked at the partition, thinking Lord Alastair must have gotten out somehow, but he was still sitting in the middle of the floor. He'd put the bowl on his head.

"He grabbed my hand and tried to tear it off. Look!" He thrust it at Lady Charlotte. "I think it's broken!"

I couldn't see any telltale redness like that on Nurse Parchtry's jaw.

"The brute tried to kill me!" he said.

"What brute?" Lady Charlotte asked.

"*What brute?* That *ape* of yours! I was walking down the corridor, and he suddenly reached out and grabbed me."

He turned to us. "I've tried to tell my sister her apes are dangerous, but she won't listen!"

"I thought that gorillas had very gentle natures," Rutgers said.

"That's what the so-called scientists at my sister's Institute say, that they're all harmless as kittens, that they wouldn't hurt a fly! Well, what about this?" he said, shaking his hand at us again. "When we're all murdered in our beds some morning, don't say I didn't warn you!"

He stormed out, but his ragings had roused Lord Alastair, who was pounding on the glass again.

"He'll go to sleep as soon as he's had his cocoa," Nurse Parchtry said pleadingly. "He always does, and today he didn't have a nap. And I'd have the monitor with me. I'd be able to hear him if he woke up. And it's Christmas Eve!"

"All right," Lady Charlotte said, relenting. "But if he wakes up, you'll have to come straight back up here."

"I will, I promise," she said, as giddily as if she were Cinderella promising to leave the ball by midnight. "Oh, this will be such fun!"

"It's hardly *my* idea of fun," I told Touffét as we were going down for dinner. "I'd much rather be at my sister's. And I'll wager Lady Charlotte would rather be, too. It's obvious why she prefers apes, with a father and a brother like that."

"The father is a millionaire," Touffét said thoughtfully. "Is that not so?"

"Billionaire," I said.

"Ah. I wonder who is it that inherits his estate when he dies? I wonder also what makes Nurse Parchtry stay with such a dis-

176 *Connie Willis*

agreeable patient?" He rubbed his hands, obviously enjoying himself. "So many mysteries. And perhaps there will be more at dinner."

There were, the first one being whether Lady Charlotte was even aware it was Christmas. There were no decorations on the table, no holly or pine garlands decking the dining room, and no heat. Leda, who had changed into a fetching little strapless dress, was shivering with cold.

And the dinner was utterly ordinary, no boar's head, no goose, no turkey, only some underseasoned cod and some overdone beef, all served by D'Artagnan, in new gloves, and Heidi. Hardly a festive holiday feast.

Lady Charlotte didn't appear to notice. She was well launched on the subject of primate intelligence, apparently grateful that her brother, James, hadn't come down to dinner. Nurse Parchtry wasn't there either. Apparently her patient hadn't gone off to sleep as easily as she'd hoped.

"One of the prejudices we're working to overcome is that primate behavior is instinctive," Lady Charlotte said. "We've done research that demonstrates conclusively their behavior is intentional. Primates are capable of conscious thought, of planning, and learning from experience, and of having insights."

Just after the soup course (tinned), Nurse Parchtry hurried in and sat down between Leda and me. She had changed out of her uniform into a gray chiffon thing with floating draperies, and she was all smiles.

"He's finally asleep," she said breathlessly, setting a white plastic box on the table. A series of wheezes and gasping noises came from it. "It's a baby monitor. So I can hear Lord Alastair if he wakes up."

How nice, I thought. Midway through dinner we shall be treated to a stream of animal screams and obscenities.

"What is it that Lord Alastair suffers from?" I asked.

"Dementia," she said, "and hatefulness, neither one of which is fatal, unfortunately. He could live for years. Thank you, Heidi," she said, as the chimpanzee set a plate of fish in front of her. "Isn't this exciting, Heidi, having Inspector Touffét here?"

Heidi nodded.

"Heidi and I are both mystery fans. We've been reading *The Case of the Crushed Skull*, haven't we?"

Heidi nodded again and signed something to Nurse Parchtry.

"She says she thinks the vicar did it," she said. She signed rapidly to Heidi. "I think it was the ex-wife. Which of us is right, Colonel Bridlings?"

Neither, as a matter of fact, though I had to give Heidi credit. *I* had thought it was the vicar, too. "I don't want to spoil the ending," I said, and Heidi bobbed her head in approval.

"He was always a dreadful man," Nurse Parchtry said, returning to the topic of Lord Alastair. "And, unfortunately, his son's just like him." She lowered her voice to a whisper. "Which is why he left everything to him in his will, I suppose. A pity. He'll only gamble it away."

"He gambles?" I said.

"He's horribly in debt," she whispered. "I heard him on the phone only this morning, pleading with his tout. You see, Lord Alastair arranged his money so it can't be touched until his death, which I suppose is a good thing. Otherwise there'd be nothing left." She shook her head. "It's Lady Charlotte I feel sorry for."

She leaned closer, her draperies drifting across my arm. "Did you know Lord Alastair stopped her from marrying her true love? She fell in love with one of his AI scientists, Phillip Davidson—Phillip was the one who got her interested in primate intelligence—and when Lord Alastair found out, he trumped up charges of industrial espionage against him, ruined his reputation, forced him to emigrate. Lady Charlotte never married."

Touffét would be interested in knowing that, I thought. I

glanced at him, but he was watching Mick Rutgers, who was listening to Lady Charlotte talk of her apes' accomplishments.

"D'Artagnan has learned eight hundred words, and over fifty sentences," she said. "We work for two hours a day on vocabulary." She smiled at D'Artagnan, who was removing the fish course. "And for an hour on serving skills."

Heidi began serving the roast beef. The snores and wheezes from the baby monitor subsided to a heavy, even breathing.

"Heidi and I work on her reading for two hours a day, and she reads on her own for another hour. Heidi," Lady Charlotte said, stopping her as she set a plate of roast beef down in front of Leda. "Tell Inspector Touffét what your favorite case is."

Heidi signed rapidly, grinning widely.

"*The Case of the Cat's Paw,*" Lady Charlotte translated.

Touffét looked pleased. "Ah, yes, a most satisfying case," he said, and launched into an account of it.

"What's a cat's paw?" Leda whispered to me. "It's not like a rabbit's foot, is it?"

"No," I said. "It's when someone uses another person for their own ends. It comes from an old tale about a monkey who used a cat's paw to pull chestnuts out of the fire."

"That's *cruel*," Nurse Parchtry said.

"No crueler than keeping apes captive and dressing them up in human clothes," Leda hissed.

"You don't approve of Lady Charlotte's work?" Nurse Parchtry said, shocked.

"N-no, of course I didn't mean that," Leda said, looking flustered. She took a forkful of roast beef and then laid it back down on her plate.

"Lady Charlotte has only the primates' best interests at heart in all her work," Nurse Parchtry said firmly. "She's utterly devoted to them, and they'd do anything for her. She saved them, you know, from terrible fates. Heidi was being *experimented* on."

Lady Charlotte had apparently heard the last part of that. "Experiments?" she said, interrupting Touffét in the middle of his case. "Primates are still being experimented on, in spite of our having proved they're conscious creatures and can feel pain just as we do. Our research has shown that they can acquire knowledge, solve complex problems, use tools, and manipulate language. Everything that humans can do."

"Not quite," Sergeant Eustis said. "They can't commit crimes or tell lies. Or cheat at cards."

"As a matter of fact," Mick Rutgers said, "primates can."

"Cheat at cards?" Sergeant Eustis said. "Don't tell me D'Artagnan plays poker, too?"

Everyone laughed.

"Various studies have shown that apes are capable of deception," Rutgers said. "Apes in the wild frequently hide food and then retrieve it when the rest of the troop is asleep, and signing apes who have done something naughty will lie when asked whether they did it. Several times Lucy hid a key in her mouth and waited until her owners were gone, and then let herself out. Their ability to lie and deceive is proof of their capability for higher forms of thinking, since it involves determining what another creature thinks and how it can be fooled."

Lady Charlotte was looking curiously at Rutgers. "You seem to know a great deal about primates, for a reporter," she said.

"It was in the informational packet you sent," he said.

"And you're quite right, they are capable of deception," she said. "But they are also capable of affection, fear, grief, gentleness, and devotion. They are far better creatures than we are."

"Is that why they attack people for no reason?" James said, coming in and sitting down next to his sister. He snapped his fingers, and Heidi hurried to bring him a plate of roast beef, looking frightened. "Is that why the University of Oklahoma had to shut down their research program after one of their apes bit the finger off a visiting surgeon? Because they're better creatures?"

He snatched the plate away from Heidi. "Has my sister told you about Lucy yet? Poor Lucy, who got sent back to the jungle to be killed by poachers? Did she tell you why Lucy got sent back? Because she attacked her owner." He smiled maliciously at Heidi. "That could happen to you, too, you know. And your friend D'Artagnan."

"I'd attack my owner, too, if I were an intelligent creature being treated like a slave," Mick Rutgers said, and Lady Charlotte gave him a grateful look, and then frowned, as if she were trying to place something.

I'd hoped there would at least be a plum pudding in honor of Christmas, but there was only vanilla custard, which reminded me unpleasantly of Lord Alastair's tapioca, but at least it meant an end to the meal. When Lady Charlotte said, "Shall we adjourn to the solarium?" I practically leaped out of my chair.

"Not yet," Touffét said. "Madam, you still have not informed me of the mystery you wished me to solve."

"All in good time," she said. "We must play a game first. No Christmas Eve is complete without games. Who wants to play Hunt the Slipper?"

"*I* do," Nurse Parchtry piped up and then looked nervous, as if she should not have called attention to herself.

"I have no intention of hunting all over the house for someone's smelly shoe," James said, and Touffét shot him an approving glance.

"How about Musical Chairs?"

"No. That's as bad as Hunt the Slipper," James said. "*I* think we should play Animal, Vegetable, or Mineral."

"That's because you're so good at it," Lady Charlotte said, but some of the bitterness seemed to have gone out of both their voices, perhaps because it was, after all, Christmas Eve.

Lady Charlotte led the way to the library. "I'm so glad Lord Alastair is still asleep," Nurse Parchtry said to me as we followed Lady Charlotte. She held the monitor up close to my ear. I could barely hear his faint, even breathing. "He won't wake up for hours," she said happily. "I *love* Christmas games."

"You should have come with me to my sister's, Touffét," I whispered to him. "You would only have had to play charades."

"Who shall be first?" Lady Charlotte said after we'd settled ourselves in the canvas chairs. "Sergeant Eustis? You must go and stand out in the corridor while we decide on an object."

Sergeant Eustis obligingly went out of the room and shut the door behind him.

"All right, what shall it be?" Lady Charlotte said brightly.

"Vegetable," Leda said.

"A Christmas tree," Nurse Parchtry said eagerly.

"He'd guess that in a minute," James said. "A literary character. It always takes them at least a dozen questions to determine it's fictional."

"Father Christmas!" Nurse Parchtry said.

Everyone ignored her.

"What do you think it should be, Inspector Touffét?" Lady Charlotte asked.

"The mystery which you asked me here to solve," Touffét said.

"No, that's too complicated," Lady Charlotte said. "I've got it! Fingerprints! It's perfect for a police officer."

A spirited discussion ensued over whether fingerprints were animal, vegetable, or mineral, and, unable to decide, they chose Goldilocks instead.

"She's a fictional character, *and* she committed a crime."

Sergeant Eustis was called in and began guessing. As predicted, he used thirteen of his twenty questions to determine that it was a fictional character, and then astonished everyone by guessing "Goldilocks" immediately.

"How *did* you guess?" Leda asked.

"It's always Goldilocks," he said. "Because I'm a police detective. Breaking and entering, you know."

One by one, everyone except Touffét took their turn at standing in the corridor and attempting to guess—a plum pudding (Nurse Parchtry's suggestion), the slipper in Hunt the Slipper, a map of Borneo, and a pair of embroidery scissors.

When it was James's turn, he demanded to be allowed to take a chair with him out into the corridor. "I don't intend to stand there forever while you all try to pick something that will fool me. I must warn you, I have never failed to guess the answer."

"He's quite right," Lady Charlotte said, smiling. "Last Christmas he guessed it in four."

"Mistletoe," Nurse Parchtry said.

"It's got to be a fictional character," Rutgers said. "He admitted himself it's the hardest to guess."

"No, his is always a fictional character. It needs to be someone real. And someone obscure. Anastasia!"

"I would hardly call Anastasia obscure," I said.

"No, but if he asks 'Is the person living?' we can say we don't know, and he'll think it's a fictional character."

"What if he's already asked if it's a fictional character and we've said no?"

"But it was a fictional character," Leda said. "I saw the Disney film when I was little."

"*And* when he asks if it's animal, vegetable, or mineral," Sergeant Eustis said. "We can say mineral. Because her body was burned to ashes."

"We don't know that," Lady Charlotte said. "Her bones have never been found."

It was a good thing James had insisted on the chair. It took us nearly fifteen minutes to decide, during which time Touffét looked increasingly as if he were going to explode.

"But, if he knows we know he always guesses fictional characters," Sergeant Eustis said, "then he'll think we won't choose one, so we should."

"King Kong," Nurse Parchtry said.

There was an embarrassed silence.

"I think perhaps we should avoid any references to primates," Lady Charlotte said finally.

We finally decided on R2D2, who was both mineral and animal (the actor inside him) and fictional and real (the actual tin can), and had the advantage of being from an old movie, which Lady Charlotte said her brother never watched.

James guessed it in four questions.

"All right," Lady Charlotte said, looking round the room. "Who hasn't gone yet? Mr. Rutgers?"

"I was a pair of embroidery scissors, remember?"

"Oh, yes. Mr. Touffét, you're the only one left. Come along. I'm sure you'll solve it even more quickly than my brother."

"Madam," Touffét said and his voice was deadly quiet. "I did not come to Marwaite Manor to play at games. I came in response to your request to solve a mystery. I wish to know what it is."

Either Lady Charlotte was tired of thinking up things, or she sensed the deadliness in Touffét's voice.

"You're quite right," she said. "It is time. What Inspector Touffét said is true. I asked him here to solve a mystery, a mystery so baffling only the greatest detective in the world could solve it."

She stood up, as if to make a speech. "The research my Institute has done has proved that primates are capable of higher-thinking skills and complex planning, that they can think and understand and speak and even write."

"Madam," Touffét said, half-rising.

She waved him back to sitting. "The mystery that I wish Inspector Touffét to solve is this: Since it has been proved that primates have thoughts and ideas equivalent to those of humans, that they *are* by every standard human, why are they not treated as human? Why do they not have legal standing in the courts? Why are they not allowed to vote and own property? Why have they not been given their civil rights? Inspector Touffét, only you can solve this mystery. Only you can give us the answer! Why are apes not given equal standing with humans?"

"You've been taken in, Touffét," I said, I must admit with some pleasure. "Lady Charlotte only invited you here as a publicity stunt. She wanted you to be a pitchman for her Institute." I laughed. "This time it's you who's the cat's paw. She's using you to get chimpanzees the vote."

"A cat's paw," he said, offended. "I do not allow myself to be used as a cat's paw." He pulled his bag off the top of the bureau. "What time is the next train to your sister's?"

"You're leaving?" I said.

"*We* are leaving," he said. "Telephone your sister and tell her we will arrive tonight. Inspector Touffét does not allow himself to be used by anyone."

Well, at any rate my sister would be happy, I thought, going downstairs to telephone her. I pulled the train schedule out of my pocket. If we were able to catch the 9:30 train, we could be there before midnight. I wondered whether Lady Charlotte would arrange for us to be driven to the station, and whether the driver would be D'Artagnan. I decided under the circumstances I'd better phone for a taxi as well. D'Artagnan was devoted to her. He might not like the idea of our leaving.

I started to open the door of the study and then stopped at the sound of a woman's voice. "No, it's going fine," she said. "You should have seen me. I was great. I even ate roast beef." There was a pause. "Tomorrow, while they're touring the compound. Listen, I've gotta go."

I backed hastily away, not wishing to be caught eavesdropping, and into the solarium. For a moment I thought there were two people standing by the window, and then I realized it was Heidi and D'Artagnan. Heidi was signing animatedly to the gorilla, and he was nodding.

They stopped as soon as they saw me, and D'Artagnan started toward me. "Help you, sir?"

"I'm looking for a telephone," I said, and he led me out into the corridor and over to the study.

I phoned my sister. "Oh, good," she said. "I'll meet you at the station. Have you had dinner?"

"Only a bite."

"I'll bring you a sandwich."

When I got back upstairs, Touffét was already waiting by the lift with our bags. "Have you telephoned for a taxi?" he asked, pushing the lift button.

"Yes," I'd started to say, when the air was split by a shrill, terrified scream from somewhere above us.

"Good Lord, Touffét!" I said. "It sounds like someone's being murdered."

"No doubt Lady Charlotte has discovered I am leaving," he said dryly, and pushed the button again.

Rutgers came tumbling out of his room, and Leda's blonde head appeared. "What was that? It sounded like an animal being tortured."

"I think we should take the stairs," I said, but before I could turn, the lift opened, and Nurse Parchtry fell into my arms.

"It's Lord Alastair!" she sobbed. "He's dead!"

"Dead?" Touffét said.

"Yes!" she said. "You must come!" She stepped back into the lift. "I think he's been murdered!"

We followed her into the lift. "Murdered?" Mick Rutgers said from down the hall, but the door was already shutting.

"See if Sergeant Eustis has gone," Touffét called through the closing door. "Now," he said to Nurse Parchtry as the lift started. "Tell me exactly what happened. Everything. After the games did you return to the nursery?"

"Yes. No, I went to my room to finish wrapping my Christmas presents," she said guiltily. "I had the baby monitor with me."

"And you heard nothing?" Touffét asked.

"No. I thought he was sleeping. He wasn't making any noise at all." She started to sob again. "I didn't know the monitor was broken."

The lift doors parted, and we stepped out. The door to the anteroom stood ajar. "Was this door open when you arrived?"

"Yes," she said, leading the way into the anteroom. "And this one, too." She pointed at the door to the nursery. "I thought he'd gotten out. But then I saw . . . him. . . ." She buried her head in my jacket.

"Come, madam," Touffét said sternly. "You must pull yourself together. You said you had always wished to see me solve a mystery. Now you shall, but you must help me."

"You're right, I did. I will," she said, but when we went into the nursery, she hung back reluctantly and then grabbed on to my arm for support.

The place was a shambles. Lord Alastair's bed had been overturned and the bedclothes dragged off it. The pillows had been torn up, the stuffing flung in handfuls about the room. The rocking chair, bowls, toys, tire—all looked as if they had been thrown about the room in a violent rage. Lord Alastair lay on his back in the middle of the floor, half on a rumpled blanket, his face swollen and purple.

"Did you touch anything?" Touffét asked, looking around the room.

"No," Nurse Parchtry said. "I knew from your cases not to." She clapped her hand to her mouth. "I did touch him. I took his pulse and listened to his heart. I thought perhaps he wasn't dead."

He looked dead to me. His face was a horrible purplish-blue color, his tongue pushing out of his mouth, his eyes bulging, his neck bruised. And she was a nurse. She should have known at a glance there was no hope of resuscitation.

"Did you touch anything else?" Touffét said, squatting down and holding out his monocle to look closely at Lord Alastair's neck.

"No," she said, "I screamed, and then I ran to find you."

"Where did you scream?"

"Where?" she said blankly. "Right here. By the body."

He stood up and looked at the glass partition and then walked over to the wall. The baby monitor lay against it, its back off and the front of the case broken in two pieces.

"That's why there was no sound from the monitor," I said. "That means he could have been killed any time after dinner."

"And no one has an alibi," Nurse Parchtry said. "We were all out in the corridor by ourselves for several minutes."

Touffét had picked up the baby monitor and was examining the switch. "Should you be doing that?" I asked. "Won't it smudge the fingerprints?"

"There are no fingerprints," he said, putting the monitor back down, "and none on the neck either."

"I warned you!" James said, appearing in the doorway. "I told you that ape was dangerous, and now he's killed my father!" He strode over to the body.

"I need to secure this crime scene," Sergeant Eustis said, coming into the room, unreeling yards and yards of yellow "Do

Not Cross" tape. "I'll have to ask all of you to leave. *Don't* touch anything," he said sharply to James, who was putting his hand to his father's neck. "This is a murder investigation. I'll want to question everyone downstairs."

"Murder investigation!" James said. "There's no need for any investigation! I'll tell you who murdered my father. It was that ape!"

"The evidence will tell us who killed him," Sergeant Eustis said, walking back over to the body. "Inspector Touffét, come look at this. It's a hair."

He pointed to a long, coarse black hair lying on Lord Alastair's pajama'd chest.

"There! Look at that!" James said. "There's your evidence!"

Sergeant Eustis took out an evidence bag and a pair of tweezers and carefully placed the hair in the bag. While all this was going on, Touffét had walked over to the far wall and was looking at the lidded cup, which had apparently hit the wall and bounced. Cocoa was splattered across the wall in a long arc. Touffét picked up the cup, pried off the lid, sniffed at the contents, and then dipped a finger in and licked it off.

"You mustn't touch that!" Sergeant Eustis said, racing over, trailing long loops of yellow. "The fingerprints!"

"You will not find any fingerprints," Touffét said. "The murderer wore gloves."

"You see!" James shouted. "Even the Great Detective knows D'Artagnan did it. Why aren't you out capturing him? He's liable to kill someone else!"

Touffét ignored him. He handed Sergeant Eustis the cup. "Have the residue analyzed. I think it will yield interesting results."

Sergeant Eustis put the cup into an evidence bag and handed it to the young constable who'd just arrived and was gaping at

Lord Alastair. "Have the residue analyzed," Sergeant Eustis said, "and take all these people downstairs. I will want to question everyone in the house."

"*Question!*" James raged. "This is a waste of time. It's obvious what happened here. I warned you!"

"Yes," Touffét said, looking curiously at James. "You did."

I was surprised that Touffét didn't object to being herded out of the nursery and into the lift by the constable, along with everyone else, but he only said, "Has Lady Charlotte been told?"

"I'll tell her," Mick Rutgers volunteered, and Touffét gazed at him for a long moment, as if his mind were elsewhere, and then nodded. He continued to look at Rutgers as he went down the corridor and then turned to me. "Who do you think committed the murder, Bridlings?"

"It seems perfectly straightforward," I said. "James said the apes were dangerous, and, unfortunately, it appears he was right."

"Appears, yes. That is because you see only the surface."

"Well, what do *you* see?" I demanded. "The old man's been strangled, furniture's been smashed, there's a gorilla hair on the body."

"Exactly. It is like a scene out of a mystery novel. I have something I wish you to do," he said abruptly. "I wish you to find Leda Fox and tell her Sergeant Eustis wishes to speak to her."

"But he didn't say he—"

"He said he wished to question everyone."

"You don't think Leda had anything to do with this?" I said. "She can't have. She's not strong enough. Lord Alastair was strangled. There was a terrific struggle."

"So it would appear," he said. He motioned me out of the room.

I went up to Leda's room and was surprised to find her packing. "I'm not staying in the same house with a killer gorilla," she said. "A *cold* house with a killer gorilla."

"No one's allowed to leave," I said. "Sergeant Eustis wants to question you."

I was surprised at her reaction. She went completely white. "Question *me*?" she stammered. "What about?"

"Who saw what, where we all were at the time of the murder, and that sort of thing, I suppose," I said, trying to reassure her.

"But I thought they knew who did it," she said. "I thought D'Artagnan did it."

"Knowing who did it and proving it are two different things," I said. "I'm certain it's just routine."

She started up to the nursery, and I went back to the study to find Touffét. He wasn't there, nor was he in his room. Perhaps he'd gone back up to the nursery, too. I went out to the lift, and it opened, revealing Lady Charlotte. She looked pale and drawn. "Oh, Colonel Bridlings," she said, "where is Inspector Touffét?"

"I'm afraid I don't—"

"I am here, madam," Touffét said, and I turned and looked at him in surprise, wondering where he'd come from.

"Oh, Inspector," she said, clutching at his hands. "I know I brought you here under false pretenses, but now you must solve this murder. D'Artagnan could not possibly have killed my father, but my brother is determined to—" She broke down.

"Madam, compose yourself," Touffét said. "I must ask you two questions. First, are any of your household keys missing?"

"I don't know," she said, pulling the bunch of keys out of her pocket and examining them. "The key to the nursery," she said suddenly. "But the keys have been with me all day. No, I didn't have them when we went up to see my father, and Nurse Parchtry had to let us in. Let's see, I had them this morning, and then I gave them to D'Artagnan because he'd misplaced his gloves—" She stopped, as if suddenly aware of what she'd said. "Oh, but you don't think he—"

"My second question is this," Touffét said, "when your father had difficult days, could you hear him on the lower floors of the house?"

"Sometimes," she said. "If only we'd heard him tonight. Poor old . . ." she clutched tearfully at Touffét's sleeve. "Please say you will stay and solve the murder."

"I have already solved it," he said. "I request that you ask everyone to come into the parlor, including Sergeant Eustis, and give them a glass of sherry. Bridlings and I will join you shortly."

As soon as she was gone, Touffét turned to me. "What time is the last train to Sussex?"

"Eleven-fourteen," I said.

"Excellent," he said, consulting his pocket watch. "More than enough time. You shall be at your sister's in time to burn your fingers on the raisins."

"We don't play Snapdragon," I said. "We play charades. And how can you have solved the crime so quickly? Sergeant Eustis's men haven't even had time to gather evidence, let alone run forensics tests."

He waved his hand dismissively. "Forensics, evidence, they tell us only how the murder was done, not why."

They also frequently tell us *who*, I would have said, if Touffét had given me the opportunity, but he was still expounding.

" 'Why' is the only question that matters," he said, "for if we know the 'why,' we know both who did the murder and how it was done. Go and tell your sister we will be on the train without fail."

I went downstairs and telephoned my sister again. "Oh, good," she said, "we're going to play Dumb Crambo this year!"

As I hung up, Touffét said, "Bridlings!"

I turned round, expecting to see him in the door. There was no one there. I went out into the corridor and looked up the stairs.

"Bridlings," Touffét said again, from inside the room. I went back in.

"Bridlings, come here at once. I need you," Touffét said, and laughed.

"Where are you?" I asked, wondering if this was some sort of ventriloquist's joke.

"In the nursery," he said. "Can you hear me?"

Well, of course I could hear him or I wouldn't be answering him. "Yes," I said, looking all round the room and finally spying the baby monitor, half hidden behind a clock on one of the bookshelves. I reached to pick it up. "Don't pick it up," he said. "You will ruin the forensic evidence you consider so important."

"Do you want me to come up to the nursery?"

"That will not be necessary. I have found out what I wished to know. Go into the parlor and make sure that Lady Charlotte has assembled everyone."

She had, though not in the parlor. "We don't have a parlor," she said, meeting me in the corridor as I came out of the library. "I've put everyone in the solarium, where we were last night. I hope that's all right."

"I'm sure it will be fine," I said.

"And I didn't have any sherry." She stopped at the door. "I had Heidi make Singapore slings."

"Probably a very good idea," I said, and opened the door.

Leda was perched on a canvas-covered hassock, with Rutgers behind her. The nurse sat in one of the canvas chairs, and the police sergeant perched next to her on the coffee table. James leaned against one of the bookshelves with a drink in his hand. D'Artagnan stood over by the windows.

As I came in, they all, except James and Heidi, who was offering him a tray of drinks, looked up expectantly and then relaxed.

"Is it true?" Leda asked eagerly. "Has Monsieur Touffét solved the crime? Does he know who murdered Lord Alastair?"

"We *all* know who murdered my father," James said, pointing at D'Artagnan. "That *animal* flew into a rage and strangled him! Isn't that right, Inspector Touffét?" he said to Touffét, who had just come in the door. "My father was killed by that *animal*!"

"So I at first thought," Touffét said, polishing his monocle. "A gorilla goes out of control, kills Lord Alastair in a violent rage, and destroys the nursery as he might his cage, throwing the furniture and the dishes against the wall. The baby monitor, also, was thrown against the wall and broken, which was why the nurse did not hear the murder being committed."

"You see!" James said to his sister. "Even your Great Detective says D'Artagnan did it."

"I said that so it seemed at first," Touffét said, looking irritated at the remark about the Great Detective, "but then I began to notice things—the fact that there were no signs of forcible entry, that the baby monitor had been switched off before it was thrown against the wall, that though it looked like a scene of great violence, none of us had heard anything—things that made me think, perhaps this is not a violent crime at all, but a carefully planned murder."

"Carefully planned!" James shouted. "The gorilla choked the life out of him in a fit of animal rage." He turned to Sergeant Eustis. "Why aren't you upstairs, gathering forensic evidence to prove that was what happened?"

"I do not need the forensic evidence," Touffét said. He took out a meerschaum pipe and filled it. "To solve this murder, I need only the motive."

"The motive?" James shouted. "You don't ask a bear what his motive is for biting off someone's head, do you? It's a *wild* animal!"

Touffét lit his pipe and took several long puffs on it. "So I begin by asking myself," he went on implacably, "who had a motive for killing Lord Alastair? Your father's will left everything to you, Lord James, did it not?"

"Yes," James said. "You're not suggesting *I* put that gorilla up to—"

"I do not suggest anything. I say only that you had a motive." He picked up his monocle and surveyed the crowd. "As does Miss Fox."

"What?" Leda said, twitching her dress down over her thighs. "I never even met Lord Alastair."

"What you say is the truth," Touffét said, "though it is the only true thing you have said since your arrival, that is. You have even lied about your name, is that not so? You are not Leda Fox, the reporter. You are Genevieve Wrigley."

Lady Charlotte gasped.

"Who's Genevieve Wrigley?" I asked.

"The head of the ARA," Touffét said, looking steadily at her. "The Animal Rescue Army."

Lady Charlotte had jumped up. "You're here to steal D'Artagnan and Heidi from me!" She turned beseechingly to Touffét. "You mustn't let her. The ARA are terrorists."

I looked wonderingly at Leda, or rather Genevieve. Lady Charlotte was right about the ARA, it was a terrorist organization, a sort of IRA for animals. I'd seen them on television, blowing up cosmetics companies and holding zookeepers hostage, but Leda—Genevieve didn't look like them at all.

Touffét said sternly, "You came here in disguise with the

intention of liberating Lady Charlotte's animals, no matter what violent means were necessary."

"That's right," Leda, or rather, Genevieve, said, rearing back dangerously, and I was grateful there wasn't room anywhere for a bomb in that dress. "But I wouldn't have killed animals. I love animals!"

"Releasing pets into a wilderness they can't survive in?" Lady Charlotte said bitterly. "Sending primates back into the jungle to be killed by poachers? You don't love animals. You don't love anyone but yourselves. Well, now you've gone too far. You've murdered my father, and I'll see you convicted."

"Why would I murder your father?" Genevieve sneered. "You're the one I wanted to murder!"

At her words, D'Artagnan and Heidi both moved protectively toward Lady Charlotte.

"Dressing primates up like servants, holding them captive here. You're slaves!" she said to D'Artagnan. "She tells you she loves you, but she just wants to enslave you!"

D'Artagnan took a threatening step toward her, his huge white-gloved fist raised. "It's all right, D'Artagnan," Lady Charlotte said. "Inspector Touffét won't let her hurt me."

Genevieve slumped back in her chair and glared at Touffét. "I can't believe you found me out," she said. "I even ate a piece of that disgusting meat at dinner."

"We were discussing your motive," Touffét said. "Terrorists do not murder secretly. Their crimes are of no use unless they take credit for them. And by killing Lord Alastair, you might have given the Institute bad publicity, but you would not necessarily have succeeded in closing the Institute. Sympathetic donations might have poured in. How much better to blow up the Institute's buildings. It is true, you might have killed primates, but your organization has been known to kill animals before, in the name of saving them."

"You can't prove that!" she said sullenly.

"There are wire and detonating caps in your luggage." He turned to Sergeant Eustis. "Ms. Wrigley was out at the compound this afternoon. When we have concluded our business here, I would suggest searching it for plastic explosives."

Sergeant Eustis nodded and came over to stand behind Genevieve's chair. She rolled her eyes in disgust and crossed her arms over her chest.

"Ms. Wrigley had a motive for murder, but she is not the only one." He took several puffs on his pipe. "Everyone in this room has a motive. Yes, even you, Captain Bridlings."

"I?" I said.

"You long to spend Christmas at your sister's house, do you not? If Lord Alastair is murdered, the Christmas celebration at Marwaite Manor will be cancelled, and you will be free to attend your sister's celebration instead."

"*If* I'm not detained for questioning," I said. "And I hardly think wanting to spend Christmas with my sister is an adequate motive for murdering a harmless, helpless old man."

Touffét held up an objecting finger. "Helpless, perhaps, but not harmless. But I quite agree with you, Bridlings, your motive is not adequate. People, though, have often murdered for inadequate motives. But you, Bridlings, are incapable of murder, and that is why I do not suspect you of the crime."

"Thank you," I said dryly.

"But. It is a motive," Touffét said. "As for Lady Charlotte, she has told all of us her motive this very evening at dinner. She has no money for her Institute. She is in danger of losing D'Artagnan and Heidi and all her other primates unless she obtains a large sum of money. And she loves them even more than she loves her father."

"But her father's will left all his money to her brother," I blurted out.

"Exactly," Touffét said, "so her brother must be eliminated as well, and what better method than to have him convicted of murder?"

"But Charlotte would never—" Rutgers said, rising involuntarily to his feet.

She looked at him in surprise.

"That is the conclusion to which I came also. Do not excite yourself, Mr. Rutgers," he said, giving the word "Rutgers" a peculiar emphasis. "I do not believe Lady Charlotte committed the murder, even though as the one who invited me here to Marwaite Manor, she was the first person I suspected."

He stopped and lit his pipe again for at least five minutes. "I said, I do not believe Lady Charlotte committed the murder, but not because I do not believe her capable of murder. I believe her desire to protect her primates could easily have driven her to murder. But that same desire would never have allowed her to let her primates be suspected of murder, even with a great detective on hand to uncover the true murderer. She would never have endangered them, even for a few hours." He turned and looked at Mick Rutgers. "You do not need to worry about Lady Charlotte, Mr. Davidson."

Now Lady Charlotte was the one who had risen involuntarily to her feet. "Phillip?" she said. "Is it really you?"

"Yes, it is Phillip Davidson," Touffét said smugly. "Who was ruined by Lord Alastair, who was kept from marrying Lady Charlotte and forced to emigrate to Australia." He paused dramatically. "Who came here determined to murder Lord Alastair for revenge."

"To murder . . ." Lady Charlotte put her hand to her bosom. "Is that true, Phillip?"

"Yes, it's true," Rutgers, or rather Davidson, said. Good Lord, just when I'd learned everyone's names. Now I was going to have to memorize them all over again.

"How did you know?" Rutg—Davidson asked.

"You called Lord Alastair 'Al,' though no one else had called him by that name," Touffét said. "It was also obvious from the way you looked at Lady Charlotte that you were still in love with her."

"It's true. I am," he said, looking at Lady Charlotte.

She was staring at him in horror. "You killed my father?"

"No," he said. "It's true, I came here to. I even brought a pistol with me. But when I saw him, I realized . . . He was a terrible man, but brilliant. To be reduced to that . . . that . . . was a worse revenge than any I could have devised." He looked at Touffét. "You have to believe me. I didn't kill him."

"I know you did not," Touffét said. "This murder required a knowledge of the house and of the people in it which you did not possess. And a revenge killer does not sedate his victim."

"Sedate?" Nurse Parchtry said.

"Yes," Touffét said. "When Sergeant Eustis completes his analysis of the cocoa, he will find the presence of sleeping medication."

I remembered the snoring on the baby monitor, subsiding into heavy, even breathing. Drugged breathing.

"Someone who murders for revenge," Touffét continued, "wishes his victim to know why he is being murdered. And you had worked with primates, Mr. Davidson, it was your interest in their intelligence that had sparked Lady Charlotte's. You would not have attempted to frame them for murder."

"Well, who would have?" Sergeant Eustis blurted.

"An excellent question," Touffét said. "And one which I will address shortly. But first we shall deal with your motive for murder, Sergeant."

"Mine?" Sergeant Eustis said, astonished. "What possible motive could I have had for murdering anyone?"

"Exactly," Touffét said, and everyone looked bewildered. "You had no motive for murdering Lord Alastair in particular, but you *did* have a motive for murdering someone."

"Aren't you forgetting he's a police officer?" James said nastily. "Or are you saying *you* have a motive for murdering my father, too?"

"No," Touffét said calmly. "For I am a great detective, with many solved cases to my credit, and none that I have failed to solve through my own incompetence. That is not, however, true of Sergeant Eustis, is it?"

Leda—Genevieve gasped. " 'Useless' Eustis. I thought you looked familiar."

"Indeed," Touffét said. "Captain Eustis, who had charge of the Tiffany Levinger case."

Tiffany Levinger. Now I remembered. It had been all over the television and the on-line tabloids. The pretty little girl who had been murdered in her own house, obviously by her own parents, but they had been acquitted because Captain Eustis had bungled the investigation so badly that it was impossible to attain a conviction. Nicknamed Useless Eustis and pilloried in the press, he had been forced to resign. And had apparently ended up here, in this remote area, demoted and disgraced.

"Another murder, the celebrated murder of a billionaire in a country manor, a sensational murder that you solved, could have redeemed your reputation, could it not?" Touffét said. "Especially with the press on the premises to record it all."

"It certainly could have," Sergeant Eustis said. "But even someone as stupid as the press claimed I was wouldn't be stupid enough to commit a murder with Inspector Touffét on the premises, now would he?"

"Exactly the conclusion I came to, Sergeant," Touffét said. "Which leaves Nurse Parchtry and James Valladay."

"Oh," Nurse Parchtry said, distressed, "you don't think I did it, do you? What motive could I have?"

"A cruel and abusive patient."

"But in that case why would I not simply have resigned?"

"That is what I asked myself," Touffét said. "You were obviously subjected to daily indignities, yet Lady Charlotte said you had been here over a year. Why? I asked myself."

"Because if she left she would forfeit the bonus I had promised her," Lady Charlotte said. She wrung her hands. "Oh, don't tell me I'm responsible for her. . . . I was so desperate. We'd been through seven nurses in less than a month. I thought if I offered her an incentive to stay . . ."

"What was the incentive?" Touffét asked Nurse Parchtry.

"Ten thousand pounds, if I stayed a full year," the nurse said dully. "I didn't think it would be so bad. I'd had difficult patients before, and it was the only way I could ever get out of debt. I didn't think it would be so bad. But I was wrong." She glared at Charlotte. "A million dollars wouldn't have been enough for taking care of that *brute*. I'm *glad* he's dead," she burst out. "I wish I'd killed him myself!"

"But you did not," Touffét said. "You are a nurse. You had at your disposal dozens of undetectable drugs, dozens of opportunities. You could have deprived him of his oxygen, given him a lethal dose of lidocaine or insulin, and it would have been assumed that he had died of natural causes. There would not even have been an autopsy. And you liked Heidi. You and she shared a passion for my cases. You would not have committed a murder that implicated her."

"No, I wouldn't have," Nurse Parchtry said tearfully. "She's a dear little thing."

"There is in fact only one person here who had a motive not only to murder Lord Alastair but also to see D'Artagnan charged with it, and that is Lord James Valladay."

"What?" James said, spilling his drink in his surprise.

"You were in considerable debt. Your father's death would

mean that you would inherit a fortune. And you hated your sister's primates. You had every reason to murder your father and frame D'Artagnan."

"B-but . . ." he spluttered. "This is ridiculous."

"You put sleeping tablets in your father's cocoa when you were in the nursery, using an attack by D'Artagnan as a distraction. During the game of Animal, Vegetable, or Mineral, you went out into the corridor, having convinced everyone that they must take considerable time in choosing your object, and you took the lift up to the nursery, putting on the gloves you had stolen from D'Artagnan earlier, and strangled your sleeping father. Then you switched off the baby monitor and overturned the bed and placed objects around the room to look as if someone had flung them violently. Then you hid the key and the gloves, and came back downstairs, where you cold-bloodedly continued playing the game."

"Oh, James, you didn't—" Lady Charlotte cried.

"Of course I didn't. You haven't any proof of any of this, Touffét. You said yourself there weren't any fingerprints."

"Ah," Touffét said, pulling a bottle of sleeping tablets out of his pocket. "This was found in your medicine cabinet, and these"—he produced a key and a pair of white gloves—"under your mattress, where you hid them, intending later to put them in the pantry to implicate D'Artagnan." He handed them to Sergeant Eustis. "I think you will find that the sleeping tablets match the residue in the cocoa cup."

"Under my mattress?" James said, doing a very good job of looking bewildered. "I don't understand— How would I have got into the nursery? I don't have a key."

"Ah," Touffét said. "D'Artagnan, come here." The gorilla lumbered forward from where he and Heidi had been watching all this and thinking God knows what. "D'Artagnan, what happened after Lady Charlotte gave you the keys?"

"Unlock," he said. "Get gloves."

"And then what?"

D'Artagnan looked fearfully at James and then back at Touffét.

"I won't let him hurt you," Sergeant Eustis said.

Lady Charlotte nodded at him. "Go ahead, D'Artagnan. Tell the truth. You won't get in trouble."

The gorilla glanced worriedly at James again and then said, "James say. Give me," pantomiming handing over a bunch of keys.

"That's a lie!" James said. "I did no such thing!"

"Then why was this under your mattress inside one of the gloves?" Touffét said, producing a key from his pocket and handing it to Sergeant Eustis.

"But I didn't—!" James said, turning to his sister. "He's lying!"

"How is that possible?" Lady Charlotte said coldly. "He's only an animal."

"A satisfying case," Touffét said as we waited for the train.

We had been driven to the station by a hairy orange orangutan named Sven. "He doesn't have a driver's license," Lady Charlotte had said, bidding us goodbye. She smiled up at Phillip Davidson, who had his arm around her. "But every policeman in the county's upstairs collecting evidence," she said, "so you won't have to worry about being ticketed."

It was easy to see why the police refused to issue Sven a driver's license. He was positively wild, and after he had nearly driven us off the road, he slapped the steering wheel with his hairy hands and grinned a teeth-baring smile at me. But he had gotten us there nearly ten minutes before train time.

Touffét was still preoccupied with the case. "It is a pity James would not confess to the murder when I confronted him. Now the police must spend Christmas Day examining evidence."

"I'm sure Sergeant Eustis won't mind," I told him. He had seemed pathetically eager to look for everything Touffét told him to, even writing it all down. "You've redeemed his reputation. And, at any rate, no one confesses these days, even when they've been caught redhanded."

"That is true," he said, checking his pocket watch. "And all has turned out well," Touffét said. "Lady Charlotte's Institute is safe, the apes no longer have to fear being homeless, and you shall arrive at your sister's in time to burn your fingers on the raisins."

"Aren't you going with me?"

"I have already endured one evening of Animal, Vegetable, or Mineral. My constitution cannot withstand another. I will disembark in London. You will convey my regrets to your sister, yes?"

I nodded absently, thinking of what he had said about the apes no longer having to fear being homeless. It was true. Until the murder, Lady Charlotte's Institute had been in great financial difficulty. She had said it might have to close. And if it did, the ARA and the other animal rights groups would have insisted on D'Artagnan and Heidi's being sent back to the wilds. Like Lucy.

Touffét had said everyone in the room had a motive, and he was right, but there were two suspects in the room he had overlooked.

James had even accused D'Artagnan of the murder, and D'Artagnan would certainly have done anything to save Lady Valladay's Institute—he was utterly devoted to her. Like D'Artagnan and the other Musketeers, who would have done anything to protect their queen. And he and Heidi were in danger of losing their home.

But killing Lord Alastair would not have saved the Institute. James would have inherited the estate. James, who had threatened to shut down the Institute, who had threatened to sell the apes to the zoo. Killing Lord Alastair would only have made the apes' situation worse.

Unless James could be made to look like the murderer. Because murderers could not inherit.

What if Heidi had put the sleeping pills into Lord Alastair's cocoa before she brought it up to the nursery, and had hidden the bottle in James's bureau? What if D'Artagnan had only pretended to lose his gloves so that Lady Charlotte would give him her keys? What if he and Heidi had gone up to the nursery while everyone was playing Animal, Vegetable, or Mineral, strangled Lord Alastair in his sleep, and then thrown the furniture about?

But that was impossible. They were *animals*, as James said. Animals who were capable of lying, cheating, deceiving. Capable of planning and executing. Executing.

What if D'Artagnan had really twisted James's wrist, so that he would accuse him, so that he'd say the apes were dangerous, and it would look as if he were trying to frame them?

No, it was too complicated. Even if they were capable of higher-level thinking, there was a huge difference between solving arithmetic problems and planning a murder.

Especially a murder that could fool Touffét, I thought, looking across the compartment at him. He was rummaging through his bag, looking for his mystery novel.

They could never have come up with a murder like that on their own. And Touffét's explanation of James's motive made perfect sense. But if James had committed the murder, why hadn't he washed the cocoa out of the cup? Why hadn't he hidden the key and the gloves in the pantry, as Touffét had said he intended to do? He'd had plenty of time after we went to our rooms. Why hadn't he dumped the sleeping tablets down the sink?

"Bridlings," Touffét said, "what have you done with my book?"

I found *The Murders in the Rue Morgue* for him.

"No, no," he said. "Not that one. I do not wish to think anymore of primates." He handed it back to me.

I stared at it. What if they hadn't had to plan the murder? What if they had only had to copy someone else's plan? "Monkey see, monkey do," I murmured.

"What?" Touffét said, rummaging irritably through his bag. "What did you say?"

"Touffét," I said earnestly, "do you remember *The Case of the Cat's Paw*?"

"Ah, yes," he said, looking pleased. "The little chimpanzee's favorite book. A most satisfying case."

"The husband did it," I said.

"*And* confessed when I confronted him," he said, looking annoyed. "You, as I recall, thought the village doctor did it."

Yes, I had thought the village doctor did it. Because the husband had made it look as though he had been framed by the doctor, so that suspicion no longer rested on him.

And *The Case of the Cat's Paw* was Heidi's favorite book. What if she and D'Artagnan had simply copied the murder in the book?

But Touffét had solved *The Case of the Cat's Paw*. How could they have been sure he would not solve this one?

"You were particularly obtuse on that case," Touffét said. "That is because you see only the facade."

"In spite of all the evidence of their intelligence," Lady Charlotte had said, "people *persist* in seeing them as animals."

As animals. Who couldn't possibly have committed a murder.

But Heidi could read. And D'Artagnan had scored 95 on IQ tests. And they would have done anything for Lady Charlotte. Anything.

"Touffét," I said. "I've been thinking—"

"Ah, but that is just the problem. You do not think. You look only at the surface. Never what lies below it."

Or behind it, I thought. To the monkey, putting the cat's paw in the fire.

Unless I told Touffét, James would be convicted of murder.

"Useless" Eustis would never discover the truth on his own, and even if he did, he wouldn't dare to contradict Touffét, who had saved his reputation.

"Touffét," I said.

"That is why I am the great detective, and you are only the scribe," Touffét said. "Because you see only the facade. That is why I do not listen to you when you tell me that you think it is the gorilla or the vicar. "Well, what is it you wished to say?"

"Nothing," I said. "I was only wondering what we should call this case. *The Case of the Country Christmas?*"

He shook his head. "I do not wish to be reminded of Christmas."

The train began to slow. "Ah, this is where I change for London." He began gathering up his belongings.

If James were allowed to inherit, he would not only shut down the Institute, he would also drink and gamble his way through all the money. And D'Artagnan and Heidi would almost certainly be shipped back to the jungle and the poachers, so it was really a form of self-defense. And even if it was murder, it would be cruel to try them for it when they had no legal standing in the courts.

And the old man had been little more than an animal in need of putting down. Less human than D'Artagnan and Heidi.

The train came to a stop, and Touffét opened the door of the compartment.

"Touffét—" I said.

"Well, what is it?" he said irritably, his hand on the compartment. "I shall miss my stop."

"Merry Christmas," I said.

The conductor called out, and Touffét bustled off toward his train. I watched him from the door of the train, thinking of Lady Charlotte. Finding out the truth, that her beloved primates were far more human than even she had imagined, would kill her. She deserved a little happiness after what her father had done to her.

And my sister would be waiting for me at the station. She would have made eggnog.

I stood there in the door, thinking of what Touffét had said about my being incapable of murder. He was wrong. We are all capable of murder. It's in our genes.

NEWSLETTER

$\mathscr{L}$ater examination of weather reports and newspapers showed that it may have started as early as October nineteenth, but the first indication I had that something unusual was going on was at Thanksgiving.

I went to Mom's for dinner (as usual), and was feeding cranberries and cut-up oranges into Mom's old-fashioned meat grinder for the cranberry relish and listening to my sister-in-law Allison talk about her Christmas newsletter (also as usual).

"Which of Cheyenne's accomplishments do you think I should write about first, Nan?" she said, spreading cheese on celery sticks. "Her playing lead snowflake in *The Nutcracker* or her hitting a home run in PeeWee Soccer?"

"I'd list the Nobel Peace Prize first," I murmured, under cover of the crunch of an apple being put through the grinder.

"There just isn't room to put in all the girls' accomplishments," she said, oblivious. "Mitch *insists* I keep it to one page."

"That's because of Aunt Lydia's newsletters," I said. "Eight pages single-spaced."

"I know," she said. "And in that tiny print you can barely read." She waved a celery stick thoughtfully. "That's an idea."

"Eight pages single-spaced?"

"No. I could get the computer to do a smaller font. That way I'd have room for Dakota's Sunshine Scout merit badges. I got the cutest paper for my newsletters this year. Little angels holding bunches of mistletoe."

Christmas newsletters are *very* big in my family, in case you couldn't tell. Everybody—uncles, grandparents, second cousins, my sister Sueann—sends the Xeroxed monstrosities to family, coworkers, old friends from high school, and people they met on their cruise to the Caribbean (which they wrote about at length in their newsletter the year before). Even my Aunt Irene, who writes a handwritten letter on every one of her Christmas cards, sticks a newsletter in with it.

My second cousin Lucille's are the worst, although there are a lot of contenders. Last year hers started:

"Another year has hurried past
And, here I am, asking, 'Where did the time go so fast?'
A trip in February, a bladder operation in July,
Too many activities, not enough time, no matter how hard I try."

At least Allison doesn't put Dakota and Cheyenne's accomplishments into verse.

"I don't think I'm going to send a Christmas newsletter this year," I said.

Allison stopped, cheese-filled knife in hand. "Why not?"

"Because I don't have any news. I don't have a new job, I didn't go on a vacation to the Bahamas, I didn't win any awards. I don't have anything to tell."

"Don't be ridiculous," my mother said, sweeping in carrying a foil-covered casserole dish. "Of course you do, Nan. What about that skydiving class you took?"

"That was last year, Mom," I said. And I had only taken it so I'd have something to write about in my Christmas newsletter.

"Well, then, tell about your social life. Have you met anybody lately at work?"

Mom asks me this every Thanksgiving. Also Christmas, the Fourth of July, and every time I see her.

"There's nobody to meet," I said, grinding cranberries. "Nobody new ever gets hired, because nobody ever quits. Everybody who works there's been there for years. Nobody even gets fired. Bob Hunziger hasn't been to work on time in eight years, and *he's* still there."

"What about . . . what was his name?" Allison said, arranging the celery sticks in a cut-glass dish. "The guy you liked who had just gotten divorced?"

"Gary," I said. "He's still hung up on his ex-wife."

"I thought you said she was a real shrew."

"She is," I said. "Marcie the Menace. She calls him twice a week complaining about how unfair the divorce settlement is, even though she got virtually everything. Last week it was the house. She claimed she'd been too upset by the divorce to get the mortgage refinanced and he owed her twenty thousand dollars because now interest rates have gone up. But it doesn't matter. Gary still keeps hoping they'll get back together. He almost didn't fly to Connecticut to his parents' for Thanksgiving because he thought she might change her mind about a reconciliation."

"You could write about Sueann's new boyfriend," Mom said, sticking marshmallows on the sweet potatoes. "She's bringing him today."

This was as usual, too. Sueann always brings a new boyfriend to Thanksgiving dinner. Last year it was a biker. And no, I don't mean one of those nice guys who wear a beard and black Harley T-shirt on weekends and work as accountants between trips to Sturgis. I mean a Hell's Angel.

My sister Sueann has the worst taste in men of anyone I have ever known. Before the biker, she dated a member of a militia group and, after the ATF arrested him, a bigamist wanted in three states.

"If this boyfriend spits on the floor, I'm leaving," Allison said, counting out silverware. "Have you met him?" she asked Mom.

"No," Mom said, "but Sueann says he used to work where you do, Nan. So *somebody* must quit once in a while."

I racked my brain, trying to think of any criminal types who'd worked in my company. "What's his name?"

"David something," Mom said, and Cheyenne and Dakota raced into the kitchen, screaming, "Aunt Sueann's here, Aunt Sueann's here! Can we eat now?"

Allison leaned over the sink and pulled the curtains back to look out the window.

"What does he look like?" I asked, sprinkling sugar on the cranberry relish.

"Clean-cut," she said, sounding surprised. "Short blond hair, slacks, white shirt, tie."

Oh, no, that meant he was a neo-Nazi. Or married and planning to get a divorce as soon as the kids graduated from college—which would turn out to be in twenty-three years, since he'd just gotten his wife pregnant again.

"Is he handsome?" I asked, sticking a spoon into the cranberry relish.

"No," Allison said, even more surprised. "He's actually kind of ordinary-looking."

I came over to the window to look. He was helping Sueann out of the car. She was dressed up, too, in a dress and a denim slouch hat. "Good heavens," I said. "It's David Carrington. He worked up on fifth in Computing."

"Was he a womanizer?" Allison asked.

"No," I said, bewildered. "He's a very nice guy. He's unmarried, he doesn't drink, and he left to go get a degree in medicine."

"Why didn't *you* ever meet him?" Mom said.

David shook hands with Mitch, regaled Cheyenne and Dakota with a knock-knock joke, and told Mom his favorite kind of sweet potatoes were the ones with the marshmallows on top.

"He must be a serial killer," I whispered to Allison.

"Come on, everybody, let's sit down," Mom said. "Cheyenne and Dakota, you sit here by Grandma. David, you sit here, next to Sueann. Sueann, take off your hat. You know hats aren't allowed at the table."

"Hats for *men* aren't allowed at the table," Sueann said, patting her denim hat. "Women's hats are." She sat down. "Hats are coming back in style, did you know that? *Cosmopolitan*'s latest issue said this is the Year of the Hat."

"I don't care what it is," Mom said. "Your father would never have allowed hats at the table."

"I'll take it off if you'll turn off the TV," Sueann said, complacently opening out her napkin.

They had reached an impasse. Mom always has the TV on during meals. "I like to have it on in case something happens," she said stubbornly.

"Like what?" Mitch said. "Aliens landing from outer space?"

"For your information, there was a UFO sighting two weeks ago. It was on CNN."

"Everything looks delicious," David said. "Is that homemade cranberry relish? I *love* that. My grandmother used to make it."

He had to be a serial killer.

For half an hour, we concentrated on turkey, stuffing, mashed potatoes, green-bean casserole, scalloped corn casserole, marsh-mallow-topped sweet potatoes, cranberry relish, pumpkin pie, and the news on CNN.

"Can't you at least turn it down, Mom?" Mitch said. "We can't even hear to talk."

"I want to see the weather in Washington," Mom said. "For your flight."

"You're leaving tonight?" Sueann said. "But you just got here. I haven't even seen Cheyenne and Dakota."

"Mitch has to fly back tonight," Allison said. "But the girls and I are staying till Wednesday."

"I don't see why you can't stay at least until tomorrow," Mom said.

"Don't tell me this is homemade whipped cream on the pump-kin pie," David said. "I haven't had homemade whipped cream in years."

"You used to work in computers, didn't you?" I asked him. "There's a lot of computer crime around these days, isn't there?"

"Computers!" Allison said. "I forgot all the awards Cheyenne won at computer camp." She turned to Mitch. "The newsletter's going to have to be at least two pages. The girls just have too many awards—T-ball, tadpole swimming, Bible-school attendance."

"Do you send Christmas newsletters in your family?" my mother asked David.

He nodded. "I love hearing from everybody."

"You see?" Mom said to me. "People *like* getting newsletters at Christmas."

"I don't have anything against Christmas newsletters," I said. "I just don't think they should be deadly dull. Mary had a root canal, Bootsy seems to be getting over her ringworm, we got new gutters on the house. Why doesn't anyone ever write about anything *interesting* in their newsletters?"

"Like what?" Sueann said.

"I don't know. An alligator biting their arm off. A meteor falling on their house. A murder. Something interesting to read."

"Probably because they didn't happen," Sueann said.

"Then they should make something up," I said, "so we don't have to hear about their trip to Nebraska and their gallbladder operation."

"You'd do that?" Allison said, appalled. "You'd make something up?"

"People make things up in their newsletters all the time, and you know it," I said. "Look at the way Aunt Laura and Uncle Phil brag about their vacations and their stock options and their cars. If you're going to lie, they might as well be lies that are interesting for other people to read."

"You have plenty of things to tell without making up lies, Nan," Mom said reprovingly. "Maybe you should do something like your cousin Celia. She writes her newsletter all year long, day by day," she explained to David. "Nan, you might have more news than you think if you kept track of it day by day like Celia. She always has a lot to tell."

Yes, indeed. Her newsletters were nearly as long as Aunt Lydia's. They read like a diary, except she wasn't in junior high, where at least there were pop quizzes and zits and your locker combination to give it a little zing. Celia's newsletters had no zing whatsoever:

"Wed. Jan. 1. Froze to death going out to get the paper. Snow got in the plastic bag thing the paper comes in. Editorial section all wet. Had to dry it out on the radiator. Bran flakes for breakfast. Watched *Good Morning America.*

"Thurs. Jan. 2. Cleaned closets. Cold and cloudy."

"If you'd write a little every day," Mom said, "you'd be surprised at how much you'd have to tell by Christmas."

Sure. With my life, I wouldn't even have to write it every day. I could do Monday's right now. "Mon. Nov. 28. Froze to death on the way to work. Bob Hunziger not in yet. Penny putting up Christmas decorations. Solveig told me she's sure the baby is going to be a boy. Asked me which name I liked, Albuquerque or Dallas. Said hi to Gary, but he was too depressed to talk to me. Thanksgiving reminds him of ex-wife's giblets. Cold and cloudy."

I was wrong. It was snowing, and Solveig's ultrasound had showed the baby was a girl. "What do you think of Trinidad as a name?" she asked me. Penny wasn't putting up Christmas decorations either. She was passing out slips of paper with our Secret Santas' names on them. "The decorations aren't here yet," she said excitedly. "I'm getting something special from a farmer upstate."

"Does it involve feathers?" I asked her. Last year the decorations had been angels with thousands of chicken feathers glued onto cardboard for their wings. We were still picking them out of our computers.

"No," she said happily. "It's a surprise. I love Christmas, don't you?"

"Is Hunziger in?" I asked her, brushing snow out of my hair. Hats always mash my hair down, so I hadn't worn one.

"Are you kidding?" she said. She handed me a Secret Santa slip. "It's the Monday after Thanksgiving. He probably won't be in till sometime Wednesday."

Gary came in, his ears bright red from the cold and a harried expression on his face. His ex-wife must not have wanted a reconciliation.

"Hi, Gary," I said, and turned to hang up my coat without waiting for him to answer.

And he didn't, but when I turned back around, he was still standing there, staring at me. I put a hand up to my hair, wishing I'd worn a hat.

"Can I talk to you a minute?" he said, looking anxiously at Penny.

"Sure," I said, trying not to get my hopes up. He probably wanted to ask me something about the Secret Santas.

He leaned farther over my desk. "Did anything unusual happen to you over Thanksgiving?"

"My sister didn't bring home a biker to Thanksgiving dinner," I said.

He waved that away dismissively. "No, I mean anything odd, peculiar, out of the ordinary."

"That *is* out of the ordinary."

He leaned even closer. "I flew out to my parents' for Thanksgiving, and on the flight home—you know how people always carry on luggage that won't fit in the overhead compartments and then try to cram it in?"

"Yes," I said, thinking of a bridesmaid's bouquet I had made the mistake of putting in the overhead compartment one time.

"Well, nobody did that on my flight. They didn't carry on hanging bags or enormous shopping bags full of Christmas presents. Some people didn't even have a carry-on. And that isn't all. Our flight was half an hour late, and the flight attendant said, 'Those of you who do not have connecting flights, please remain seated until those with connections have deplaned.' And they did." He looked at me expectantly.

"Maybe everybody was just in the Christmas spirit."

He shook his head. "All four babies on the flight slept the whole way, and the toddler behind me didn't kick the seat."

That *was* unusual.

"Not only that, the guy next to me was reading *The Way of All Flesh* by Samuel Butler. When's the last time you saw anybody on an airplane reading anything but John Grisham or Danielle Steele? I tell you, there's something funny going on."

"What?" I asked curiously.

"I don't know," he said. "You're sure you haven't noticed anything?"

"Nothing except for my sister. She always dates these losers, but the guy she brought to Thanksgiving was really nice. He even helped with the dishes."

"You didn't notice anything else?"

"No," I said, wishing I had. This was the longest he'd ever talked to me about anything besides his ex-wife. "Maybe it's something in the air at DIA. I have to take my sister-in-law and her little girls to the airport Wednesday. I'll keep an eye out."

He nodded. "Don't say anything about this, okay?" he said, and hurried off to Accounting.

"What was that all about?" Penny asked, coming over.

"His ex-wife," I said. "When do we have to exchange Secret Santa gifts?"

"Every Friday, and Christmas Eve."

I opened up my slip. Good, I'd gotten Hunziger. With luck I wouldn't have to buy any Secret Santa gifts at all.

Tuesday I got Aunt Laura and Uncle Phil's Christmas newsletter. It was in gold ink on cream-colored paper, with large gold bells in the corners. "Joyeux Noël," it began. "That's French for Merry Christmas. We're sending our newsletter out early this year because we're spending Christmas in Cannes to celebrate Phil's promotion to assistant CEO and my wonderful new career! Yes, I'm starting my own business—Laura's Floral Creations—and orders are pouring in! It's already been written up in *House Beautiful*, and you will *never* guess who called last week—Martha Stewart!" Et cetera.

I didn't see Gary. Or anything unusual, although the waiter who took my lunch order actually got it right for a change. But he got Tonya's (who works up on third) wrong.

"I *told* him tomato and lettuce only," she said, picking pickles off her sandwich. "I heard Gary talked to you yesterday. Did he ask you out?"

"What's that?" I said, pointing to the folder Tonya'd brought with her to change the subject. "The Harbrace file?"

"No," she said. "Do you want my pickles? It's our Christmas schedule. *Never* marry anybody who has kids from a previous marriage. Especially when *you* have kids from a previous marriage. Tom's ex-wife, Janine, my ex-husband, John, and four sets of grandparents all want the kids, and they all want them on Christmas morning. It's like trying to schedule the D-Day invasion."

"At least your husband isn't still hung up on his ex-wife," I said glumly.

"So Gary didn't ask you out, huh?" She bit into her sandwich, frowned, and extracted another pickle. "I'm sure he will. Okay, if we take the kids to Tom's parents at four on Christmas Eve, Janine could pick them up at eight. . . . No, that won't work." She switched her sandwich to her other hand and began erasing. "Janine's not speaking to Tom's parents."

She sighed. "At least John's being reasonable. He called yesterday and said he'd be willing to wait till New Year's to have the kids. I don't know what got into him."

When I got back to work, there was a folded copy of the morning newspaper on my desk.

I opened it up. The headline read "City Hall Christmas Display to Be Turned On," which wasn't unusual. And neither was tomorrow's headline, which would be "City Hall Christmas Display Protested."

Either the Freedom Against Faith people protest the Nativity scene or the fundamentalists protest the elves or the environmental people protest cutting down Christmas trees or all of them protest the whole thing. It happens every year.

I turned to the inside pages. Several articles were circled in red, and there was a note next to them which read "See what I mean? Gary."

I looked at the circled articles. "Christmas Shoplifting Down," the first one read. "Mall stores report incidences of shoplifting are down for the first week of the Christmas season. Usually prevalent this time of—"

"What are you doing?" Penny said, looking over my shoulder.

I shut the paper with a rustle. "Nothing," I said. I folded it back up and stuck it into a drawer. "Did you need something?"

"Here," she said, handing me a slip of paper.

"I already got my Secret Santa name," I said.

"This is for Holiday Goodies," she said. "Everybody takes turns bringing in coffee cake or tarts or cake."

I opened up my slip. It read "Friday Dec. 20. Four dozen cookies."

"I saw you and Gary talking yesterday," Penny said. "What about?"

"His ex-wife," I said. "What kind of cookies do you want me to bring?"

"Chocolate chip," she said. "Everybody loves chocolate."

As soon as she was gone, I got the newspaper out again and took it into Hunziger's office to read. "Legislature Passes Balanced Budget," the other articles read. "Escaped Convict Turns Self In," "Christmas Food Bank Donations Up."

I read through them and then threw the paper into the wastebasket. Halfway out the door I thought better of it and took it out, folded it up, and took it back to my desk with me.

While I was putting it into my purse, Hunziger wandered in.

"If anybody asks where I am, tell them I'm in the men's room," he said, and wandered out again.

Wednesday afternoon I took the girls and Allison to the airport. She was still fretting over her newsletter.

"Do you think a greeting is absolutely necessary?" she said in the baggage check-in line. "You know, like 'Dear Friends and Family'?"

"Probably not," I said absently. I was watching the people in line ahead of us, trying to spot this unusual behavior Gary had talked about, but so far I hadn't seen any. People were looking at their watches and complaining about the length of the line, the ticket agents were calling, "Next. Next!" to the person at the head of the line, who, after having stood impatiently in line for forty-five minutes waiting for this moment, was now staring blankly into space, and an unattended toddler was methodically pulling the elastic strings off a stack of luggage tags.

"They'll still know it's a Christmas newsletter, won't they?" Allison said. "Even without a greeting at the beginning of it?"

With a border of angels holding bunches of mistletoe, what else could it be? I thought.

"Next!" the ticket agent shouted.

The man in front of us had forgotten his photo ID, the girl in front of us in line for the security check was wearing heavy metal, and on the train out to the concourse a woman stepped on my foot and then glared at me as if it were my fault. Apparently all the nice people had traveled the day Gary came home.

And that was probably what it was—some kind of statistical clump where all the considerate, intelligent people had ended up on the same flight.

I knew they existed. My sister Sueann had had an insurance actuary for a boyfriend once (he was also an embezzler, which is why Sueann was dating him) and he had said events weren't evenly distributed, that there were peaks and valleys. Gary must just have hit a peak.

Which was too bad, I thought, lugging Cheyenne, who had demanded to be carried the minute we got off the train, down the concourse. Because the only reason he had approached me was because he thought there was something strange going on.

"Here's Gate 55," Allison said, setting Dakota down and getting out French-language tapes for the girls. "If I left off the 'Dear Friends and Family,' I'd have room to include Dakota's violin recital. She played 'The Gypsy Dance.'"

She settled the girls in adjoining chairs and put on their headphones. "But Mitch says it's a letter, so it has to have a greeting."

"What if you used something short?" I said. "Like 'Greetings' or something. Then you'd have room to start the letter on the same line."

"Not 'Greetings.'" She made a face. "Uncle Frank started his letter that way last year, and it scared me half to death. I thought Mitch had been *drafted*."

I had been alarmed when I'd gotten mine, too, but at least it had given me a temporary rush of adrenaline, which was more than Uncle Frank's letters usually did, concerned as they were with prostate problems and disputes over property taxes.

"I suppose I could use 'Holiday Greetings,'" Allison said. "Or 'Christmas Greetings,' but that's almost as long as 'Dear Friends and Family.' If only there were something shorter."

"How about 'hi'?"

"That might work." She got out paper and a pen and started writing. "How do you spell 'outstanding'?"

"O-u-t-s-t-a-n-d-i-n-g," I said absently. I was watching the moving sidewalks in the middle of the concourse. People were standing on the right, like they were supposed to, and walking on the left. No people were standing four abreast or blocking the entire sidewalk with their luggage. No kids were running in the opposite direction of the sidewalk's movement, screaming and running their hands along the rubber railing.

"How do you spell 'fabulous'?" Allison asked.

"Flight 2216 to Spokane is now ready for boarding," the flight attendant at the desk said. "Those passengers traveling with small children or those who require additional time for boarding may now board."

A single old lady with a walker stood up and got in line. Allison unhooked the girls' headphones, and we began the ritual of hugging and gathering up belongings.

"We'll see you at Christmas," she said.

"Good luck with your newsletter," I said, handing Dakota her teddy bear, "and don't worry about the heading. It doesn't need one."

They started down the passageway. I stood there, waving, till they were out of sight, and then turned to go.

"We are now ready for regular boarding of rows 25 through 33," the flight attendant said, and everybody in the gate area stood up. Nothing unusual here, I thought, and started for the concourse.

"What rows did she call?" a woman in a red beret asked a teenaged boy.

"25 through 33," he said.

"Oh, I'm Row 14," the woman said, and sat back down.

So did I.

"We are now ready to board rows 15 through 24," the flight attendant said, and a dozen people looked carefully at their tickets and then stepped back from the door, patiently waiting their turn. One of them pulled a paperback out of her tote bag and began to read. It was *Kidnapped* by Robert Louis Stevenson. Only when the flight attendant said, "We are now boarding all rows," did the rest of them stand up and get in line.

Which didn't prove anything, and neither did the standing on the right of the moving sidewalk. Maybe people were just being nice because it was Christmas.

Don't be ridiculous, I told myself. People aren't nicer at Christmas. They're ruder and pushier and crabbier than ever. You've seen them at the mall, and in line for the post office. They act worse at Christmas than any other time.

"This is your final boarding call for Flight 2216 to Spokane," the flight attendant said to the empty waiting area. She called to me, "Are you flying to Spokane, ma'am?"

"No." I stood up. "I was seeing friends off."

"I just wanted to make sure you didn't miss your flight," she said, and turned to shut the door.

I started for the moving sidewalk, and nearly collided with a young man running for the gate. He raced up to the desk and flung his ticket down.

"I'm sorry, sir," the flight attendant said, leaning slightly away from the young man as if expecting an explosion. "Your flight has already left. I'm really terribly sor—"

"Oh, it's okay," he said. "It serves me right. I didn't allow enough time for parking and everything, that's all. I should have started for the airport earlier."

The flight attendant was tapping busily on the computer. "I'm afraid the only other open flight to Spokane for today isn't until 11:05 this evening."

"Oh, well," he said, smiling. "It'll give me a chance to catch up on my reading." He reached down into his attaché case and pulled out a paperback. It was W. Somerset Maugham's *Of Human Bondage*.

"Well?" Gary said as soon as I got back to work Thursday morning. He was standing by my desk, waiting for me.

"There's definitely something going on," I said, and told him about the moving sidewalks and the guy who'd missed his plane. "But what?"

"Is there somewhere we can talk?" he said, looking anxiously around.

"Hunziger's office," I said, "but I don't know if he's in yet."

"He's not," he said, led me into the office, and shut the door behind him.

"Sit down," he said, indicating Hunziger's chair. "Now, I know this is going to sound crazy, but I think all these people have been possessed by some kind of alien intelligence. Have you ever seen *Invasion of the Body Snatchers*?"

"What?" I said.

"*Invasion of the Body Snatchers,*" he said. "It's about these parasites from outer space who take over people's bodies and—"

"I *know* what it's about," I said, "and it's *science fiction*. You think the man who missed his plane was some kind of pod-person? You're right," I said, reaching for the doorknob. "I do think you're crazy."

"That's what Donald Sutherland said in *Leechmen from Mars*. Nobody ever believes it's happening, until it's too late."

He pulled a folded newspaper out of his back pocket. "Look at this," he said, waving it in front of me. "Holiday credit-card fraud down twenty percent. Holiday suicides down thirty percent. Charitable giving up *sixty* percent."

"They're coincidences." I explained about the statistical peaks and valleys. "Look," I said, taking the paper from him and turning to the front page. "People Against Cruelty to Our Furry Friends Protests City Hall Christmas Display. Animal Rights Group Objects to Exploitation of Reindeer."

"What about your sister?" he said. "You said she only dates losers. Why would she suddenly start dating a nice guy? Why would an escaped convict suddenly turn himself in? Why would people suddenly start reading the classics? Because they've been taken over."

"By aliens from outer space?" I said incredulously.

"Did he have a hat?"

"Who?" I said, wondering if he really was crazy. Could his being hung up on his horrible ex-wife have finally made him crack?

"The man who missed his plane," he said. "Was he wearing a hat?"

"I don't remember," I said, and felt suddenly cold. Sueann had worn a hat to Thanksgiving dinner. She'd refused to take it off at the table. And the woman whose ticket said Row 14 had been wearing a beret.

"What do hats have to do with it?" I asked.

"The man on the plane next to me was wearing a hat. So were most of the other people on the flight. Did you ever see *The Puppet Masters*? The parasites attached themselves to the spinal cord and took over the nervous system," he said. "This morning here at work I counted nineteen people wearing hats. Les Sawtelle, Rodney Jones, Jim Bridgeman—"

"Jim Bridgeman always wears a hat," I said. "It's to hide his bald spot. Besides, he's a computer programmer. All the computer people wear baseball caps."

"DeeDee Crawford," he said. "Vera McDermott, Janet Hall—"

"Women's hats are supposed to be making a comeback," I said.

"George Frazelli, the entire Documentation section—"

"I'm sure there's a logical explanation," I said. "It's been freezing in here all week. There's probably something wrong with the heating system."

"The thermostat's turned down to fifty," he said, "which is something else peculiar. The thermostat's been turned down on all floors."

"Well, that's probably Management. You know how they're always trying to cut costs—"

"They're giving us a Christmas bonus. And they fired Hunziger."

"They fired Hunziger?" I said. Management never fires anybody.

"This morning. That's how I knew he wouldn't be in his office."

"They actually fired Hunziger?"

"And one of the janitors. The one who drank. How do you explain that?"

"I–I don't know," I stammered. "But there has to be some other explanation than aliens. Maybe they took a management course or got the Christmas spirit or their therapists told them to do good deeds or something. Something besides leechmen. Aliens coming from outer space and taking over our brains is impossible!"

"That's what Dana Wynter said in *Invasion of the Body Snatchers*. But it's not impossible. It's happening right here, and we've got to stop it before they take over everybody and we're the only ones left. They—"

There was a knock on the door. "Sorry to bother you, Gary," Carol Zaliski said, leaning in the door, "but you've got an urgent phone call. It's your ex-wife."

"Coming," he said, looking at me. "Think about what I said, okay?" He went out.

I stood looking after him and frowning.

"What was that all about?" Carol said, coming into the office. She was wearing a white fur hat.

"He wanted to know what to buy his Secret Santa person," I said.

Friday Gary wasn't there. "He had to go talk to his ex-wife this morning," Tonya told me at lunch, picking pickles off her sandwich. "He'll be back this afternoon. Marcie's demanding he pay for her therapy. She's seeing this psychiatrist, and she claims Gary's the one who made her crazy, so he should pick up the bill for her Prozac. *Why* is he still hung up on her?"

"I don't know," I said, scraping mustard off my burger.

"Carol Zaliski said the two of you were talking in Hunziger's office yesterday. What about? Did he ask you out? Nan?"

"Tonya, has Gary talked to you since Thanksgiving? Did he ask you about whether you'd noticed anything unusual happening?"

"He asked me if I'd noticed anything bizarre or abnormal about my family. I told him, in my family bizarre *is* normal. You won't believe what's happened now. Tom's parents are getting a divorce, which means five sets of parents. Why couldn't they have waited till after Christmas to do this? It's throwing my whole schedule off."

She bit into her sandwich. "I'm sure Gary's going to ask you out. He's probably just working up to it."

If he was, he had the strangest line I'd ever heard. Aliens from outer space. Hiding under hats!

Though, now that he'd mentioned it, there were an awful lot of people wearing hats. Nearly all the men in Data Analysis had baseball caps on, Jerrilyn Wells was wearing a wool stocking cap, and Ms. Jacobson's secretary looked like she was dressed for a wedding in a white thing with a veil. But Sueann had said this was the Year of the Hat.

Sueann, who dated only gigolos and Mafia dons. But she had been bound to hit a nice boyfriend sooner or later, she dated so many guys.

And there weren't any signs of alien possession when I tried to get somebody in the steno pool to make some copies for me. "We're *busy*," Paula Grandy snapped. "It's Christmas, you know!"

I went back to my desk, feeling better. There was an enormous dish made of pine cones on it, filled with candy canes and red and green foil-wrapped chocolate kisses. "Is this part of the Christmas decorations?" I asked Penny.

"No. They aren't ready yet," she said. "This is just a little something to brighten the holidays. I made one for everyone's desk."

I felt even better. I pushed the dish over to one side and started through my mail. There was a green envelope from Allison and Mitch. She must have mailed her newsletters as soon as she got off the plane. I wonder if she decided to forgo the heading or Dakota's Most Improved Practicing Piano Award, I thought, slicing it open with the letter opener.

"Dear Nan," it began, several spaces down from the angels-and-mistletoe border. "Nothing much new this year. We're all okay, though Mitch is worried about downsizing, and I always seem to be running from behind. The girls are growing like weeds and doing okay in school, though Cheyenne's been having some problems with her reading and Dakota's still wetting the bed. Mitch and I decided we've been pushing them too hard, and we're working on trying not to overschedule them for activities and just letting them be normal, average little girls."

I jammed the letter back into the envelope and ran up to fourth to look for Gary.

"All right," I said when I found him. "I believe you. What do we do now?"

We rented movies. Actually, we rented only some of the movies. *Attack of the Soul-Killers* and *Invasion from Betelgeuse* were both checked out.

"Which means somebody else has figured it out, too," Gary said. "If only we knew who."

"We could ask the clerk," I suggested.

He shook his head violently. "We can't do anything to make them suspicious. For all we know, they may have taken them off the shelves themselves, in which case we're on the right track. What else shall we rent?"

"What?" I said blankly.

"So it won't look like we're just renting alien invasion movies."

"Oh," I said, and picked up *Ordinary People* and a black-and-white version of *A Christmas Carol*.

It didn't work. *"The Puppet Masters,"* the kid at the rental desk, wearing a blue-and-yellow Blockbuster hat, said inquiringly. "Is that a good movie?"

"I haven't seen it," Gary said nervously.

"We're renting it because it has Donald Sutherland in it," I said. "We're having a Donald Sutherland film festival. *The Puppet Masters*, *Ordinary People*, *Invasion of the Body Snatchers*—"

"Is Donald Sutherland in this?" he asked, holding up *A Christmas Carol*."

"He plays Tiny Tim," I said. "It was his first screen appearance."

"You were great in there," Gary said, leading me down to the other end of the mall to Suncoast to buy *Attack of the Soul Killers*. "You're a very good liar."

"Thanks," I said, pulling my coat closer and looking around the mall. It was freezing in here, and there were hats everywhere, on people and in window displays, Panamas and porkpies and picture hats.

"We're surrounded. Look at that," he said, nodding in the direction of Santa Claus's North Pole.

"Santa Claus has always worn a hat," I said.

"I meant the line," he said.

He was right. The kids in line were waiting patiently, cheerfully. Not a single one was screaming or announcing she had to go to the bathroom. "I want a Masters of Earth," a little boy in a felt beanie was saying eagerly to his mother.

"Well, we'll ask Santa," the mother said, "but he may not be able to get it for you. All the stores are sold out."

"Okay," he said. "Then I want a wagon."

Suncoast was sold out of *Attack of the Soul Killers*, but we bought *Invasion from Betelgeuse* and *Infiltrators from Space* and went back to his apartment to screen them.

"Well?" Gary said after we'd watched three of them. "Did you notice how they start slowly and then spread through the population?"

Actually, what I'd noticed was how dumb all the people in these movies were. "The brain-suckers attack when we're asleep," the hero would say, and promptly lie down for a nap. Or the hero's girlfriend would say, "They're on to us. We've got to get out of here. Right now," and then go back to her apartment to pack.

And, just like in every horror movie, they were always splitting up instead of sticking together. And going down dark alleys. They deserved to be turned into pod-people.

"Our first order of business is to pool what we know about the aliens," Gary said. "It's obvious the purpose of the hats is to conceal the parasites' presence from those who haven't been taken over yet," he said, "and that they're attached to the brain."

"Or the spinal column," I said, "like in *The Puppet Masters*."

He shook his head. "If that were the case, they could attach themselves to the neck or the back, which would be much less conspicuous. Why would they take the risk of hiding under hats, which are so noticeable, if they aren't attached to the top of the head?"

"Maybe the hats serve some other purpose."

The phone rang.

"Yes?" Gary answered it. His face lit up and then fell.

His ex-wife, I thought, and started watching *Infiltrators from Space*.

"You've got to believe me," the hero's girlfriend said to the psychiatrist. "There are aliens here among us. They look just like you or me. You have to believe me."

"I do believe you," the psychiatrist said, and raised his finger to point at her. "Ahhhggghhh!" he screeched, his eyes glowing bright green.

"Marcie," Gary said. There was a long pause. "A friend." Longer pause. "No."

The hero's girlfriend ran down a dark alley, wearing high heels. Halfway through, she twisted her ankle and fell.

"You know that isn't true," Gary said.

I fast-forwarded. The hero was in his apartment, on the phone. "Hello, Police Department?" he said. "You have to help me. We've been invaded by aliens who take over your body!"

"We'll be right there, Mr. Daly," the voice on the phone said. "Stay there."

"How do you know my name?" the hero shouted. "I didn't tell you my address."

"We're on our way," the voice said.

"We'll talk about it tomorrow," Gary said, and hung up.

"Sorry," he said, coming over to the couch. "Okay, I downloaded a bunch of stuff about parasites and aliens from the Internet," he said, handing me a sheaf of stapled papers. "We need to discover what it is they're doing to the people they take over, what their weaknesses are, and how we can fight them. We need to know when and where it started," Gary went on, "how and where it's spreading, and what it's doing to people. We need to find out as much as we can about the nature of the aliens so we can figure out a way to eliminate them. How do they communicate with each other? Are they telepathic, like in *Village of the Damned*, or do they use some other form of communication?

If they're telepathic, can they read our minds as well as each other's?"

"If they could, wouldn't they know we're on to them?" I said.

The phone rang again.

"It's probably my ex-wife again," he said.

I picked up the remote and flicked on *Infiltrators from Space* again.

Gary answered the phone. "Yes?" he said, and then warily, "How did you get my number?"

The hero slammed down the phone and ran to the window. Dozens of police cars were pulling up, lights flashing.

"Sure," Gary said. He grinned. "No, I won't forget."

He hung up. "That was Penny. She forgot to give me my Holiday Goodies slip. I'm supposed to take in four dozen sugar cookies next Monday." He shook his head wonderingly. "Now, *there's* somebody I'd like to see taken over by the aliens."

He sat down on the couch and started making a list. "Okay, methods of fighting them. Diseases. Poison. Dynamite. Nuclear weapons. What else?"

I didn't answer. I was thinking about what he'd said about wishing Penny would be taken over.

"The problem with all of those solutions is that they kill the people, too," Gary said. What we need is something like the virus they used in *Invasion*. Or the ultrasonic pulses only the aliens could hear in *War with the Slugmen*. If we're going to stop them, we've got to find something that kills the parasite but not the host."

"Do we have to stop them?"

"What?" he said. "Of course we have to stop them. What do you mean?"

"All the aliens in these movies turn people into zombies or monsters," I said. "They shuffle around, attacking people and killing them and trying to take over the world. Nobody's done anything like that. People are standing on the right and walking on the left, the suicide rate's down, my sister's dating a very nice guy. Everybody who's been taken over is nicer, happier, more polite. Maybe the parasites are a good influence, and we shouldn't interfere."

"And maybe that's what they want us to think. What if they're acting nice to trick us, to keep us from trying to stop them? Remember *Attack of the Soul Killers*? What if it's all an act, and they're only acting nice till the takeover's complete?"

If it was an act, it was a great one. Over the next few days, Solveig, in a red straw hat, announced she was naming her baby Jane, Jim Bridgeman nodded at me in the elevator, my cousin Celia's newsletter/diary was short and funny, and the waiter, sporting a soda-jerk's hat, got both Tonya's and my orders right.

"No pickles!" Tonya said delightedly, picking up her sandwich. "Ow! Can you get carpal tunnel syndrome from wrapping Christmas presents? My hand's been hurting all morning."

She opened her file folder. There was a new diagram inside, a rectangle with names written all around the sides.

"Is that your Christmas schedule?" I asked.

"No," she said, showing it to me. "It's a seating arrangement for Christmas dinner. It was crazy, running the kids from house to house like that, so we decided to just have everybody at our house."

I took a startled look at her, but she was still hatless.

"I thought Tom's ex-wife couldn't stand his parents."

"Everybody's agreed we all need to get along for the kids' sake. After all, it's Christmas."

I was still staring at her.

She put her hand up to her hair. "Do you like it? It's a wig. Eric got it for me for Christmas. For being such a great mother to the boys through the divorce. I couldn't believe it." She patted her hair. "Isn't it great?"

"They're hiding their aliens under wigs," I told Gary.

"I know," he said. "Paul Gunden got a new toupee. We can't trust anyone." He handed me a folder full of clippings.

Employment rates were up. Thefts of packages from cars, usually prevalent at this time of year, were down. A woman in Minnesota had brought back a library book that was twenty-two years overdue. "Groups Praise City Hall Christmas Display," one of the clippings read, and the accompanying picture showed the People for a Non-Commercial Christmas, the Holy Spirit Southern Baptists, and the Equal Rights for Ethnics activists holding hands and singing Christmas carols around the crèche.

On the ninth, Mom called. "Have you written your newsletter yet?"

"I've been busy," I said, and waited for her to ask me if I'd met anyone lately at work.

"I got Jackie Peterson's newsletter this morning," she said.

"So did I." The invasion apparently hadn't reached Miami. Jackie's newsletter, which is usually terminally cute, had reached new heights:

> "M is for our trip to Mexico
> E is for Every place else we'd like to go
> R is for the RV that takes us there. . . ."

And straight through MERRY CHRISTMAS, A HAPPY NEW YEAR, and both her first and last names.

"I do wish she wouldn't try to put her letters in verse," Mom said. "They never scan."

"Mom," I said. "Are you okay?"

"I'm fine," she said. "My arthritis has been kicking up the last couple of days, but otherwise I've never felt better. I've been thinking, there's no reason for you to send out newsletters if you don't want to."

"Mom," I said, "did Sueann give you a hat for Christmas?"

"Oh, she told you," Mom said. "You know, I don't usually like hats, but I'm going to need one for the wedding, and—"

"Wedding?"

"Oh, didn't she tell you? She and David are getting married right after Christmas. I am so relieved. I thought she was never going to meet anyone decent."

I reported that to Gary. "I know," he said glumly. "I just got a raise."

"I haven't found a single bad effect," I said. "No signs of violence or antisocial behavior. Not even any irritability."

"*There* you are," Penny said crabbily, coming up with a huge poinsettia under each arm. "Can you help me put these on everybody's desks?"

"Are these the Christmas decorations?" I asked.

"No, I'm still waiting on that farmer," she said, handing me one of the poinsettias. "This is just a little something to brighten up everyone's desk." She reached down to move the pine-cone dish on Gary's desk. "You didn't eat your candy canes," she said.

"I don't like peppermint."

"Nobody ate their candy canes," she said disgustedly. "They all ate the chocolate kisses and left the candy canes."

"People like chocolate," Gary said, and whispered to me, "*When* is she going to be taken over?"

"Meet me in Hunziger's office right away," I whispered back, and said to Penny, "Where does this poinsettia go?"

"Jim Bridgeman's desk."

I took the poinsettia up to Computing on fifth. Jim was wearing his baseball cap backward. "A little something to brighten your desk," I said, handing it to him, and started back toward the stairs.

"Can I talk to you a minute?" he said, following me out into the stairwell.

"Sure," I said, trying to sound calm. "What about?"

He leaned toward me. "Have you noticed anything unusual going on?"

"You mean the poinsettia?" I said. "Penny does tend to go a little overboard for Christmas, but—"

"No," he said, putting his hand awkwardly to his cap, "people who are acting funny, people who aren't themselves?"

"No," I said, smiling. "I haven't noticed a thing."

I waited for Gary in Hunziger's office for nearly half an hour. "Sorry I took so long," he said when he finally got there. "My ex-wife called. What were you saying?"

"I was saying that even you have to admit it would be a good thing if Penny was taken over," I said. "What if the parasites aren't evil? What if they're those—what are those parasites that benefit the host called? You know, like the bacteria that help cows produce milk? Or those birds that pick insects off of rhinoceroses?"

"You mean symbiotes?" Gary said.

"Yes," I said eagerly. "What if this is some kind of symbiotic relationship? What if they're raising everyone's IQ or enhancing their emotional maturity, and it's having a good effect on us?"

"Things that sound too good to be true usually are. No," he said, shaking his head. "They're up to something, I know it. And we've got to find out what it is."

· · ·

On the tenth when I came to work, Penny was putting up the Christmas decorations. They were, as she had promised, something special: wide swags of red velvet ribbons running all around the walls, with red velvet bows and large bunches of mistletoe every few feet. In between were gold-calligraphic scrolls reading "And kiss me 'neath the mistletoe, For Christmas comes but once a year."

"What do you think?" Penny said, climbing down from her stepladder. "Every floor has a different quotation." She reached into a large cardboard box. "Accounting's is 'Sweetest the kiss that's stolen under the mistletoe.' "

I came over and looked into the box. "Where did you get all the mistletoe?" I asked.

"This apple farmer I know," she said, moving the ladder.

I picked up a big branch of the green leaves and white berries. "It must have cost a fortune." I had bought a sprig of it last year that had cost six dollars.

Penny, climbing the ladder, shook her head. "It didn't cost anything. He was glad to get rid of it." She tied the bunch of mistletoe to the red velvet ribbon. "It's a parasite, you know. It kills the trees."

"Kills the trees?" I said blankly, staring at the white berries.

"Or deforms them," she said. "It steals nutrients from the tree's sap, and the tree gets these swellings and galls and things. The farmer told me all about it."

As soon as I had the chance, I took the material Gary had downloaded on parasites into Hunziger's office and read through it.

Mistletoe caused grotesque swellings wherever its rootlets attached themselves to the tree. Anthracnose caused cracks and then spots of dead bark called cankers. Blight wilted trees' leaves. Witches' broom weakened limbs. Bacteria caused tumor-like growths on the trunk, called galls.

We had been focusing on the mental and psychological effects when we should have been looking at the physical ones. The heightened intelligence, the increase in civility and common sense, must simply be side effects of the parasites' stealing nutrients. And damaging the host.

I stuck the papers back into the file folder, went back to my desk, and called Sueann.

"Sueann, hi," I said. "I'm working on my Christmas newsletter, and I wanted to make sure I spelled David's name right. Is Carrington spelled C-A-R-R or C-E-R-R?"

"C-A-R-R. Oh, Nan, he's so wonderful! So different from the losers I usually date! He's considerate and sensitive and—"

"And how are you?" I said. "Everybody at work's been down with the flu."

"Really?" she said. "No, I'm fine."

What did I do now? I couldn't ask "Are you sure?" without making her suspicious. "C-A-R-R," I said, trying to think of another way to approach the subject.

Sueann saved me the trouble. "You won't believe what he did yesterday. Showed up at work to take me home. He knew my ankles had been hurting, and he brought me a tube of Ben-Gay and a dozen pink roses. He is so thoughtful."

"Your ankles have been hurting?" I said, trying not to sound anxious.

"Like crazy. It's this weather or something. I could hardly walk on them this morning."

I jammed the parasite papers back into the file folder, made sure I hadn't left any on the desk like the hero in *Parasite People from Planet X*, and went up to see Gary.

He was on the phone.

"I've got to talk to you," I whispered.

"I'd like that," he said into the phone, an odd look on his face.

"What is it?" I said. "Have they found out we're on to them?"

"Shh," he said. "You know I do," he said into the phone.

"You don't understand," I said. "I've figured out what it's doing to people."

He held up a finger, motioning me to wait. "Can you hang on a minute?" he said into the phone, and put his hand over the receiver. "I'll meet you in Hunziger's office in five minutes," he said.

"No," I said. "It's not safe. Meet me at the post office."

He nodded, and went back to his conversation, still with that odd look on his face.

I ran back down to second for my purse and went to the post office. I had intended to wait on the corner, but it was crowded with people jockeying to drop money into the Salvation Army Santa Claus's kettle.

I looked down the sidewalk. Where was Gary? I went up the steps and scanned the street. There was no sign of him.

"Merry Christmas!" a man said, half-tipping a fedora and holding the door for me.

"Oh, no, I'm—" I began, and saw Tonya coming down the street. "Thank you," I said, and ducked inside.

It was freezing inside, and the line for the postal clerks wound out into the lobby. I got in it. It would take an hour at least to work my way to the front, which meant I could wait for Gary without looking suspicious.

Except that I was the only one not wearing a hat. Every single person in line had one on, and the clerks behind the counter were wearing mail carriers' caps. And broad smiles.

"Packages going overseas should really have been mailed by November fifteenth," the middle clerk was saying, not at all disgruntledly, to a little Japanese woman in a red cap, "but don't worry, we'll figure out a way to get your presents there on time."

"The line's only about forty-five minutes long," the woman in front of me confided cheerfully. She was wearing a small black hat with a feather and carrying four enormous packages. I wondered if they were full of pods. "Which isn't bad at all, considering it's Christmas."

I nodded, looking toward the door. Where was he?

"Why are you here?" the woman said, smiling.

"What?" I said, whirling back around, my heart pounding.

"What are you here to mail?" she said. "I see you don't have any packages."

"S-stamps," I stammered.

"You can go ahead of me," she said. "If all you're buying is stamps. I've got all these packages to send. You don't want to wait for that."

I *do* want to wait, I thought. "No, that's all right. I'm buying a *lot* of stamps," I said. "I'm buying several sheets. For my Christmas newsletter."

She shook her head, balancing the packages. "Don't be silly. You don't want to wait while they weigh all these." She tapped the man in front of her. "This young lady's only buying stamps," she said. "Why don't we let her go ahead of us?"

"Certainly," the man, who was wearing a Russian karakul hat, said, and bowed slightly, stepping back.

"No, really," I began, but it was too late. The line had parted like the Red Sea.

"Thank you," I said, and walked up to the counter. "Merry Christmas."

The line closed behind me. They know, I thought. They know I was looking up plant parasites. I glanced desperately toward the door.

"Holly and ivy?" the clerk said, beaming at me.

"What?" I said.

"Your stamps." He held up two sheets. "Holly and ivy or Madonna and Child?"

"Holly and ivy," I said weakly. "Three sheets, please."

I paid for the sheets, thanked the mob again, and went back out into the freezing-cold lobby. And now what? Pretend I had a box and fiddle with the combination? *Where* was he?

I went over to the bulletin board, trying not to seem suspicious, and looked at the Wanted posters. They had probably all turned themselves in by now and were being model prisoners. And it really was a pity the parasites were going to have to be stopped. *If* they could be stopped.

It had been easy in the movies (in the movies, that is, in which they had managed to defeat them, which wasn't all that many. Over half the movies had ended with the whole world being turned into glowing green eyes). And in the ones where they did defeat them, there had been an awful lot of explosions and hanging precariously from helicopters. I hoped whatever we came up with didn't involve skydiving.

Or a virus or ultrasonic sound, because even if I knew a doctor or scientist to ask, I couldn't confide in them. "We can't trust anybody," Gary had said, and he was right. We couldn't risk it. There was too much at stake. And we couldn't call the police. "It's all in your imagination, Miss Johnson," they would say. "Stay right there. We're on our way."

We would have to do this on our own. And *where* was Gary?

I looked at the Wanted posters some more. I was sure the one in the middle looked like one of Sueann's old boyfriends. He—

"I'm sorry I'm late," Gary said breathlessly. His ears were red from the cold, and his hair was ruffled from running. "I had this phone call and—"

"Come on," I said, and hustled him out of the post office, down the steps, and past the Santa and his mob of donors.

"Keep walking," I said. "You were right about the parasites, but not because they turn people into zombies."

I hurriedly told him about the galls and Tonya's carpal tunnel syndrome. "My sister was infected at Thanksgiving, and now she can hardly walk," I said. "You were right. We've got to stop them."

"But you don't have any proof of this," he said. "It could be arthritis or something, couldn't it?"

I stopped walking. "What?"

"You don't have any proof that it's the aliens that are causing it. It's cold. People's arthritis always acts up when it's cold out. And even if the aliens are causing it, a few aches and pains is a small price to pay for all the benefits. You said yourself—"

I stared at his hair.

"Don't look at me like that," he said. "I haven't been taken over. I've just been thinking about what you said about your sister's engagement and—"

"Who was on the phone?"

He looked uncomfortable. "The thing is—"

"It was your ex-wife," I said. "She's been taken over, and now she's nice, and you want to get back together with her. That's it, isn't it?"

"You know how I've always felt about Marcie," he said guiltily. "She says she never stopped loving me."

When something sounds too good to be true, it probably is, I thought.

"She thinks I should move back in and see if we can't work things out. But that isn't the only reason," he said, grabbing my arm. "I've been looking at all those clippings—dropouts going back to school, escaped convicts turning themselves in—"

"People returning overdue library books," I said.

"Are we willing to be responsible for ruining all that? I think we should think about this before we do anything."

I pulled my arm away from him.

"I just think we should consider all the factors before we decide what to do. Waiting a few days can't hurt."

"You're right," I said, and started walking. "There's a lot we don't know about them."

"I just think we should do a little more research," he said, opening the door of our building.

"You're right," I said, and started up the stairs.

"I'll talk to you tomorrow, okay?" he said when we got to second.

I nodded and went back to my desk and put my head in my hands.

He was willing to let parasites take over the planet so he could get his ex-wife back, but were my motives any better than his? Why had I believed in an alien invasion in the first place, and spent all that time watching science-fiction movies and having huddled conversations? So I could spend time with him.

He was right. A few aches and pains were worth it to have Sueann married to someone nice and postal workers nondisgruntled and passengers remaining seated till those people with connecting flights had deplaned.

"Are you okay?" Tonya said, leaning over my desk.

"I'm fine," I said. "How's your arm?"

"Fine," she said, rotating the elbow to show me. "It must have been a cramp or something."

I didn't *know* these parasites were like mistletoe. They might cause only temporary aches and pains. Gary was right. We needed to do more research. Waiting a few days couldn't hurt.

The phone rang. "I've been trying to get hold of you," Mom said. "Dakota's in the hospital. They don't know what it is. It's something wrong with her legs. You need to call Allison."

"I will," I said, and hung up the phone.

I logged on to my computer, called up the file I'd been working on, and scrolled halfway through it so it would look like I was away from my desk for just a minute, took off my high heels and changed into my sneakers, stuck the high heels into my desk drawer, grabbed my purse and coat, and took off.

The best place to look for information on how to get rid of the parasites was the library, but the card file was on-line, and you had to use your library card to get access. The next best was a bookstore. Not the independent on Sixteenth. Their clerks were far too helpful. And knowledgeable.

I went to the Barnes & Noble on Eighth, taking the back way (but no alleys). It was jammed, and there was some kind of book signing going on up front, but nobody paid any attention to me. Even so, I didn't go straight to the gardening section. I wandered casually through the aisles, looking at T-shirts and mugs and stopping to thumb through a copy of *How Irrational Fears Can Ruin Your Life*, gradually working my way back to the gardening section.

They had only two books on parasites: *Common Garden Parasites and Diseases* and *Organic Weed and Pest Control*. I grabbed them both, retreated to the literature section, and began to read.

"Fungicides such as Benomyl and Ferbam are effective against certain rusts," *Common Garden Parasites* said. "Streptomycin is effective against some viruses."

But which was this, if either? "Spraying with Diazinon or Malathion can be effective in most cases. Note: These are dangerous chemicals. Avoid all contact with skin. Do not breathe fumes."

That was out. I put down *Common Garden Parasites* and picked up *Organic Weed and Pest Control*. At least it didn't recommend spraying with deadly chemicals, but what it did recommend wasn't much more useful. Prune affected limbs. Remove and destroy berries. Cover branches with black plastic.

Too often it said simply: Destroy all infected plants.

"The main difficulty in the case of parasites is to destroy the parasite without also destroying the host." That sounded more like it. "It is therefore necessary to find a substance that the host can tolerate that is intolerable to the parasite. Some rusts, for instance, cannot tolerate a vinegar and ginger solution, which can be sprayed on the leaves of the host plant. Red mites, which infest honeybees, are allergic to peppermint. Frosting made with oil of peppermint can be fed to the bees. As it permeates the bees' systems, the red mites drop off harmlessly. Other parasites respond variously to spearmint, citrus oil, oil of garlic, and powdered aloe vera."

But which? And how could I find out? Wear a garlic necklace? Stick an orange under Tonya's nose? There was no way to find out without their figuring out what I was doing.

I kept reading. "Some parasites can be destroyed by rendering the environment unfavorable. For moisture-dependent rusts, draining the soil can be beneficial. For temperature-susceptible pests, freezing and/or use of smudge pots can kill the invader. For light-sensitive parasites, exposure to light can kill the parasite."

Temperature-sensitive. I thought about the hats. Were they to hide the parasites or to protect them from the cold? No, that couldn't be it. The temperature in the building had been turned down to freezing for two weeks, and if they needed heat, why hadn't they landed in Florida?

I thought about Jackie Peterson's newsletter. She hadn't been affected. And neither had Uncle Marty, whose newsletter had come this morning. Or, rather, Uncle Marty's dog, who ostensibly dictated them. "Woof, woof!" the newsletter had said. "I'm lying here under a Christmas saguaro out on the desert, chewing on a bone and hoping Santa brings me a nice new flea collar."

So they hadn't landed in Arizona or Miami, and none of the

newspaper articles Gary had circled had been from Mexico or California. They had all been datelined Minnesota and Michigan and Illinois. Places where it was cold. Cold and cloudy, I thought, thinking of Cousin Celia's Christmas newsletter. Cold and cloudy.

I flipped back through the pages, looking for the reference to light-sensitive parasites.

"It's right back here," a voice said.

I shut the book, jammed it in among Shakespeare's plays, and snatched up a copy of *Hamlet*.

"It's for my daughter," the customer, who was, thankfully, hatless, said, appearing at the end of the aisle. "That's what she said she wanted for Christmas when I called her. I was so surprised. She hardly ever reads."

The clerk was right behind her, wearing a mobcap with red and green ribbons. "Everybody's reading Shakespeare right now," she said, smiling. "We can hardly keep it on the shelves."

I ducked my head and pretended to read the *Hamlet*. "O villain, villain, smiling, damned villain!" Hamlet said. "I set it down, that one may smile, and smile, and be a villain."

The clerk started along the shelves, looking for the book. "*King Lear, King Lear* . . . let's see."

"Here it is," I said, handing it to her before she reached *Common Garden Parasites*.

"Thank you," she said, smiling. She handed it to the customer. "Have you been to our book signing yet? Darla Sheridan, the fashion designer, is in the store today, signing her new book, *In Your Easter Bonnet*. Hats are coming back, you know."

"Really?" the customer said.

"She's giving away a free hat with every copy of the book," the clerk said.

"*Really?*" the customer said. "Where, did you say?"

"I'll show you," the clerk said, still smiling, and led the customer away like a lamb to the slaughter.

As soon as they were gone, I pulled out *Organic Gardening* and looked up "light-sensitive" in the index. Page 264. "Pruning branches above the infection and cutting away surrounding leaves to expose the source to sunlight or artificial light will usually kill light-sensitive parasites."

I closed the book and hid it behind the Shakespeare plays, laying it on its side so it wouldn't show, and pulled out *Common Garden Pests*.

"Hi," Gary said, and I nearly dropped the book. "What are you doing here?"

"What are *you* doing here?" I said, cautiously closing the book.

He was looking at the title. I stuck it on the shelf between *Othello* and *The Riddle of Shakespeare's Identity*.

"I realized you were right." He looked cautiously around. "We've got to destroy them."

"I thought you said they were symbiotes, that they were beneficial," I said, watching him warily.

"You think I've been taken over by the aliens, don't you?" he said. He ran his hand through his hair. "See? No hat, no toupee."

But in *The Puppet Masters* the parasites had been able to attach themselves anywhere along the spine.

"I thought you said the benefits outweighed a few aches and pains," I said.

"I wanted to believe that," he said ruefully. "I guess what I really wanted to believe was that my ex-wife and I would get back together."

"What changed your mind?" I said, trying not to look at the bookshelf.

"You did," he said. "I realized somewhere along the way what a dope I'd been, mooning over her when you were right there in front of me. I was standing there, listening to her talk about how great it was going to be to get back together, and all of a sudden I realized that I didn't want to, that I'd found somebody nicer, prettier, someone I could trust. And that someone was you, Nan." He smiled at me. "So what have you found out? Something we can use to destroy them?"

I took a long, deep breath, and looked at him, deciding.

"Yes," I said, and pulled out the book. I handed it to him. "The section on bees. It says in here that introducing allergens into the bloodstream of the host can kill the parasite."

"Like in *Infiltrators from Space*."

"Yes." I told him about the red mites and the honeybees. "Oil of wintergreen, citrus oil, garlic, and powdered aloe vera are all used on various pests. So if we can introduce peppermint into the food of the affected people, it—"

"Peppermint?" he said blankly.

"Yes. Remember how Penny said nobody ate any of the candy canes she put out? I think it's because they're allergic to peppermint," I said, watching him.

"Peppermint," he said thoughtfully. "They didn't eat any of the ribbon candy Jan Gundell had on her desk either. I think you've hit it. So how are you going to get them to ingest it? Put it in the water cooler?"

"No," I said. "In cookies. Chocolate chip cookies. Everybody loves chocolate." I pushed the books into place on the shelf and started for the front. "It's my turn to bring Holiday Goodies tomorrow. I'll go to the grocery store and get the cookie ingredients—"

"I'll go with you," he said.

"No," I said. "I need you to buy the oil of peppermint. They should have it at a drugstore or a health food store. Buy the most concentrated form you can get, and make sure you buy it from somebody who hasn't been taken over. I'll meet you back at my apartment, and we'll make the cookies there."

"Great," he said.

"We'd better leave separately," I said. I handed him the *Othello*. "Here. Go buy this. It'll give you a bag to carry the oil of peppermint in."

He nodded and started for the checkout line. I walked out of Barnes & Noble, went down Eighth to the grocery store, ducked out the side door, and went back to the office. I stopped at my desk for a metal ruler, and ran up to fifth. Jim Bridgeman, in his backward baseball cap, glanced up at me and then back down at his keyboard.

I went over to the thermostat.

And this was the moment when everyone surrounded you, pointing and squawking an unearthly screech at you. Or turned and stared at you with their glowing green eyes. I twisted the thermostat dial as far up as it would go, to ninety-five.

Nothing happened.

Nobody even looked up from their computers. Jim Bridgeman was typing intently.

I pried the dial and casing off with the metal ruler and stuck them into my coat pocket, bent the metal nub back so it couldn't be moved, and walked back out to the stairwell.

And now, please let it warm up fast enough to work before everybody goes home, I thought, clattering down the stairs to fourth. Let everybody start sweating and take off their hats. Let the aliens be light-sensitive. Let them not be telepathic.

I jammed the thermostats on fourth and third, and clattered down to second. Our thermostat was on the far side, next to Hunziger's office. I grabbed up a stack of memos from my desk, walked purposefully across the floor, dismantled the thermostat, and started back toward the stairs.

"Where do you think you're going?" Solveig said, planting herself firmly in front of me.

"To a meeting," I said, trying not to look as lame and frightened as the hero's girlfriend in the movies always did. She looked down at my sneakers. "Across town."

"You're not going anywhere," she said.

"Why not?" I said weakly.

"Because I've got to show you what I bought Jane for Christmas."

She reached for a shopping bag under her desk. "I know I'm not due till May, but I couldn't resist this," she said, rummaging in the bag. "It is so cute!"

She pulled out a tiny pink bonnet with white daisies on it. "Isn't it adorable?" she said. "It's newborn size. She can wear it home from the hospital. Oh, and I got her the cutest—"

"I lied," I said, and Solveig looked up alertly. "Don't tell anybody, but I completely forgot to buy a Secret Santa gift. Penny'll kill me if she finds out. If anybody asks where I've gone, tell them the ladies' room," I said, and took off down to first.

The thermostat was right by the door. I disabled it and the one in the basement, got my car (looking in the backseat first, unlike the people in the movies) and drove to the courthouse and the hospital and McDonald's, and then called my mother and invited myself to dinner. "I'll bring dessert," I said, drove out to the mall, and hit the bakery, the Gap, the video-rental place, and the theater multiplex on the way.

Mom didn't have the TV on. She did have the hat on that Sueann had given her. "Don't you think it's adorable?" she said.

"I brought cheesecake," I said. "Have you heard from Allison and Mitch? How's Dakota?"

"Worse," she said. "She has these swellings on her knees and ankles. The doctors don't know what's causing them." She took the cheesecake into the kitchen, limping slightly. "I'm so worried."

I turned up the thermostats in the living room and the bedroom and was plugging the space heater in when she brought in the soup. "I got chilled on the way over," I said, turning the space heater up to high. "It's freezing out. I think it's going to snow."

We ate our soup, and Mom told me about Sueann's wedding. "She wants you to be her maid of honor," she said, fanning herself. "Aren't you warm yet?"

"No," I said, rubbing my arms.

"I'll get you a sweater," she said, and went into the bedroom, turning the space heater off as she went.

I turned it back on and went into the living room to build a fire in the fireplace.

"Have you met anyone at work lately?" she called in from the bedroom.

"What?" I said, sitting back on my knees.

She came back in without the sweater. Her hat was gone, and her hair was mussed up, as if something had thrashed around in it. "I hope you're not still refusing to write a Christmas newsletter," she said, going into the kitchen and coming out again with two plates of cheesecake. "Come sit down and eat your dessert," she said.

I did, still watching her warily.

"Making up things!" she said. "What an idea! Aunt Margaret wrote me just the other day to tell me how much she loves hearing from you girls and how interesting your newsletters always are." She cleared the table. "You can stay for a while, can't you? I hate waiting here alone for news about Dakota."

"No, I've got to go," I said, and stood up. "I've got to . . ."

I've got to . . . what? I thought, feeling suddenly overwhelmed. Fly to Spokane? And then, as soon as Dakota was okay, fly back and run wildly around town turning up thermostats until I fell over from exhaustion? And then what? It was when people fell asleep in the movies that the aliens took them over. And there was no way I could stay awake until every parasite was exposed to the light, even if they didn't catch me and turn me into one of them. Even if I didn't turn my ankle.

The phone rang.

"Tell them I'm not here," I said.

"Who?" Mom asked, picking it up. "Oh, dear, I hope it's not Mitch with bad news. Hello?" Pause. "It's Sueann," she said, putting her hand over the receiver, and listened for a long interval. "She broke up with her boyfriend."

"With David?" I said. "Give me the phone."

"I thought you said you weren't here," she said, handing the phone over.

"Sueann?" I said. "Why did you break up with David?"

"Because he's so deadly dull," she said. "He's always calling me and sending me flowers and being nice. He even wants to get married. And tonight at dinner, I just thought, '*Why* am I dating him?' and we broke up."

Mom went over and turned on the TV. "In local news," the CNN guy said, "special-interest groups banded together to donate fifteen thousand dollars to City Hall's Christmas display."

"Where were you having dinner?" I asked Sueann. "At McDonald's?"

"No, at this pizza place, which is another thing. All he ever wants is to go to dinner or the movies. We never do anything *interesting*."

"Did you go to a movie tonight?" She might have been in the multiplex at the mall.

"*No*. I *told* you, I broke up with him."

This made no sense. I hadn't hit any pizza places.

"Weather is next," the guy on CNN said.

"Mom, can you turn that down?" I said. "Sueann, this is important. Tell me what you're wearing."

"Jeans and my blue top and my zodiac necklace. What does that have to do with my breaking up with David?"

"Are you wearing a hat?"

"In our forecast just ahead," the CNN guy said, "great weather for all you people trying to get your Christmas shopping d—"

Mom turned the TV down.

"Mom, turn it back up," I said, motioning wildly.

"No, I'm not wearing a hat," Sueann said. "What does that have to do with whether I broke up with David or not?"

The weather map behind the CNN guy was covered with 62, 65, 70, 68. *"Mom,"* I said.

She fumbled with the remote.

"You won't *believe* what he did the other day," Sueann said, outraged. "Gave me an engagement ring! Can you imag—"

"—unseasonably warm temperatures and *lots* of sunshine," the weather guy blared out. "Continuing right through Christmas."

"I mean, what was I thinking?" Sueann said.

"Shh," I said. "I'm trying to listen to the weather."

"It's supposed to be nice all next week," Mom said.

It was nice all the next week. Allison called to tell me Dakota was back home. "The doctors don't know what it was, some kind of bug or something, but whatever it was, it's completely gone. She's back taking ice skating and tap-dancing lessons, and next week I'm signing both girls up for Junior Band."

"You did the right thing," Gary said grudgingly. "Marcie told me her knee was really hurting. When she was still talking to me, that is."

"The reconciliation's off, huh?"

"Yeah," he said, "but I haven't given up. The way she acted proves to me that her love for me is still there, if I can only reach it."

All it proved to me was that it took an invasion from outer space to make her seem even marginally human, but I didn't say so.

"I've talked her into going into marriage counseling with me," he said. "You were right not to trust me either. That's the mistake they always make in those body-snatcher movies, trusting people."

Well, yes and no. If I'd trusted Jim Bridgeman, I wouldn't have had to do all those thermostats alone.

"You were the one who turned the heat up at the pizza place where Sueann and her fiancé were having dinner," I said after he told me he'd figured out what the aliens' weakness was after seeing me turn up the thermostat on fifth. "You were the one who'd checked out *Attack of the Soul Killers*."

"I tried to talk to you," he said. "I don't blame you for not trusting me. I should have taken my hat off, but I didn't want you to see my bald spot."

"You can't go by appearances," I said.

By December fifteenth, hat sales were down, the mall was jammed with ill-tempered shoppers, at City Hall an animal-rights group was protesting Santa Claus's wearing fur, and Gary's wife had skipped their first marriage-counseling session and then blamed it on him.

It's now four days till Christmas, and things are completely back to normal. Nobody at work's wearing a hat except Jim, Solveig's naming her baby Durango, Hunziger's suing management for firing him, antidepressant sales are up, and my mother called just now to tell me Sueann has a new boyfriend who's a terrorist, and to ask me if I'd sent out my Christmas newsletters yet. And had I met anyone lately at work.

"Yes," I said. "I'm bringing him to Christmas dinner."

Yesterday Betty Holland filed a sexual harassment suit against Nathan Steinberg for kissing her under the mistletoe, and I was nearly run over on my way home from work. But the world has been made safe from cankers, leaf wilt, and galls.

And it makes an interesting Christmas Newsletter.

Whether it's true or not.

Wishing you and yours a very Merry Christmas and a Happy New Year,

Nan Johnson

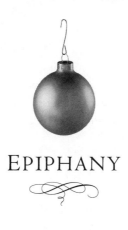

EPIPHANY

*"But pray ye that your flight be not in the winter,
neither on the sabbath day."*

— MATTHEW 24:20

little after three, it began to snow. It had looked like it was going to all the way through Pennsylvania, and had even spit a few flakes just before Youngstown, Ohio, but now it was snowing in earnest, thick flakes that were already covering the stiff dead grass on the median and getting thicker as he drove west.

And this is what you get for setting out in the middle of January, he thought, without checking the Weather Channel first. He hadn't checked anything. He had taken off his robe, packed a bag, gotten into his car, and taken off. Like a man fleeing a crime.

The congregation will think I've absconded with the money in the collection plate, he thought. Or worse. Hadn't there been a minister in the paper last month who'd run off to the Bahamas with the building fund and a blonde? They'll say, "I *thought* he acted strange in church this morning."

But they wouldn't know yet that he was gone. The Sunday night Mariners' Meeting had been cancelled, the elders' meeting wasn't till next week, and the interchurch ecumenical meeting wasn't till Thursday.

He was supposed to play chess with B.T. on Wednesday, but he could call him and move it. He would have to call when B.T. was at work and leave him a message on his voice mail. He couldn't risk talking to him—they had been friends too many years. B.T. would instantly know something was up. And he would be the last person to understand.

I'll call his voice mail and move our chess game to Thursday night after the ecumenical meeting, Mel thought. That will give me till Thursday.

He was kidding himself. The church secretary, Mrs. Bilderbeck, would miss him Monday morning when he didn't show up in the church office.

I'll call her and tell her I've got the flu, he thought. No, she would insist on bringing him over chicken soup and zinc lozenges. I'll tell her I've been called out of town for a few days on personal business.

She will immediately think the worst, he thought. She'll think I have cancer, or that I'm looking at another church. And anything they conclude, he thought, even embezzlement, would be easier for them to accept than the truth.

The snow was starting to stick on the highway, and the windshield was beginning to fog up. Mel turned on the defroster. A truck passed him, throwing up snow. It was full of gold-and-white Ferris wheel baskets. He had been seeing trucks like it all afternoon, carrying black Octopus cars and concession stands and lengths of roller-coaster track. He wondered what a carnival was doing in Ohio in the middle of January. And in this weather.

Maybe they were lost. Or maybe they suddenly had a vision telling them to head west, he thought grimly. Maybe they suddenly had a nervous breakdown in the middle of church. In the middle of their sermon.

He had scared the choir half to death. They had been sitting there, midway through the sermon, and thinking they had plenty of time before they had to find the recessional hymn, when he'd stopped cold, his hand still raised, in the middle of a sentence.

There had been silence for a full minute before the organist thought to play the intro, and then a frantic scramble for their bulletins and their hymnals, a frantic flipping of pages. They had straggled unevenly to their feet all the way through the first verse, singing and looking at him like he was crazy.

And were they right? Had he really had a vision or was it some kind of midlife crisis? Or psychotic episode?

He was a Presbyterian, not a Pentecostal. He did not have visions. The only time he had experienced anything remotely like this was when he was nineteen, and that hadn't been a vision. It had been a call to the ministry, and it had only sent him to seminary, not haring off to who knows where.

And this wasn't a vision either. He hadn't seen a burning bush or an angel. He hadn't seen anything. He had simply had an overwhelming conviction that what he was saying was true.

He wished he still had it, that he wasn't beginning to doubt it now that he was three hundred miles from home and in the middle of a snowstorm, that he wasn't beginning to think it had been some kind of self-induced hysteria, born out of his own wishful thinking and the fact that it was January.

He hated January. The church always looked cheerless and abandoned, with all the Christmas decorations taken down, the sanctuary dim and chilly in the gray winter light, Epiphany over and nothing to look forward to but Lent and taxes. And Good Friday. Attendance and the collection down, half the congregation out with the flu and the other half away on a winter cruise, those who were there looking abandoned, too, and like they wished they had somewhere to go.

That was why he had decided against his sermon on Christian duty and pulled an old one out of the files, a sermon on Jesus' promise that He would return. To get that abandoned look off their faces.

"This is the hardest time," he had said, "when Christmas is over, and the bills have all come due, and it seems like winter is never going to end and summer is never going to come. But Christ tells us that we 'know not when the master of the house cometh, at even, or at midnight, or at the cockcrowing, or in the morning,' and when he comes, we must be ready for him. He may come tomorrow or next year or a thousand years from now. He may already be here, right now. At this moment . . ."

And as he said it, he had had an overwhelming feeling that it was true, that He had already come, and he must go find Him.

But now he wondered if it was just the desire to be somewhere else, too, somewhere besides the cold, poinsettialess sanctuary.

If so, you came the wrong way, he thought. It was freezing, and the windshield was starting to fog up. Mel kicked the defrost all the way up to high and swiped at the windshield with his gloved hand.

The snow was coming down much harder, and the wind was picking up. Mel switched on the radio to hear a weather report.

". . . and in the last days, the Book of Revelation tells us," a voice said, " 'there will be hail and fire mingled with blood.' "

He hoped that wasn't the weather report. He hit the scan button on the radio and listened as it cycled through the stations. ". . . for the latest on the scandal involving the President and . . ." the voice of Randy Travis, singing "Forever and Ever, Amen" . . .

"hog futures at" . . . "and the disciples said, 'Lord, show us a sign. . . .'"

A sign, that was what he needed, Mel thought, peering at the road. A sign that he was not crazy.

A semi roared past in a blinding blast of snow and exhaust. He leaned forward, trying to see the lines on the pavement, and another truck went by, full of orange-and-yellow bumper cars. Bumper cars. How appropriate. They were all going to be riding bumper cars if this snow kept up, Mel thought, watching the truck pull into the lane ahead of him. It fishtailed wildly as it did, and Mel put his foot on the brake, felt it skid, and lifted his foot off.

Well, he had asked for a sign, he thought, carefully slowing down, and this one couldn't be clearer if it was written in fiery letters: Go home! This was a crazy idea! You're going to be killed, and then what will the congregation think? Go home!

Which was easier said than done. He could scarcely see the road, let alone any exit signs, and the windshield was starting to ice up. He kicked the defroster all the way up and swiped at the window again.

He didn't dare pull over and stop—those semis would never see him—but he was going to have to. The defroster wasn't having any effect on the ice on the windshield, and neither were the windshield wipers.

He rolled down the window and leaned out, trying to grab the wiper and slap it against the windshield to shake the ice off. Snow stabbed his face, stinging it.

"All right, all right," he shouted into the wind. "I get the message!"

He rolled the window back up, shivering, and swiped at the inside of the windshield again. The only kind of sign he wanted now was an exit sign, but he couldn't see the side of the road.

If I'm *on* the road, he thought, trying to spot the shoulder, a telltale outline, but the whole world had disappeared into a featureless whiteness. And what would keep him from driving right off the road and into a ditch?

He leaned forward tensely, trying to spot something, anything, and thought he saw, far ahead, a light.

A yellow light, too high up for a taillight—a reflector on a motorcycle, maybe. That was impossible, there was no way a motorcycle could be out in this. One of those lights on the top corners of a semi.

If that was what it was, he couldn't see the other one, but the light was moving steadily in front of him, and he followed it, trying to keep pace.

The windshield wipers were icing up again. He rolled down the window, and in the process lost sight of the light. Or the road, he thought frightenedly. No, there was the light, still high up, but closer, and it wasn't a light, it was a whole cluster of them, round yellow bulbs in the shape of an arrow.

The arrow on top of a police car, he thought, telling you to change lanes. There must be some kind of accident up ahead. He strained forward, trying to make out flashing blue ambulance lights.

But the yellow arrow moved steadily ahead, and as he got closer, he saw that the arrow was pointed down at an angle. And that it was slowing. Mel slowed, too, focusing his whole attention on the road and on pumping his brakes to keep the car from skidding.

When he looked up again, the arrow had slowed nearly to a stop, and he could see it clearly. It was part of a lighted sign on the back of a truck. "Shooting Star" it said in a flowing script, and next to the arrow in neon pink, "Tickets."

The truck came to a complete stop, its turn light blinking, and then started up again, and in its headlights he caught a glimpse of snow-spattered red. A stop sign.

And this was an exit. He had followed the truck off the highway onto an exit without even knowing it.

And now he was hopefully following it into a town, he thought, clicking on his right-turn signal and turning after the truck, but in the moment he had hesitated, he had lost it. And the blowing snow was worse here than on the highway.

There was the yellow arrow again. No, what he saw was a Burger King crown. He pulled in, scraping the snow-covered curb, and saw that he was wrong again. It was a motel sign. "King's Rest," with a crown of sulfur-yellow bulbs.

He parked the car and got out, slipping in the snow, and started for the office, which had, thank goodness, a "Vacancy" sign in the same neon pink as the "Tickets" sign.

A little blue Honda pulled up beside him and a short, plump woman got out of it, winding a bright purple muffler around her head. "Thank goodness you knew where you were going," she said, pulling on a pair of turquoise mittens. "I couldn't see a thing except your taillights." She reached back into the Honda for a vivid green canvas bag. "Anybody who'd be on the roads in weather like this would have to be crazy, wouldn't they?"

And if the blizzard hadn't been sign enough, here was proof positive. "Yes," he said, although she had already gone inside the motel office, "they would."

He would check in, wait a few hours till the storm let up, and then start back. With luck he would be back home before Mrs. Bilderbeck got to the office tomorrow morning.

He went inside the office, where a balding man was handing the plump woman a room key and talking to someone on the phone.

"Another one," he said when Mel opened the door. "Yeah."

He hung up the phone and pushed a registration form and a pen at Mel.

"Which way'd *you* come from?" he asked.

"East," Mel said.

The man shook his balding head. "You got here in the nick of time," he said to both of them. "They just closed all the roads east of here."

> *"And thus I saw the horses in the vision, and them that sat upon them."*
>
> — REVELATION 9:17

In the morning, Mel called Mrs. Bilderbeck. "I won't be in today. I've been called out of town."

"Out of town?" Mrs. Bilderbeck said, interested.

"Yes. On personal business. I'll be gone most of the week."

"Oh, dear," she said, and Mel suddenly hoped that there was an emergency at the church, that Gus Uhank had had another stroke or Lottie Millar's mother had died, so that he would have to go back.

"I told Juan you'd be in," Mrs. Bilderbeck said. "He's putting the sanctuary Christmas decorations away, and he wanted to know if you want to save the star for next year. And the pilot light went out again. The church was *freezing* when I got here this morning."

"Was Juan able to get it relit?"

"Yes, but I think someone should look at it. What if it goes out on a Saturday night?"

"Call Jake Adams at A-1 Heating," he said. Jake was a deacon.

"A-1 Heating," she said slowly, as if she were writing it down. "What about the star? Are we going to use it again next year?"

Is there going to *be* a next year? Mel thought. "Whatever you think," he said.

"And what about the ecumenical meeting?" she asked. "Will you be back in time for that?"

"Yes," he said, afraid if he said "no," she would ask more questions.

"Is there a number where I can reach you?"

"No. I'll check in tomorrow." He hung up quickly, and then sat there on the bed, trying to decide whether to call B.T. or not. He hadn't done anything major in the fifteen years they'd been friends without telling him, but Mel knew what he'd say. They'd met on the ecumenical committee, when the Unitarian chairman had decided that, to be truly ecumenical, they needed a resident atheist and Darwinian biologist. And, Mel suspected, an African-American.

It was the only good thing that had ever come out of the ecumenical committee. He and B.T. had started by complaining about the idiocies of the ecumenical committee, which seemed bent on proving that denominations couldn't get along, progressed to playing chess and then to discussing religion and politics and disagreeing on both, and ended by becoming close friends.

I have to call him, Mel thought, it's a betrayal of our friendship not to.

And tell him what? That he'd had a holy vision? That the Book of Revelation was coming literally true? It sounded crazy to Mel, let alone to B.T., who was a scientist, who didn't believe in the First Coming, let alone the Second. But if it *was* true, how could he not call him?

He dialed B.T.'s area code and then put down the receiver and went to check out.

The roads east were still closed. "You shouldn't have any trouble heading west, though," the balding man said, handing Mel his credit-card receipt. "The snow's supposed to let up by noon."

Mel hoped so. The interstate was snow-packed and unbelievably slick, and when Mel positioned himself behind a sand truck, a rock struck his windshield and made a ding.

At least there was hardly any traffic. There were only a few semis, and a navy-blue pickup with a bumper sticker that said "In case of the Rapture, this car will be unoccupied." There was no sign of the blue Honda or of the carnival. They had seen the light and were still at the King's Rest, sitting in the restaurant, drinking coffee. Or headed south for the winter.

He passed a snow-obscured sign that read "For Weather Info, Tune to AM 1410."

He did. ". . . and in the last days Christ Himself will appear," an evangelist, possibly the one from yesterday, or a different one— they all had the same accent, the same intonation—said. "The Book of Revelation tells us He will appear riding a white horse and leading a mighty army of the righteous against the Antichrist in that last great battle of Armageddon. And the unbelievers— the fornicators and the baby-murderers—will be flung into the bottomless pit."

The ultimate "Wait till your father gets home," threat, Mel thought.

"And how do I know these things are coming?" the radio said. "I'll *tell* you how. The Lord came to me in a dream, and He said, 'These shall be the signs of my coming. There will be wars and rumors of wars.' Iraq, my friends, that's what he's talking about. The sun's face will be covered, and the godless will prosper. Look around you. Who do you see prospering? Abortion doctors and homosexuals and godless atheists. But when Christ comes, they will be punished. He's told me so. The Lord spoke to me, just like he spoke to Moses, just like he spoke to Isaiah. . . ."

He switched off the radio, but it didn't do any good. Because this was what had been bothering him ever since he started out. How did he know his vision wasn't just like some radio evangelist's?

Because his is born out of hatred, bigotry, and revenge, Mel thought. God no more spoke to him than did the man in the moon.

And how do you know He spoke to you? Because it *felt* real? The voices telling the bomber to destroy the abortion clinic felt real, too. Emotion isn't proof. Signs aren't evidence. "Do you have any outside confirmation?" he could hear B.T. saying skeptically.

The sun came out, and the glare off the white road, the white fields, was worse than the snow had been. He almost didn't see the truck off to the side. Its emergency flashers weren't on, and at first he thought it had just slid off the road, but as he went past, he saw it was one of the carnival trucks with its hood up and steam coming out. A young man in a denim jacket was standing next to it, hooking his thumb for a ride.

I should stop, Mel thought, but he was already past, and picking up hitchhikers was dangerous. He had found that out when he'd preached a sermon on the Good Samaritan last year. "Let us not be like the Levite or the Pharisee who passes by the stranded motorist, the injured victim," he had told his congregation. "Let us be like the Samaritan, who stopped and helped."

It had seemed like a perfectly harmless sermon topic, and he had been totally unprepared for the uproar that ensued. "I cannot believe you told people to pick up hitchhikers!" Dan Crosby had raged. "If one of my daughters ends up raped, I'm holding you responsible."

"What were you thinking of?" Mrs. Bilderbeck had said, hanging up after fending off Mable Jenkins. "On CNN last week there was a story about somebody who stopped to help a couple who was out of gas, and they cut off his head."

He had had to issue a retraction the next Sunday, saying that women had no business helping anyone (which had made Mamie Rollet mad, for feminist reasons) and that the best thing for everyone else to do was to alert the state patrol on their cell phones and let them take care of it, unless they knew the person, although somehow he couldn't imagine the Good Samaritan with a cell phone.

There was a median crossing up ahead, but it was marked with a sign that read "Authorized Vehicles Only." And if I get my head cut off, he thought, the congregation will have no sympathy at all.

But it was threatening to snow again, and the green interstate sign up ahead said "Wayside, 28 Mi." And the carnival had been his Good Samaritan last night.

" 'Inasmuch as ye have done it unto one of the least of these, you have done it unto me,' " he murmured, and turned into the median crossing and onto the eastbound side of the highway, and started back.

The truck was still there, though he couldn't see the driver. Good, he thought, looking for a place to cross. Some other Samaritan's picked him up. But when he pulled up behind the truck, the man got out of the truck's cab and started over to the car, his hands jammed into his denim jacket. Mel began to feel sorry he'd stopped. The man had a ragged scar across his forehead, and his hair was lank and greasy.

He slouched over to the side of the car, and Mel saw that he was much younger than he'd looked at first. He's just a kid, Mel thought.

Yeah, well, so was Billy the Kid, he reminded himself. And Andrew Cunanan.

Mel leaned across and pulled down the passenger window. "What's the trouble?"

The kid leaned down to talk to him. "Died," he said, and grinned.

"Do you need a lift into town?" he asked, and the kid immediately opened the car door, keeping his right hand in his jacket pocket. Where the gun is, Mel thought.

The kid slid in and shut the door, still using only one hand. When they find me robbed and murdered, they'll be convinced I was involved in some kind of drug deal, Mel thought. He started the car.

"Man, it was cold out there," the kid said, taking his right hand out of his pocket and rubbing his hands together. "I been waiting forever."

Mel kicked the heater over to high, and the kid leaned forward and held his hands in front of the vent. There was a peace sign tattooed on the back of one of them and a fierce-looking lion on the other. Both looked like they'd been done by hand.

The kid rubbed his hands together, wincing, and Mel took another look. His hands were red with cold and between the tattoo lines there were ugly white splotches. The kid started rubbing them again.

"Don't—" Mel said, putting out his hand unthinkingly to stop him. "That looks like frostbite. Don't rub it. You're supposed to . . ." he said, and then couldn't remember. Put them in warm water? Wrap them up? "They're supposed to warm up slowly," he said finally.

"You mean like by warming 'em up in front of a heater?" the kid said, holding his hands in front of the vent again. He put up his hand and touched the ding in the windshield. "That's gonna spread," he said.

His hand looked even worse now that it was warming up. The sickly white splotches stood out starkly against the rest of his skin.

Mel took off his gloves, switching hands on the steering wheel and using his teeth to get the second one off. "Here," he said, handing them to the kid. "These are insulated."

The kid looked at him for a minute and then put them on.

"You should get your hands looked at," Mel said. "I can take you to the emergency room when we get to town."

"I'll be okay," the kid said. "You get used to being cold, working a carny."

"What's a carnival doing here in the middle of winter, anyway?" Mel asked.

"Best time," the kid said. "Catches 'em by surprise. What're you doin' out here?"

He wondered what the kid would say if he told him. "I'm a minister," he said instead.

"A preacher, huh?" he said. "You believe in the Second Coming?"

"The Second Coming?" Mel gasped, caught off-guard.

"Yeah, we had a preacher come to the carny the other day telling us Jesus was coming back and was gonna punish everybody for hanging him on the cross, knock down the mountains, burn the whole planet up. You believe all that's gonna happen?"

"No," Mel said. "I don't think Jesus is coming back to punish anybody."

"The preacher said it was all right there in the Bible."

"There are lots of things in the Bible. They don't always turn out to mean what you thought they did."

The kid nodded sagely. "Like the Siamese twins."

"Siamese twins?" Mel said, unable to remember any Siamese twins in the Bible.

"Yeah, like this one carny up in Fargo. It had a big sign saying 'See the Siamese twins,' and everybody pays a buck, thinking they're gonna see two people hooked together. And when they get there it's a cage with two Siamese kittens in it. Like that."

"Not exactly," Mel said. "The prophecies aren't a scam to cheat people, they're—"

"What about Roswell? The alien autopsy and all that. You think that's a scam, too?"

Well, there was some outside confirmation for you. Mel was in a class with scam artists and UFO nuts.

"After what happened the first time, I don't know if I'd wanta come back or not," the kid said, and it took Mel a minute to realize he was talking about Christ. "If I did, I'd wear some kind of disguise or something."

Like the last time, Mel thought, when He came disguised as a baby.

The kid was still preoccupied with the ding. "There's stuff you could do to keep it from spreading for a little while," he said, "but it's still gonna spread. There ain't nothing that can stop it." He pointed out the window at a sign. "Wayside, exit 1 mile."

Mel pulled off and into a Total station, apparently all there was to Wayside. The kid opened the door and started to take off the gloves.

"Keep them," Mel said. "Do you want me to wait till you find out if they've got a tow truck?"

The kid shook his head. "I'll call Pete." He reached into the pocket of the denim jacket and handed Mel three orange cardboard tickets. They were marked "Admit One Free."

"It's a ticket to the show," the kid said. "We got a triple Ferris wheel, three wheels one inside the other. And a great roller coaster. The Comet."

Mel splayed the tickets apart. "There are three tickets here."

"Bring your friends," the kid said, slapped the car door, and ambled off toward the gas station.

Bring your friends.

Mel got back on the highway. It was getting dark. He hoped the next exit wasn't as far, or as uninhabited, as this one.

Bring your friends. I should have told B.T., he thought, even though he would have said, Don't go, you're crazy, let me recommend a good psychiatrist.

"I still should have told him," he said out loud, and was as certain of it as he had been of what he should do in that moment in the church. And now he had cut himself off from B.T. not only by hundreds of miles of closed highways and "icy and snow-packed conditions," but by his deception, his failure to tell him.

The next exit didn't even have a gas station, and the one after that nothing but a Dairy Queen. It was nearly eight by the time he got to Zion Center and a Holiday Inn.

He walked straight in, not even stopping to get his luggage out of the trunk, and across the lobby toward the phones.

"Hello!" The short plump woman he'd seen the night before waylaid him. "Here we are again, orphans of the storm. Weren't the roads awful?" she said cheerfully. "I almost went off in the ditch twice. My little Honda doesn't have four-wheel drive, and—"

"Excuse me," Mel interrupted her. "I have a phone call I *have* to make."

"You can't," she said, still cheerfully. "The lines are down."

"Down?"

"Because of the storm. I tried to call my sister just now, and the clerk told me the phone's been out all day. I don't know what she's going to think when she doesn't hear from me. I promised *faithfully* that I'd call her every night and tell her where I was and that I'd gotten there safely."

He couldn't call B.T. Or get to him. "Excuse me," he said, and started back across the lobby to the registration desk.

"Has the interstate going east opened up yet?" he asked the girl behind the counter.

She shook her head. "It's still closed between Malcolm and Iowa City. Ground blizzards," she said. "Will you be checking in, sir? How many are there in your party?"

"Two," a voice said.

Mel turned. And there, leaning against the end of the registration desk, was B.T.

> "And there appeared another wonder in heaven, and
> behold a great red dragon."
>
> —REVELATION 12:3

For a moment he couldn't speak for the joy, the relief he felt. He clutched the check-out counter, vaguely aware that the girl behind the counter was saying something.

"What are you doing here?" he said finally.

B.T. smiled his slow checkmate smile. "Aren't I the one who should be asking that?"

And now that he was here, he would have to tell him. Mel felt the relief turn into resentment. "I thought the roads were closed," he said.

"I didn't come that way," B.T. said.

"And how would you like to pay for that, sir?" the clerk said, and Mel knew she had asked him before.

"Credit card," he said, fumbling for his wallet.

"License number?" the clerk asked.

"I flew to Omaha and rented a car," B.T. said.

Mel handed her his MasterCard. "TY 804."

"State?"

"Pennsylvania." He looked at B.T. "How did you find me?"

" 'License number?' " B.T. said, mimicking the clerk. " 'Will you be putting this on your credit card, sir?' If you've got a computer, it's the easiest thing in the world to find someone these days, especially if they're using that." He gestured at the MasterCard the clerk was handing back to Mel.

She handed him a folder. "Your room number is written inside, sir. It's not on the key for security purposes," the clerk said, as if his room number weren't in the computer, too. B.T. probably already knew it.

"You still haven't answered my question," B.T. said. "What are you doing here?"

"I have to go get my suitcase," Mel said, and walked past him and out to the parking lot and his car. He opened the trunk.

B.T. reached past him and picked up Mel's suitcase, as if taking it into custody.

"How did you know I was missing?" Mel asked, but he already knew the answer to that. "Mrs. Bilderbeck sent you."

B.T. nodded. "She said she was worried about you, that you'd called and something was seriously wrong. She said she knew because you hadn't tried to get out of the ecumenical meeting on Thursday. She said you always tried to get out of it."

They say it's the little mistakes that trip criminals up, Mel thought.

"She said she thought you were sick and were going to see a specialist," B.T. said, his black face gray with worry. "Out of town, so nobody in the congregation would find out about it. A brain tumor, she said." He shifted the suitcase to his other hand. "Do you have a brain tumor?"

A brain tumor. That would be a nice, convenient explanation. When Ivor Sorenson had had a brain tumor, he had stood up during the offertory, convinced there was an ostrich sitting in the pew next to him.

"*Are* you sick?" B.T. said.

"No."

"But it is something serious."

"It's freezing out here," Mel said. "Let's discuss this inside."

B.T. didn't move. "Whatever it is, no matter how bad it is, you can tell me."

"All right. Fine. 'For ye know neither the day nor the hour wherein the Son of Man cometh.' Matthew 25:13," Mel said. "I had a revelation. About the Second Coming. I think He's here already, that the Second Coming's already happened."

Whatever B.T. had imagined—terminal illness or embezzlement or some other, worse crime—it obviously wasn't as bad as this. His face went even grayer. "The Second Coming," he said. "Of Christ?"

"Yes," Mel said. He told him what had happened during

the sermon Sunday. "I scared the choir half out of their wits," he said.

B.T. nodded. "Mrs. Bilderbeck told me. She said you stopped in the middle of a sentence and just stood there, staring into space with your hand up to your forehead. That's why she thought you had a brain tumor. How long did this . . . vision last?"

"It wasn't a vision," Mel said. "It was a revelation, a conviction . . . an epiphany."

"An epiphany," B.T. said in a flat, expressionless voice. "And it told you He was here? In Zion Center?"

"No," Mel said. "I don't know where He is."

"You don't know where He is," B.T. repeated. "You just got in your car and started driving?"

"West," Mel said. "I knew He was somewhere west."

"Somewhere west," B.T. said softly. He rubbed his hand over his mouth.

"Why don't you say it?" Mel said. He slammed the trunk shut. "You think I'm crazy."

"I think we're both crazy," he said, "standing out here in the snow, fighting. Have you had supper?"

"No," Mel said.

"Neither have I," B.T. said. He took Mel's arm. "Let's go get some dinner."

"And a dose of antidepressants? A nice straitjacket?"

"I was thinking steak," B.T. said, and tried to smile. "Isn't that what they eat here in Iowa?"

"Corn," Mel said.

> "And when I looked, behold . . . the appearance of
> the wheels was as the colour of a beryl stone and . . .
> as if a wheel had been in the midst of a wheel."
>
> —JEREMIAH 10:9–10

Epiphany   275

Neither corn nor steak was on the menu, which had the Holiday Inn star on the front, and they were out of nearly everything else. "Because of the interstate being closed," the waitress said. "We've got chicken teriyaki and beef chow mein."

They ordered the chow mein and coffee, and the waitress left. Mel braced himself for more questions, but B.T. only asked, "How were the roads today?" and told him about the problems he'd had getting a flight and a rental car. "Chicago O'Hare was shut down because of a winter storm," he said, "*and* Denver *and* Kansas City. I had to fly into Albuquerque and then up to Omaha."

"I'm sorry you had to go to all that trouble," Mel said.

"I was worried about you."

The waitress arrived with their chow mein, which came with mashed potatoes and gravy and green beans.

"Interesting," B.T. said, poking at the gravy. He made a half-hearted attempt at the chow mein, and then pushed the plate away.

"There's something I don't understand," he said. "The Second Coming is when Christ returns, right? I thought He was supposed to appear in the clouds in a blaze of glory, complete with trumpets and angel choirs."

Mel nodded.

"Then how can He already be here without anybody knowing?"

"I don't know," Mel said. "I don't understand any of this any more than you do. I just know He's here."

"But you don't know where."

"No. I thought when I got out here there would be a sign."

"A sign," B.T. said.

"Yes," Mel said, getting angry all over again. "You know. A burning bush, a pillar of fire, a star. A *sign*."

He must have been shouting. The waitress came scurrying over with the check. "Are you through with this?" she said, looking at the plates of half-eaten food.

"Yes," Mel said. "We're through."

"You can pay at the register," the waitress said, and scurried away with their plates.

"Look," B.T. said, "the brain's a very complicated thing. An alteration in brain chemistry—are you on any medications? Sometimes medications can cause people to hear voices or—"

Mel picked up the check and stood, reaching for his wallet. "It wasn't a voice."

He put down money for a tip and went over to the cash register.

"You said it was a strong feeling," B.T. said after Mel had paid. "Sometimes endorphins can—nothing like this has ever happened to you before, has it?"

Mel walked out into the lobby. "Yes," he said, and turned to face B.T. "It happened once before."

"When?" B.T. said, his face gray again.

"When I was nineteen. I was in college, studying pre-law. I went to church with a girlfriend, and the minister gave a hellfire-and-brimstone sermon on the evils of dancing and associating with anyone who did. He said Jesus said it was wrong to associate with nonbelievers, that they would corrupt and contaminate you. Jesus, who spent all His time with lowlifes, tax collectors and prostitutes and lepers! And all of a sudden I had this overwhelming feeling, this—"

"Epiphany," B.T. said.

"That I had to do something, that I had to fight him and all the other ministers like him. I stood up and walked out in the middle of the sermon," Mel said, remembering, "and went home and applied to seminary."

B.T. rubbed his hand across his mouth. "And the epiphany you had yesterday was the same as that one?"

"Yes."

"Reverend Abrams?" a woman's voice said.

Mel turned. The short plump woman who'd been on the phone and at the motel the night before was hurrying toward them, lugging her bright green tote bag.

"Who's that?" B.T. said.

Mel shook his head, wondering how she knew his name.

She came up to them. "Oh, Reverend Abrams," she said breathlessly, "I wanted to thank you—I'm Cassie Hunter, by the way." She stuck out a plump, beringed hand.

"How do you do?" Mel said, shaking it. "This is Dr. Bernard Thomas, and I'm Mel Abrams."

She nodded. "I heard the desk clerk say your name. I didn't thank you the other night for saving my life."

"Saving your life?" B.T. said, looking at Mel.

"There was this awful whiteout," Cassie said. "You couldn't see the road at all, and if it hadn't been for the taillights on Reverend Abrams's car, I'd have ended up in a ditch."

Mel shook his head. "You shouldn't thank me. You should thank the driver of the carnival truck *I* was following. He saved both of us."

"I *saw* those carnival trucks," Cassie said. "I wondered what a carnival was doing in Iowa in the middle of winter." She laughed, a bright, chirpy laugh. "Of course, you're probably wondering what a retired English teacher is doing in Iowa in the middle of winter. Of course, for that matter, what are *you* doing in Iowa in the middle of winter?"

"We're on our way to a religious meeting," B.T. said before Mel could answer.

"Really? I've been visiting famous writers' birthplaces," she said. "Everyone back home thinks I'm *crazy*, but except for the last few days, the weather's been *fine*. Oh, and I wanted to tell you, I just talked to the clerk, and she thinks the phones will be working again by tomorrow morning, so you should be able to make your call."

She rummaged in her voluminous tote bag and came up with

a room-key folder. "Well, anyway, I just wanted to thank you. It was nice meeting you," she said to B.T., and bustled off across the lobby toward the coffee shop.

"Who were you trying to call?" B.T. asked.

"You," Mel said bitterly. "I realized I owed it to you to tell you, even if you did think I was crazy."

B.T. didn't say anything.

"That *is* what you think, isn't it?" Mel said. "Why don't you just say it? You think I'm crazy."

"All right. I think you're crazy," B.T. said, and then continued angrily, "Well, what do you expect me to say? You take off in the middle of a blizzard, you don't tell anyone where you're going, because you saw the Second Coming in a *vision?*"

"It wasn't—"

"Oh, right. It wasn't a vision. You had an epiphany. So did the woman in *The Globe* last week who saw the Virgin Mary on her refrigerator. So did the Heaven's Gate people. Are you telling me *they're* not crazy?"

"No," Mel said, and started down the hall to his room.

"For fifteen years you've raved about faith healers and cults and preachers who claim they've got a direct line to God being frauds," B.T. said, following him, "and now you suddenly believe in it?"

He kept walking. "No."

"But you're telling me I'm supposed to believe in *your* revelation because it's different, because this is the real thing."

"I'm not telling you anything," Mel said, turning to face him. "You're the one who came out here and demanded to know what I was doing. I told you. You got what you came for. Now you can go back and tell Mrs. Bilderbeck I don't have a brain tumor, it's a chemical imbalance."

"And what do you intend to do? Drive west until you fall off the Santa Monica pier?"

"I intend to find Him," Mel said.

B.T. opened his mouth as if to say something and then shut it and stormed off down the hall.

Mel stood there, watching him till a door slammed, down the hall.

Bring your friends, Mel thought. Bring your friends.

> *"For now we see through a glass darkly, but then face to face."*
>
> —I CORINTHIANS 13:12

"I intend to find Him," Mel had said, and was glad B.T. hadn't shouted back "How?" because he had no idea.

He had not had a sign, which meant that the answer must be somewhere else. Mel sat down on the bed, opened the drawer of the bedside table, and got out the Gideon Bible.

He propped the pillows up against the headboard and leaned back against them and opened the Bible to the Book of Revelation.

The radio evangelists made it sound like the story of the Second Coming was a single narrative, but it was actually a hodge-podge of isolated scriptures—Matthew 24 and sections of Isaiah and Daniel, verses out of Second Thessalonians and John and Joel, stray ravings from Revelation and Jeremiah, all thrown together by the evangelists as if the authors were writing at the same time. If they were even writing about the same thing.

And the references were full of contradictions. A trumpet would sound, and Christ would come in the clouds of heaven with power and great glory. Or on a white horse, leading an army of a hundred and forty-four thousand. Or like a thief in the night. There would be earthquakes and pestilences and a star falling out of heaven. Or a dragon would come up out of the sea, or four great beasts, with the heads of a lion and a bear and a leopard and eagles' wings. Or darkness would cover the earth.

But in all the assorted prophecies there were no locations mentioned. Joel talked about a desolate wilderness and Jeremiah about a wasteland, but not about where they were. Luke said the faithful would come "from the east, and from the west, and from the north" to the kingdom of God, but neglected to say where it was located.

The only place mentioned by name in all the prophecies was Armageddon. But Armageddon (or Har-Magedon or 'Ar Himdah) was a word that appeared only once in the Scriptures and whose meaning was not known, a word that might be Hebrew or Greek or something else altogether, that might mean "level" or "valley plain" or "place of desire."

Mel remembered from seminary that some scholars thought it referred to the plain in front of Mt. Megiddo, the site of a battle between Israel and Sisera the Canaanite. But there was no Mt. Megiddo on ancient or modern maps. It could be anywhere.

He put on his shoes and his coat and went out to the parking lot to get his road atlas out of the car.

B.T. was leaning against the trunk.

"How long have you been out here?" Mel asked, but the answer was obvious. B.T.'s dark face was pinched with cold, and his hands were jammed into his pockets like the carnival kid's had been.

"I've been thinking," he said, his voice shivering with the cold. "I don't have to be back until Thursday, and I can fly out of Denver just as easily as out of Omaha. If we drive as far as Denver together, it'll give us more time—"

"For you to talk me out of this," Mel said, and then was sorry when he saw the expression on B.T.'s face.

"For us to talk," B.T. said. "For me to figure this—epiphany—out."

"All right," Mel said. "As far as Denver." He opened the car door. "You can come inside now. I'm not going anywhere till morning." He leaned inside the car and got the atlas. "It's a good thing I came out for this. You didn't actually intend to stand out here all night, did you?"

He nodded, his teeth chattering. "You're not the only one who's crazy."

*"By hearing ye shall hear, and shall not understand,
and seeing ye shall see and shall not perceive."*
—MATTHEW 13:14

There wasn't a Hertz rental car agency in Zion Center. "The nearest one's in Redfield," B.T. said unhappily.

"I'll meet you there," Mel said.

"Will you?" B.T. said. "You won't take off on your own?"

"No," Mel said.

"What if you see a sign?"

"If I see a burning bush, I'll pull off on the side and let you know," Mel said dryly. "We can caravan if you want."

"Fine," B.T. said. "I'll follow you."

"I don't know where the rental place is."

"I'll pull ahead of you once we get to Redfield," B.T. said, and got into his rental car. "It's the second exit. What are the roads supposed to be like?"

"Icy. Snow-packed. But the weather report said clear."

Mel got into his car. The kid from the carnival had been right. The ding had started to spread, raying out in three long cracks and one short one.

He led the way over to the interstate, being careful to signal lane changes and not to get too far ahead, so B.T. wouldn't think he was trying to escape.

The carnival must have stayed the night in Zion Center, too. He passed a truck carrying the Tilt-a-Whirl and one full of stacked, slanted mirrors for, Mel assumed, the Hall of Mirrors. A Blazer roared past him with the bumper sticker "When the Rapture comes, I'm outta here!"

As soon as he was on the interstate, he turned on the radio. ". . . and snow-packed. Partly cloudy becoming clear by midmorning. Interstate 80 between Victor and Davenport is closed, also U.S. 35 and State Highway 218. Partly cloudy skies, clearing by midmorning. The following schools are closed: Edgewater, Bennett, Olathe, Oskaloosa, Vinton, Shellsburg. . . ."

Mel twisted the knob.

". . . but the Second Coming is not something we believers have to be afraid of," the evangelist, this one with a Texas accent, said, "for the Book of Revelation tells us that Christ will protect us from the final tribulation, and when He comes to power we will dwell with Him in His Holy City, which shines with jewels and precious stones, and we will drink from living fountains of water. The lion shall lie down with the lamb, and there . . . be . . . more—"

The evangelist sputtered into static and then out of range, which was just as well because Mel was heading into fog and needed to give his whole attention to his driving.

The fog got worse, descending like a smothering blanket. Mel turned on his lights. They didn't help at all, but Mel hoped B.T. would be able to see his taillights the way Cassie had. He couldn't see anything beyond a few yards in front of him. And if he had wanted a sign of his mental state, this was certainly appropriate.

"God has told us His will in no uncertain terms," the radio evangelist thundered, coming suddenly back into range. "There can't be any question about it."

But he had dozens of questions. There had been no Megiddo on the map of Nebraska last night. Or of Kansas or Colorado or

New Mexico, and nothing in all the prophecies about location except a reference to the New Jerusalem, and there was no New Jerusalem on the map either.

"And how do I know the Second Coming is at hand?" the evangelist roared, suddenly back in range. "Because the Bible *tells* us so. It tells us *how* He is coming and when!"

And that wasn't true either. "Ye know neither the day nor the hour wherein the Son of man cometh," Matthew had written, and Luke, "The Son of man cometh at an hour when ye think not," and even Revelation, "I will come on thee as a thief, and thou shalt not know what hour I will come." It was the only thing they were all agreed on.

"The signs are *all* around us," the evangelist shouted. "They're as plain as the nose on your face! Air pollution, liberals outlawing school prayer, wickedness! Why, anybody'd have to be *blind* not to recognize them! Open your eyes and see!"

"All I see is fog," Mel said, turning on the defrost and wiping his sleeve across the windshield, but it wasn't the windshield. It was the world, which had vanished completely in the whiteness.

He nearly missed the turnoff to Redfield. Luckily, the fog was less dense in town, and they were able to find not only the rental car place, but the local Tastee-Freez. Mel went over to get some lunch to take with them while B.T. checked the car in.

It was full of farmers, all talking about the weather. "Damned meter-ologists," one of them, redfaced and wearing a John Deere cap and earmuffs, grumbled. "Said it was supposed to be clear."

"It is clear," another one in a down vest said. "He just didn't say *where*. You get up above that fog, say thirty thousand feet, and it's clear as a bell."

"Number six," the woman behind the counter called.

Mel went up to the counter and paid. There was a fluorescent green poster for the carnival taped up on the wall beside the counter. "Come have the time of your life!" it read. "Thrills, chills, excitement!"

Chills is right, Mel thought, thinking of how cold being up in a Ferris wheel in this fog would be.

It was an old sign. "Littletown, Dec. 24," it read. "Ft. Dodge, Dec. 28. Cairo, Dec. 30."

B.T. was already in the car when Mel got back with their hamburgers and coffee. He handed him the sack and got back on the highway.

That was a mistake. The fog was so thick he couldn't even take a hand off the wheel to hold the hamburger B.T. offered him. "I'll eat it later," he said, leaning forward and squinting as if that would make things clearer. "You go ahead and eat, and we'll switch places in a couple of exits."

But there were no exits, or Mel couldn't see them in the fog, and after twenty miles of it, he had B.T. hand him his coffee, now stone cold, and took a couple of sips.

"I've been looking at the Second Coming scientifically," B.T. said. " 'A great mountain burning with fire was cast into the sea and the third part of the sea became blood.' "

Mel glanced over. B.T. was reading from a black leather Bible. "Where'd you get that?" he asked.

"It was in the hotel room," B.T. said.

"You *stole* a Gideon Bible?" Mel said.

"They put them there for people who need them. And I'd say we qualify. 'There was a great earthquake, and the sun became black as sackcloth of hair and the moon became as blood. And the stars of heaven fell into the earth. And every mountain and island were moved out of their places.'

"All these things are supposed to happen along with the Second Coming," B.T. said. "Earthquakes, wars and rumors of wars, pestilence, locusts." He leafed through the flimsy pages. " 'And there arose a smoke out of the pit, as the smoke of a great furnace, and the sun and the air were darkened. And there came out of the smoke locusts upon the earth.' "

He shut the Bible. "All right, earthquakes happen all the time, and there have been wars and rumors of wars for the last ten thousand years, and I guess this—'and the stars shall fall from the sky'—could refer to meteors. But there's no sign of any of these other things. No locusts, no bottomless pit opening up, no 'third part of trees and grass were burnt up and a third part of the creatures which were in the sea died.' "

"Nuclear war," Mel said.

"What?"

"According to the evangelists, that's supposed to refer to nuclear war," Mel said. "And before that, to the Communist threat. Or fluoridation of water. Or anything else they disapprove of."

"Well, whatever it stands for, no bottomless pit has opened up lately or we would have seen it on CNN. And volcanoes don't cause locust swarms. Mel," he said seriously, "let's say your experience was a real epiphany. Couldn't you have misinterpreted what it meant?"

And for a split second, Mel almost had it. The key to where He was and what was going to happen. The key to all of it.

"Couldn't it have been about something else?" B.T. said. "Something besides the Second Coming?"

No, Mel thought, trying to hang on to the insight, it *was* the Second Coming, but—it was gone. Whatever it was, he'd lost it.

He stared blindly ahead at the fog, trying to remember what had triggered it. B.T. had said, "Couldn't you have misunderstood what it meant?" No, that wasn't right. "Couldn't you—"

"What is it?" B.T. was pointing through the windshield. What is that? Up ahead?"

"I don't see anything," Mel said, straining ahead. He couldn't see anything but fog. "What was it?"

"I don't know. I just saw a glimpse of lights."

"Are you sure?" Mel said. There was nothing there but whiteness.

"There it is again," B.T. said, pointing. "Didn't you see it? Yellow flashing lights. There must be an accident. You'd better slow down."

Mel was already barely creeping along, but he slowed further, still unable to see anything. "Was it on our side of the highway?"

"Yes . . . I don't know," B.T. said, leaning forward. "I don't see it now. But I'm sure it was there."

Mel crawled forward, squinting into the whiteness. "Could it have been a truck? The carnival truck had a yellow arrow," he said, and saw the lights.

And they were definitely not a sign for a carnival ride. They filled the road just ahead, flashing yellow and red and blue, all out of synch with each other. Police cars or fire trucks or ambulances. Definitely an accident. He pumped the brakes, hoping whoever was behind him could see his taillights, and slowed to a stop.

A patrolman appeared out of the fog, holding up his hand in the sign for "stop." He was wearing a yellow poncho and a clear plastic cover over his brown hat.

Mel rolled his window down, and the patrolman leaned in to talk to them. "Road up ahead's closed. You need to get off at this exit."

"Exit?" Mel said, looking to the right. He could just make out a green outline in the fog.

"It's right there, up about a hundred yards," the patrolman said, pointing into nothingness. "We'll come tell you when it's open again."

"Are you closing it because of the weather?" B.T. asked.

The patrolman shook his head. "Accident," he said. "Big mess. It'll be a while." He motioned them off to the right.

Mel felt his way to the exit and off the highway. At least it had a truck stop instead of just a gas station. He and B.T. parked and went into the restaurant.

It was jammed. Every booth, every seat at the counter was full. Mel and B.T. sat down at the last unoccupied table, and it immediately became clear why it had been unoccupied. The draft when the door opened made B.T., who had just taken his coat off, put it back on and then zip it up.

Mel had expected everyone to be angry about the delay, but the waitresses and customers all seemed to be in a holiday mood. Truckers leaned across the backs of the booths to talk to each other, laughing, and the waitresses, carrying pots of coffee, were smiling. One of them had, inexplicably, a plastic kewpie doll stuck in her beehive hairdo.

The door opened again, sending an Arctic blast across their table, and a paramedic came in and went up to the counter to talk to the waitress. ". . . accident . . ." Mel heard him say and shake his head, ". . . carnival truck . . ."

Mel went over. "Excuse me," he said. "I heard you say something about a carnival truck. Is that what had the accident?"

"Disaster is more like it," the paramedic said, shaking his head. "Took a turn too sharp and lost his whole load. And don't ask me what a carnival's doing up here in the middle of winter."

"Was the driver hurt?" Mel asked anxiously.

"Hurt? Hell, no. Not a scratch. But that road's going to be closed the rest of the day." He pulled a bamboo Chinese finger trap out of his pocket and handed it to Mel. "Truck was carrying all the prizes and stuff for the midway. The whole road's covered in stuffed animals and baseballs. And you can't even see to clean 'em up."

Mel went back to the table and told B.T. what had happened.

"We could go south and pick up Highway 33," B.T. said, consulting the road atlas.

"No, you can't," the waitress, appearing with two pots of coffee, said. "It's closed. Fog. So's 15 north." She poured coffee into their cups. "You're not going anywhere."

The draft hit them again, and the waitress glanced over at the door. "Hey! Don't just stand there—shut the door!"

Mel looked toward the door. Cassie was standing there, wearing a bulky orange sweater that made her look even rounder, and scanning the restaurant for an empty booth. She was carrying a red dinosaur under one arm and her bright green tote bag over the other.

"Cassie!" Mel called to her, and she smiled and came over.

"Put your dinosaur down and join us," B.T. said.

"It's not a dinosaur," she said, setting it on the table. "It's a dragon. See?" she said, pointing to two pieces of red felt on its back. "Wings."

"Where'd you get it?" Mel said.

"The driver of the truck that spilled them gave it to me," she said. "I'd better call my sister before she hears about this on the news," she said, looking around the restaurant. "Do you think the phones are working?"

B.T. pointed at a sign that said "Phones," and she left.

She was back instantly. "There's a line," she said, and sat down. The waitress came by again with coffee and menus, and they ordered pie, and then Cassie went to check the phones again.

"There's still a line," she said, coming back. "My sister will have a fit when she hears about this. She already thinks I'm crazy. And out there in that fog today I thought so, too. I wish my grandmother had never looked up verses in the Bible."

"The Bible?" Mel said.

She waved her hand dismissively. "It's a long story."

"We seem to have plenty of time," B.T. said.

"Well," she said, settling herself. "I'm an English teacher— *was* an English teacher—and the school board offered this early-retirement bonus that was too good to turn down, so I retired in June, but I didn't know what I wanted to do. I'd always wanted to travel, but I hate traveling alone, and I didn't know where I wanted to go. So I got on the sub list—our district has a terrible time getting subs, and there's been all this flu."

It is going to be a long story, Mel thought. He picked up the finger trap and idly stuck his finger into one end. B.T. leaned back in his chair.

"Well, anyway, I was subbing for Carla Sewell, who teaches sophomore lit, *Julius Caesar,* and I couldn't remember the speech about our fate being in the stars, dear Brutus."

Mel stuck a forefinger into the other side of the finger trap.

"So I was looking it up, but I read the page number wrong, so when I looked it up, it wasn't *Julius Caesar*, it was *Twelfth Night.*"

Mel stretched the finger trap experimentally. It tightened on his fingers.

" 'Westward, ho!' it said," Cassie said, "and sitting there, reading it, I had this epiphany."

"Epiphany?" Mel said, yanking his fingers apart.

"Epiphany?" B.T. said.

"I'm sorry," Cassie said. "I keep thinking I'm still an English teacher. Epiphany is a literary term for a revelation, a sudden understanding, like in James Joyce's *The Dubliners*. The word comes from—"

"The story of the wise men," Mel said.

"Yes," she said delightedly, and Mel half-expected her to announce that he had gotten an A. "Epiphany is the word for their arrival at the manger."

And there it was again. The feeling that he knew where Christ was. The wise men's arrival at the manger. James Joyce.

"When I read the words 'Westward, ho!' " Cassie was saying, "I thought, that means me. I have to go west. Something important is going to happen." She looked from one to the other. "You probably think I'm crazy, doing something because of a line in *Bartlett's Quotations*. But whenever my grandmother had an important decision to make, she used to close her eyes and open her Bible and point at a Scripture, and when she opened her eyes, whatever the Scripture said to do, she'd do it. And, after all, *Bartlett's* is the Bible of English teachers. So I tried it. I closed the book and my eyes and picked a quotation at random, and it said, 'Come, my friends, 'tis not too late to seek a newer world.' "

"Tennyson," Mel said.

She nodded. "So here I am."

"And has something important happened?" B.T. asked.

"Not yet," she said, sounding completely unconcerned. "But it's going to happen soon—I'm sure of it. And in the meantime, I'm seeing all these wonderful sights. I went to Gene Stratton Porter's cabin in Geneva, and the house where Mark Twain grew up in Hannibal, Missouri, and Sherwood Anderson's museum."

She looked at Mel. "Struggling against it doesn't work," she said, pushing her index fingers together, and Mel realized he was struggling vainly to free his fingers from the finger trap. "You have to push them together."

There was a blast of icy air and a patrolman wearing three pink plastic leis around his neck and carrying a spotted plush leopard came in.

"Road's open," he said, and there was a general scramble for coats. "It's still real foggy out there," he said, raising his voice, "so don't get carried away."

Mel freed himself from the finger trap and helped Cassie into her coat while B.T. paid the bill. "Do you want to follow us?" he asked.

"No," she said, "I'm going to try to call my sister again, and if she's heard about this accident, it'll take forever. You go on."

B.T. came back from paying, and they went out to the car, which had acquired a thin, rock-hard coating of ice. Mel, chipping at the windshield with the scraper, started a new offshoot in the rapidly spreading crack.

They got back on the interstate. The fog was thicker than ever. Mel peered through it, looking at objects dimly visible at the sides of the road. The debris from the accident—baseballs and plastic leis and Coke bottles. Stuffed animals and kewpie dolls littered the median, looking in the fog like the casualties of some great battle.

"I suppose you consider this the sign you were looking for," B.T. said.

"What?" Mel said.

"Cassie's so-called epiphany. You can read anything you want into random quotations," B.T. said. "You realize that, don't you? It's like reading your horoscope. Or a fortune cookie."

"The Devil can quote scripture to his own ends," Mel murmured.

"Exactly," B.T. said, opening the Gideon Bible and closing his eyes. "Look," he said "Psalm 115, verse 5. 'Eyes have they, but they see not.' Obviously a reference to the fog.' "

He flipped to another page and stabbed his finger at it. " 'Thou shalt not eat any abominable thing.' Oh, dear, we shouldn't have ordered that pie. You can make them mean anything. And you heard her, she'd retired, she liked to travel, she was obviously looking for an excuse to go somewhere. And her epiphany only said something important was going to happen. It didn't say a word about the Second Coming."

"It told her to go west," Mel said, trying to remember exactly what she had said. She had been looking for a speech from *Julius Caesar* and had stumbled on *Twelfth Night* instead. Twelfth night. Epiphany.

"How many times is the word 'west' mentioned in *Bartlett's*

Quotations?" B.T. said. "A hundred? 'Oh, young Lochinvar is come out of the west'? 'Go west, young man'? 'One flew east, one flew west, one flew over the cuckoo's nest'?" He shut the Bible. "I'm sorry," he said. "It's just—" He turned and looked out his window at nothing. "It looks like it might be breaking up."

It wasn't. The fog thinned a little, swirling away from the car in little eddies, and then descended again, more smothering than ever.

"Suppose you do find Him? What do you do then?" B.T. said. "Bow down and worship Him? Give Him frankincense and myrrh?"

"Help Him," Mel said.

"Help Him what? Separate the sheep from the goats? Fight the battle of Armageddon?"

"I don't know," Mel said. "Maybe."

"You really think there's going to be a battle between good and evil?"

"There's always a battle between good and evil," Mel said. "Look at the first time He came. He hadn't been on earth a week before Herod's men were out looking for Him. They murdered every baby and two-year-old in Bethlehem, trying to kill Him."

And thirty-three years later they succeeded, Mel thought. Only killing couldn't stop Him. Nothing could stop Him.

Who had said that? The kid from the carnival, talking about the windshield. "Nothing can stop it. There's stuff you could do to keep it from spreading for a while, but it's still going to spread. There ain't nothing that can stop it."

He felt a flicker of the feeling again. Something about the kid from the carnival. What had he been talking about before that? Siamese twins. And Roswell. No. Something else.

He tried to think what Cassie had said at the truck stop. Something about the wise men arriving at the manger. And not struggling. "You have to push them together," she had said.

It stayed tantalizingly out of reach, as elusive as a road sign glimpsed in the fog.

B.T. reached forward and flicked on the radio. "Foggy tonight, and colder," it said. "In the teens for eastern Nebraska, down in the . . ." it faded to static. B.T. twisted the knob.

"And do you know what will happen to us when Jesus comes?" an evangelist shouted, "The Book of Revelation tells us we will be tormented with fire and brimstone, unless we repent *now*, before it's too late!"

"A little fire and brimstone would be welcome right about now," B.T. said, reaching forward to turn the heater up to high.

"There's a blanket in the backseat," Mel said, and B.T. reached back and wrapped himself up in it.

"We will be scorched with fire," the radio said, "and the smoke of our torment will rise up forever and ever."

B.T. leaned his head against the doorjamb. "Just so it's warm," he murmured and closed his eyes.

"But that's not all that will happen to us if we do not repent," the evangelist said, "if we do not take Jesus as our personal Savior. The Book of Revelation tells us in Chapter 14 that we will be cast into the winepress of God's wrath and be *trodden* in it till our blood covers the ground for a thousand *miles*! And don't fool yourselves, that day is coming *soon*! The signs are all around us! Wait till your father gets home."

Mel switched it off, but it was too late. The evangelist had hit it, the problem Mel had been trying to avoid since that moment in the sanctuary.

I don't believe it, he had thought when he'd heard the minister talking about Jesus forbidding believers to associate with outcasts. And he had thought it again when he heard the radio evangelist that first day talking about Christ coming to get revenge.

"I don't believe it," he thought, and when B.T. stirred in his corner, he realized he had spoken aloud.

"I don't believe it," he murmured. God had so loved the world, He had sent His only begotten Son to live among men, to be a helpless baby and a little boy and a young man, had sent Him to be cold and confused, angry and overjoyed. "To share our common lot," the Nicene Creed said. To undergo and understand and forgive. "Father, forgive them," He had said, with nails driven through His hands, and when they had arrested Him, he had made the disciples put away their weapons. He had healed the soldier's ear Peter had cut off.

He would never, *never* come back in a blaze of wrath and revenge, slaughtering enemies, tormenting unbelievers, wreaking fire and pestilence and famine on them. Never.

And how can I believe in a revelation about the Second Coming, he thought, when I don't believe in the Second Coming?

But the revelation wasn't about the Second Coming, he thought. He hadn't seen earthquakes or Armageddon or Christ coming in a blaze of clouds and glory. He's already here, he had thought, now, and had set out to find Him, to look for a sign.

But there aren't any, he thought, and saw one off in the mist. "Prairie Home 5, Denver 468."

Denver. They would be there tomorrow night. And B.T. would want him to fly home with him.

Unless I figure out the key, Mel thought. Unless I'm given a sign. Or unless the roads are closed.

> *"And, lo, the star, which they saw in the east, went before them. . . ."*
>
> — MATTHEW 2:9

"They should be open," the woman at the Wayfarer Motel said. The Holiday Inn and the Super 8 and the Innkeeper had all been full up, and the Wayfarer had only one room left. "There's supposed to be fog in the morning, and then it's supposed to be nice all the way till Sunday."

"What about the roads east?" B.T. asked.

"No problem," she said.

The Wayfarer didn't have a coffee shop. They ate supper at the Village Inn on the other end of town. As they were leaving, they ran into Cassie in the parking lot.

"Oh, good," she said. "I was afraid I wouldn't have a chance to say goodbye."

"Goodbye?" Mel said.

"I'm heading south tomorrow to Red Cloud. When I consulted Bartlett's, it said, 'Winter lies too long in country towns.'"

"Oh?" Mel said, wondering what this had to do with going south.

"Willa Cather," Cassie said. "*My Ántonia*. I didn't understand it either, so I tried the Gideon Bible in my hotel, it's so nice of them to leave them there, and it was Exodus 13:21, 'And the Lord went before them by day in a pillar of a cloud, to lead them the way; and by night in a pillar of fire.'"

She smiled expectantly at them. "Pillar of fire. Red Cloud. Willa Cather's museum is in Red Cloud."

They said goodbye to her and went back to the motel. B.T. sat down on his bed and took his laptop out of his suitcase. "I've got some e-mail I've got to answer," he said.

And send? Mel wondered. "Dear Mrs. Bilderbeck, we'll be in Denver tomorrow. Am hoping to persuade Mel to come home with me. Have straitjacket ready."

Mel sat down in the room's only chair with the Rand McNally and looked at the map of Nebraska, searching for a town named Megiddo or New Jerusalem. There was Red Cloud, down near the southern border of Nebraska. Pillar of fire. Why couldn't he have had a nice straightforward sign like that? A pillar of smoke by day and a pillar of fire by night. Or a star.

But Moses had wandered around in the wilderness for forty years following said pillar. And the star hadn't led the wise men to Bethlehem. It had led them straight into King Herod's arms. They hadn't had a clue where the newborn Christ was. "Where is He that is born king of the Jews?" they'd asked Herod.

"Where is He?" Mel murmured, and B.T. glanced up from his laptop and then back down at it again, typing steadily.

Mel turned to the map of Colorado. Beulah. Bonanza. Firstview.

"Even if your—epiphany—was real," B.T. had asked him this afternoon, "couldn't you have misinterpreted what it means?"

Well, if he had, he wouldn't have been the first one. The Bible was full of people who had misinterpreted prophecies. "Dogs have compassed me; the assembly of the wicked have enclosed me," the Scriptures said, "they pierced my hands and my feet." But nobody saw the Crucifixion coming. Or the Resurrection.

His own disciples didn't recognize Him. Easter Sunday they walked all the way to Emmaus with Him without figuring out who He was, and even when He told them, Thomas refused to believe Him and demanded to see the scars of the nails in His hands.

They had never recognized Him. Isaiah had plainly predicted a virgin who would bring forth a child "out of the root of Jesse," a child who would redeem Israel. But nobody had thought that meant a baby in a stable.

They had thought he was talking about a warrior, a king who would raise an army and drive the hated foreigners out of their country, a hero on a white horse who would vanquish their enemies and set them free. And He had, but not in the way they expected.

Nobody had expected Him to be a poor itinerant preacher from an obscure family, with no college degree and no military training, a nobody. Even the wise men had expected Him to be royalty. "Where is the *king* whose star we have seen in the east?" they had asked Herod.

And Herod had promptly sent soldiers out to search for a usurper, a threat to his throne.

They had been looking for the wrong thing. And maybe B.T.'s right, maybe I am, too, and that's the answer. The Second Coming isn't going to be battles and earthquakes and falling stars, and Revelation means something else, like the prophecies of the Messiah.

Or maybe it wasn't the Second Coming, and Christ was here only in a symbolic sense, in the poor, the hungry, in those in need of help. "As ye have done this unto the least of these—"

"Maybe the Second Coming really is here," B.T. said from the bed. "Look at this."

He turned the laptop around so Mel could see the screen. "Watch, therefore," it read, "for ye know neither the day nor the hour wherein the Son of man cometh."

"It's a website," B.T. said. "www.watchman."

"It probably belongs to one of the radio evangelists," Mel said.

"I don't think so," B.T. said. He hit a key, and a new screen came up. It was full of entries.

"Meteor, 12-23, 4 mi. NNW Raton."

"Examined area. 12-28. No sign."

"Weather Channel 11-2, 9:15 a.m. PST. Reference to unusual cloud formations."

"Latitude and longitude? Need location."

"8.6 mi. WNW Prescott AZ 11-4."

"Denver Post 914P8C2—Headline: 'Unusually high lightning activity strikes Carson National Forest. MT2427.' "

"What do you think that stands for?" B.T. said, pointing at the string of letters and numbers.

"Matthew 24, verse 27," Mel said. " 'For the lightning cometh out of the west and shineth even unto the east, so shall also the coming of the Son of man be.' "

B.T. nodded and scrolled the screen down.

"Triple lightning strike. 7-11, Platteville, CO. Nov. 28. Two injured."

"Lightning storm, Dec. 4, Truth or Consequences."

"What about that one?" B.T. said, pointing at "Truth or Consequences."

"It's a town in southern New Mexico," Mel said.

"Oh." He scrolled the screen down some more.

"Falling star, 12-30, 2 mi. W of U.S. State Hwy 191, west of Bozeman, mile marker 161."

"Coma patient recovery, Yale–New Haven Hosp. Connection?"

"Negative. Too far east."

"Possible sighting Nevada."

"Need location."

Need location. " 'Go search diligently for the young child,' " Mel murmured, " 'and when ye have found him, bring me word again, that I may come and worship him.' "

"What?" B.T. said.

"It's what Herod said when the wise men told him about the star." He stared at the screen:

"L.A. Times Jan 2 P5C1. Fish die-off. RV89?"

"Possible sighting. Old Faithful, Yellowstone Nat'l Pk, Jan. 2."

And over and over again:

"Need location."

"Need location."

"Need location."

"They obviously think the Second Coming's happened," B.T. said, staring at the screen.

"Or aliens have landed at Roswell," Mel said. He pointed to the convenience store entry. "Or Elvis is back."

"Maybe," B.T. said, staring at the screen.

Mel went back to looking at the maps. Barren Rock. Deadwood. Last Chance.

Need location, he thought. Maybe he and Cassie and

whoever had written "Too far east" on the website had all misinterpreted the message, and it was not "west" but "West."

He turned to the gazetteer in the back. West. Westwood Hills, Kansas. Westville, Oklahoma. West Hollywood, California. Westview. Westgate. Westmont. There was a Westwood Hills in Kansas. Colorado had a Westcliffe, a Western Hills, and a Westminster. Neither Arizona nor New Mexico had any Wests. Nevada didn't either. Nebraska had a West Point.

West Point. Maybe it wasn't even in the west. Maybe it was West Orange, New Jersey, or West Palm Beach. Or West Berlin.

He shut the atlas and looked over at B.T. He had dozed off, his face tired and worried-looking even in sleep. His laptop was on his chest, and the Gideon Bible he had stolen from the Holiday Inn lay beside him.

Mel shut the laptop off and quietly closed it. B.T. didn't move. Mel picked up the Bible.

The answer had to be in the Scriptures. He opened the Bible to Matthew. "Then if any man shall say unto you, Lo, here is Christ, or there; believe it not."

He read on. Disasters and devastation and tribulation, as the prophets had spoken.

The prophets. He found Isaiah. "Hear ye indeed but understand not; and see ye indeed but perceive not."

He shut the Bible. All right, he thought, standing it on its spine on his hand. Let's have a sign here. I'm running out of time.

He opened his eyes. His finger was on I Samuel 23, verse 14. "And Saul sought him every day, but God delivered him not into his hand."

> "For all these things must come to pass, but the end is not yet."
>
> — MATTHEW 24:6

All the roads were open, and, from Grand Island, clear and dry, and the fog had lifted a little.

"With roads like this, we ought to be in Denver by tonight," B.T. said.

Yes, Mel thought, finishing what B.T. had said, if you fly back with me, we could be there in time for the ecumenical meeting. Nobody'd ever have to know he'd been gone, except Mrs. Bilderbeck, and he could tell her he'd been offered a job by another church, but had decided not to take it, which was true.

"It just didn't work out," he would tell Mrs. Bilderbeck, and she would be so overjoyed that he wasn't leaving, she wouldn't even ask for details.

And he could go back to doing sermons and giving the choir plenty of warning, storing the star, and keeping the pilot light going, as if nothing had happened.

"Exit 312" a green interstate sign up ahead said. "Hastings, 18. Red Cloud, 57."

He wondered if Cassie was already at Willa Cather's house, convinced she had been led there by *Bartlett's Quotations*.

Cassie had no trouble finding signs—she saw them everywhere. And maybe they are everywhere, and I'm just not seeing them. Maybe Hastings is a sign, and the truck full of mirrors, and those stuffed toys all over the road. Maybe that Chinese finger-trap I got stuck in yesterday was—

"Look," B.T. said. "Wasn't that Cassie's car?"

"Where?" Mel said, craning his neck around.

"In that ditch back there."

This time Mel didn't wait for an "Authorized Vehicles Only" crossing. He plunged into the snowy median and back along the other side of the highway, still unable to see anything.

"There," B.T. said, pointing, and he turned onto the median.

He had crossed both lanes and was onto the shoulder before

he saw the Honda, halfway down a steep ditch and tilted at an awkward angle. He couldn't see anyone in the driver's seat.

B.T. was out of the car before Mel got the car stopped and plunging down the snowy bank, with Mel behind him. B.T. wrenched the car door open.

Cassie's green tote bag was on the floor of the passenger seat. B.T. peered into the backseat. "She's not here," he said unnecessarily.

"Cassie!" Mel called. He ran around the front of the car, though she couldn't have been thrown out. The door would have been open if she'd been thrown out. "Cassie!"

"Here," a faint voice said, and Mel looked down the slope. Cassie lay at the bottom in tall dry weeds.

"She's down here," he said, and half-walked, half-slid down the ravine.

She was lying on her back with her leg bent under her. "I think it's broken," she said to Mel.

"Go flag a semi down," Mel said to B.T., who'd appeared above them. "Have them call an ambulance."

B.T. disappeared, and Mel turned back to Cassie. "How long have you been here?" he asked her, pulling off his overcoat and tucking it around her.

"I don't know," she said, shivering. "There was a patch of ice. I didn't think anybody'd see the car, so I got out to climb up to the road, and that's when I slipped. My leg's broken, isn't it?"

At that angle, it had to be. "I think it probably is," Mel said.

She turned her face away in the dry weeds. "My sister was right."

Mel took off his jacket, rolled it up, and put it under her head. "We'll have an ambulance here for you in no time."

"She told me I was crazy," Cassie said, still not looking at Mel, "and this proves it, doesn't it? And she didn't even know about the epiphany." She turned and looked at Mel. "Only it wasn't an epiphany. Just low estrogen levels."

"Conserve your strength," he said, and looked anxiously up the slope.

Cassie grabbed at his hand. "I lied to you. I wasn't offered early retirement. I asked for it. I was so sure 'Westward ho!' meant something. I sold my house and took out all my savings."

Her hand was red with cold. Mel wished he had taken his gloves back when the kid from the carnival offered them. He took her icy hand between his own and held it tightly.

"I was so *sure*," she said.

"Mel," B.T. called from above them. "I've had four semis go by without stopping. I think it's the color." He pointed to his black face. "You need to come up and try."

"I'll be right there," Mel called back up to him. "I'll be right back," he said to Cassie.

"No," she said, clutching his hand. "Don't you see? It didn't mean anything. It was nothing but menopause, like my sister said. She tried to tell me, but I wouldn't listen."

"Cassie," Mel said, gently releasing her hand, "we need to get you out of here and into town to a hospital. You can tell me all about it then."

"There's nothing to tell," she said, and let go of his hand.

"Come on, there's another truck coming," B.T. called down, and Mel started up the slope. "No, never mind," B.T. said. "The cavalry's here," he said, and, amazingly, he laughed.

There was a screech of hydraulic brakes. Mel scrambled up the rest of the way. A truck was stopping. It was one of the carnival's, loaded with merry-go-round horses, white and black and palomino, with red-and-gold saddles and jeweled bridles. B.T. was already running toward the cab, asking, "Do you have a CB?"

"Yeah," the driver said, and came around the back of the

truck. It was the kid Mel had picked up, still wearing the gloves he had given him.

"We need an ambulance," Mel said. "There's a lady hurt here."

"Sure thing," the kid said, and disappeared back around the truck.

Mel skidded back down the slope to Cassie. "He's calling an ambulance," he said to her.

She nodded uninterestedly.

"They're on their way," the kid called down from above them. He went over to the Honda, B.T. following, and stuck his head under the back of it. He walked all around it, squatting next to the far wheels, and then disappeared back up the slope again.

"He says his truck doesn't have a tow rope," B.T. said, coming back to report, "and he doesn't think he could get the car out anyway, so he's calling a tow truck."

Mel nodded. "I saw a sign that said the next town was only ten miles. They'll have you in out of the cold before you know it."

She didn't answer. Mel wondered if perhaps she was going into shock. "Cassie," he said, taking her hands again and rubbing them in spite of what he'd told the kid about frostbite. "We were so surprised to see your car," he said, just to be saying something, to get her to talk. "We thought you were going down to Red Cloud. What made you change your mind?"

"Bartlett's," she said bitterly. "When I was putting my tote bag in the car, it fell out onto the parking lot, and when I picked it up, the first thing I read was from William Blake. 'Turn away no more,' it said. I thought it meant I shouldn't turn south to Red Cloud, that I should keep going west. Can you imagine anybody being that stupid?"

Yes, Mel thought.

The ambulance pulled up, sirens and yellow lights blazing,

and two paramedics leaped out with a stretcher, skidded down the slope to where Cassie was, and began maneuvering her expertly onto it.

Mel went over to B.T. "You go in with her in the ambulance," he said, "and I'll wait here for the tow truck."

"Are you sure?" B.T. said. "I can wait here."

"No," Mel said. "I'll follow the tow truck to the garage and find out what I can about her car. Then I'll meet you at the hospital. What time's the earliest flight home from Denver tomorrow?"

"Flight?" B.T. said. "No. I'm not going home without you."

"You won't have to," Mel said. "What time's the earliest flight?"

"I don't understand—"

"Or we can drive back. If we take turns driving we can be back in time for the ecumenical meeting."

"But—" B.T. said bewilderedly.

"I wanted a sign. Well, I got it," he said, waving his arm at Cassie, at her car. "I don't have to be hit over the head to get the message. I'm out here in the middle of nowhere in the middle of winter on a fool's errand."

"What about the epiphany?"

"It was a hallucination, a seizure, a temporary hormonal imbalance."

"And what about your call to the ministry?" B.T. said. "Was that a hallucination, too? What about Cassie?"

"The Devil can quote Scripture, remember?" Mel said bitterly. "And *Bartlett's Quotations*."

"Can you give us a hand here?" one of the paramedics called. They had Cassie on the stretcher and were ready to carry it up the slope.

"Coming," Mel said, and started toward them.

B.T. took his arm. "What about the others who are looking for Him? The watchman website?"

"UFO nuts," Mel said, and went over to the stretcher. "It doesn't mean anything."

Cassie lay under a gray blanket, her head turned to the side, the way it had been when Mel found her.

"Are you all right?" B.T., taking hold of the other side of the stretcher, asked.

"No," she said, and a tear wobbled down her plump cheek. "I'm sorry I put you to all this trouble."

The kid from the carnival took hold of the front of the stretcher. "Things aren't always as bad as they look," he said, patting the blanket. "I saw a guy fall off the top of the Ferris wheel once, and he wasn't even hurt."

Cassie shook her head. "It was a mistake. I shouldn't have come."

"Don't say that," B.T. said. "You got to see Mark Twain's house. And Gene Stratton Porter's."

She turned her face away. "What good are they? I'm not even an English teacher anymore."

Things might not have been as bad as they looked for the guy who fell off the Ferris wheel, but they were even worse than they looked when it came to the snowy slope and getting Cassie up it. By the time they got her into the ambulance, her face was as gray as the blanket and twisted with pain. The paramedics began hooking her up to a blood-pressure cuff and an IV.

"I'll meet you at the hospital," Mel said. "You can call Mrs. Bilderbeck and tell her we're coming."

"What if the roads are closed?" B.T. said.

"You heard the clerk last night. Clear both directions." He looked at B.T. "I thought this was what you wanted, for me to come to my senses, to admit I was crazy."

B.T. looked unhappy. "Animals don't always leave tracks," he said. "I learned that five years ago banding deer for a Lyme disease project. Sometimes they leave all sorts of sign, other times they're invisible."

The paramedics were shutting the doors. "Wait," he said. "I'm going with her."

He clambered up into the back of the ambulance. "Do you know the only way you can tell for sure the deer are there?"

Mel shook his head.

"By the wolves," he said.

> *"Therefore the Lord himself shall give you a sign . . ."*
>
> —ISAIAH 7:14

It took nearly an hour for the tow truck to get there. Mel waited in his car with the heater running for a while and then got out and went over to stare at Cassie's Honda.

Wolves, B.T. had said. Predators. " 'For wheresoever the carcass is,' " he quoted, " 'there will the eagles be gathered together.' MT2428."

"The Devil can quote Scripture," he said aloud, and got back into the car.

The crack in the windshield had split again, splaying out in two new directions from the center. A definite sign.

You've had dozens of signs, he thought. Blizzards, road closures, icy and snow-packed conditions. You just chose to ignore them.

"Why, anybody'd have to be *blind* not to recognize them," the radio evangelist had said, and that was what he had been, willfully blind, pretending the yellow arrow, the roads closing behind him, were signs he was going in the right direction, that Cassie's "Westward, ho!" was outside confirmation.

"It didn't mean anything," he said.

It was getting dark by the time the tow truck finally got there, and pitch black by the time they got Cassie's Honda pulled up the slope.

And that was a sign, too, Mel thought, following the tow truck. Like the fog and the carnival truck jackknifed across the highway and the "No Vacancy" signs on the motels. All of them flashing the same message. It was a mistake. Give up. Go home.

The tow truck had gotten far ahead of him. He stepped on the gas, but a very slow pickup pulled in front of him, and an even slower recreation vehicle was blocking the right lane. By the time he got to the gas station, the mechanic was already sliding out from under the Honda and shaking his head.

"Snapped an axle and did in the transmission," he said, wiping his hands on a greasy rag. "Cost at least fifteen hundred to fix it, and I doubt if it's worth half that." He patted the hood sympathetically. "I'm afraid it's the end of the road."

The end of the road. All right, all right, Mel thought, I get the message.

"So what do you want to do?" the mechanic asked.

Give up, Mel thought. Come to my senses. Go home. "It's not my car," he said. "I'll have to ask the owner. She's in the hospital right now."

"She hurt bad?"

Mel remembered her lying there in the weeds, saying, "It didn't mean anything."

"No," he lied.

"Tell her I can do an estimate on a new axle and a new transmission if she wants," the mechanic said reluctantly, "but if I was her I'd take the insurance and start over."

"I'll tell her," Mel said. He opened the trunk and took out her suitcase, and then went around to the passenger side to get her green bag out of the backseat.

There was a bright yellow flyer rolled up and jammed in the door handle. Mel unrolled it. It was a flyer from the carnival. The kid must have stuck it there, Mel thought, smiling in spite of himself.

There was a drawing of a trumpet at the top, with "Come one, come all!" issuing from the mouth of it.

Underneath that, there was a drawing of the triple Ferris wheel, and scattered in boxes across the page, "Marvel at the Living Fountains," "Ride the Sea Dragon!," "Popcorn, Snow Cones, Cotton Candy!," "See a Lion and a Lamb in a Single Cage!"

He stared at the flyer.

"Tell her if she wants to sell it for parts," the mechanic said, "I can give her four hundred."

A lion and a lamb. Wheels within wheels. "For the Lamb shall lead them unto living fountains of waters."

"What's that you're reading?" the mechanic said, coming around the car.

A midway with stuffed animals for prizes—bears and lions and red dragons—and a ride called the Shooting Star, a hall of mirrors. "For now we see in a glass darkly but then we shall see face to face."

The mechanic peered over his shoulder. "Oh, an ad for that crazy carnival," he said. "Yeah, I got a sign for it in the window."

A sign. "For behold, I give you a sign." And the sign was just what it said, a sign. Like the Siamese twins. Like the peace sign on the back of the kid's hand. "For unto us a son is given, and his name shall be called Wonderful, Counsellor, the Prince of Peace." On the kid's scarred hand.

"If she wants an estimate, tell her it'll take some time," the mechanic said, but Mel wasn't listening. He was gazing blindly at the flyer. "Peer into the Bottomless Pit!" it said. "Ride the Merry-Go-Round!"

"And thus I saw the horses in the vision," Mel murmured, "and them that sat upon them." He started to laugh.

The mechanic frowned at him. "It ain't funny," he said. "This car's a real mess. So what do you think she'll want to do?"

"Go to a carnival," Mel said, and ran to get in his car.

> "And there shall be no night there; and they need no
> candle, neither light of the sun . . ."
>
> —REVELATION 22:15

The hospital was a three-story brick building. Mel parked in front of the emergency entrance and went in.

"May I help you?" the admitting nurse asked.

"Yes," he said, "I'm looking for—" and then stopped. Behind the desk was a sign for the carnival with dates at the bottom. "Crown Point, Dec. 14" it read. "Gresham, Jan. 13th, Empyrean, Jan. 15."

"May I help you, sir?" the nurse said again, and Mel turned to ask her where Empyrean was, but she wasn't talking to him. She was asking two men in navy-blue suits.

"Yes," the taller one said, "we're starting a hospital outreach, ministering to people who are in the hospital far from home. Do you have any patients here from out of town?"

The nurse looked doubtful. "I'm afraid we're not allowed to give out information about patients."

"Of course, I understand," the man said, opening his Bible. "We don't want to violate anyone's privacy. We'd just like to be able to say a few words of comfort, like the Good Samaritan."

"I'm not supposed to . . ." the nurse said.

"We understand," the shorter man said. "Will *you* join us in a moment of prayer? Precious Lord, we seek—"

The door opened, and as they all turned to look at a boy with a bleeding forehead, Mel slipped down the hall and up the stairs.

Where would they have taken her? he wondered, peering into rooms with open doors. Did a hospital this small even have separate wards, or were all the patients jumbled together?

She wasn't on the first floor. He hurried up the stairs to the second, keeping an eye out for the men in the navy-blue suits. They didn't know her name yet, but they would soon. Even if they couldn't get it out of the admitting nurse, Cassie would have given them her health-insurance card. It would all be in the computer. *Where* would they have taken her? X-ray, he thought.

"Can you tell me how to get to X-ray?" he asked a middle-aged woman in a pink uniform.

"Third floor," she said, and pointed toward the elevator.

Mel thanked her, and as soon as she was out of sight, he took the stairs two at a time.

Cassie wasn't in X-ray. Mel started to look for a technician to ask and then saw B.T. down at the end of the hall.

"Good news," B.T. said as he hurried up to him. "It's not broken. She's got a sprained knee."

"Where is she?" Mel asked, taking B.T.'s arm.

"Three-oh-eight," B.T. said, and Mel propelled him into the room and shut the door behind them.

Cassie, in a white hospital gown, was lying in the far bed, her head turned away from them as it had been in the frozen weeds. She looked pale and listless.

"She called her sister," B.T. said, looking anxiously at her. "She's on her way down from Minnesota to get her."

"She told me I was lucky I hadn't gotten into worse trouble

than a sprained knee," Cassie said, turning to look at Mel. "How's my car?"

"A dead loss," Mel said, stepping up to the head of the bed. "But it doesn't matter. We—"

"You're right," she said, and turned her head on the pillow. "It doesn't matter. I've come to my senses. I'm going home." She smiled wanly at Mel. "I'm just sorry you had to go to all this trouble for me, but at least it won't be for much longer. My sister should be here tomorrow night, and the hospital is keeping me overnight for observation, so you two don't have to stay. You can go to your religious meeting."

"We lied to you," Mel said. "We're not on our way to a religious meeting," and realized they were. "You aren't the only one who had an epiphany."

"I'm not?" she said, and pushed herself partway up against the pillows.

"No. I got a message to go west, too," Mel said. "You were right. Something important *is* going to happen, and we want you to come with us."

B.T. cut in, "You know where He is?"

"I know where He's going to be," Mel said. "B.T., I want you to go get the road atlas and look up a town called Empyrean and see where it is."

"*I* know where it is," Cassie said, and sat up all the way. "It's in Dante."

They both looked at her, and she said, half-apologetically, "I'm an English teacher, remember? It's the highest circle of Paradise. The Holy City of God."

"I doubt if that's going to be in Rand McNally," B.T. said.

"It doesn't matter," Mel said. "We'll be able to find it by the lights. But we've got to get her out of here first. Cassie, do you think you can walk if we help you?"

"Yes." She flung the covers off and began edging her bandaged knee toward the side of the bed. "My clothes are in the closet there."

Mel helped her hobble to the closet.

"I'll go check her out," B.T. said, and went out.

Cassie pulled her dress off the hanger and began unzipping it. Mel turned his back and went over to the door to look out. There was no sign of the two men.

"Can you help me get my boots on?" Cassie said, hobbling over to the chair. "My knee's feeling a lot better," she said, lowering herself into the chair. "It hardly hurts at all." Mel knelt and eased her feet into her fur-edged boots.

B.T. came in. "There are two men down at the admissions desk," he said, out of breath, "trying to find out what room she's in."

"Who are they?" Cassie asked.

"Herod's men," Mel said. "It'll have to be the fire escape. Can you manage that?"

She nodded. Mel helped her to her feet and went and got her coat. He and B.T. helped her into it, and each took an arm, and helped her to the door, opening it cautiously and looking both ways down the hall, and then over to the fire escape.

"I should call my sister," Cassie said, "and tell her I've changed my mind."

"We'll stop at a gas station," B.T. said, opening the door fully and looking both ways again. "Okay," he said, and they went down the hall, through the emergency exit door, and onto the fire escape.

"You go bring the car around," B.T. said, and Mel clattered down the metal mesh steps and ducked across the parking lot to the car.

The emergency-room door opened and two men stood in its light for a moment, talking to someone.

Mel jammed the key into the ignition, switched it on, and pulled the car around to the side of the hospital, where B.T. and Cassie were working their way down the last steps.

"Come on," he said, grabbing Cassie under the arm, "hurry," and hustled her across to the car.

A siren blared. "Hurry," Mel said, yanking the door open and pushing her into the backseat, slamming the door shut. B.T. ran around to the other side.

The siren came abruptly closer and then cut off, and Mel, reaching for the door handle, looked back toward the entrance. An ambulance pulled in, red and yellow lights flashing, and the two men in the door reached forward and took a stretcher off the back.

And this is crazy, Mel thought. Nobody's after us. But they would be, as soon as the nurse saw Cassie was missing, and if not then, as soon as Cassie's sister got there. "I saw two men push a woman into a car and then go peeling out of here," one of the interns unloading that stretcher would say. "It looked like they were kidnapping her." And how would they explain to the police that they were looking for the City of God?

"This is insane," Mel started to say, reaching for the door handle.

There was a flyer wedged in it. Mel unrolled it and read it by the parking lot's vapor light. "Hurry, hurry, hurry! Step right up to the Greatest Show on Earth!" it read in letters of gold. "Wonders, Marvels, Mysteries Revealed!"

Mel got into the car and handed the flyer to B.T. "Ready?" he asked.

"Let's go," Cassie said, and leaned forward to point at the front door. Two men in navy-blue suits were running down the front steps.

"Keep down," Mel said, and peeled out of the parking lot. He turned south, drove a block, turned onto a side street, pulled up to the curb, switched off the lights, and waited, watching in his rearview mirror until a navy-blue car roared past them going south.

He started the car and drove two blocks without lights on and then circled back to the highway and headed north. Five miles out of town, he turned east on a gravel road, drove till it ended, turned south, and then east again, and north onto a dirt road. There was no one behind them.

"Okay," he said, and B.T. and Cassie sat up.

"Where are we?" Cassie asked.

"I have no idea," Mel said. He turned east again and then south on the first paved road he came to.

"Where are we going?" B.T. asked.

"I don't know that either. But I know what we're looking for." He waited till a beat-up pickup truck full of kids passed them and then pulled over to the side of the road and switched on the dome light.

"Where's your laptop?" he asked B.T.

"Right here," B.T. said, opening it up and switching it on.

"All right," Mel said, holding the flyer up to the light. "They were in Omaha on January fourth, Palmyra on the ninth, and Beatrice on the tenth." He concentrated, trying to remember the dates on the sign in the hospital.

"Beatrice," Cassie murmured. "That's in Dante, too."

"The carnival was in Crown Point on December fourteenth," Mel went on, trying to remember the dates on the sign in the hospital, "and Gresham on January twelfth."

"The carnival?" B.T. said. "We're looking for a carnival?"

"Yes," Mel said. "Cassie, have you got your *Bartlett's Quotations*?"

"Yes," she said, and began rummaging in the emerald-green tote bag.

"I saw them between Pittsburgh and Youngstown on Sunday,"

Mel said to B.T., who had started typing, "and in Wayside, Iowa, on Monday."

"And the truck spill was at Seward," B.T. said, tapping keys.

"What have you got, Cassie?" Mel said, looking in the rearview mirror.

She had her finger on an open page. "It's Christina Rossetti," she said. " 'Will the day's journey take the whole long day? From morn to night, my friend.' "

"They're skipping all over the map," B.T. said, turning the laptop so Mel could see the screen. It was a maze of connecting lines.

"Can you tell what general direction they're headed?" Mel asked.

"Yes," B.T. said. "West."

"West," Mel repeated. Of course. He started the car again and turned west on the first road they came to.

There were no cars at all, and only a few scattered lights, a farm and a grain elevator, and a radio tower. Mel drove steadily west across the flat, snowy landscape, looking for the distant glittering lights of the carnival.

The sky turned navy blue and then gray, and they stopped to get gas and call Cassie's sister.

"Use my calling card," B.T. said, handing it to Cassie. "They're not looking for me yet. How much cash do we have?"

Cassie had sixty and another two hundred in traveler's checks. Mel had a hundred sixty-eight. "What did you do?" B.T. asked. "Rob the collection plate?"

Mel called Mrs. Bilderbeck. "I won't be back in time for the services on Sunday," he told her. "Call Reverend Davidson and ask if he'll fill in. And tell the ecumenical meeting to read John 3: 16–18 for a devotion."

"Are you sure you're all right?" Mrs. Bilderbeck asked. "There were some men here looking for you yesterday."

Mel gripped the receiver. "What did you tell them?"

"I didn't like the looks of them, so I told them you were at a ministerial alliance meeting in Boston."

"You're wonderful" Mel said, and started to hang up.

"Oh, wait, what about the furnace?" Mrs. Bilderbeck said. "What if the pilot light goes out again?"

"It won't," Mel said. "Nothing can put it out."

He hung up and handed the phone and the calling card to Cassie. She called her sister, who had a car phone, and told her not to come, that she was fine, her knee hadn't been sprained after all, just twisted.

"And I think it must have been," she said to Mel, walking back to the car. "See? I'm not limping at all."

B.T. had bought juice and doughnuts and a large bag of potato chips. They ate them while Mel drove, going south across the interstate and down to Highway 34.

The sun came up and glittered off metal silos and onto the star-shaped crack in the windshield. Mel squinted against its brilliance. They drove slowly through McCook and Sharon Springs and Maranatha, looking for flyers on telephone poles and in store windows, calling out the towns and dates to B.T., who added them to the ones on his laptop.

Trucks passed them, none of them carrying Tilt-a-Whirls or concession stands, and Cassie consulted *Bartlett's* again. "A cold coming we had of it," it said. "Just the worst time of the year."

"T. S. Eliot," Cassie said wonderingly. " 'Journey of the Magi.' "

They stopped for gas again, and B.T. drove while Mel napped. It began to get dark. B.T. and Mel changed places, and Cassie got in front, moving stiffly.

"Is your knee hurting again?" Mel asked.

"No," Cassie said. "It doesn't hurt at all. I've just been sitting in the car too long," she said. "At least it's not camels. Can you *imagine* what that must have been like?"

Yes, Mel thought, I can. I'll bet everyone thought they were crazy. Including them.

It got very dark. They continued west, through Glorieta and Gilead and Beulah Center, searching for multicolored lights glimmering in a cold field, a spinning Ferris wheel and the smell of cotton candy, listening for the screams of the roller coaster and the music of a merry-go-round.

And the star went before them.

A Final Word

$\mathcal{T}$he giving (and getting) of gifts is inextricably bound up with Christmas and the Christmas story—from the Magis' gold, frankincense, and myrrh to the partridge in the pear tree, from the turkey "bigger than a boy" that the formerly stingy Scrooge sends the Cratchits to the small bottle of cologne the still-stingy Amy buys for Marmee so she'll have enough money to buy some drawing pencils. From heart's desires like Ralphie's "Red Ryder repeating carbine with a compass mounted in the stock" and Susan's "a *real* house," to the more symbolic, like Amahl's crutch and the ham the Herdmans brought the Holy Family.

So it seemed fitting to end this book by giving some sort of gift. This is easier said than done. I can't get you a BB gun. You'd shoot your eye out. And I don't know what size you wear or what color you like, whether you have long hair or have sold it to buy a watch fob or the money for a train ticket for Marmee. I don't know anything about you, really, except that you like reading Christmas stories.

When I was a kid, one of my chief joys was finding a wonderful new book or author, especially if the place I found it was in the pages of a book. When the little women read *The Pickwick Papers*, and played *Pilgrim's Progress*, it was as if Jo was personally recommending them to me.

Kip's father in Robert A. Heinlein's *Have Space Suit Will Travel* wasn't listening to Kip, because he was reading Jerome K. Jerome's *Three Men in a Boat*, and the three men in the boat were singing Gilbert and Sullivan. Anne of Green Gables acted out "The Lady of Shalott" by Tennyson, who wrote "Le Morte d'Arthur," which led me to T. H. White's *The Once and Future King*, which was right next to Charles Williams's *All Hallow's Eve* on the library bookshelf, and Williams had been friends with J. R. R. Tolkien, who led me to Middle Earth, which led me to . . .

I've plugged some favorites in these stories—*A Little Princess*, by Frances Hodgson Burnett in "Adaptation," *Miracle on 34th Street* in "Miracle"—but there are lots of Christmas stories and movies I couldn't manage to fit in, stories and movies I love and that my family reads out loud and watches together every Christmas.

So it seems like a perfect Christmas present to introduce you to them, the way Anne Shirley introduced me to *Ben Hur* and Kip Russell introduced me to *The Tempest*.

So here they are, twelve of them, in honor of the Twelve Days of Christmas, *Twelfth Night,* and Epiphany.

Merry Christmas!

Twelve Terrific Things to Read at Christmas

1. THE ORIGINAL (Matthew Chapter 1:18–25, 2:1–18, Luke Chapter 1:5–80, 2:1–52): The best Christmas story ever. This one's got everything you could ask for in a story: adventure, excitement, love, betrayal, special effects. Good guys, bad guys, narrow escapes, reversals, mysterious strangers, and a great chase scene. And the promise of a great sequel.

2. A CHRISTMAS CAROL by Charles Dickens: The perfect Christmas story, which proves beyond a shadow of a doubt that the only way to begin a Christmas story is with, "Marley was dead: to begin with." And just because you know it all by heart—Scrooge and Tiny Tim and the Ghost of Christmas Past, "I forged these chains in life," and the bedcurtains and the turkey and "God bless us, one and all!"—is no reason not to read it again.

3. **THE BEST CHRISTMAS PAGEANT EVER by Barbara Robinson:** This modest children's story of a church Nativity pageant invaded by the horrible Herdman kids, who steal and swear and smoke cigars (even the girls), accomplishes the nearly impossible—the creation of a new classic—and makes the reader look at the story of Mary and Joseph and the baby "wrapped in wadded-up clothes," as the Herdmans do, with new eyes.

4. **"JOURNEY OF THE MAGI" by T. S. Eliot:** The Bible doesn't tell us anything about what the wise men's journey to Bethlehem was like, or how much it must have cost them to make it. Or what happened to them afterwards, when it was time to go back home.

5. **"THE TREE THAT DIDN'T GET TRIMMED" by Christopher Morley:** Obviously inspired by Hans Christian Andersen's sickeningly sentimental "The Fir Tree," this story of a tree that doesn't get bought by anyone and instead gets thrown away not only avoids all the sins of its antecedent, but ends by telling a touching parable of those ultimate Christmas themes, suffering and redemption.

6. **"THE STAR" by Arthur C. Clarke:** One of the classics of science fiction by one of the masters in the field, this tells the troubling story behind the star that guided the wise men to Bethlehem.

7. **"DANCING DAN'S CHRISTMAS" by Damon Runyon:** When the dust settles on the twentieth century, it's my belief that Damon Runyon will finally be appreciated for his

clever plots, his unerring ear for language, and his cast of guys, dolls, gangsters, bookies, chorus girls, crapshooters, Salvation Army soul-savers, high rollers, lowlifes, louts, and lovable losers. I chose "Dancing Dan's Christmas," a story involving a mean mobster, a Santa Claus suit, a diamond vanity case, and a few too many Tom and Jerrys, but it was a tough call. "Palm Beach Santa Claus" and "The Three Wise Guys" were both a close second.

8. **"THE GIFT OF THE MAGI" by O. Henry:** O. Henry is another underappreciated author, as witness the fact that dozens of stories, screenplays, and sitcoms have copied the plot of this story. But none of them have ever managed to copy the charm or the style of this simple little tale of a watch fob and a set of tortoiseshell combs.

9. **"RUMPOLE AND THE SPIRIT OF CHRISTMAS" by John Mortimer:** If you've encountered the irascible Old Bailey hack, Horace Rumpole, on PBS's *Mystery*, he seems like the last person to have any Christmas spirit. And he is. Which is why this story works so well. Leave it to John Mortimer to teach us a new meaning of "the Christmas spirit."

10. **"THE SANTA CLAUS COMPROMISE" by Thomas Disch:** This story of a future in which six- and seven-year-olds have finally gotten their political rights and have exercised them by exposing the Santa scandal could have been written in today's group-rights-activism climate. The fact that it was written back in 1975, when satire was still possible, makes it chilling as well as funny.

11. **"ANOTHER CHRISTMAS CAROL" by P. G. Wodehouse**: There's no way to describe a P. G. Wodehouse story, so I won't even try. I'll just say that this is the only Christmas story I know of that involves the bubonic plague and tofu, and that, if you've never read him, there could be no better Christmas gift than discovering P. G. Wodehouse.

12. **"FOR THE TIME BEING: A CHRISTMAS ORATORIO" by W. H. Auden**: Part play, part poem, part masterpiece, this long work is what you should read in January, when you're taking down the Christmas decorations and your sense of goodwill toward men and putting them away for another year, and then facing the bleak post-Bethlehem world we all find ourselves living in.

And Twelve to Watch

1. **MIRACLE ON 34TH STREET:** The best Christmas movie ever made. (See Introduction.) I am of course talking about the original, with Natalie Wood and Edmund Gwenn. In black-and-white. Don't even *think* about either of the wretched remakes.

2. **A CHRISTMAS STORY:** A close second, this Jean Shepherd story of a kid who desperately wants a BB gun ("You'll shoot your eye out!") for Christmas is that rarest of things—nostalgic without a trace of sentimentality. It has a number of hilarious scenes—the tongue stuck to the flagpole, the Bumpus dogs and the turkey, the trip to see the department-store Santa. (Pick your favorite. Mine is the Major Award, no, wait, the Ovaltine magic decoder ring, no, wait . . .) But it's not just a series of comic set pieces. More than any other Christmas story, *A Christmas Story* captures

just how badly you want things when you're a kid and how central Christmas is to the kid's year.

3. **THE SURE THING**: I almost didn't go see this movie. The previews (and the title) made it look like a beery remake of *Porky's*. But then I noticed that certain scenes looked an awful lot like *It Happened One Night* and decided to take a chance. Now, every year we watch this great road picture about Allison, who's going to visit her boyfriend for Christmas, and Gibb, who's trying to get to California for "a sure thing" and who happens to hitch a ride in the same car with Allison.

4. **MEET JOHN DOE**: Frank Capra's other Christmas movie—you know the one I mean—is a lot more famous than this one (and shown approximately 987 times a day through the entire month of December), but this one, which stars Gary Cooper as a down-and-out hobo and Barbara Stanwyck as an enterprising reporter, is *really* interesting, especially in these days of religious cults, hungry-for-power politicians, a rampant press, and even more rampant cynicism.

5. **THE MIRACLE OF MORGAN'S CREEK**: Most movies made during World War II were about brave soldiers and the girls who waited faithfully for them on the home front. Preston Sturges instead decided to tell the story of a girl who goes to an army dance and ends up getting married (maybe) and pregnant (definitely), and of her 4-F boyfriend, Norville, who tries to help her out of her predicament. But everything they attempt only makes things worse, till nothing short of a miracle can save them, and you can't even imagine a miracle that would do any good.

6. **AMAHL AND THE NIGHT VISITORS**: This one-act opera by Gian Carlo Menotti about the wise men stopping at a poor widow's on their way to Bethlehem was originally produced for television. It's out on video, but, even better, it's often performed at Christmas by churches, colleges, and community theater groups, and I definitely recommend seeing it live. The story is haunting, the music is heartbreaking, and every production adds something to the simple story of the crippled shepherd boy, his embittered mother, and their distinguished visitors.

7. **A CHRISTMAS CAROL (THE MOVIES)**: There are a jillion versions of this, starring everybody from Alastair Sim to Captain Picard to Bill Murray. My two favorites are The Muppets' and Mr. Magoo's. Not only are they the most literarily faithful (okay, okay, the Muppet one has two Marleys, but it also has Charles Dickens as a character—and Rizzo the Rat), but they're the most fun. And they have wonderful scores. The Muppets' songs were written by Paul Williams. Mr. Magoo's were done by the Broadway team of Jule Styne and Bob Merrill, and include the wonderful "When You're Alone in the World."

8. **WHILE YOU WERE SLEEPING**: This sweet and romantic comedy with Sandra Bullock and Bill Pullman is about the loony complications that can result from being all alone at Christmastime and wishing you were part of a family.

9. **THE THREE GODFATHERS**: A Christmas story in the last place you'd ever expect to find one—a John Ford Western starring John Wayne—*The Three Godfathers* tells

the story of three bank robbers who find a pioneer woman in a godforsaken place and about to give birth. This is the perfect movie to watch when you've overdosed on mistletoe and Santas and snow, and it may introduce you to John Ford's Westerns, which are all wonderful, and convince you to go on to *The Searchers* and *She Wore a Yellow Ribbon*.

10. **THE LEMON DROP KID**: Not only is this based on a Damon Runyon story (see comments on Runyon under "Dancing Dan's Christmas"), but it has Bob Hope. And the song "Silver Bells."

11. **WHITE CHRISTMAS**: This wasn't the movie that introduced the song, but who cares? It's got Bing Crosby, Danny Kaye, Vera-Ellen, Rosemary Clooney, fifteen Irving Berlin songs, soldiers, snow, sentiment, and killer costumes.

12. **LITTLE WOMEN**: This isn't really a Christmas movie, but it starts out at Christmas, and the book has one of the great Christmas-story first lines ever: " 'Christmas won't be Christmas without any presents,' grumbled Jo, lying on the rug." And I watched it every Christmas when I was a kid. There are three versions to choose from: the one I grew up on was the June Allyson one (with Elizabeth Taylor perfectly cast as snotty Amy), the Katharine Hepburn version is generally acknowledged to be a classic, and my personal favorite is the new one with Winona Ryder and Kirsten Dunst.